AM

NO

ONE

I Am No One

Patrick Flanery

ATLANTIC BOOKS
LONDON

First published in hardback in Great Britain in 2016 by
Atlantic Books, an imprint of Atlantic Books Ltd.

This edition published in 2017 by Atlantic Books.

Copyright © Patrick ... ...

the moral right of the author ... ...

the author

... work has been asserted ... in accordance with the

... Patents Act 1988.

with the

All rights reserved. ... ... may be reproduced, stored ... ... in any

... or transmitted ... in any form or by any ... opying,

recording, or otherwise ... ... of both of both

... ... ook.

This novel is entirely a work of fiction. ... names, characters and ... racters and

... events portrayed in it are the work of the ... ... nagination nagination

... not to be construed as real. Any ... ... tual persons,

... events or locales ... ... tal.

e
d in any
opying,
of both
ook.
racters and
nagination
tual persons,
tal.

A CIP catalogue record for this book is available from
the British Library.

Paperback ISBN 9781782397984
E-book ISBN 9781782397977

Excerpt from *The Spirit of Utopia* by Ernst Bloch, translated by
Anthony A. Nassar, copyright © 2000 by the Board of Trustees
of the Leland Stanford Jr. University

All rights reserved. Reprinted by permission of the publisher,
Stanford University Press, sup.org.

Printed in Great Britain

Atlantic Books
An imprint of Atlantic Books Ltd
Ormond House
26–27 Boswell Street
London WCIN 3JZ

www.atlantic-books.co.uk

For AEV & GLF

I
AM
NO
ONE

AT THE TIME OF my return to New York earlier this year I had been living in Oxford for more than a decade. Having failed to get tenure at Columbia I believed Britain might offer a way to restart my career, though I always planned to move back to America, imagining I would stay abroad for a few years at most. In the interim, however, America has changed so radically—by coincidence I left just after the attacks on New York—that I find myself feeling no less alienated now than I did during those long years in Britain.

Although I acquired British citizenship and owned a house in East Oxford on the rather optimistically named Divinity Road, which becomes gradually more affluent as it rises to the crest of a hill, Britain has no narrative of immigrant assimilation, so for my British colleagues and friends and students, it mattered little that I was legally one of them. First and last, I was and would always be an American. Perhaps if one comes at a younger age total acculturation is possible, but as a man in his forties my habits were too firmly in place to undergo whatever changes might have allowed me to become British in anything other than law.

When I was fresh out of my doctorate at Princeton, New York University was not one of the places I would have chosen to work, but I was thrilled when NYU's History Department approached me to apply for a professorship and even happier when I was offered the position, assured at last that my years away from home were finished. It is surprising how much displacement can alter the mind, and while I went to Britain entirely of my own accord, I became restive after the first few years and increasingly resentful that I was being denied— it seemed to me then—access to a fully American life. I blamed my former colleagues at Columbia and whatever machinations had led to my not being awarded tenure and having thus to begin afresh as a rather lowly sounding Fellow and University Lecturer at one of Oxford's older Colleges, which, though founded in the fifteenth century, does not attract the brightest students or have the largest endowment.

Nonetheless, I came to see it as a comfortable place to be, despite the workload being substantially greater than at a comparable American institution since Oxford has continued to teach students individually or in small groups, and there is an ever-expandable duty of pastoral care unlike anything in American academia. I became accustomed to the College chef sending me lunch in my rooms if he was not too busy, often including some tidbit (or as the British say, *titbit*) from the previous night's High Table dinner. There were excellent wines in the College cellars and life ticked on as it had for centuries, with few changes other than the admission of women, which some dons in my time still regarded as an ill-thought-out modernization that had, they insisted, altered the character of Oxford irremediably.

I was lucky with the property market and before returning to New York this past July sold the house on Divinity Road for a staggering million dollars' profit, which I invested in a house and some land overlooking the Hudson River a couple hours north of the city, while taking up NYU's generously subsidized housing in the Silver Towers on Houston Street. Beautiful this apartment is not, but it is a five-minute walk to Bobst Library and I have relished being back in a city that feels global in a way Oxford certainly did not despite the great number of international students and scholars hustling around its quadrangles.

Coming home, of course, meant knowing that I would see my daughter more than once or twice a year, as was our custom during my time in Britain. My loss of tenure coincided with the breakdown of my marriage, though the two were unrelated and no one was really at fault. Nonetheless, it had felt at the time as if there were doubly good reason to seek new opportunities, not only because my career in American academia was finished, so far as I could tell, but because my marriage was also over.

A few weeks ago, just months into my first semester back in New York, I had a meeting scheduled with a doctoral student to whose committee I had been assigned. Life in Oxford has produced a kind of informality in my relations with students, graduate students in particular, and so I proposed meeting Rachel at a café on the Saturday afternoon before Thanksgiving. It was one of a series of Italian-themed places on MacDougal Street that claimed a lineage longer than seemed likely, but I enjoyed its cheap coffees and the variety of authentic pastries for sale in the glass display case. It helped soften some of the culture shock I have been feeling on my return to America, allowing me to believe for a moment that those markers of European life towards which I have grown fond remain accessible even on this side of the Atlantic. Accordingly I made Caffè Paradiso a regular stop in my weekly life, as it provided the kind of quiet and spacious venue where friends and students could be met and conversation lingered over without the sense that a waiter or waitress was going to rush us out the door. It has more atmosphere and élan than any of the chain coffee shops and less hectic bustle than the faux-artisanal places so packed that one has to compete for a table and then feel the pressure of other guests helicoptering with eyes peeled for the first movements building to a departure. Caffè Paradiso is not chic or hip but it has understated style and that, I suspect, is what has kept it in business for so many years—either that or it's a front for money laundering, which is always a possibility in this town.

Rachel was usually prompt in our communications and we had met once before, in September, for what in Oxford I would have called a supervision but which now was perhaps better called a meeting or, if that felt too businesslike, then simply *coffee*. In the intervening two months I had heard little from Rachel until she sent me a completed draft of a chapter. This work, on the organizational history of the Ministry for State Security in the German Democratic Republic, was very assured. I had only a few suggestions for how she might fine-tune her methodological framework but wrote to say I thought it would be productive to meet again before the holidays.

Since I am always early wherever I go I had brought a book with me, though I did not expect Rachel to keep me waiting. She gave the impression in our first meeting and in all our subsequent communications of being a young woman of exceptional meticulousness and punctuality, even punctiliousness. Several days prior to our previous meeting she had written to confirm the time and place before I had done so and when I arrived for that appointment, in the coffee shop near the southeastern corner of Washington Square, she was already waiting for me.

On this second meeting, just a few weeks ago, I ordered an Americano, took a table near the window, and opened my book. I cannot now remember what the book was, it might have been Paul Virilio's *Open Sky*, or something of that sort, but I soon found that I had read ten pages and when I looked at my watch it was nearly a quarter past four, fifteen minutes after the appointed time of the meeting. I took out my phone, an antiquated black plastic wedge unable to send or receive emails, but at least, I thought, I could send Rachel a text message, as I sometimes did to my daughter if

I was arranging to meet her and got stuck in traffic. When I scrolled through my list of contacts I was surprised to discover that Rachel's name was not among them, although I was certain I had entered her details when we met in September.

Another ten minutes passed and I took out my phone again, checked to be sure I had not overlooked her number, perhaps it was filed under last name instead of first, but there was nothing. It was possible that at some point I had accidentally deleted the entry, my fingers are not as dexterous as they once were and the tiny keys on my phone are difficult for me to punch accurately, or maybe, I reasoned, the memory of putting Rachel's name and number into the list of contacts was nothing more than willful invention or a false memory of an intention left unfulfilled.

I had been nursing the coffee and now decided there was no point in waiting longer so I raised the cup to my mouth and in so doing caught the gaze of a young man, perhaps in his late twenties or early thirties, sitting at a table across from me. I cannot say how long he had been sitting there, whether he had already been present when I walked in or if he had arrived after me, but he nodded or perhaps did not nod but made some acknowledgment or greeting and then began speaking in a way so casually familiar that I was taken off guard. This is not something that tends to happen in Britain, where suspicion of strangers is so deeply ingrained in the national psyche, perhaps from the years of the IRA threat, or even more distantly, from the suspicion of German spies during the Second World War, that strangers often do not even make eye contact let alone speak with one another, unless they are from elsewhere, and then, by happy chance, it becomes possible to bond with someone in a public place, both shaking your heads over the confounding maze of London's transportation network or the cost of living or the difficulty inherent in walking down the street because whatever laws of left-side walking that might once have been in force have been confused by London's transformation into an international microstate, and though distant enough from the capital, Oxford is a satellite of this phenomenon, its Englishness gradually giving way to a cosmopolitanism that moves with brutal transformative force. Perhaps the day will soon come when strangers in Britain talk to each other in ways that will feel normal rather than extraordinary.

But here, in New York, on a cold day in November, there was a stranger engaging me in conversation, and because of my habituation to an English attitude of reticence it seemed so astonishing that at first I did not believe he could possibly be speaking to me.

'Stood up?'

I did a double take, looking round the room. 'You talking to me?'

'*You talking to me?* That's funny,' he laughed, 'like De Niro, right? *You talkin' to me?*'

'Yeah, I suppose so.'

'So? Stood up?'

'No. It's not like that. I was waiting for a student.'

'Male or female?'

Again, I surveyed the room. The café was not very full and there was something sufficiently strange in the young man's tone that I was unsure whether it was safe to continue the conversation and thought of ending it right there by excusing myself. If I had any common sense remaining, that is precisely what I should have done, given what has come to pass, but clearly, in retrospect, I had taken leave of my senses, or perhaps, I think now, taken leave of my British senses and allowed the American ones to seize control.

'Female.'

'Pretty?'

Once more I looked around, this time to be sure there was no one I knew within earshot.

'Excuse me?'

'That means no. You sound British.'

'I lived there for more than a decade. To the British I always sounded American.'

'Well, you sound British to me. Anyone else tell you that?'

'A number of people. Americans tend not to have a good ear. They think that British actor, what's his name, who plays a doctor on TV, they think he does a faultless American accent. He doesn't. It sounds like an accent that was cooked up in a laboratory rather than grown from seed, as it were.'

'See, that's what I mean. Americans would never say *as it were*. You totally sound British. That's awesome.'

'Thank you, I guess.'

'So she's not pretty, the student who stood you up?'

'She's attractive enough, but that's not the point. She's an excellent student.'

'But a flake.'

'No, not a flake. It's just not like her.'

'Then call her.'

'I don't have her number. Thought I did . . .'

'Senior moment?'

'Listen, I'm not that old.'

'You could be my granddad.'

'I'm not even fifty-five.'

'Okay, calm down, I'm just messing with you. What do you teach?'

'Modern History and Politics, and a senior seminar on Film.'

'Cool.'

'Are you a student?'

'Nope. Not anymore.'

'You know what I do. Don't you want to tell me what you do?'

'Just another corporate shill.'

And that, as far as I remember it, was the end of the conversation. He struck me as not much younger or older than my daughter, with sandy hair and a pale complexion that made him look like a corn-fed Midwesterner, the kind of face that hosts the slightly haunted-looking eyes of poverty from a few generations back—not his parents or grandparents necessarily, but one or more of the great-grandparents, I suspected, had not eaten well for much of his or her life and somehow that hunger had taken hold of their genes and been passed down to the kid who struck up a conversation with me in an Italian café in Greenwich Village at the end of last month. It was a face that reminded me of the portraits by Mike Disfarmer, those sepia photographs of ordinary Arkansas folk, too tanned, most of them lean and a little hungry or hunted looking, as though in hunting to put meat on the table they had at some moment in the chase realized they were themselves being tracked by an unseen predator.

The meeting was not in itself unsettling, although this young man was the sort of person who left me glancing over my shoulder as I walked back to my building in the afternoon dark, and then as I stood in the lighted window overlooking Houston Street—or, rather, staring at my own reflection as I was thinking about the passing traffic outside—it occurred to me just how visible I was, only a few floors up from street level, the blinds open and me standing there, listening to Miles Davis and drinking a glass of scotch because it was, after all, already half past five in the afternoon and it was November and dark and I felt alone, in fact quite lonely, and realizing that the reason I had not ended the conversation immediately, even when it took its stranger turns, was because I had not yet managed to reconnect with my old friends in this city, had in fact allowed those friendships to slide during my years in Oxford, so that now I no longer feel able to phone up the people who were once my intimates and ask them if we could meet for a coffee as easily as I proposed such meetings with my students, female or not, pretty or otherwise. I decided I should invite a small group of colleagues for dinner, then remembered the reason I was feeling unsettled in the first place, and the fact that I had briefly forgotten why I was unsettled compounded my sense of unease. I opened my laptop and there, right at the top of the sent messages in my email, was a message to Rachel that I had apparently written that afternoon, at just past 2pm, so only a few hours earlier, in which I asked her if we might reschedule our meeting until Monday at 4pm in my office because another commitment had unexpectedly arisen and I could not, I was terribly sorry, find a way to get out of it, and would she please forgive me. And there was her reply, which I had apparently read, assuring me it was no problem whatsoever and Monday at 4pm in my office suited her perfectly.

Now, I had no memory of writing the message, or of having read her reply, and while it is true that I was having my first drink before 6pm, it was definitely my first of the day. Moreover, I had not had a drink all week, though one might think that because I have to mention such a thing perhaps I have had a problem in the past, which is not the case either, unlike a great many of my former colleagues at Oxford, a majority of whom I would guess were functional—and some not remotely functional—alcoholics of the kind not readily tolerated in American academe. The point being: I had not blacked out, had not forgotten this exchange with Rachel because of alcoholism, although it would have been reassuring if I had completely blanked out the episode because of something external to my own mind and not because of a black hole in my memory. It may be a point of regret but in those moments in my newly re-Americanized life when I feel suddenly ill at ease or simply lonelier than any contact with students and colleagues can remedy, I phone my daughter, and this is what I did on that Saturday a few weeks ago. I turned down

Miles Davis and picked up the phone and asked Meredith how she and Peter were doing.

'Fine, Dad, a little crazed, to be honest. We have a dinner tonight.'

'Anyone important?'

'Yes, but I can't—I mean, I shouldn't really say.'

'Am I untrustworthy?'

'No, of course not, it's just, phone lines these days, you never know. Maybe I'm being paranoid. But how are you?'

'Okay. Something—it's . . . nothing really. I just wanted to hear your voice.'

'Come tonight if you like. I could use another person. And it would be good to see you.'

I could not tell whether it was a genuine invitation or if my daughter was simply throwing pity on me, but I made a brief show of protest before accepting. The thought of spending the night alone in that apartment in the Village, or even taking myself out to eat and then going off to see some deeply earnest Iranian or Turkish or even French film at the Angelika or walking an hour up to Central Park just to feel the sensation of moving among other people, to imagine I was not alone in the world, failed and a failure because I had to throw myself into the company of strangers to create the illusion of connection, was more than I could stomach. Such perambulations, all the attempts at distracting myself from my loneliness, only made the sense of isolation worse.

When I accepted the job at NYU I did not give much thought to how this change, my return to a city I still thought of as home despite more than a decade's absence, would affect my social life, which in Oxford was stuffed with colleagues. Many of them, it has to be said, were foreigners like me, banding together in our shared sense of alienation from the English, or from Englishness, which I gradually came to understand was distinct from Scottishness or Welshness (though the latter is a word one does not commonly hear) and was often conflated in the minds of the English with Britishness. I once heard an anchor on Sky News describe the tennis player Andy Murray as 'England's great hope, and he's a Scot,' as if the whole country were truly England, only one part of a federal country, and not the United Kingdom. Despite the alienations of Englishness, which is really about the exclusionary quality apparent in some quarters of Englishness, its unwillingness to assimilate its immigrants, I was not, not ever, not even in the first months of my life in Oxford, ever truly lonely. There were endless garden parties and High Table dinners and gaudies and drinks receptions, and it remains a small enough place that the like-minded seem instinctively to seek each other out, making time despite the onerousness of the workload to keep conviviality at the heart of their experience of that ancient city. The socializing, I came to understand, was as much a part of the educational and intellectual atmosphere as the libraries and lecture theaters.

So in the late afternoons or evenings, feeling a sudden void of loneliness in New York—the city I love, a love that sustained me when I was in Oxford, a city I also came to love for its own peculiar charms—I find myself too often phoning my daughter, especially on weekends, and perhaps too suggestively asking if she and Peter have any plans. Three out of five times Meredith invites me to their apartment for dinner or to meet at a restaurant, or I discover that she has an event in the Village or Meatpacking District—a gallery opening or party—and she swings by to see me before heading home. I have learned that my daughter, who until recently I still thought of as a child even though she is married and by all measures successful in her own right, with a gallery bearing her name and a rising reputation, has, like her father, a taste for single malts, and especially for those earthy and almost medicinally peaty ones from Islay. Together we will sit in my living room with Miles Davis or Ornette Coleman on the record player, because I have taken to buying ink-black vinyl LPs in what my daughter calls, with not a little contempt, one of my 'aging hipster affectations.' All that remains missing is a Cuban cigar between us, though that sounds unduly Freudian now that I think about it, or might suggest that what I really wanted—what I want, what I most desire now—is a son. Meredith is the greatest joy of my life, and will always be, I remain certain, no matter whoever else may yet—I hope—become a part of my family.

ON THAT SATURDAY IN November when the meeting with my student Rachel did not materialize, I took the subway up to Columbus Circle and stopped in a grocery store in the basement of a building that wasn't there when I last lived in the city; in fact Columbus Circle has changed so much over the years that it is scarcely recognizable to me every time I return. If I emerge from the subway without thinking where I am, the disorientation is so acute I have to look at a map or ask directions just to find my way onto Central Park South.

Perhaps it's related to the divorce, or to the fact that I packed up and moved away when my daughter was only thirteen, leaving her in the care of her mother, or even the humbling way in which she and Peter have transformed my own life by granting me access to luxuries I never thought would be within my reach (travel is always First Class, zipping through fast lanes and pre-approval lines at airports, resting in executive lounges before departures and helping myself to free food and drink), but I find it impossible now to arrive empty-handed at her door. How much I owe her, how much I feel I have to compensate for the years of my absence. That night I brought a bottle of Laphroaig because she likes it, though it is neither expensive nor rare, and an autumnal bouquet from that overpriced basement grocery store.

Meredith answered the door and my God, the effect! For a father it was nothing short of breathtaking to see her like that, in an exquisite black dress, a string of pearls, her dark hair swept behind her shoulders, her whole presence perfectly composed in every imaginable way except in the eyes, and there, in her gaze, I could recognize total panic and guessed she had invited me not as a favor, but because she needed help getting through the kind of gathering that would once have been extraordinary to her and to me, but is now meant to be no more significant than any other business dinner. Why she had not invited me in the first place I can only guess; perhaps she thought I would find it boring, or Peter vetoed it, or, after my long absence from their lives, it had not occurred to them, although we have seen each other frequently over the past few months, which suggested to me that a conscious decision had been made at some point—or at some level, I thought, because it has always been clear that Peter regards himself as the 'decider' in the marriage—that on this occasion I should not be present.

As I handed Meredith the flowers and scotch she leaned over to kiss me on both cheeks. How sophisticated we've become in the space of two generations. My parents would never have imagined greeting anyone with such European flair. But before I could get any further two security men in suits appeared.

'Sorry, Dad, you understand, no one gets inside tonight without the onceover. You know how it goes.'

The men passed a metal detecting wand around me and patted me down and once I had been given the all-clear, assured that I was unarmed and therefore not a risk to whoever was in the next room, I followed my daughter into the kitchen, which was thronged with cater waiters and a chef. Since my return to New York, and in fact since Meredith and Peter married two years ago, I had never seen my daughter so much as boil water for tea. Usually the housekeeper does the cooking, but for an event like that night's dinner they needed a larger staff and it was only later that I understood how important the evening was, and what a risk, in a sense, Meredith had taken by inviting me at the last minute (I later discovered there had been a late cancellation, one of Peter's colleagues whose child fell ill with food poisoning, and I presented myself, as if by fate, to make up the numbers). I don't know in retrospect whether there was an element of calculation on Meredith's part but I like to think there was not, that there was and is enough affection between us that she was moved as much by her own need of my support as by a desire to support me, to lift me out of my all too obvious loneliness.

'I'm so grateful you could come, Dad. I need you this evening.'

'Don't be silly, it's my very great pleasure.'

'You've become so British,' she smiled, straightening my tie. 'Would you like a glass of something? There's champagne.'

'That would be lovely.'

'God! *So* British.'

'How is that British, sweetheart?'

'Americans just don't say lovely in the same way.'

'Is it wrong? Should I try to change?'

'No! Of course not.' She handed me a glass of champagne that had been passed to her by a waiter with whom she communicated by a slight tilt of the head in my direction.

'Who's here tonight? Can you tell me now?'

'Sorry for the subterfuge, it's a working dinner for Peter. Albert Fogel and his wife, and Fogel's mother. The rest are all Peter's colleagues,' and here she dropped her voice, 'most of whom I can't stand, but you know, they were all at the same prep schools and colleges and they're all millionaires many times over. These are the people who are really running the country, and most of the time they have no idea how pervasive the effects of their power are, but there you go, this is the world we live in.'

It broke my heart a little to hear my daughter sound so jaded and I wondered if marrying into money was responsible for that, not that her mother and I were poor, her mother especially, and one has to acknowledge that Meredith went to one of those colleges and one of those private schools and it was because of that educational access, not to mention her distinctive, slightly old-fashioned beauty, the face of a Vermeer, the creamy pale skin of a Manet, all those random genetic inheritances, in combination with her fine mind and exceptional taste, that made her so attractive to a certain population of wealthy young men who had an eye for beauty but also for intelligence, who could see that my daughter, not spoiled from birth but well looked after, nurtured and kept level-headed, would be a stable partner at least for the first decade of their professional lives. A colleague at Oxford quipped on hearing of Meredith's engagement a few years ago, one can but hope to see one's children reach their tenth wedding anniversary: to hope for any more would be foolish, even hubristic. The age of constancy has passed.

That evening Albert Fogel, New York's newly elected Mayor, was seated next to Peter at one end of the table, the Mayor's wife next to Meredith at the other, and I was saddled with Caroline, the Mayor's widowed mother, who fancied herself an artist. The rest of the places were taken up by Peter's colleagues, most of them either editors at his magazine or at other magazines or newspapers, although I wondered whether they actually called their publications by such old-fashioned names these days, if instead they thought of themselves as the titans of 'news outlets' or 'information platforms' or even 'media ecosystems.'

'And what do you do?' Caroline asked me over the monkfish, by which time I had spent half an hour listening as she rhapsodized about Meredith's brilliant career, and what a bright light she was already becoming and how she hoped that perhaps I might put in a good word for her with my daughter, because in her day she had been lucky enough to have shows at some of the big galleries, and she was still producing art, not yet out of the game, she was working on a series of paintings about the aging human body, 'self-portraits of my own isolated body parts. And what do you work on, Jeremy?'

'Twentieth-century German history and political thought, some political theory. I wrote a history of East Germans who worked as coerced informants for the Stasi.' Mrs. Fogel nodded, but I sensed I had lost her attention. 'Now I'm teaching a course on film, and I guess that's what I'm most interested in at the moment, perhaps it's a sign that my brain is beginning to atrophy, that I no longer have the patience for the hard archival work and would rather just watch movies.'

'Film. How interesting,' she said, and I was certain I had lost her. 'My first husband was a director. He was always trying to film me in the nude. I finally dumped the schmuck and married Albert's father. He was a lawyer. Just as prying, you know, but not so invasive. I think he might have been a homosexual. Don't look so shocked! He was never very interested in sex or even in seeing me naked, and frankly that suited me fine, but God, he wanted to know everything about my *mind*. It was exhausting but he moved me out to Connecticut, which was heaven.'

'You don't like New York?'

'It's so dirty, so busy. I hate all the dog crap on the sidewalks. It makes me sick.'

'I've just moved back after more than a decade in Oxford.'

'Why would you want to come back to New York? Oxford is pretty, so peaceful. I used to dream of having a little English cottage with a thatched roof surrounded by a meadow. Something like *Howards End*, you know, with the tree and the pigs' teeth in the bark and all that. *So* romantic. *So* English. Why would you leave all that behind? There's nothing like that here, not in New York, and the

American countryside is so *wild*, so dangerous. You can take a breath and fall over dead.'

'It's not quite that bad.'

'All I know is that I love the pastoral quality of the English countryside, the Constable landscapes, the coziness of it, nothing that can kill you but your own stupidity. Oh, you're making me want to go! I should plan a trip for next spring, when the bluebells are in bloom. I remember a bluebell wood outside of Oxford, back in the '60s, and I felt like I'd stumbled into fairyland. Albert was only a baby then and the three of us had this delightful two-week holiday driving around the south of England. How could you bear to leave all that behind?'

I thought of the trucks that thundered past my Oxford house, shaking the windows even though it was a residential street, and the student parties next door that would sometimes require phoning the police, or the banal ugliness of so much of East Oxford, the construction that seemed to go on for years along the Cowley Road, the unstable sidewalks made of one-foot-square concrete slabs that would subside in the rain and flip up to drench my legs, not to mention the drone of the ring road circling the city. There is little truly peaceful about Oxford these days.

'The truth is, I missed America. And NYU offered me more money and less teaching. And of course Meredith and Peter are here, and my mother is in Rhinebeck. It was about family as much as anything.' I told Caroline this because people never want to hear that a place about which they have romantic associations is just as mundane and imperfect as anywhere else, and I know that Oxford is beautiful in a way that is quite special, despite its flaws, but I was also still in the first flush of my renewed love affair with New York, with this great global city that seems truly unlike anywhere else in the western world, and that night I did not want to hear anyone trying to convince me that Oxford would have been a better place to see out my professional life, in my cushy College Fellowship and university professorship. Nothing could possibly have kept me from staying despite a desire to do less work and to be paid more money and to see my daughter more than twice a year and to live again in the city that once gave me so much.

I did not think then about all that New York had taken away, namely my wife, my marriage, an unbroken career in America, and thus an uncomplicated sense of what home means. Of course I found Oxford beautiful, particularly on those uncanny long summer evenings, sprawling with friends in the University Parks or punting on the Cherwell, steering the boats over to the shore to picnic on the water as swans floated past, the hawthorns dropping white blossoms. Perhaps the shabbiness around the edges, the ugliness that licked against the idyll, was a large part of why all that remained beautiful seemed so exquisite, so transformative, able to foster a desire to make myself one with the beauty, to soften the cadences of my speech and adapt my vowels. Returning to America I have discovered with ever greater frequency that many Americans no longer see me in the same way, that I have become something other than an American to them, although I know that with work and a studied determination to undo the verbal and behavioral tics I acquired in Britain, I may yet pass as my old self, or a subtly altered version of my old self.

'I think you'll find America has changed since you've been away,' Caroline said, leaning to one side as a waiter took her plate. 'When the Republicans no longer had the Cold War to let them do what they liked, they had to invent a new one, that badly named War on Terror. What they could not have imagined is that the War on Terror, by turning its eye everywhere, even within the borders of this country, laid the groundwork for a new Civil War. That's what the Tea Party and its ilk want, although they'd call it Revolution probably, but the reality isn't revolution at all. It's one part of the population determined to live and govern in a way that's anathema to most of us. I don't know, I'm just a painter, and maybe what I'm describing is the very definition of Revolution, but it's not one with universal support, however much they might want to present it as such.'

As the evening progressed I realized the Mayor's mother was more intelligent than at first she seemed. She looked and sounded like Lauren Bacall, whom I had once seen stepping into a car on Park Avenue; Caroline had the same elegance and grace and the kind of deep voice that suggested either an unusual physiognomy or else long years of marinating her vocal cords in whisky and cigarette smoke. She must have been in her eighties, so could easily have been my mother, and she spoke in the often irritating way of the aged and coherent, who insist on their wisdom and on imparting their knowledge to those who will listen. I was willing to listen politely for the sake of my daughter and her husband, not that Peter has done much to encourage my affection, I find him a rather stiff son-of-a-bitch, not unlike the Hooray Henrys of Oxford's Bullingdon Club, the American equivalent of those self-satisfied toffs with no interest in ordinary people and no real understanding of how the poor suffer. The difference with Peter, however, is that his politics and heart are ostensibly in the right place, which is to say, from my perspective, the left, although with the super rich, and I think it's fair to put Peter in this category, for those people who have been rich from birth, who have, as his mother jokes, been paying taxes since they were in utero, they can never entirely understand the realities faced by most Americans, never mind the realities of the profoundly impoverished people elsewhere in the world, to whom America's poor would look comparatively well off.

I met the new Mayor and his wife that evening, we spoke briefly over coffee, all of us stepping out onto the terrace despite the cold to look at the lights in Central Park and the glow of buildings over on the Upper East Side. *This*, I thought, *this* is why I came back to New

York, because I have been nowhere else that affords such urban views. London is a city of great pre-war beauty and much post-war ugliness, Paris for all its splendor can be monotonous and museum-like, Rome is chaotic, Berlin a hodgepodge, but New York has, despite the recent proliferation of new skyscrapers, cracked a kind of urban code that makes it one of the most dynamic cities in the world. Admittedly I have not been to Asia, and colleagues tell me that to see the urban future I have to go to Shanghai and Tokyo and a dozen other cities that will tell me a quite different story. Perhaps one day, although the promise of that kind of travel now grows more and more dim as the days pass and I sit in this room, scribbling these pages and wondering just what kind of future may yet be mine, what the purpose of my account here will be, who will read it, whether it will be little more than an eccentric legacy left to my heirs, or one day soon entered into evidence, a matter to be classified rather than kept public. You who read it, whoever you are, in whatever number, are undoubtedly already drawing conclusions about me, reading between the lines and making assumptions despite my protestations of innocence.

Fogel was charming but I sensed his judgment that I was a person of no great importance. The only reason to chat to me over coffee was because I was the father of his hostess and because he relied on the goodwill of media titans like Peter and his colleagues to convince the city that what he wanted to do, the plan he had to make it a fairer, more egalitarian place, would not undo the economic growth attributed to the policies of his predecessor. We spoke only briefly and he showed no real interest in me. I cannot blame him. What am I but an academic historian, a professor who may teach another fifteen or twenty years, perhaps influence a generation or two of other scholars, although now that future—all aspects of my future—seem genuinely in doubt. Each word I put on paper I imagine may be the last I write in freedom.

WHEN EVERYONE HAD GONE home that night and I was left alone with Peter and Meredith while the staff washed the dishes, the three of us sat down in the den. I thought Meredith might open the Laphroaig and was surprised when she did not, although we had all been drinking throughout the evening, three different white wines, one for each course, of a quality I had come to expect from Peter.

'Why don't you stay the night, Dad?'

'No, I should get home.'

'Don't be silly. It's after one. We have nothing to do tomorrow, so stay. We'll have a late breakfast.'

'You're sure it's no trouble?'

'You're very welcome, Jeremy.'

'As a matter of fact, I wanted to talk with you about something, although maybe I should leave it until tomorrow.'

'Go ahead, Dad, I'm feeling wide awake.'

Peter, though, looked exhausted. 'If you want to go to bed, it's fine. I don't have to talk about it now. It's really no big deal.'

'No, please, Jeremy, you've piqued our interest.'

'Something slightly strange happened today. I was supposed to meet a student and I confirmed it by email earlier in the week. I saw her after a lecture I gave yesterday and we spoke again about the meeting. So I went to the café at the appointed time and she didn't show. I walked home and was going to email her to ask why she hadn't shown up, only to discover that I appear to have written to her earlier today to ask if I could reschedule and she responded saying that was fine. Now the problem is, I have no memory of writing that email asking to reschedule, nor do I remember reading her reply, and yet both messages are there.'

Meredith shifted on the couch, drawing her feet up under her legs and covering herself with a gray wool blanket I remembered having sent them after a trip I made to Stockholm for a conference last year. It was gratifying to see it was in use and had not been stowed in a cupboard, forgotten, or re-gifted to some less affluent friend. 'I guess that is kind of strange. Have there been, you know, any other incidents like this?'

'No, sweetheart, not that I'm aware of, which is why I wanted to talk to you about it. Have you noticed anything? Am I losing it?'

'No, absolutely not. I haven't noticed anything like that. Have you, Peter?'

Peter shook his head. 'Honestly, I swear, Jeremy, your memory is better than mine. I haven't detected anything strange. I mean, you drive me crazy a lot of the time, but that's not the same.' He smiled because it was a teasing, generous thing to say, rather than an expression of real irritation. It was the kind of banter that made me like the kid a little more each time I saw him, and I felt he was gradually relaxing around me, accepting me as part of the family, though I had met his parents only a couple of times and had the sense that Meredith was becoming integrated into Peter's family more completely than he had become a part of ours, perhaps because there was no 'ours'; there was now my family, which was Meredith and my mother, and Meredith's mother, who was really on her own, she has no siblings, her parents are dead, so less scope for Peter to become a part of *us* in the way that Meredith could become a part of *them*. I felt this as a loss, it is true, because I knew that to a large degree the dissolution of our family was my fault and not Susan's, although the decline of any relationship is almost always multilateral, and my ex-wife was not without fault.

They tried to reassure me, Meredith and Peter, and by the time it was two in the morning we were all struggling to stay awake and Meredith went in search of something I could wear to bed, returning after a few minutes with a pair of pajamas that had never been worn, as well as a brand-new bamboo toothbrush, still in its packaging, and a razor.

'Were you expecting me to stay?'

'We're prepared for just about any eventuality. Security to the power of ten.'

'Or more.'

'Probably a great deal more.'

I wondered whether the guest bedrooms were always made up, or if Meredith had anticipated there might be last-minute guests and had asked the housekeeper, a Dominican woman, to put on clean sheets and set out fresh towels. There was reassurance in taking off my clothes and putting on new pajamas, particularly ones of such lovely quality—*lovely*, not very American, it's true, but I can't get rid of it, *nice* tastes like Wonder Bread on my tongue—and then sliding in between those high thread-count sheets and pulling the duvet up around my chin, looking out at the lights across the park and knowing my daughter is in such a position that I need never worry about my own security for the rest of my life. This had happened in a way I could not have predicted and with such speed it sometimes threatened to destabilize my sense of our relationship. She was not yet thirty, hardly out of childhood it seemed, and yet she was also a fully functioning adult with a career, with her own business, and with a husband who is one of the most influential men in America, and all of this at such a young age! Youth has somehow effected a bloodless revolution and it is foolish, I know, to imagine that the young people of America are not ultimately in charge. That night I could go to sleep confident that if I woke the next morning and remembered nothing of the previous days or weeks, or had forgotten the sum total of my adult life, then Meredith and Peter would look after me. I would be shipped off to the top facility on the East Coast and until my death I would be contained and cared for, never having to worry if I might end up wandering the sewers of New York City or sleeping in the Amtrak tunnels in which I remember once seeing informal encampments on the way to visit my mother upstate. Whatever happens, I will not be one of the destitute fated to fall off the grid, no matter how much a part of me might now wish that were possible.

THE FOLLOWING DAY, SUNDAY, we were slow to get up, but when we finally convened, a little after ten that morning, the house-keeper had already made waffles and there was a bowl of fruit salad and hot coffee and *The New York Times*, satisfyingly thick, all laid out on the white marble kitchen counter. I could see almost at once, however, that Meredith and Peter had been talking and there was something they needed to say, as if they had—this turned out to be the case—made a decision about me in the hours following my confession of the unexplainable lacuna in my memory, or so it then seemed.

They waited until we were alone in the kitchen, in the glassed-in breakfast area overlooking the park. It was not the first time I had stayed with them, but I could see how the longer they lived together they were settling into a pattern of routinized comfort that suggested a pursuit of the ideal, of the best possible way of drinking coffee and eating breakfast and enjoying the beauty of their view, not to mention the beauty of each other. They are, without question, a stun-ning young couple whose attractiveness is not about youth alone, but about the way they wear that privilege of age without worry, or with worries always mediated by the knowledge that security will, barring a revolution, be permanently theirs.

'We've been talking, and we'd like to arrange for you to see a really great doctor.'

'My dad has been to see her, Jeremy. She's one of the top memory specialists in the city.'

'So you do think there's a problem with me?'

'No, Dad, honestly, neither of us has noticed anything. We just think—'

'Isn't it better to rule out the possibility of anything actually being wrong, Jeremy? Wouldn't you rather know, and catch it at an early stage, instead of living with the uncertainty and the worry?'

They both sounded sincere. Sincerity is not one of their failings.

'Of course you're right.'

'Can I make you an appointment for this week? I'm sure we could get you in before Thanksgiving.'

True to his word, Peter arranged an appointment for Monday, when I had no classes and no commitments other than the rescheduled 4pm meeting in my office with Rachel. I was grateful to Peter for leveraging his influence, and I hope, even still, after all that has happened since that week when I first became conscious of the strange changes pressing against the trajectory of my life, that I demonstrated sufficient gratitude for his assistance.

After brunch I went home. Meredith offered to send me in a car and for once I accepted because I was still feeling tired from the late night and I wanted to indulge, if only for another half-hour or so, in the knowledge that someone was looking after me. How different my life would be if I had remained in Britain, if I had not sold that house on Divinity Road but continued to live there in my slightly cramped if comfortable way, making the occasional excursion to some European city and leading what was in many ways a very un-English life, or at least a life not representative of the constricted lives so many people in Britain suffer. Not that I have more space in my NYU apartment, slightly less in fact, and no garden just outside the dining room, but nor do I have the sense of vertiginous insecurity that sometimes came over me in Oxford when I was lying alone in bed and wondering whether the house was locked. In New York, as a white man of a certain age and class, I have tended to feel secure, despite the city's unpredictability and its problems with police corruption and crime and terror, though Oxford was not immune from terror either, or at least from those who would seek to spread the contagion of terror even to the sleepier corners of the world.

Riding in the back of the black town car down Seventh Avenue, I thought of a Syrian doctoral student who arrived in Oxford almost at the same time as me, and I think of him now, wondering if my brief association with him might have been a foretaste of what was to come. The young man made odd threats against me and my colleagues, demanding special treatment for no better reason than because he had recently been working for Syria's mission at the United Nations in New York. When his demands were rebuffed he threatened the entire department. At first no one took it seriously, but when the threats escalated I reported the young man to the terrorist hotline that Britain had then set up and within a few days he disappeared and no more was heard of him.

I did not then and still do not regret what I did, and the fact that he disappeared suggests to me I was not mistaken in reporting him to the authorities. It occurs to me now how easily a single tip-off, a phone call lasting no more than five minutes, might change the course of a stranger's life. Am I, I wonder, any different from the ordinary East Germans who turned themselves into informers for the Stasi? I assumed the young Syrian was a threat but had no evidence other than my suspicions and fears. I remember now that he said something to me along the lines of, 'things are going to change around here. You'll see who really runs the show.' It was perhaps nothing more than a young man's boast. In fact it sounds, thinking about it once more, like little more than ill-advised swagger, the sort of threat someone who has been on the receiving end of an authoritarian boss might then turn around and use against the next weak person he or she encounters—the kind of boast I can imagine I myself could have made to a senior colleague at Columbia, much to my regret. Perhaps there was nothing suspicious about that young Syrian, but the British security services must have thought otherwise, since he disappeared. It is possible, I suppose, that he was not detained but simply chose to leave. His face came back to me that Sunday as we turned onto Bleecker and suddenly a group of young Middle Eastern men surrounded the car as they crossed the street. I had more or less inoculated myself against seeing threat in a brown face during my years in Oxford, particularly after buying the house on Divinity Road, which required, for the fastest possible commute to my College, walking along the Cowley Road where so many Pakistanis and people from elsewhere in the Muslim world have shops and make their homes, as well as go to worship. From my back garden I could see the dome and white spire of the Central Oxford Mosque and on more than one occasion had to listen to the music of a party in some neighboring garden, melodies and rhythms such that I fancied I might as well have been in Lahore or Istanbul. No, living in Oxford in the immediate aftermath of the attacks on New York and Washington was like having immersion therapy by exposure to the thing one fears most.

THERE ARE SEVERAL doormen who work in my building but the guy on duty that Sunday was a clean-cut Puerto Rican called Rafa.

'Professor O'Keefe! Package for you.'

From behind the desk he pointed to the area where packages are left, near the mailboxes and the windows looking out on the courtyard between the three buildings. Odd that a package would arrive on a Sunday, but perhaps it had been delivered on Saturday and I had simply failed to check whether there was anything for me.

'Do you know if this came yesterday, Rafa?'

'Can't tell you, boss. I came on at ten this morning and it was here when I arrived. Ignacio was on duty yesterday. You can ask him tomorrow.'

The box was wrapped in brown paper and was the size of the old cosmetics cases my mother used as a young woman, the variety of luggage no one takes on airplanes anymore but which were once a staple of women's accouterments; I remember that the last one she owned, before they became extinct in the age of strict bag limitations, was covered in turquoise vinyl, part of a larger set of suitcases all in the same color, with brass locks and fasteners. It must have dated from the 1960s, and after my mother no longer used it for makeup it became the repository of photographs that had never made it into albums and which she now keeps under her bed and for all I know has continued to open every day, inhaling the case's old cosmetic smell and the odor of the slowly decaying vinyl and whatever toxic chemical complexity went into fixing the turquoise dye. The box was that size, and had the heaviness of the cosmetic case when it was fully packed with bottles and vials, and as I held it in the elevator going up to the third floor, examining the unfamiliar handwriting that had addressed it to me, Professor Jeremy O'Keefe, I imagined all the possibilities it might contain. There was no return address, no indication of a sender or origin, no postage, and thus no postmark, so truly no way of determining where it might have originated, at least not before I had opened it.

I put the box on the coffee table in the living room and it is possible I forgot about it or that I was disturbed enough by its arrival and mystery that I feared opening it, or it could be nothing more than the fact that Meredith phoned to tell me Peter had spoken with Dr. Sebastian and confirmed I could come for an appointment at ten on Monday morning, which would give me ample time to get back to my office for the meeting with Rachel at 4pm. 'Maybe,' Meredith said, 'it's time to get a smartphone. That way you'll always have access to email and something like this would be less likely to happen next time.'

'I'll think about it.'

'Come on, I know that means you won't think about it.'

'Okay, sweetheart, I'll get one tomorrow or the next day, if that makes you happy.'

'It would make your life easier, that's all.'

'I don't know that it would have made any difference to what happened yesterday. I still would have gone to the café, and if I'd had one of those things then perhaps I wouldn't have waited for half an hour to see if she arrived, so it might have saved me time, but the mistake would still have happened.'

'I know it's unsettling.'

'If you notice anything, or if you and Peter remember any occasion when I seemed to have been forgetful, but more than just in an ordinary way like struggling for a name or something, then you have to tell me.'

'I will, but we talked about it again, and neither of us can remember anything of the kind. You seem fine to us . . . just a little lonely.'

For a moment I could not speak. A cry swelled in my throat. I was surprised that she was addressing my loneliness, having imagined that by appearing ebullient every time we met, I might have concealed just how depressed I felt. I swallowed a few times and said, 'Yes, I've been a little lonely lately. Missing people in Oxford. I had very good friends there.'

'But you still know people in New York.'

'Not any close friends. And everyone in Oxford has gone unexpectedly silent, as if they resent my leaving. You're the only person I can really talk to, Meredith. I'm sorry if I've seemed needy.'

'You don't have to be sorry! It's nice to have you around. You don't ever have to feel bad for wanting to see me.'

'But if I call and you're busy, or it isn't a good time, I want you to promise you'll say so. I don't want to be a burden.'

'Please, Dad, my life isn't that busy, I swear.'

She gave me the address, the doctor would be working from her home office instead of the hospital, because, I supposed, it was the week of Thanksgiving, or perhaps memory specialists were not based in hospitals, or for initial consultations they thought it not so threatening to see the patients in a less medicalized space, where the prospect of long years locked in a dementia ward would not open off every corridor glimpsed in the walk from the entrance to the examining room. The address was on the Upper West Side, on West End Avenue, and I entered it in my online calendar so that I would receive an email reminder on Monday morning.

Having spoken to Meredith, and then spending some time reading the news and checking my email—no messages in the personal account, more messages than I wanted to read in my work account—I decided to find something to watch on TV, an old western or even a football game, if there was one of any interest, but the box that had arrived loomed before me on the coffee table and I felt compelled to open it, though it's true that sometimes I leave my bank statements unopened for weeks or months, and there have been times in the past when a letter has arrived (when letters were still routinely sent) that I so little wanted to read it might sit unopened for days or weeks or even—I remember a letter from a French ex-girlfriend in college that I only opened after the color of the envelope had faded, changing from blue to violet to pink—for years. I went back to the kitchen for a knife and slit open the brown wrapping paper, revealing a brown cardboard box taped shut with brown packing tape, but with no other marks or writing. I looked at it for some time and even thought of calling the police, because I had no idea what it might contain, whether it might be a bomb, since every professor has his host of disgruntled former students, and my mind wandered—in a careening, full-tilt way—to my attachments at Oxford whose loose ends might yet be curling round to bite me. After pressing my ear against the cardboard and hearing nothing, seeing no signs of leakage or other hints that a threat might be packed inside, and having shaken it with no conclusive results—it sounded, simply, *full*, and I had no sense of parts moving inside when I shook it—I took up the paring knife and slit along the tape to open the top flaps.

For children the opening of packages is almost always a matter of joyful expectation, but as the years progress and one discovers that some packages may not bring happiness and can just as frequently deliver disappointment or anxiety, one looks upon boxes, particularly ones as mysterious as that which arrived at my apartment on the Sunday before Thanksgiving, with a vague feeling of trepidation or even sometimes dread. Perhaps, for me, this shift in the possibility of packages dates from my move to Oxford, when, after six weeks, the shipping container finally arrived in Britain and the vanload of possessions I had thought I could not live without—books, music, a few pieces of art, clothes, but no furniture, since I did not go to Oxford thinking I was staying permanently—was unloaded at the College's lodge. For the first year I lived in rooms on site, so the porters helped me carry the boxes around the front quad and up the staircase to the top floor, where my furnished rooms were in the eaves, the windows overlooking the sandstone battlements. When I began opening those boxes from home, I found the anticipation and happiness of being reunited with my possessions quickly give way to small irritations— the covers of some valuable books had been damaged, the glass in several framed pictures was cracked—and then to an overwhelming sense of nostalgia that crested only to leave in its wake a sense of despair and regret. I could smell not only New York on my belongings, my books and clothes in particular, but the apartment on the Upper West Side I had so recently shared with my wife and daughter and which I had left of my own accord because I believed the marriage to be finished; I was the one who chose to leave, though it was Susan who had made clear the relationship was coming to an end and our legal severing came only a year later. Sitting in that Oxford room with its cream-colored walls and institutional furniture, surrounded by the carnage of boxes that came freighted with memories of a life abandoned, I wept, and wept so loudly that my neighbor across the corridor, a postdoctoral Fellow from Geneva, knocked on the door to offer me a sherry and then, because he was sensible and helpful and became one of my closest friends during my first year in that city, helped me unpack my books and arrange them on the shelves. If I had been left to do the unpacking alone, it might never have happened. Since then, if not before, a taped-up box has been an object of threat more than one of desire or expectation.

I opened the flaps of the box on my coffee table and realized on catching sight of the contents that it was some kind of file carton, because it contained an unbroken stack of 8½ × 11 sheets on which were printed, in dense, single-spaced type, thousands upon thousands of web addresses. At first I thought the top layer of paper might conceal something else beneath, but as I paged through—there must have been twenty-five hundred sheets of paper or more—it was all the same, one address after another, separated only by a comma and a space, no returns, no paragraph breaks. I thought there might be some kind of message, though I did not at first look at each page individually; that was a process that took parts of a few days. There was no message, however, and it was only later that I would understand the full significance of what was before me. Some of the addresses were familiar—websites for newspapers and magazines—while others meant nothing to me, or seemed to have been composed almost entirely of numbers and a random assortment of characters. It was a puzzle, but because there was no message, no explanation, it was one that only a small part of me had any interest in tackling. My mind is not the puzzling kind, it takes no joy in crosswords or number games, I have never been a card or chess player, I would much rather read a book or watch a movie to make the time pass. I assumed it must be an error, that whatever this list of addresses might be it had nothing to do with me. I put the pages back in the box, closed the flaps, and slid it under a side table.

So I switched on the television and by chance happened upon Francis Ford Coppola's *The Conversation*, which I am teaching on my senior seminar later this semester. Since I had not watched it recently, I slumped into the couch with that satisfying relaxation that comes from finding the kind of distraction which can be relied upon to last for two hours and lull one gradually towards sleep. I had first seen *The Conversation* as a boy, and it was possible to imagine that it might then have put me to sleep, at least in the beginning, because it starts slow and even when the pace begins to pick up and Hackman flushes the toilet, which overflows with blood, it remains deeply adult in the sense that it is a sober vision of the consequences—psychological as much as tangible or physical—of snooping, consequences so profound that the snooper becomes the snooped upon, driven crazy by the skill he has perfected when it is turned against him. It had been some years since I last saw the film and in the interim I had watched *Das Leben der Anderen*, which now seemed to me to be engaged in a subtle conversation with Coppola's film, the two main characters isolated men working for institutions or corporations that are somehow distant, if only in the minds of the men, who seem to hold themselves at arm's length from the higher echelons of their respective organizations, listening to the people they have been charged with monitoring before finding, at some point late in each film, that all they thought they knew and understood, all the received wisdom that has supported their appreciation—perhaps even passion—for the work they undertake, is held together with little more than the illusion of some higher moral purpose, its bankruptcy disguised and defended by cultures of fear that they both, too late, discover at great risk to themselves. Florian Henckel von Donnersmarck's film, like Coppola's, presents its subject, the man charged with surveillance, as a species of obsessive monk who has discovered a vocation in monitoring the lives of others—targets who may or may not be innocent, whose guilt, if indeed they are guilty, occurs only because the laws are themselves so ludicrous or, in the case of Coppola's film, because of a dark conspiracy, though the work of the Stasi could itself be judged a sort of dark conspiracy, however virtuous the organization might have believed its mission to be. Gradually he cultivates his work into an art, a private virtuosity, but one that only he can fully appreciate. In contrast, Gene Hackman's character, Harry Caul, is paranoid about defending and policing his own privacy.

The broadcast of *The Conversation* was part of a double bill on whatever channel I was watching, and as Coppola's film ended and Antonioni's *Blowup* began, I ordered out for Vietnamese food and decided to settle in for the evening, trying to take my mind off the appointment with the doctor scheduled for the next morning. Ordering takeout, the ability to get whatever you want at almost any hour delivered to your door, has been one of the great pleasures of returning to New York. The food came well before the scene where David Hemmings blows up the photographs taken in the park, enlarging and re-enlarging until the images lose all definition, pixelating before pixels existed in photography, becoming a field of indecipherable grain right at the moment when they are about to reveal the full horror of what he, the photographer, has captured, which is to say, Vanessa Redgrave's participation in a plot to kill a man, just as Cindy Williams, a few years later, played her own white-bread-American-hotel-room murderess. I noticed for the first time that at the beginning, when we first see Hemmings, we know nothing about his character. Having left the doss house in disguise, he goes to his car, and as he drives he speaks on a radio in a way that suggests he might be a spy or an undercover police detective; it is only gradually that we realize he is nothing more sinister than a photographer, another kind of spy. In his white jeans and blue shirt and hard-soled shoes he has a poisonous yet angelic beauty, a charisma I long tried to emulate, believing it might be the key to attracting the rather brittle young women I so often desired but who seemed, in my youth, oblivious to my bookish charms. The barely clothed models he abuses become a metaphor for surveillance, offering glimpses of what we (or what Antonioni) think we want to see, those expanses of exposed skin drawing attention to the dominance of the photographer's voyeuristic gaze, standing in for the gaze of the audience, the viewers viewing the viewer viewing the viewed.

As I watched Hemmings mince through dingy South London I indulged in my food, I ate sloppily, I enjoyed seeing those 1960s British models mess around topless in lengths of colored paper. The weird oral fixation Redgrave seemed to betray as she tried to make Hemmings give up the film he had shot was more powerful than I had remembered, her fingers always flying to her mouth, and perhaps it was on account of Caroline Fogel's comment from dinner the previous night but I remembered how, in James Ivory's adaptation of *Howards End*, Vanessa Redgrave raised her hand to her mouth as she told Emma Thompson about the pigs' teeth in the tree at the eponymous house, and how that gesture, her middle finger tapping her teeth, had always struck me as so profoundly erotic as to be almost obscene, quite out of place in the world of Edwardian England. Perhaps that was the point, however, that sex was erupting everywhere, even from beneath the bark of the trees themselves, and in the almost subconscious gestures of the nouveaux riches.

The mimes playing their fantasy tennis game at the end of *Blowup* were a disappointment, as they were every time I had ever seen the picture, but unlike some of my friends and colleagues who insist it has not stood up well over the years, I remain convinced that *Blowup* achieves greatness precisely because it is so unquestionably of its particular moment: like *The Conversation*, it tells us a great deal about the psychological preoccupations and mania of those decades, the ways in which surveillance, undertaken for intelligence gathering as well as other more nefarious purposes, was beginning to work on the collective unconscious of the movie-going public.

Having watched both films and feeling that slight numbness that comes from too much exposure to a screen, I went to bed to read a collection of essays by the late historian Tony Judt, someone who was never quite a friend although we knew each other, and I found that within half an hour of climbing under the duvet and expecting sleep would come after I had read one or two short essays I was in fact wide awake, so much so that I finished the book. Although by then it was after midnight and I knew I had the appointment with the memory specialist, Dr. Sebastian, the next morning, I got out of bed and went through to the living room, found myself standing at the window, the blinds open, in my T-shirt and shorts, feeling a draft coming in around the expanse of glass. Because the room was dark I could see clearly down to Houston Street and I thought, for a moment, that someone was standing there watching me, or had perhaps already been standing there as if he were waiting for me to come to the window and when he saw that I had noticed him he immediately began walking towards Broadway. Perhaps I was already edging into unconsciousness, but my mind both registered and did not register the event of this acknowledgment, the nod I think I made and his slightly flustered forward movement. Part of my mind thought it was nothing more than coincidence, that he had not been looking up but instead consulting the screen of his smartphone, reading an email or checking directions. I was certain, however, of a reciprocal acknowledgment, that by nodding I was telling him I saw him watching me, the two of us watching each other: *Hello, hey you, my watcher, I can see you! I know what you're doing!*

There was something about the encounter that made me double-check the locks on the door to the apartment and when I returned to bed I also locked the bedroom door, almost as a reflex. One would think I must have been suffering from paranoia, locking myself in, behind two doors, in a building protected by a doorman and CCTV cameras. If there were a break-in, campus security and even the NYPD would respond and all would be well. Nonetheless, I lay in bed thinking of that man's dark shape on the street, of the head cocked in my direction and the frisson of communication I felt when my nod seemed to act as a trigger for his movement. Who? Who would be watching me?

Though at the time I did not quite understand why it should be so, the exchange with the man on the street made me begin thinking about all that had happened so recently in Oxford. Perhaps the effects of the complicated life I led during my later years in Britain had somehow followed me across the Atlantic.

Now, as the evidence grows around me, that seems all but certain.

I SHOULD HAVE RECOGNIZED the address when Peter gave it to me but, like other bits of information in my life, I had blocked out the associations that might have been conjured by West End Avenue and was surprised when I arrived there on Monday morning to find Dr. Sebastian's office just around the corner from the apartment where I last lived in New York, with Susan and Meredith, on the top floor of a converted brownstone, a school across the street and the sound of garbage trucks often waking me on a Saturday morning before dawn.

I had not been back to 75th Street in more than a decade, not since the summer when I moved out of the apartment and, for a brief period, up to my mother's house in Rhinebeck, before the subsequent and more significant migration to Oxford. When I moved out of the family home I conceded nearly all the furniture, which is also why I took not so much as a lamp or end table across the ocean. At the time I tried half-heartedly to fight Susan for the sleek four-slice toaster I had bought only a few months earlier because I was tired of making toast in the oven, but when I saw Meredith's face fall, it seemed as though losing the toaster might just be too much to bear, that losing her father *and* the possibility of toast when she wanted it would push her into juvenile delinquency in a way that the more serious ructions on their own might not. So I left home only with clothes and books and photographs and the art that was indisputably mine, some of it acquired before Susan and I were married, much of it—including an early Neo Rauch bought before his prices rose beyond my means—purchased with money left to me by my father and thus, I argued, not a matter for negotiation. The art was my inheritance in a real sense, although some of that money had also helped us buy the apartment, which I relinquished to Susan (although really, I convinced myself, to Meredith) with no more argument than when I abandoned my toaster and my favorite floor lamp and even the black acoustic guitar my parents gave me in high school and which Meredith had inexplicably named Bobo, taking it to play with her friends when they congregated on the promenade in Riverside Park, channeling some kind of nostalgic hippy vibe Susan and I had both been too young to impart.

That Monday morning in November I was too early to spend half an hour reading magazines in Dr. Sebastian's waiting room, so I walked down 75th Street past the building where I knew Susan still lived. Knowing she was on sabbatical, and likely at home, I nearly pressed the buzzer, until I thought better of it, certain she would not be in the mood to speak to her ex-husband. In fairness to Susan, we have managed to remain friends since the divorce, and in many ways I feel closer to her than anyone other than Meredith, who has a fairly difficult relationship with her mother. After Meredith graduated from high school and moved to Boston for college, even though I was in Oxford, Susan would phone me to find out how our daughter was doing because at the time the two had still not recovered from several fallings out over high school boyfriends and Meredith's decision to major in Art History. Susan worried this was an impractical choice and felt there was no need for Meredith to decide even before she had started college what she might want to do. In fact, Susan believed that Meredith should major in Business, and things between them only began to improve when a Masters in Arts Administration eventually capped off that BA in Art History. This suggested to Susan that there was a practical streak in the daughter who seemed so often to live in a world of the imagination. 'What else would you expect from an economist?' I once said to Meredith. 'Your mother thinks in terms of logic and illogic, equations, balances, expectations, futures. Think of it this way: she is only concerned about your future.' Meredith, I remember, had grimaced: 'And not about my happiness.'

It was too cold to walk to Riverside Park that morning a few weeks ago, but I went anyway, pulling the coat closer around my neck as I passed the enclosed dog run where I had spent so many early mornings and late evenings while Lotte, our dog, did her business, her habits often forcing me into conversations with people I would not otherwise have met, even on one occasion the actress Kathleen Turner. We dog-run regulars tried to act as if Ms. Turner was no one in particular, to give her space, I suppose, although we all must have felt the frisson of a celebrity in our midst, being able to observe her in ordinary life, a person of more than ordinary presence, walking her dog and being normal in a way that looked like the enactment of a borrowed identity. I could not help thinking of the performance I had seen her give a few years earlier in *Indiscretions*, based on Cocteau's *Les Parents terribles*, in which she played Yvonne, the more-than-half-mad mother to Michel, played in that production by Jude Law, then a virtual unknown who caused a sensation by getting out of a bath in the second act and standing with great naturalness, wet and nude, on the stage. It was a show about different forms of nakedness, most of them psychological and emotional, and Turner, though she remained clothed, was as naked as anyone on that extraordinary set. The pleasure for the audience, even more acutely than with most plays, came from engaging in a communal act of voyeurism, enjoying the spectacle of one family parading its psychic wounds. At the end of the play the set split apart, walls and ceiling flying away from one another, penetrated by a searchingly brilliant light, which struck me then as a symbol or stand-in for the audience's own collective act of observation: staring with such intensity that by our combined force of scrutiny we tore the characters' home apart at its seams.

Only a few dog walkers were in the park that morning, most of them elderly women, one with half a dozen Bichons moving like a fog along the pathways arcing down to the river. When the wind whipped up off the Hudson and caught my neck, I decided to turn back. No longer such a young man, I feared a cold would lay me out for a week. As it happened, Dr. Sebastian had no other appointments and directed me into her consulting room almost as soon as I walked in the door. I remember the room being spare, with white walls and modern furniture, a severe space stripped of distractions or anything that might trigger strong associations in the mind.

'Customarily I take this week off each year, but seeing as you are Peter's father-in-law I make an exception,' she said and smiled. She was my age, not a native English speaker, and somehow that made the situation seem even more serious. I realized how worried I had been since the events of Saturday and, perhaps more to the point, since telling Peter and Meredith about my strange confusion. What I had really been hoping for, I understood, was for my daughter and son-in-law to reassure me that there was nothing to worry about, encourage me instead just to get on with life, not to refer me to a memory specialist who might discover something seriously amiss in the workings of my brain. I realized too that 'memory specialist' was a euphemism: the woman was nothing less than a neurologist, and *that* term, more than the other, gave me palpitations. I was seeing a neurologist for the first time in my life because the people closest to me suspected problems with my brain. How could I blame them given the glitch I had revealed? It begins with such blips, failures of ordinary language, searching for common phrases that remain elusive, blacking out an entire recent conversation or correspondence and proceeding as if whatever agreement has been reached, whatever information rehearsed, had never been mooted.

'I would like you to begin by telling me what you have been detecting,' Dr. Sebastian said from behind her desk. She used a pen that looked antique, taking notes in a ledger of the kind that might be used for financial accounts, a reckoning of profit and loss.

I told her what I had experienced over the weekend, recounting the confusion about the appointment with Rachel just as I had to Meredith and Peter.

'And previously? This has occurred other times?'

'I am not aware of anything like this ever happening in the past.'

Dr. Sebastian nodded, made a few notes, and then took me through a series of questions to ascertain whether I was experiencing any aspects of dementia. She asked me the year and the season, the date and day, she wanted to know where we were, both generally and precisely, she gave me three words to remember and asked me to recall them later in the consultation, wanted me to spell various other words and then to spell them again in reverse, to count backwards from one hundred by a factor of seven, asked me to identify and name a number of everyday objects that she produced from a box, had me repeat particular phrases, write complete sentences, follow written commands, and draw a simple design of geometric shapes. I felt like a child. When it was all over I asked her how I had scored.

'Faultless. You did not miss a solitary one. I would like to refer you for a scan, just to be certain there is nothing irregular internally, to exclude stroke or tumor and suchlike.'

'Stroke or tumor?'

'Listen, Professor O'Keefe,' she said, stretching her hands and bringing the fingertips together into a steeple, 'it is improbable, but in the absence of any observable memory or cognitive problems, I would like to corroborate there is nothing wrong inside. There is no history of Parkinson's in your family?'

'None whatsoever.'

'Alzheimer's?'

'Not that I know of.'

'No discussion ever of forgetful family members?'

'Everyone died of cancer, heart failure, or old age.'

'Meaning?'

'They slipped off in their sleep at a very advanced age, so I suppose that was heart failure as well.'

Dr. Sebastian nodded and told me I could get the scan done on Wednesday if I did not mind, and of course that suited me fine. By the end of the appointment I wanted certainty rather than further questions.

'But what does it mean, if there doesn't end up being any sign of a neurological problem?'

Twirling her pen between her fingers, she averted her gaze.

'Then we must consider if there may be some psychological explanation.'

Dr. Sebastian looked over the tops of her glasses in a way that reminded me of a teacher administering a stern lesson or warning. Under other circumstances, in a different context, I would not have thought twice about making my interest in this woman as clear as modesty and respect might allow. She wore no wedding ring, although I knew that this did not necessarily signal availability. There were no photographs on her desk or on the walls of her office, only her degrees, all of them from Harvard, mounted and framed and hung in such an orderly grid I knew professionals must have done it. That precision, as well as the care she took with her grooming and clothes, the black wool slacks and black shoes, the creamy silk blouse, the total absence of jewelry except for a watch, made from a silvery metal, reminded

me of the only other woman with whom I had recently been in love—
the only woman I had loved in a very long time—and made me wish
that Dr. Sebastian and I were not meeting for the first time in this
particular situation, that I might have met her when I did not look so
undone by the odd experiences of the previous weekend.

'I take you to mean I might be going crazy.'

She raised her chin so that she could look at me straight through
the lenses.

'No, Professor O'Keefe, I mean there are some number of reasons,
or ways, that the mind can *blot out* certain events.' What was her
nationality, I wondered? German, possibly, in which case we might
have had an easier conversation in her mother tongue than in mine.
'It would be worth speaking to someone. Do you already have a
therapist?'

'I've never been in therapy.'

'Do you know any therapists socially?'

'Not in New York.'

'I could make a referral.'

'I'll have to think about it.'

I left the appointment wondering what psychological causes could
possibly produce such a specific void in my memory. As I walked
back to the subway at 72nd Street I tried to think about trauma as
the potential cause of that blackout, but could come up with no
particular reason why planning to meet Rachel, who strikes me as a
solid student unlikely to prompt any variety of strong emotional or
psychological response, could have triggered traumatic amnesia. Nor
did I know for certain whether this was what Dr. Sebastian meant,
or if the mind even acted in this way. Then it occurred to me that
perhaps something had happened on Saturday afternoon, some other
form of trauma unrelated to Rachel, and the communication with
her was swept away with my forgetting whatever that other trauma

might have been. Possible though it remained, this hypothesis did not seem convincing.

In those minutes walking through my old neighborhood I thought of the innumerable evenings when, returning from Columbia after a day of teaching, I would stop for groceries at Fairway, for fresh fish or oysters at Citarella, a nice cake for dessert, and then go home to whip up a dinner for my wife and daughter, back when it still seemed— despite the small irritations of an ordinary married life—that I was in a family capable of persisting in one form or another until the day I died. My parents did not divorce and I believed when I married Susan that she and I would be together forever. Her own parents provided a much different model, but I wanted to believe in the permanence of our relationship, in the possibility of finding ways to adjust our behavior as the decades progressed, accommodating ourselves to the shifting needs and desires of the other, that in so doing we would be able to continue returning to the marital bed with a sense of security as well as hope, or if not hope then an ever diminishing mystery, a broadening knowledge of the other person, the idiosyncrasies of her desire, the textures of her body, the way parts expanded and contracted quickly or over longer periods of time. I could not then imagine, not on those nights of impromptu cooking, that Susan had lost interest and that her losing interest would infect my professional life, forcing not only my departure from the home, but from my own country.

In that first, lonely year spent living in College rooms in the front quad overlooking a perfect postage stamp of lawn, woken at odd hours by carousing Oxford students, finding myself sleepless in a twin bed for the first time since I had left college myself, I resented Susan for her failure to remain interested in me, and just when that resentment was about to turn corrosive, at the moment when I became conscious of having drunk a whole bottle of wine each evening for weeks on end and could see myself being looked at by the young students who came to my rooms for tutorials with a mixture of perplexity and vague disgust, I decided that, as Rilke would have insisted, I had to change my life before I, too, became a ruin. I cut back on the drink and started running, despite the English rain, and kept running as a way of reclaiming the man I had been. I was not going to age like most male academics, I decided, and so turned to some of my female colleagues for inspiration. The older they grew, the more carefully they attended to their appearance, so that a woman of sixty who had the rooms next to mine looked scarcely a day over forty-five. I asked her once why she did it, if all the effort was only for herself, or for her partner. 'The students already think we're ancient,' she said. 'Why give them more ammunition?'

WHEN RACHEL KNOCKED on my office door that afternoon, in the townhouse overlooking Washington Square, I was already wondering whether to bring up the confusion about our previous appointment or to pretend nothing had happened. Rachel is one of those graduate students who appears always to be on her way to an interview, usually dressed in a suit, more often—like Dr. Sebastian, who was still much on my mind—in conservative slacks and blouse and stylish black leather boots with a low heel and gently pointed toe that suggested power and professionalism, but without making men like me feel insecure.

I had no sense what Rachel's background might be, it is often difficult to tell with students just how much money is in the family, but she looked as though she had enjoyed a solid middle-class upbringing, with enough resources to be comfortable. The suit she was wearing that Monday was good quality, it might have been bought by her parents or grandparents, and yet there was a slight edge of professionalism and striving, as though she knew she needed to work to get the kind of coveted tenure-track position that has become ever more difficult to secure because institutions like NYU and Columbia are hiring fewer people for permanent jobs, relying instead on adjuncts with contracts so limited they have little choice but to work at three or four universities just to make ends meet. Rachel had the look of the student who says to herself, 'That is not going to be me, I'm going to be one of *you*, Professor O'Keefe, and I want you to know that when it comes to writing a reference next year, I'm the one about whom you will say, *you would be fools to hire anyone other than Rachel.*' Among the undergraduate students she was a well-liked TA, which is to say there was a healthy balance of those who complained she was too demanding and those who thought she was a genius, the best teacher they had ever encountered. Because of this response, not to mention the strength of her scholarship, I felt certain I would provide a reference urging hiring committees that Rachel, above all my other doctoral candidates, was the best one for the job. Even still, it was unlikely she would be hired until several more years had passed, and then she might have to spend the first part of her professional life in Louisiana or Utah or Alabama.

'How was your weekend, Professor O'Keefe? You said something came up? Did that go okay, whatever it was? Sorry, I don't mean to pry, I just wanted to make sure everything was okay.'

I had been hoping Rachel would not ask such a question.

'My daughter was hosting a business dinner, and she wanted my advice,' I lied. 'I'm sorry, I don't make a habit of rescheduling like that, but it was a very important occasion for her.'

As Rachel listened to the excuse, which felt even stupider the more I talked myself into it, her eyes began to narrow in a way that made me anxious, and when I had finished speaking I saw them pop wide again, whatever confusion there might have been giving way to surprise, or at least the affectation of surprise.

'So I didn't realize your daughter lives in New York, too?'

'That was one of the attractions of this job, to be near my daughter again after too much time away from her, you know, and as you get older that desire to be close to your children only becomes more acute, I can't really explain why, it's as much about wanting them close if something goes wrong as wanting to be available to help them, not that I'm old and need help and not that my daughter needs much in the way of assistance, but you understand what I mean.'

Rachel was nodding vigorously, trying to maintain eye contact even as my own gaze wandered out the window to Washington Square Park, which changed during my absence from the city in ways that seem both subtle and curiously profound, as though it is the same park but a cleaner and tidier version of itself. A man across the street paused, looked towards my office window, stood still for twenty seconds or so staring, and then continued on his walk.

'So what's it like moving to America?' Rachel asked. As I watched the man walk across the park, turn, and then loop back to pass my window once more, I felt a flutter of unease. Second encounter? Third? I began to feel as though I needed a ledger, a way of recording moments that felt strange or uncanny. After the events of Saturday and Sunday, this was the next occasion of what I can only think to call weirdness. 'Professor O'Keefe?'

'Sorry? The . . . ?'

'I meant is it difficult, moving to America? Do you feel welcomed?'

In a comparable situation in Britain such small talk would be kept to a minimum; this being a professional relationship, there is no requirement or expectation on my part that we should become friends. The point of our meeting was to discuss the work on which I am charged with giving advice and guidance in the hope that my substantial foundation of knowledge in the field will help Rachel or whatever student might be sitting before me not to look like an idiot when it comes time to let a wider group of scholars read what she has written. Rachel, though, is not going to look like an ass. She works like the devil and has an almost preternatural ability to see the problems before they are even on the horizon, and, having realized they are approaching, reroute herself to avoid them or acquire the necessary tools to attack and disable the problems when they arrive (i.e. improve her German so as to read Ernst Bloch in the original, master enough French to read Bernard Stiegler, also in the original, spend a little more time with the work of Hayden White). The question she had asked me, though, was perhaps the real source of my irritation, because it betrayed her failure to understand that I am not British in anything other than a legal sense. One might even say that my Britishness is a legal fiction, except legally it is true, but the legality of it produces a fiction of belonging or acculturation that is nothing short of fantasy for me now. When I was still living in Britain, and believed I might go on living there for the rest of my life or at least until my retirement, it was, perhaps, a matter of self-delusion or even of wishful thinking.

'What can I say, Rachel? It's like coming home.'

Once again, the moment I started speaking, she began nodding. I wondered whether, if I said something preposterous, like our planet is simply a simulation run by an unseen and unseeable computer and free will is only an illusion, or if I began spouting racist or sexist bile, if she would continue to signal her agreement so robotically.

'Wow, how interesting,' she smiled, cocking her head as if to suggest the weight of a thought, 'I guess that's because American culture is so dominant globally?'

'No, Rachel, it's because I'm American.'

Her face clouded with an expression of total confusion, almost bordering on disgust. 'But you *sound* British. Were your parents British?'

'No, we're all-American Americans, here for centuries. My

mother's side was English, but they came over at the end of the seventeenth century, and my father's side, all of them Irish, arrived in the 1840s, like so many others.'

'I just assumed because of the accent . . .'

'I don't have a British accent. The British don't think so either. To them I sound American.'

'But you don't, not at all.'

'It's a question of intonation. If you listen to my vowels, they're entirely American. It's just the phrasing and the emphases, maybe the vocabulary as well, that has drifted from origins.'

She was still shaking her head but by then I'd had quite enough of her insistence that I was not what I am, so I asserted in a rather English way—with an excess of understatement—that if we did not get to work there was little point in such meetings and at the end of the hour we would both feel the result was rather unsatisfactory. Thus, from a state of confusion, we moved on to Rachel's chapter, which we discussed for the next forty-five minutes. She was relieved to hear I thought it needed very little work. Still, throughout the meeting, there was a look of puzzlement on her face, as though some part of her brain was continuing to think about the sound of my voice, the way I speak, listening for the roundness of my vowels, the vocabulary and idioms I use, and when she tried to put it together with her idea of what a fellow American sounds like—although one may be American in every sense and still not necessarily a first-language English speaker— she found I did not fit her paradigm of American-ness.

'It's not just intonation. I think it's about cadence,' she told me at the end of the hour, 'it's the cadences you use and the volume, which is softer than most Americans speak, and it's also your constructions and vocabulary, you're right, you have British-English constructions and words slip in that Americans just don't use, which is why a lot of us assumed you must be British, and also of course because we know you just came from Oxford, so you have that origin story if you know what I mean—'

I nodded, but was distracted again by the same young man in Washington Square Park, pausing for an instant outside my window. It was impossible to see his face in the twilight, even with the park's lamps on, but it was obvious he was standing there just long enough to check that I was still in my office. As Rachel was speaking, I stood up and closed the blinds.

'—and because of that, because of your recent history, knowing where you came from and whatnot, and having seen you give that lecture last spring when you were here for the interviews and all, and you sounded really, *really* British then, probably because you'd just come from Oxford and hadn't been around Americans very long, you know what I mean? Well, we just assumed, I mean I'm not the only one, other people must have mistaken you for British?'

'Some, yes, but only strangers.'

What I meant to imply was that Rachel's confusion could so easily have been dispelled if she had spent five minutes on my Faculty web page, where a brief academic biography makes my trajectory unambiguously clear. This, however, is something I have noticed in Rachel's generation, and even more so in younger students: despite having all the world's information available to them, they seem even more likely than earlier generations to leap to assumptions, or to wait for someone to explain to them what they have failed to understand or investigate for themselves, and in so failing have gone on living in a state of uncertainty or false belief. It surprised me at the time, but even in Oxford there were occasions when it became apparent in the course of a tutorial or supervision that a student had woefully misinterpreted some aspect of the work because he or she had not known the meaning of certain words, and despite having the *Oxford English Dictionary* freely accessible online, had failed to look up unfamiliar vocabulary, instead reading in so superficial a way that he or she had reached wildly erroneous conclusions about the text in question. I had hoped that in returning to America I would not find this same intellectual laziness, such absence of curiosity. I was, it has to be said, disappointed by Rachel's failure to figure out that I was as American, probably much more and much longer American, as she. Frankly, I was more than a little pissed off and I thought of what the man had asked me in Caffè Paradiso on Saturday, whether the student who had failed to arrive was female and if she was attractive. No, I said to myself sitting before Rachel that Monday afternoon, she was well dressed and neatly groomed, but she was not attractive. Genetics had dealt her a rather poor hand. I am ashamed to admit her homeliness (a confusing word, meaning something entirely different in British English, almost the opposite of what it means in America) heightened the bitterness I felt as the hour drew to a close and she, this homely but very bright, very promising girl, felt compelled to tell me why I did not sound American to her untrained and largely untraveled ear.

As I showed her to the door, I turned and said, before thinking about the words or what their effect might be, 'You know, Rachel, one of the great things about America, one of the reasons I wanted to come home to my country, is that anyone can speak any language in any possible accent and still be accorded the status of American.'

Rachel blushed and muttered something almost unintelligible, a kind of half apology that did not go far enough by half, as some British acquaintances of mine might have said.

'Sorry,' I said, 'I didn't quite hear that,' which was true, although I could not help noticing she looked crushed, and in that moment I felt sick with myself. I was behaving badly in a way I had not in a very long time.

'I'm sorry, Professor O'Keefe,' she mumbled, 'I find, I don't know, I just—interacting with people is really difficult sometimes, because,

I guess, I don't find other people very transparent.'

'You should move to Germany. Germans are very transparent. If they hate you, they'll tell you.'

And with that she rustled off into the cold November night. I had not meant to speak with such vehemence, but as I did, little though Rachel knew it, I was thinking of an encounter I had at a High Table dinner at Exeter College a few years before, when the matter of my nationality arose for the umpteenth time. I had by then acquired dual citizenship, having done so for the pragmatic reasons that it made travel back and forth between Britain and America much easier, and so when a Fellow of the College, a woman my age born and bred in London, asked me where I was from, I said, 'I'm American, but now I'm also British, I'm a dual citizen,' and she shook her head and corrected me, saying, 'No, no, no. You're American.' When I protested, insisting, 'It's more complicated than that, I've lived in Britain for a decade and have acculturated to a certain extent, and don't have any plans to return to America,' she again shook her head, scolding me, 'No, you are American, first and last, and even if you spent the rest of your life here you would never be British.' I was so irritated by the woman, a Professor of English whose own family were themselves Austrian immigrants to Britain in the 1930s, that I did not speak to her for the remainder of the meal, or for the drinks afterward in the Senior Common Room, and ignored her whenever we passed each other on the street in the months and years that followed. I could not imagine a similar conversation happening in America. I could not imagine a born and bred American saying to an immigrant who had been in the country legally for a decade or more, someone who had acquired American citizenship, that they were not and would never be *American*; such a stance would be antithetical to the foundational concepts of American national identity.

The encounter with Rachel unsettled me, mostly because since returning to New York from Oxford there had been a number of such exchanges with strangers who assumed on first introductions that I was British, and on a few occasions some of the less astute strangers persisted, even after I had explained the situation and my personal history, convinced that *I myself* was somehow confused about my own nationality, that I was in fact *not* American, or that my parents must be British. Sometimes these exchanges would turn into confrontations; I would begin to lose my temper at a party or other social event, alcohol perhaps muddying the argument while also prolonging it, until I was finally forced to say something to the effect of, 'Listen, I was born in the state of New York to parents who were born in the state of New York to grandparents who were born somewhere between Maine and Pennsylvania. I grew up in New York, I was a child in this state, I was a student here, I lived in America until I was in my late thirties, and then by the whims of a career in academia I happened to take a job in Britain and move there for a period of more than a decade. Some Americans are capable of living abroad and never losing their native accent. I am not one of them. Call me a chameleon or poseur or snob or whatever else you like, but I tried, perhaps unconsciously, perhaps intentionally at some points, to blend into British life because it became exhausting to be asked twice or three times what I meant when I said a word or phrase or whole sentence that was misunderstood as a direct result of my thoroughly American accent or vocabulary or some concatenation of the two, and so I made micro adjustments the better to be understood by the people who were, in a very real sense, my hosts. In making such adjustments I made myself sound foreign to you and people like you but I am no less American than I was when I moved to Britain all those years ago.' And then, because I might have made the mistake of mentioning the year in which I moved to Oxford, a shadow would fall between me and the person who had misinterpreted my nationality to the point of offending me, and he or she would say something to the effect of, 'Oh, did you leave before or after the attacks?' and then I would have to say that the move occurred in the weeks following the attacks on New York and Washington, although this was merely a matter of coincidence. In a few cases one of these tin-eared interlocutors would look at me sharply and grumble, 'If it had been me, I wouldn't have deserted my country in that hour for the sake of a job,' and, having made such a statement, the person would take their drink or canapé and flounce away, as if there could be no retort from me that would change their mind. It was dispiriting, and this succession of encounters, including the encounter with the English don at Exeter College that Rachel's confusion recalled, all bled into my exchange with her that dark Monday afternoon. Conversations, perhaps especially ones involving some element of miscommunication or misapprehension that leads to a sense of conflict unfolding unexpectedly in the course of the exchange, are necessarily informed by the whole panoply of other remembered conversations about the same or similar subjects, conversations that devolved into a state of tension or open conflict. Sometimes that process of recall is triggered by nothing more than the physical stance of the person to whom one is talking, the way she cocks her head or uses a finger to draw her hair behind her shoulder, or by a word, a phrase, a tone of voice that suggests a prior exchange with a different person in a distant location. Then the catalog of past conversations begins to poison the present, so that, in this particular case, I was responding not only to Rachel's confusion and stubbornness, but to the confusion and stubbornness, the rudeness and exclusiveness, of the Professor of English I had encountered at Exeter, and the Americans who have wanted to place me in the narrowest possible national category, who have seemed to think that they know my identity better than I do myself.

*

MY WALK HOME should have taken me directly across Washington Square Park, but instead, without making a conscious decision to do so, I skirted its northern and eastern perimeter, as if the vision of that young man passing my office earlier, his circling round and round again, acted as a repellent force, though as the autumn days grew shorter I had been finding it more difficult to brave the park after nightfall, despite it being well lit and, particularly in late afternoon and early evening, full of people walking to their homes or jobs or simply exercising their dogs. It did not seem to be the zone of criminality and licentiousness I remembered from the past, a park where one could scarcely walk ten feet without being offered drugs or noticing the invitation of some person's gaze.

As I walked round the edge of the park, I felt a spasm of regret for the tone I had adopted with Rachel. Such truculence was not like me, and I began to compose a message to her in my mind, apologizing for the confusion while also explaining, in brief, the history behind my irritation with the subject, and then assuring her that it was not a big deal and finishing by asserting my sincere hope that I had not upset her. The more I thought about it the more I began to realize that the confusion and insistence by others that they knew better who I was than I did myself was only partly the cause of the intense irritation I was feeling. What was really irritating me was that I had taken the job at Oxford out of a sense of desperation since Columbia's failure to grant me tenure seemed effectively to have ended my career in America at the time. After such a decision there is little one can do, nowhere one can go in America but down, to some lesser institution, perhaps even to a community college, or worse, to a high school, and faced with the prospect of becoming a high school History teacher to teenagers who cared nothing for the subject and would become ever more hostile to an aging teacher who, God only knows, might have developed a cancer the treatment for which his job's poor medical insurance would not have begun to cover and instead of turning to the production of crystal meth, as in that unlikely television drama, I might have been moved to do something no less illegal like applying my linguistic and historical knowledge to treasonous ends, that is to say by turning spy, though as soon as I thought of this the more ridiculous it seemed since I have no access to government files or secrets, and my loyalty, though engaged and interrogative, a loyalty that marks its fidelity by the robustness of its critique, has never been in doubt. I would have been no one but a failed and failing high school History teacher with scant knowledge that any foreign government might wish to acquire. I am still in possession of nothing—no information, no secrets, no connections (at least I believe this is true)—that can possibly be of use to anyone other than myself, perhaps my heirs and a few of my students and colleagues. I know nothing that would or should make me a person of interest to the authorities on either side of whatever divisions now carve up our world.

Although I was exceptionally lucky to get the position at Oxford given what had happened at Columbia, moving there did not feel like a choice made freely, since the alternative—a life of poorly paid secondary school teaching or criminality of whatever stripe—was so horrific that I could do nothing *but* leave the country of my birth to find better work elsewhere. It was that which niggled, the resentment I felt for having been forced into a more complicated relationship with the idea of home.

In any case, I vowed to write out my apology to Rachel and send it the next day, then to put it from my mind since I will have no occasion to see her again until this coming spring.

When I got home—though it is strange to think of this apartment as home, since for so many years home was a redbrick Victorian house with a beech hedge in the small front courtyard shielding the living room windows from the street—there was another box waiting for me, the same size as the first, with the address written in the same hand. Would there be forensic traces if I turned it over to the police? Had the sender worn gloves? Could the police even be trusted?

I took this second box up in the elevator and opened it as I had the first, again finding some two thousand pages or so filled with web addresses. I put the boxes next to each other, wondering what I should do about them; neither had postage, both were unmistakably intended for me, which suggested there was a clear intention about the delivery, but what it meant or who might be sending the packages I could not imagine. I phoned the doorman, Manu, and asked him who had dropped it off.

'Sorry, Professor, I don't know anything about the guy.'

'What do you mean?'

'He looked like a bike messenger, you know, and he had one of those exhaust masks on, with the mesh, like a gas mask? And sunglasses and a hat, so I couldn't tell much about him.'

'Did he say anything?'

'Just to make sure you got it.'

'Nothing else?'

'Nah. He was kind of unfriendly. Most of these guys, you know, even if they're in a rush and having a shitty day—oh, sorry, Professor O'Keefe—'

'Never mind about that.'

'What I mean is, even when they're having a really, really bad day, most of these guys, you know, they'll still be polite, and this guy was seriously not polite. He was a fucking asshole.'

I thanked Manu, hung up the phone, and poured a glass of wine, but then became curious and pulled the boxes out again and sat with them open before me, turning the pages over one at a time, thinking that I would look at every one, at least skim what was printed on each, even if it took me all night. Living in a doorman building, which is to say living with an intermediary between my domestic space and the outside world, offers a considerable sense of comfort and security. One of the unexpected outcomes of living on Divinity Road in Oxford was the profound vulnerability I felt when I moved in and discovered for the first time since leaving my childhood home for college, what it feels like to have someone arrive unexpected at my front door, not to have at least an intercom between me and the outside world. At the worst, when I was living with Susan and Meredith on 75th Street, we got the occasional drunk in the middle of the night pressing our buzzer and waking us up. Sometimes Meredith would be crying at the door by the time I woke and there was one terrible occasion when Susan had taken Meredith on a mother–daughter trip to Amsterdam and I was alone in the apartment and someone pressed the buzzer repeatedly at three in the morning and I was convinced it was not a mistake, that even if the person—it turned out to be a man—was drunk, he knew exactly where he was; in fact this was true, because between bouts of buzzing he stood back on the sidewalk, swaying unsteadily and looking up at our apartment as I cowered behind a curtain looking down at him, and though he did not shout or scream, because this might have attracted the attention of neighbors or police, he was pointing his finger at our apartment, stabbing it in the air, and the more animated he became the more I was convinced he must have been a student I had offended or who believed I had wronged him in some way, ruining his chances for graduate school, or who knows what, because students can, some of them, become incredibly volatile, unpredictable, and even dangerous.

In Oxford, the intrusions on my privacy were more acute; anyone could walk up to my door on Divinity Road and ring the doorbell or hammer his fist, or, as some British people are apt to do, bang the letter slot, though this is something often done by tradesmen or delivery people and always felt to me like the most intrusive act of all, since those strangers' hands were effectively entering *into* my home, *into* my private domestic space. It eventually became so upsetting that I put up a small sign that said PLEASE RING THE BELL and after that the letter-slot banging became much less frequent. Nonetheless, on a great number of occasions the kinds of visitors I had were so alarming that it reached the point where, if I was not expecting someone, if they did not phone or text in advance of their arrival, I simply did not answer the door. Before taking this radical decision, I had had a number of unpleasant encounters on my doorstep. Some were benign: local councillors—or as we say in America, city council members— canvassing to see if residents had any concerns; sometimes political campaigners would come, other times people collecting for charities who would want me to sign up with my bank details to provide a monthly payment to their organization. None of these encounters troubled me unduly. On other occasions, however, I sensed a more malign purpose, or was faced with a man or woman, often working for a corporation, a public utility or broadband provider or something of the kind, who would not take no for an answer and begin to argue with me, wondering why I should not wish to switch my energy supplier when I was undoubtedly paying too much, or why I would not want to get faster broadband when it was being offered at this very special price, and when I told the individual that even if I did choose to change my energy supplier or switch my internet service provider I would not do so in person on my doorstep but over the phone or the internet, they often became incensed, as if I was impugning them, suggesting they were untrustworthy, which was in fact the case. I have always had difficulty in trusting strangers.

Then there were other more ambiguous encounters. Once a woman came to the door, a Polish woman, who claimed to be an art student, peddling her drawings of kittens and kitsch English country houses. I turned her down but she came back every day for a week until I told her that if she came again I would phone the police. I discovered later that she had also tormented my neighbors, even some of my colleagues who lived in other neighborhoods in Oxford. This was in the early days of large numbers of Poles moving to Britain. On another occasion, a day when I was feeling weak, or rather low, or perhaps just tired of living outside of America where things like this did not seem to happen, or at least never happened to me, a couple of Middle Eastern men rang the bell. I had failed to look through the peephole before opening the door and was taken aback when I saw them standing there, bearded and smiling. My first thought was that they were from the local mosque and had come on a community-relations campaign going door-to-door, but they explained they were gathering signatures and contributions to fight against the regime in Syria. I allowed them, standing there on my multicolored Victorian tile walkway, to tell me about the dictatorship and the many human rights abuses taking place in their country. Because, frankly, I was a little afraid of the men, I signed my name to their petition and wrote a check for twenty-five pounds, made out to an innocuous-sounding organization that had 'Democratic' or 'Democracy' in its name—I no longer remember precisely what it was. The check cleared within the week, though I had thought for a moment after the men left and I was standing in my front hall holding my checkbook and shaking unac-countably that perhaps I should cancel the check, but then worried that if they discovered it was no good these men might return, and who could say what measures they might take to get the twenty-five pounds I had given in apparent good faith. An unpleasant part of my mind insisted that Muslims or Arabs, or that section of the human population where the two groups intersect, are funny about money, or rather that they have a different sense of ethics relating to money than Christians or Jews, and that my failure to give money in good faith might have been regarded as some breach of Sharia law, though that system is not in place in Britain, but Britain was, by halfway through my time there, feeling like a more actively Islamic place than when I had first arrived. These men must have come to my door on Divinity Road after the bombings in London, and by that point I remembered having seen a poster at Modern Art Oxford depicting the city transformed into an Islamic paradise, with minarets and domes rising around the Oxford skyline and women in burqas and niqabs populating the cityscape, reclining on Persian carpets. That poster had inspired a kind of visceral anger in me that I could not entirely understand or explain to myself. At the time, I had few Muslim friends and little knowledge of the religion except the crude versions of it depicted in much of the western media during the early years of the War on Terror. I know now that there are as many kinds of Muslim as there are Christian or Jew or Buddhist or Hindu, and I would like to think that if the same thing happened today my response would be quite different, owing to the very good Muslim friends I have made, and the marvelous colleagues from the Middle East I have come to know and whose work I respect, not to mention the more intimate relationship I had (I still have? The question remains open, if only just) a few years later, a relationship that has altered my sense of Islam more profoundly than I might have thought possible. But at the time, the imagining of Oxford, a great seat of Christian tradition and learning, transformed into the outpost of some new caliphate seemed as grotesque to me as if one were to depict Mecca as the home of a holy roller Evangelical Christian church or a Midwestern shopping mall, and the intersection of that imagined remaking of Oxford with the men on my doorstep campaigning for Syria almost undid me.

All this was spinning in my thoughts as I sat in my New York apartment, turning over the pages of web addresses, which, though unremarkable at first, began to alarm me. I thought I recognized some of them, and not just in the obvious way that I would notice the root address for *The New York Times* or *National Public Radio* or *The New Yorker* or *The Guardian* or any number of other websites I frequent, but because I started to spot complete addresses for news stories that I knew I had read in recent days, and then I saw addresses that, frankly, made me begin to panic, not because my name appeared, but because they were addresses for two email inboxes, one in the NYU server, and the other from Google's mail system. I reached for my laptop, logged into my Gmail account, and began entering addresses that were on the printout in front of me. Messages I had sent and received began to appear on the screen, and at this point my stomach dropped, I felt a chill pass through me, and my heart started hammering. This, I understood, these thousands of pages before me with who knows how many tens or hundreds of thousands of addresses on them, was a printout of my own web history. How many days or weeks or months or years were represented by twenty-five hundred pages of addresses, or even by five thousand if the second box was not just a set of duplicates? (I checked and the pages appeared to be different.) How much of my life was before me, and who on earth might have sent it? What might they be trying to tell me, other than the obvious, which is to say that they could see exactly where I had been, and that someone has been monitoring my activity for quite some time? The fact of digital surveillance was not itself a surprise, but surely the government would not present the information gathered to the person surveilled? No, this was, I felt certain, the work of some private entity, perhaps someone with a grievance who was preparing to blackmail me. This—I knew, I suddenly felt, I could see very clearly—was all too real a possibility, for there were without question secrets from the past decade that might well be exposed by my activity online, which someone might use against me, either in an attempt to shame me publicly—this was possible, truly, though I feel certain I have never done anything that would be judged, in the end, as intrinsically evil—or, and this seemed less probable, to try to get me fired from my job, though why anyone would wish this I cannot say. I have held no grudges against my former colleagues at Columbia, I got on exceptionally well with my colleagues at Oxford, both in the College and the Faculty of History, and in the months since starting at NYU I have found all my colleagues professional and, frankly, charming.

For hours that night I read through my history, in the telegraphic style of web addresses. I say read, though in fact I barely made a dent in those five thousand pages because once I had confirmed what was before me the temptation to check the addresses against my memory, to ascertain whether every email I had sent and received was there accounted for (they were, to my astonishment, every one of them, beginning from a week before the first box arrived and going backwards in time, though how far I could not quite discern on first reading), and in so reliving my recent activity I felt both the futility and waste of my hours but also the horror of being watched, of knowing that even if someone was not actively monitoring everything I did then they were surely *recording for future use* everything I read and wrote and viewed online. I do not imagine, I am sensitive enough for this to be true, that the intrusion I felt in those hours alone on a cold Monday night in my apartment was as painful or traumatic as rape, but rape was the metaphor for which my mind first grasped. The violation felt like a hand punching up through my viscera and seizing my heart. I could not begin to go to sleep. It is one thing to imagine a faceless government entity somewhere logging my activity, quite another to have someone go to the trouble of printing out the record of such activity on white paper, placing it in a standard cardboard box, wrapping it in brown paper, and addressing it in permanent marker before having it delivered, or delivering it himself, in person, in disguise, to my home address.

UNABLE TO SLEEP, I watched Tuesday dawn knowing I could not possibly teach that morning. On the radio, *Democracy Now* was reporting that the United Nations had scheduled peace talks between rebels and the Syrian government, while the government of Pakistan was protesting America's ongoing drone war, which seems, according to *The Washington Post*, to be under the control of the CIA rather than the US military. On the *New York Times* website I read about the effective banning of street protests in Egypt, and because I suddenly wondered about the wisdom of reading such an article in a form that was traceable, and, more to the point, because the story itself was something I did not wish to think about, I turned off my computer and stared out the window at the dull November light, seeing a face in my mind, in the movements of cloud behind the projection of memory: a face I had been trying, unsuccessfully, to forget, along with the three syllables, the arrangement of phonemes, attached to its image.

Since it was the week of Thanksgiving and a major storm was threatening the East Coast, no one would complain if I canceled my classes, which I promptly did. With nowhere else to be I stayed in bed all morning listening to the radio, reading the news about Egypt and Syria and Iran and Iraq and Pakistan and Yemen even when I wanted not to think about such places, listening and reading as I lay surrounded by the record of my recent life, sometimes moved to bouts of shaking and weeping. There was more of my life recorded in those pages than I cared to remember. Not that I have done anything about which I should be truly embarrassed. A sex life lived out alone, in isolation, with still images on a screen, not even with another adult interacting in some live if remote way on the other end of an anonymized connection, did not seem extraordinary, since so very many people view porn and the porn I had looked at over the years was not even terribly exceptional, I would hazard. Yet seeing in glimpses the perambulations of my own fantasies and desires mapped in this way so galled me that I felt I could not even leave the apartment, terrified that the shame would flare on my cheeks and brow, visible for all.

What, in fact, if the pages had come from a current student, perhaps even Rachel? She had behaved slightly out of character the day before, and it was not unreasonable to suspect that, as one of my closest advisees, one of the students I had come to know best in those first months back in New York, she might have taken offense at something I said in the welter of comments I have made on her work. It is possible I unwittingly provoked her anger, such that she might attempt to persecute or threaten me. Something like this had happened in Oxford, I have to admit, actually on more than one occasion.

I cannot explain why I have attracted this particular breed of student over the years. In one of my tutorial groups during my first year at Oxford I had a student named Jayanti, and in that small group (I think perhaps there were at most only half a dozen second-year undergraduate students), Jayanti was always the least prepared, had sometimes not prepared at all, failing to do the reading, or writing nothing she might present. Halfway through the course of the eight-week term in which the trouble occurred (I think it was Michaelmas, I remember the leaves turning, or rather I remember taking walks to try to sort out what was happening and being conscious of rotting leaves underfoot), Jayanti began missing tutorials. With each tutorial she missed I would send her an email noting her absence, enquiring if she had been unwell, hoping she would be able to attend the next tutorial, reminding her that tutorials were compulsory and she should send me the work she had failed to deliver in person. Always I copied in the Senior Tutor. At first Jayanti responded in a measured way, apologizing, claiming illness, offering a doctor's note, asking to arrange to make up the missed class, though I was under no obligation to provide such a service and I do not think we had any meetings outside of the ordinary tutorial sessions.

For a couple weeks Jayanti came to class, although she still did not seem very well prepared and the essays she had written sounded as though they might have been the work of someone else. Then, in the final two weeks of term, as we were approaching the Christmas holidays, she failed to turn up for a tutorial and failed to write to explain her absence, so in response I wrote a firm but professional email, again copying the Senior Tutor, to make note of her absence and remind her once more that tutorials were compulsory and illness required a doctor's note to be excused.

That was when the real trouble began. Jayanti replied within minutes, accusing me of lying, claiming she had come to the tutorial but found my rooms empty, that she knocked and knocked on the door and called my name but no one had answered. This was a complete fabrication, or else she was herself mistaken and had gone to the wrong rooms, or perhaps was delusional, I began to think. She claimed I had been 'riding her hard' all semester, that I was belittling and high-handed and patronizing and any number of other things, all unfounded accusations. She concluded her email by threatening to throw herself off the roof of the College or to jump from Folly Bridge into the Thames. Because she had copied her message not only to the Senior Tutor but also to the College Principal, the Domestic Bursar, and to a number of my colleagues in the History Faculty, an investigation was opened into my behavior, which involved the lengthy interviewing of all my students. To my great satisfaction, all my other students reported that Jayanti was lying, that I was demanding but also a fair and respectful teacher and that we had all been sitting in my rooms during the tutorial in question and not once had anyone knocked on the door, let alone called out my name. The investigation was closed before the end of that Michaelmas term but I spent the holidays—the *vac* as the British call it, which I always heard as 'vacuum', an association not entirely misplaced for me in my first year at Oxford when I did not return to the US—alone, whiling away those dark weeks in my rooms, or failing to find occupation in a city that largely shuts down for Christmas, or going, out of despair, to spend a few expensive days in London visiting the galleries and attending concerts. I had never felt so isolated in my life. I missed my wife and daughter. I missed my mother and my late father. I wondered why I had ever come to Britain and why I had not had the sense to go home for Christmas, even if that would have meant sleeping on the couch of a friend in New York or spending it with my mother at her house in Rhinebeck. I did not make the same mistake ever again, and always thereafter, whatever the cost, flew back to New York for Christmas.

My experience with Jayanti was so upsetting I almost quit, there and then, because despite the problems I had faced at Columbia, and they were in their own way unfounded, I had never before been accused of misconduct by a student, never been lied about so outrageously, nor had anyone threatened to commit suicide because of my teaching. This was, I think now, the most distressing aspect of the affair, that a young woman's psychology was so troubled she would threaten to kill herself. The College authorities, to their credit, handled the matter with care, placing Jayanti on academic probation. She left the university without finishing her degree, but remained in Oxford living with her boyfriend, who was also in the College, and I continued to see her throughout my years there, often at the most inopportune moments, so that it began to feel as though she might be stalking me, trying to get revenge for the part I had played in the stalling of her higher education.

Perhaps the addresses for those messages that passed between Jayanti and me were now before me on the bed, on one of those five thousand sheets of paper, probably near the bottom of the pile, though as I turned them over they became a lapping sea of black on white and any order that might have been was lost. It hardly mattered; I knew what was before me, what the pages represented, and knew that someone, perhaps very close at hand, wanted me to know I was being watched.

A LARGE PART OF growing up in society, which is to say growing up in any kind of community, involves acculturating oneself from infancy to the experience of being observed. One might go so far as to say that the human condition is one of observation. Not to be observed is, in fact, regarded as a crime, the crime of parental neglect or abandonment. The unobserved child becomes the abandoned child, the wild child, the girl or boy raised by wolves, discovered often in adolescence when some attempt is made forcibly to acculturate them to being monitored, to observation, to the modes of behavior a given society requires for a person of whatever age in order to remain an accepted member of the community. I think back to the ways in which I became aware of being attended to as a child, the means by which I was conscious of my parents in the first instance paying attention to what I was doing, observing me and punishing me if I did something they regarded as inappropriate or simply 'naughty,' though when I say punishment I should be clear my parents did not believe in corporal chastisement: I was never hit or spanked or slapped or, as the British would say, *smacked*. As punishment my parents would send me to my room. Being a sociable child not readily given to reflection, this was quite effective chastisement, although it was always couched in reasonable terms: 'Jeremy, please go to your room and think about what you have done and come out when you are ready to behave like a civilized human being.' In my rage or tantrum, galled that whatever I had done was regarded as naughty or uncivilized, I would stomp off to my room, close the door—I learned quickly not to slam it, for this would increase the punishment to an active form of correction, such as having to polish all the silver or pull every weed in my mother's flowerbeds or collect every twig or branch that had fallen on the lawn—and sit at my desk drawing pictures or lie on my bed, hyperventilating at first, but then reading to calm myself. As I read or drew, my thoughts would wander to whatever I might have done to incur this punishment and I remember on occasion being astonished that my parents had discovered the wrong I had committed because it might have seemed like the kind of thing no one would notice at the time.

The process of learning that one's actions are observed, that if I arranged snails on the kitchen sink my mother would immediately know I had put them there and that they had not, as I believed she might think, crawled there themselves, meant that by degrees I learned to self-correct, or to monitor my own behavior and act within the boundaries of what was regarded in my home as 'civilized.' By chance and chance alone my parents had a quite narrow sense of what was civilized, at least compared to the wider world, so by the time I went to school I was recognized by teachers as a 'good boy,' and because this was gratifying and I responded positively to such attention and reinforcement, I continued to follow the rules and behave well, lest I become a 'bad boy' or a 'naughty boy.'

School expanded the universe of observation and monitoring. It was no longer just a matter of my behavior being attended to: the products of my intellectual and creative efforts were subject to analysis, critique, grading, etc. This process of having my work assessed and scrutinized compounded my desire to be both a 'good boy' and a 'good student.' I knew that whatever I wrote or drew or painted in class would be looked at by someone else and therefore, unlike some of my peers who for whatever reason did not feel the same impetus, I tried to perfect everything I did, to be as accurate as I could be, always to know the answer, to draw and paint objects, people, and animals in ways that aspired to verisimilitude, even perhaps to realism, though I did not know the meaning of that word until I went to college.

The scrutiny of one's peers is also, of course, a part of that process of becoming acculturated to observation, knowing that Kelly and Jason and Emily and Chad were watching me as much as I was watching them, and that if I did something naughty or uncivilized out of view of my teachers, there was often the very good chance, the near certainty, that one of my classmates would turn tattle and tell the nearest adult whatever it was I had done. I knew this was the case because I, too, was a tattler, although tattling often occupied an ambiguous position in the culture of the school since teachers maligned the act of tattling as much as they rewarded, in various immaterial ways, the child who revealed serious wrong done by classmates. We were, thus, taught to observe and report while also being told that the act of reporting, of telling what we had seen, was somehow dirty, that being a tattler was not so different from being a snitch, and being a snitch not so different from being a spy, which is to be someone who trades in deception, who might easily be turned by an opposing force to spy on *us*. I tattle on Shelley but the next time I see her doing something wrong she offers me a bribe to remain silent and the moment I accept that bribe and keep the secret of her wrongdoing, perhaps even keeping watch in case Mrs. Stuyvesant approaches wherever the illicit behavior of whatever variety is taking place, in that moment I become a foreign agent in the realm of the school, acting against the best interests of the community culture, against the power of the school's system of government and control, and that is because I have proven myself an effective spy who is also beset by his own weakness, perhaps simply the weakness of wishing to be liked, or because I desire something that my own allowance cannot procure for me, but with the money from Shelley I will be able to afford whatever it might be that makes me turn against the wider culture. Children are trained in the arts of observation and betrayal from the moment they are left to play together, beyond the full observation of adults, but with the promise that the adults will ultimately return to remind them that any sense of freedom is false. To be human is to be watched, to be part of society, because we are social animals, but we do not expect that observation by community or government will extend into our private adult lives. Those of us who are rational believe that as long as we are not breaking any laws, there is no reason the government should be watching what we do inside our homes, within the confines of our private property, and yet this apparently rational belief has been demonstrated, time and again, by the behavior of law enforcement and intelligence services, to be profoundly false.

THAT TUESDAY, NOVEMBER 26TH, two days before Thanksgiving, I did not eat well. I remained in bed except to go to the bathroom, to make myself coffee in the morning, to eat a bowl of cereal and some fruit for breakfast, a sandwich for lunch. For dinner I ordered in spring rolls and vegetarian pho and ate in bed like a dissolute sultan pondering the course of his life, surveying the record of his thoughts and whims, his petty histories, the banality of his triumphs and defeats, printed so coldly before him.

I remembered the last time I ate in bed, more than a decade ago, in that bleak Christmas vacation during my first year in England. Though at the time I was still unsure if my marriage to Susan was definitively over, whether the separation would translate itself into a divorce or if some renegotiation of the terms of our bond might yet be possible, I had decided to see other people, or rather Susan and I had agreed that as part of the separation we would, in her words, 'explore the widest spectrum of our desires.' I have a rather limited palate, so I went looking for someone who, I see in retrospect, was merely a different shade of Susan, another academic woman, a person of learning and intellect and mild attractiveness.

There was a young postdoctoral Fellow in the College, then in her late twenties, working on some aspect of post-war British history, though it was never entirely clear to me what the subject or point of it was, it seemed more philosophy than historiography. We had, after a particularly dissolute High Table dinner, found ourselves alone in the front quad at three in the morning. Our rooms were on opposite stair-cases, though both on the top floor so that on several occasions, when the days were warm—and there were some lovely warm autumn days during my first weeks in Oxford—we had glimpsed each other sitting on the battlements in the sunshine and as a consequence started chat-ting whenever we met in the Senior Common Room. By the night of debauchery, which was also in late November, we were calling each other Jeremy and Bethan. I am certain she made the first move, offer-ing me yet another drink in her rooms. I followed her up the narrow unvarnished wooden stairs and found myself struggling to remain conscious as she fumbled with the key to her door and then, alone in her suite, which was very like my own, she poured us both a whisky that I could not bring myself to drink. We talked, half reclining next to each other on her couch, the black skirt inching up her legs, shoes kicked off, and after an hour we both began to fall asleep. The couch was deep enough that we could lie next to each other comfortably and so remained there until dawn. Since it was a Saturday there was no scout coming to clean the room and the sun woke us, or at least me, and when I opened my eyes I also became conscious of Bethan's finger tracing a legend in my back. She leaned her face into mine and we kissed, though both of us, I think, were aware of the foulness of our breath and the scents of the previous evening's meal on our clothes and the complexities and complications that might arise if we took the moment further.

'We should talk, perhaps,' I said, and she nodded as someone knocked at the door.

I slipped from the couch and tiptoed into her kitchen where I waited as she made excuses to the youngest of the College porters, Robert, who had a crush on her. He had brought her a package that was delivered that morning, though usually it would have been left in the College lodge for her to pick up later in the day. My first encounter with Bethan went nowhere, but we tentatively began meeting for coffees and dinners outside of College, a rather old-fashioned round of dating without sex, since Bethan did not seem in any hurry to go to bed with me and, though I found she had nice legs and a reasonably fine face, she was not beautiful, not nearly as beautiful as Susan; I felt little in the way of passion, scant desire to complicate my new life in College or the Faculty by making love to a younger colleague. If sex alone was what I was missing, I knew I could wait.

Left alone that Christmas, however, discovering that in Britain everything closes down for Christmas Day itself and it is impossible to go to the movies, as had been my and Susan and Meredith's habit in the years before our family split apart, I slipped into a state of such profound depression that I knew I had to get out of Oxford, where there was no snow, just a thin layer of ice that covered the sidewalks and seemed perfectly to reflect the state of my heart. I knew Bethan had gone home to Derbyshire for the holidays and was staying with her parents, but I phoned her nonetheless to see how she was doing. I admit now that I was hoping for an invitation, telling her how lonely Oxford seemed and how deserted it was with all the students gone for the vac.

'Why don't you come here for New Year's?' she said at last. 'There's plenty of room. But you'll have to be prepared for the disco on New Year's Eve.'

Her parents managed an inn in the Peak District, living in a flat at the back of the establishment, above the kitchen. It seemed an opportunity to see a different version of British life, though Bethan warned me that her parents were negotiating a separation, possibly a divorce, her father was an alcoholic, and he and Bethan's mother were no longer sharing a bedroom, her mother having taken over Bethan's own childhood room while she slept on a couch in the lounge or in a room in the inn if one happened to be free, on the understanding she would be responsible for cleaning it the next morning.

The inn was near the Chatsworth estate and I took the train from Oxford to Chesterfield, where Bethan met me at the station in her mother's Mercedes, a late-model silver sedan, which surprised me because she had mentioned money problems and the difficulties they had keeping the inn profitable despite the near constant flow of drinkers. Apparently they had not managed to tap the lucrative market of ramblers and backpackers who seemed to favor establishments with more character than the Cock & Boot. It was on the edge of a village, overlooking that gentle, managed landscape of hills and woodland, but with an interior which spoke more of the 1980s than the 1780s, lacking those qualities sought by tourists, the air of *olde worlde Englande* that Americans in particular so desire, many of them assuming, as I once did, that the whole country will look like a Merchant Ivory film or a Jane Austen adaptation.

When I met them Bethan's parents were the age I am now, in their early fifties. I have little sense how she described me before my arrival, perhaps as the rather sad American colleague who was alone for the holidays and knew no one else well enough in the whole of Britain to have another invitation. They welcomed me with what I would later come to recognize as a Northern working-class friendliness, rough at the edges but quite genuine, without ever plumbing very deep beneath the surface. They asked me few questions about myself and I only gradually discovered, or inferred, that people like Bethan's parents tend not to probe in the way Americans almost certainly will, trying to place a person socially, geographically, and professionally within minutes of being introduced. So they appeared little interested in me at first, except as a friend of their daughter, who drove me out to a neighboring village where we had dinner alone the first night, in a pub with a disused well in the middle of the dining room, its opening capped with Perspex, a light burning forty feet below, and a little plaque on the wall next to it claiming it was haunted by the soul of a Fenian fugitive drowned there by locals in the late nineteenth century.

I had brought Bethan a late Christmas present, a book on Paul Klee, in whose work she had expressed interest, with a card that read, 'For Bethan, who is not ignored, Love, Jeremy.' She had complained on the phone of feeling her parents were so convulsed by the drama of their dying relationship that they seemed unaware of her presence. When I presented the book she blushed and became flustered and later insisted on buying me dinner. I understood I had made a misstep. We were not at the gift-giving stage of our friendship, although in America, I was certain, this would not have been so. The expectations were different, and I had no sense of their parameters.

That night, the first night I spent at the Cock & Boot, was also the first of two nights I spent getting drunk with Bethan and her mother, Peggy. We started in the pub itself, rather warily circling Bethan's father, Tom, a small solid man, not much more than five-foot-five but with muscular arms and a chest of the kind that made me think he might once have been a boxer and could certainly still throw a punch if he had to eject someone from his pub. When I tried to pay, he raised a hand and grumbled, refusing my money.

I spent the night in one of their guest rooms (again, they refused payment), and while I thought Bethan might come to visit me after her parents had gone to bed, I spent the night alone. The following day I came down for breakfast at eight but there was no one about. I was starving and walked into the village hoping to find something to eat but nothing was open. I didn't know if this was because it was New Year's Eve or simply the reality of life in a small English village but I returned to the Cock & Boot to find Tom readying the pub for opening. I had a stabbing headache and was nearly doubled over with hunger when he looked up in my direction.

'Can I get you some breakfast?' he mumbled.

'That would be great, Tom. Whatever you have.'

Without replying he ducked into the kitchen and a few minutes later returned with a plate of fried eggs, sausages, baked beans, a grilled tomato, and toast, which he served to me at the bar.

'That looks delicious,' I lied. The plate was a sea of grease.

'I always do the breakfasts. The Missus can't cook to save her life.'

As I began to eat Tom polished glasses behind the bar, his jowls hanging, bulldoggish, checking from time to time on my progress but for the most part preoccupying himself with what looked like busy work.

'You like my daughter?' he asked at one point, his back to me.

'She's very nice.'

'She's a good girl. Any man would be lucky.'

'She's an intelligent woman.'

Tom glanced over his shoulder, mouth breaking into a smirk as he cracked his neck, put down a glass, then cracked his knuckles before reaching out to turn a bottle of whisky ten degrees to the right so the label was aligned with all the others on the shelf.

'Told me to be nice to you. I hope you're, you know, nice to her.'

I was unsure what he might be implying. It was the kind of oblique statement that fell short of asking what my intentions might be, but was close enough to make me more uncomfortable than I already felt.

'I appreciate your concern, but we're only just getting to know each other.'

'Says you have a wife.'

'That's right.'

'And a daughter.'

'Also right.'

'Love her I bet.'

'Very much,' I said.

'So you understand.'

He said the words so quietly they sounded like a threat.

'Yes, I do understand.'

He was silent then, as though thinking, though he did not give the impression of being thoughtful. Ruminative, perhaps—it was possible he was the kind of man who turned a single thought over in his head until it accumulated mass enough to burst from his mouth. 'O'Keefe. That Irish?'

'Long way back.'

'My older brother was killed in the Birmingham bombings.'

'I'm sorry. Bethan never mentioned it.'

'Happened before she was born. IRA.'

'That must have been very upsetting.'

'Was only a boy,' he said, as if this made the loss of his brother even more profound, as if the Irish, in killing his brother when Tom was only a child, had amplified the wound. '1974. Drinking in the Mulberry Bush.' His eyes popped and he stared at me, face reddening.

'I imagine that's the kind of thing you never really get over.'

There was another long pause. The fat congealed on my plate.

'Your daughter in New York?'

'She is.'

'Must miss her.'

'Very much.'

'Couldn't have left myself. If I were you, I mean. That's all I'm saying.'

His words poked a finger into the most sensitive part of me, where the guilt was raw.

'I accepted the job at Oxford before the attacks, and I was already separated from my wife.'

Smoking was then still legal in English pubs and Tom pulled a pack of cigarettes from his pocket and lit one, blowing smoke towards the ceiling. When I had eaten all I could, I pushed the plate across the bar, wiped my mouth on the paper napkin, and left the room.

What kind of man was I to leave my young daughter in New York and move to Oxford at the very moment of the city's worst crisis in its history? Though Susan and Meredith were comparatively unaffected, their lives being almost wholly on the Upper West Side with no reason to venture much farther south than 59th Street, every time I was made to think about my choice I felt queasy with guilt. At the time of the attacks I had already been out of the city for more than two months and was preparing for my transatlantic move from the upstate safety of my mother's house. Even there, knowing I would have to leave America in only ten days, I was paralyzed by panic. When my mother and I woke in the middle of the night to the keening of sirens we were convinced that terrorists had found their way to our corner of the state, and in the first months in Oxford I could not hear a siren without my blood pressure rising. No one had bothered to warn me about Bonfire Night and Guy Fawkes', the weeks of fireworks at the end of October and beginning of November, fireworks that sounded more like explosions than acts of celebration, so that as I tried to go to sleep in my narrow twin bed in College I would suddenly sit upright, often banging my head against the frame, when what sounded like a mortar shell exploded somewhere nearby.

A friend who lived in Tribeca had been jogging down Greenwich Street but was already at work in Midtown by the time the first plane hit. It was the closest I had come to being touched by the attacks, though a tremor rippled through my psyche in the ensuing days as I tried to get my affairs together to make a move that suddenly felt foolhardy: how could I possibly leave my daughter? What if there were more attacks? What if planes never flew again? What if the world as we had known it was suddenly coming to a catastrophic end?

That brief exchange with Tom picked away at my guilt, and during my remaining time at the Cock & Boot we did not say another word to each other. I admit I avoided him as much as I could. Loneliness had delivered me to this strange situation, in which I felt, if anything, even more isolated and alienated than I had sitting alone in my College rooms in Oxford.

Bethan and I spent the rest of that day walking in the countryside, crossing the Chatsworth estate, eating lunch in yet another pub, this one in Bakewell. Every meal apart from breakfast involved an alcoholic drink and this, I knew even then, was a habit to which I would never be able to accommodate myself. Night fell by half past three in the afternoon, and as the people around me slipped into intoxication, I again wondered why I had left New York. I knew of course. I had little choice, at least no other choice that made sense to me then.

The New Year's disco at the Cock & Boot was a sad occasion, and sadder still because Bethan tried to make herself an irrelevance, to pretend she was not one of the elect by virtue of her intelligence and hard work and yet that was exactly what she did, becoming so drunk there was no point in my sticking around. I disappeared without saying goodnight and fled the next morning before anyone was up, leaving behind a note of apology that made some excuse about a crisis requiring my immediate return to New York. In truth I took a taxi to the Chesterfield station and caught the next train back to Oxford, where I holed up in my College rooms behind the battlements, cooking and eating alone until the rest of the College began to return.

Bethan and I managed to achieve a quite British understanding that there was nothing more to be said, and whatever brief romantic spark might have flared between us was allowed to die. The awkwardness

I feared never materialized, at least not in a way I was aware of, and by the time I left Oxford she was married to a Professor of Theology whose Bohemian family had left him an elegant villa in Park Town, where Bethan turned herself into a North Oxford bluestocking of the kind who bathes twice a month, trailing children of similarly recherché hygiene.

LYING IN BED alone in New York all this came back to me, the flashback leaving a sour taste on my tongue and a cramp in my gut, though perhaps it was the Vietnamese food. Before returning to bed I took a turn around my empty apartment, glancing out the windows at the dark length of Houston Street and feeling, despite myself, a pang of nostalgia and longing for Oxford, which for so many years had felt like a place of semi-voluntary exile. Perhaps people like me, people of my strangely *unheimlich* temperament, always long to be somewhere other than where we are, to live in a state of unhomeliness as a way of distancing ourselves from other people.

As I stood there looking at the city to which I had returned but which had not, in some essential way, returned itself to me, for I still felt apart from it even in the moment of being a part of it, I noticed a man on the sidewalk pause and look up at my window. This time there was no doubt in my mind. He was staring at me and conscious of me staring back. We were looking at each other, as openly as two people can who are separated by glass and distance and the optical confusions of light and reflection. Who is this man who watches me? Who is the person who tracks my virtual life? Are they one and the same? The room was dark, so I could see him clearly, but there was no hope of identifying the man's face, because he was wearing a ski mask, only his eyes exposed, glinting in the frosty night.

ON WEDNESDAY I WENT for the brain scan on Park Avenue because that is where Peter and Meredith and Dr. Sebastian insisted I go, no doubt at ridiculous cost although I never saw the bills, and as I lay in the clunking, hammering white tunnel, listening to music through earphones, a kind of helmet surrounding my head and a mirror above me offering a view of the technician, I already suspected nothing would appear on the image to suggest my brain was functioning in any way that might be judged abnormal. Observation and assessment: how long, I wondered, before they invent a machine capable of reading our thoughts better than we can ourselves?

Perhaps because I had seen the man standing out on the sidewalk the night before, I believed that I was not sick, and the confusion over my Saturday appointment with Rachel could not have had anything to do with me, which is to say I had become certain that although an email from my account had been sent asking to reschedule our appointment, I had never written it, I had not pressed send, nor had I read Rachel's answer confirming she had received the message I had never written. Someone, without question, was playing with my life. I changed my email passwords but now kept the accounts open, obsessively checking to be sure nothing was amiss, that no one was sending messages pretending to be me, and no alerts were appearing that might indicate the account was open in another location.

On the way home from the scan I stopped to buy a bottle of wine to take to Meredith and Peter's for Thanksgiving. They had offered to host an extended family celebration, beginning in the morning with a balloon-level view of the parade from their terrace, or from the sunroom if the weather was too cold. As I stepped out of the liquor store a man at the corner—a tall black man in a suit and tie—shouted out to me, 'Excuse me! Sir, sir!'

I recognized that the black man was hailing me and I looked instantly in his direction. How this kind of recognition remains possible even in crowded urban spaces is, I think, one of the great mysteries of humanity, that one may be addressed merely with a title or an informal noun and still *know* by the tone, timbre, and directionality of the voice calling that you are the one intended. I looked at the man, expecting perhaps that he was going to tell me my fly was open or that I had dropped my keys or wallet or receipt, or that the bottle of rather expensive Châteauneuf-du-Pape I had just purchased was about to slip through the bottom of its brown paper bag, but instead he looked at me with a concern I found profoundly touching and beckoned me over, as though he was about to tell me I was being secretly filmed for some sort of man-on-the-street show about bumbling nobodies, my little tiff with the clerk in the liquor store which ended with me calling him a 'jerk' and disputing the price of the bottle having been captured for the amusement of millions. As I drew closer, the man dropped his voice and leaned close so he could speak quietly but still be heard above the midday traffic, and said, 'I thought you should know, somebody's *watching* you. He went around the corner toward Lexington just as you came out of the store, but he'd been following you all the way down the block and stood there staring while you were inside. I could be mistaken, but it was weird. I thought you should know.'

I looked him square in the eye and could see that this was not a man given to delusions or affected by any substance, not that I would have suspected either of those things, although the encounter was odd enough I could have been forgiven for thinking he might be unhinged.

'I appreciate it. Thank you very much. It's—no, I don't think you're wrong.'

I turned the corner and scanned the street ahead to see if there was any likely person, but 59th was curiously deserted and I hurried through the cold to the subway, looking over my shoulder as I walked, feeling certain that the man, whoever the watcher might be, had waited for me to pass and was now tailing me, ducking into doorways the moment he noticed me starting to turn. Though the black man outside the liquor store was certainly not crazy, I felt my own mind beginning to fray at the edges, or rather it would be more accurate to say that I began to be conscious, perhaps for the first time in my life, of the boundaries of my own sanity, such that I felt I was walking a border and could see another, wilder territory just within reach. The most alarming thing about this experience or realization or epiphany was that there was no discernible barrier between sanity and insanity, all it would take is a single step across the demarcating line and yet I knew, just as clearly, that while it is all too easy to defect *out* of sanity, just as simple as taking a step, to go back in the other direction and *regain* the territory of sanity, to *leave* the realm of insanity, which totally encompasses its more rational neighbor, a kind of perforated state where insanity is the largest of the two territories and sanity merely the unaffiliated enclave within it, a Vatican or San Marino of the mind (or indeed a West Berlin surrounded by the menace of the German Democratic Republic), would require an effort only the superhuman might be capable of achieving. Allow myself to step over the border and leave the kingdom of sanity and I might never manage to return.

The question I faced was who to tell. I feared telling Meredith and Peter, worrying they would think I had lost my mind until the results from the scan came back and even then it might take going to a psychiatrist to convince them I was not suffering from any class of delusion.

HAVING RETURNED HOME, I sat down at my desk and tried to think as clearly as possible about the events of the previous few days and to look at my own psyche, if such an act is possible, so as to assess whether I might be going crazy. The boxes of paper containing a history of my recent life online, all the sites visited, all the emails sent, seemed to militate against any conclusion that I might be insane, but I wanted nonetheless not to rule it out. Was it possible I had sent the boxes to myself? Was it possible I had somehow saved the complete browsing histories of all my computers over the past several years, dumped those histories into a single word-processing document, printed it out in the department, boxed it up, addressed it, and arranged with a courier service to deliver the boxes to my apartment without now having any memory of such actions? I could, I suppose, find a surveillance record of the time I had spent in my university office—security camera footage, card access records, etc. If it could be proved that I had spent long hours there in the previous week, say on Friday night, and if I had no memory of putting in such long hours at my office then it is possible that I did this myself. Or, and here was another possibility: my memory of looking at the pages and seeing their contents was itself a fabrication.

I returned to the papers, which I had repacked in their boxes, to be certain they were not, in fact, blank. With both relief and horror I confirmed they were as I remembered them being, though that still left me with the possibility I might have generated them, that I— another I from the I now writing, from the I who sat at his desk on the day before Thanksgiving—was either presenting them to myself—the myself that is the me now writing, some weeks later, the me I call myself at my desk puzzling over the contortions of my life—as a kind of record keeping, or a taking stock, or a warning, or a reminder of that which I have tried, actively, to forget. As I stared at one of the densely printed pages, an image began to emerge, a fragmentary arc, two arcs, a strong dividing line, the rolled silk of a mouth, but when I held it up and stood at arm's length from the image I could no longer see the face that had been there a moment earlier.

Turning away from myself, trying to ignore the possibility that either I was going crazy or someone was persecuting me, I listened to the headlines on the radio. An Egyptian prosecutor had charged two activists for protesting against the anti-protest law, while a number of others had been detained. Further revelations from American whistle-blowers suggested the NSA has been gathering information about the online sexual habits of a number of Islamist leaders in the hopes, one suspects, of demonstrating to followers of these men that because they have a taste for pornography they should not be taken seriously, though it remains unclear whether the NSA has attempted to use the information they have discovered. Meanwhile, the United Nations is moving forward with a resolution drafted by Germany and Brazil asserting that all citizens have the right not to be subjected to the unwarranted surveillance of their own or any other government. How, I wondered, would 'unwarranted' be defined? In strictly legal terms, meaning that a warrant would always be required? Or in a broader sense, as in *unjustified* or *unfounded* as well as being *unauthorized* by a court? Where does the authority of a court stand in a country that has allowed its intelligence services to operate outside the law?

IT WAS LATE afternoon when the phone rang from the front desk and Ernesto, who was then on duty, told me a package had arrived.

Not another one, I thought, but I went downstairs and with a sickening shudder in my heart saw a box just like the first two.

'Can you tell me who dropped it off?' Ernesto was slumped behind the reception desk. I have to admit I have trouble keeping these young men straight, Ignacio and Rafa and Manu and Ernesto, they are so much alike to my eye, except for the few very fat ones, Jorge and DeJuan, all of them polite and respectful, all of them unfailingly pleasant and friendly, so much so that on my loneliest evenings I am sometimes tempted to come sit in the lobby, little seating though there is, and spend an hour or two shooting the breeze with whoever might be on duty, if only I could be assured that none of my colleagues or graduate students might chance to see me there, appearing both needy and grateful for the conversation of a doorman. 'Was it a bike messenger? I think the last package I had was a bike messenger delivery.'

Ernesto shook his head. 'This guy, he just comes in and puts it down on the desk without even saying nothing. Really rude. No hello and no goodbye. I mean that's just weird, ain't it? I was all, "have a nice day," but dude didn't even look back, just ran out the door.'

'Did he actually run?'

'You know, in a manner of speaking. He was walking fast, I guess, but it's cold, so . . .' He paused, as if there might be more.

'But?'

'Nah, I don't know. It's just, this day and age, you don't drop a box like that in a lobby and not say nothing. How do we know what's inside? And if the guy looks like he's in a hurry and there's no return address and no postage, then you kinda wonder. That's why I phoned you.'

'You mean it might be a bomb.'

Ernesto sat back in his chair as if the idea had not occurred to him until I said it.

'You think we oughta call campus police?'

I lifted the box and considered the possibility that it might blow up in my face. It was the same weight as the first two packages, more or less, and when I shook it—rolling on the casters, Ernesto pushed his chair away from me—there was nothing to suggest it contained anything capable of causing physical damage.

'It's just paper,' I said, 'probably one of my doctoral students. Chapter drafts or something.' I took the box in my arms and marched towards the elevator.

'If I hear a bang I'll call 911,' Ernesto laughed. Did New Yorkers always have this knack for gallows humor, or is it a more recent development?

Back upstairs I almost dumped this third box down the trash chute, but then curiosity got the better of me and I opened what was by now a familiarly wrapped parcel, only this time the pages stacked within did not contain internet addresses but a log of telephone calls with originating number, number called, date and duration of the call. I immediately recognized Meredith and Peter's number, the number of my daughter's gallery, the number of my house upstate, and then when I paged deeper into the pile, there was the number of my mother's house, of my house in Oxford, of various friends in Oxford and London, Berlin, Heidelberg, Hamburg, Munich, Leipzig, Jena, Dresden, etc. It was the history of who I had called, who had called me, at my home, office, or on my various cell numbers, when the calls occurred and for what length of time, going back nearly a decade, although it seemed impossible, inconceivable that someone had been paying attention to my activity for such a long time, had been making note of this kind of detail. The more I thought about it the more it occurred to me that, unlike with the history of my activity on the internet, which could have been followed by any ordinary hacker, to amass such detailed information about my phone activity—unless those records were themselves susceptible to hackers—suggested the involvement of the government, or some intelligence-gathering contractor affiliated with the government to be more specific, and while I knew this was possible, given recent revelations, it was difficult to imagine why I might have become a person of interest to my own government, or to whatever intelligence division has seen fit to pay such close attention to my telecommunications. Moreover, I could not begin to imagine why someone within that organization would then turn around and send me evidence of the monitoring, for surely I might bring such evidence out into the open, as it were, to expose the level of intrusion—unless, of course, there was something within these pages that might cause me profound embarrassment, although what that would be, well, I could only begin to guess. Or perhaps the guess was not so difficult to imagine. The only relief I found was that this third box seemed proof of my sanity: I could not have produced such a record unless I had kept a log of every phone call made and received every day of my life, and that, I remain certain, is something I have never done.

The phone rang. It was Ernesto from the lobby.

'I wanted to make sure you were okay, Professor O'Keefe. I didn't hear no explosion . . .'

'Thanks, it was just some files, old correspondence, from my ex-wife. I still have all my limbs. My apologies for the behavior of the delivery man.'

'Nah, that's okay, Professor. If I don't see you later you have a happy Thanksgiving. You going to see your family?'

'I'll be with my daughter tomorrow, and my son-in-law. What about you?'

'With my sister in Queens.'

'Happy Thanksgiving, Ernesto.'

'Catch you Sunday maybe, Professor.'

So, I am not crazy, I thought, hanging up the phone. Someone was messing with my life, or at least monitoring it, and perhaps the messing around part, the monkeying with my email, was a first sally, a play to make me see that 'they' could do what they liked because 'they', whoever 'they' were, had full knowledge of what I did and when I did it. What I needed was to get away from the city, and while I could not very well duck out on Thanksgiving, I decided to go upstate on Friday morning and have a couple nights in the country just to think, away from phones and the internet. I was about to buy the ticket online until I thought to myself, if someone is watching all the time then perhaps I don't want them knowing that I'm going away, perhaps it will be some kind of test. I would go to Penn Station on Friday morning, buy my ticket with cash, and disappear for the weekend. If I could return to the city feeling as though an actual escape had been possible, some sense of slipping away from the world of constant surveillance, then perhaps I would be able to extend my territory of sanity back to the proportions whereby the boundary is no longer visible.

I took the three boxes of unwanted warnings—for how could I see them except as warnings, whether sent benevolently or menacingly?—and put them in the back of the hall closet where it was easier not to think about them. I tried to spend the evening diverting my attention elsewhere, making dinner, listening to NPR, and then, after loading the dishwasher, sitting down to look at a new book of photography drawn from the Stasi archives. Some photos were of agents and employees in risible disguises, each agent assuming various different personae, suggesting actors in a porn film, while others were reminiscent of Jeff Wall's work or Cindy Sherman's or even Rineke Dijkstra's, images achieving a strangely artful quality even within their artlessness. The highly artificed poses and arrangements of people in space suggested authorial intention, which was not out of keeping, I supposed, with the wider ethos of a totalitarian society, whereby intentionality is present in every moment of being, life both in private and public arranged and patterned by ideology as much as by human needs and impulses. Despite the interest I took in these images, my mind kept chewing at the question of why I should have been a person of interest to the surveillance entities of our government. Why would the NSA—for who else could it be?—have any desire to keep me so closely in its sights? I was no one of interest before I left America. I had not been politically active, nor had my parents, so much so that I cannot remember them ever even putting a campaign sign in our front yard, though I know they always voted through a kind of instinctively faithful spirit, loyal both to the Democratic Party and to America, loyal in an unthinking way because they had come of age in the 1950s, spent their childhoods under Roosevelt and Truman, the children of people whose natural affiliations were with organized labor. I suppose they were political in a rather matter-of-fact way, politics being an unconsidered part of their intellectual and social lives, but mostly they just got on with their work and did not raise me to be a political animal. I vote and I had—still have—strong positions and opinions, but have never been a campaigner. Perhaps the very fact of moving to Britain brought me to the attention of the intelligence community, perhaps all Americans who move abroad are scrutinized in this way.

There was, of course, the other matter. My mind spent that evening dancing a great wide arc all the way round the most likely reason my government might see fit to pay such close attention to my behavior. But *that* reason was comparatively recent, and the surveillance had quite obviously been going on for a longer time. I was ruminating about this and not really thinking about what I was doing—this happens more often than I would like to admit, my mind goes whirring along a given track and my hands and arms and feet and legs get on with other business—when I found myself back at the window in my living room overlooking the lamp-lit length of Houston Street. The man I had seen before was again stopped on the sidewalk, standing quite still and looking up at my window. The difference on this occasion was that the lights were on in my apartment, so he had a very clear view of me from where he was standing, and I had an even less clear view of him. I raised my hand as if to wave and the man, again wearing a ski mask (what the British call a *balaclava*), shook his head, his eyes flashing briefly in the street lamps, and began walking off towards Broadway, as he had done on the previous occasion. Why didn't anyone look at him and think *there is a potential terrorist and I should call the police*, although if you see a woman in a niqab and burqa you do not, if you're a good liberal, try to think anything of the kind, but a man in western clothes wearing a ski mask in the middle of the city has, by now, come to look like our image of a criminal, someone intent on robbing a bank or a convenience store or perhaps even worse, with those black leather gloves he might easily have been intending to commit murder, a quick killing with a stealthy knife or silenced pistol or his hands alone, before blending into the crowds on Broadway.

I grabbed my coat and keys, waited for the elevator, pounding the call button to hurry it along, fidgeted during the descent, and then ran past Ernesto, out into the plaza, around to Houston Street, and up the sidewalk in the direction of Broadway, but there was no sign anywhere of a man in a ski mask. I knew how easily he could have ducked into a building, even perhaps the Angelika Film Center, or continued on the sidewalk after having removed the mask so that I would not easily be able to identify him. I tried to think what else he had been wearing but could not be more specific to myself than to say, 'the man was wearing a black coat and black pants and perhaps black leather shoes or boots, he had black gloves and a black ski mask.'

I ran up Mercer to Bleecker, along to Broadway, down to Prince, staring at every man I met, and there was no one who seemed to fit. Sensing that the boundary between my territory of sanity and the perforation state of insanity was well within sight, that I might in fact be dancing perilously close to the border, I walked back along Prince to Wooster and home. Ernesto gazed up at me as I entered.

'You okay, Professor?'

An amiable guy, Ernesto, and there was a vacant chair next to him, which I indicated with a nod of the head, 'May I?'

'Sure, please, sit down.'

'I think someone's following me.'

'I got that feeling *all* the time.'

'No, I mean someone is actually following me. A man stopped me on Park Avenue earlier today and told me he saw someone watching me from outside on the street while I was in a store, and then, there's this guy in a ski mask who stands out on the sidewalk on Houston at night and he just looks up at my apartment. I know he's staring at me, because tonight I waved at him and he shook his head and ran away. And—' I hesitated, wondering if I should tell the doorman about the contents of the boxes I had received, and then decided it might be better to keep that to myself. '—And other things have been happening as well.'

'That sounds pretty heavy, Professor.'

'Please call me Jeremy.'

'Whatever you say, boss.'

'And please don't call me boss.'

'Okay, Jeremy,' he smiled, and gave me his hand to shake, as if we were meeting for the first time.

'You think I'm crazy? I worry I might be going a little crazy.'

'Nah, man, that sounds like some serious shit. I mean, I feel like someone's following me but that's just because my ex, I broke up with her cause she really was crazy, and I know she's following me around, but you, what you got, that sounds like, I don't know, for real?'

'Yes, I'm afraid it is for real.'

'You get on the wrong side of the mob or something?'

'Nothing like that. Nothing—criminal.'

'I don't know what to tell you then. Maybe go to the police?'

We both looked at each other and the laughter was instantaneous.

'Let me ask you this, without saying anything to any of the other guys who work here, I wonder if you would do me a favor?'

'Sure, anything.'

'If someone delivers a package for me again, would you mind taking a picture of him, but try to do it so he doesn't notice. Take a picture as he's leaving, or just as he's outside, passing by the windows.'

'Yeah, I can do that for you.'

'Thank you, Ernesto, and Happy Thanksgiving to you and your sister.'

I fished a fifty from my wallet and put it in the doorman's hand. Though he tried to protest, I waved in dismissal and took the stairs back up to the third floor, knowing at the same time that the satisfaction I got from giving him fifty dollars was a cheap kind of pleasure, and really it should have been double that since fifty does not buy what it once did, especially not in New York, and I made a mental note to be sure I gave him more at Christmas, for when have I ever given enough to anyone, except perhaps Meredith, and even to her I owe more than I will ever be able to repay because I left, I see now, when she undoubtedly needed me most. It is not enough in one's adolescence to see a father or mother only twice or three times a year, to be robbed of their annoying and nagging presence or their consolation or protection or supervision after having spent all one's life in the expectation of such care and frustration, and now there is nothing I can give my Meredith, who has everything, except the solace and aggravation of my presence, and of course these words, this text, which may end up being all I can leave her.

I WENT OUT EARLY on Thanksgiving morning to avoid the crush, knowing there would be crowds despite the forecast of high winds, but I had the taxi go up 10th Avenue and drop me at Amsterdam and 62nd so I could walk past Lincoln Center, which brought back so many fond memories of taking Meredith to the ballet and opera when she was little, and then across Broadway as I made my way to the side entrance of the Century Building so I wouldn't have to fight the crowds and cops on Central Park West. But then, just as I crossed Broadway, I noticed the Lincoln Plaza Cinemas, which I hadn't been to for more than a decade, the last thing I saw there was either Von Trier's *Dancer in the Dark* or Raúl Ruiz's strange but wonderful *Time Regained* with its stagey moving scenery and Marcello Mazzarella vamping as an oddly voyeuristic Marcel, a peeping-tom pervert spying on the lives of his friends, and so I stopped to see what was playing, half thinking that if the party at Meredith and Peter's got too boring I might duck out early and catch a matinee.

I was looking at the posters when I noticed him, as though he had come up behind me. It was the young guy in his late twenties from the café on Saturday, the guy I had spoken with when Rachel did not show up, the one who described himself as a 'corporate shill' and wondered whether Rachel was pretty, and there he was, also at the Lincoln Plaza Cinemas, also looking at the posters, though now

I can no longer remember what was showing, perhaps some Italian film indebted to Fellini or an American independent that thought it was radical to shoot in black and white, either one of which might have caught my eye, but what I do remember is turning to the young man and saying, 'Happy Thanksgiving,' and he turned to me, seemed surprised, and said, 'Coincidence! We meet again,' in a cheery tone that made me think it really was just a coincidence, of the kind that so often seemed to happen to me in New York before I left for Oxford but which, in the months since my return, had thus far been a rarity, or seemed so, perhaps because after even a month in Oxford it becomes impossible to go anywhere without seeing faces one recognizes, either colleagues or students, or simply townspeople and scholars in other disciplines, the habitués of Bodleian and Taylorian library reading rooms, daylight dwellers of the Turf and the King's Arms and the Bear, although this is the phenomenon of a small city of 150,000 people. When coincidental meetings happen in New York, by contrast, they necessarily carry more symbolic weight, it seems as though something astonishing has occurred, particularly when you meet the same stranger several times in different parts of the city; it feels almost as though fate or God, for those who believe, must be trying to send a message, to say 'this is a person you should know, you should pay attention, the two of you have been thrown together for better or ill and there is a reason you continue to meet, do not imagine there is any such thing as total coincidence.' I remember once, the year before I left for Oxford, going to an exhibition at the Yale Center for British Art, a show of Bloomsbury painters, and on the train up to New Haven there was a woman reading Lytton Strachey's *Eminent Victorians*, and though I expected to see her in the gallery itself she was not there. A few days later I saw her again, on the subway, again reading Strachey, and then a third time a few days after that. She was perhaps a decade older than me and on the third encounter I went up to her and said that by chance we'd been on the same trains three times in a week, each time I'd seen her reading Strachey, and it seemed like more than coincidence, because I had been reading Roger Fry and John Maynard Keynes in recent weeks. The woman looked at me with horror.

'Is this a joke?' she asked. 'You've been following me? What the fuck do you want?'

'Nothing, nothing at all,' I protested. 'I just thought it was an interesting coincidence, that I should see you three times in such quick succession and because we seem to have similar interests.'

Sneering, she glared at my hand. 'You're married. Go back to your fucking wife.'

Romance was the last thing on my mind but I blushed as she rose from her seat and got off at the next stop, people around us looking at me and shifting away, as if I might be carrying plague. As a consequence, standing outside the Lincoln Plaza Cinemas that Thanksgiving morning, I was wary of being too friendly, lest this young man also think I might be making a pass at him. In the end, however, he was the first to speak.

'Did you ever find your ugly girl?' he asked, a wry, cocksure look on his face, as if he enjoyed rude conversations with strangers.

'Excuse me? I'm not sure—'

'That student you were supposed to meet at Caffè Paradiso on Saturday, the one who didn't show up and you couldn't find her number.'

'Why would you call her an ugly girl? She's not ugly at all.'

'On Saturday I asked you if she was pretty and you said *no, not really*, and so I said it didn't matter whether she showed up or not.'

I could not remember having said anything of the kind, though looking back over this document I see that in my account of the conversation I implied as much. It was embarrassing to think I had been coaxed into such an unpleasant assertion, the sort of thing one man might say to another as a way of building a little unsavory misogynistic capital. Thinking back on my life, I doubted I had said anything like this since becoming a father, and the regret I felt towards Rachel, the way I had been thinking about and treating her since Saturday, tightened my chest. 'That's a crude way of looking at it.'

The young man kept smiling, showing his long white canines, teeth that had either grown naturally straight or had the benefit of expensive orthodonture. I had not paid much attention to what he looked like on our first meeting but I could see now that he was of average height, perhaps thinner than he should have been, with limp hair, and a hungry look. He was wearing dark wool slacks and black shoes and a black wool pea coat, all of them well made, expensive (designer clothes, I would have said, though I pay no attention to fashion), and he spoke with an accent I associated with well-educated East Coast families, so much so that he might have been part of Peter's set, one of Peter's former friends or classmates, the kind of privileged Ivy League frat boy who remains unmarried into his thirties, shying away from commitment or perhaps being passed over by women who see him for the jerk he is.

'I'm a crude guy. So is she ugly or not?'

'No, not ugly. I'm sure I never said she was ugly.'

'But not pretty, you definitely said she wasn't pretty, which means either she must be fat or she's hairy.'

This young man was not, himself, particularly handsome, not objectively so, although he was no uglier than Rachel, which is to say he was neither handsome nor ugly, just as Rachel is neither pretty nor ugly, but quite unexceptional, an ordinary-looking person in a world of ordinary-looking people. In his case, the young man was too thin to be handsome, his chin too prominent, cheeks gaunt, as if he might have a drug problem or eating disorder, though eating disorders among men are, I know, a rarity. He did not look athletic, did not have the build or musculature of a runner or cyclist or triathlete, which might otherwise have explained the leanness of his face. His trousers were snug and his legs looked unhealthily thin, his neck sticking out above the broad collar of the coat was vulnerable in a way that made him seem pathetic. His hair was straight and aggressively parted on one side, slicked back in the way I knew was in fashion, the extension of a recent 1950s nostalgia that had unexpectedly started looking even further back, to the 1930s, with Hitler Youth haircuts now so common in London and parts of New York that for a historian of twentieth-century Germany it is unsettling to see this hallmark of fascism embraced by young men with so little knowledge of history that they can see their chosen style simply as a marker of urban sophistication and ironic appropriation of the past; whether they even know its fascist associations I cannot say (I suppose the great majority do not), but I hoped that if they discovered what those associations really signified they would lose no time in growing their hair long and affecting a progressive bohemianism, a fin-de-siècle extravagance to counter the global lurch to the right, at least esthetically speaking, though so much of this revivification of the signifiers of fascism has been accompanied by a swing towards ultranationalist political movements that one cannot help feeling emboldened to trot out the old maxim that history repeats itself. Please may it not.

I wanted to get away from him but also, instinctively, felt he might be the sort of maniac who carries a concealed weapon and would hold me hostage. For all I knew, he afforded his expensive wardrobe through armed muggings, and so I tried to make an exit that would be definitive without provoking him. 'Listen, it's Thanksgiving, and we're strangers, we don't know anything about each other, and I'm not really comfortable with this conversation. In any case, I'm expected somewhere.'

The young man's smirk deepened, cutting a sneer into his pale right cheek. 'Parade party?'

'Something like that.'

'Me too. Friend of mine in the Century Building.'

For a moment I thought of cancelling, or saying I had another errand to run before I went to the party, just to avoid him, but no one runs last-minute errands on Thanksgiving morning and I knew the lie would be transparent. 'What a coincidence. That's where I'm going.' No such thing as coincidence, I reminded myself, not when it comes to meeting strangers multiple times in a short span of days, not when you speak to a man you do not know about intimate subjects twice in the same week, not when those conversations happen at times and locations where you have planned in advance to be present, especially not when you know between Meeting One and Meeting Two that someone is monitoring all of your communications. This sequence of thoughts flashed through my mind very rapidly without my reaching a definite conclusion, but as they did I looked at the thin young man with a greater sense of suspicion. He was smiling as I spoke, and then laughed, as if he found the situation extravagantly funny. Unhinged, I thought, unstable, already canvassing the wilderness beyond the borders of his personal microstate of sanity.

'No kidding! Wouldn't it be funny if it was the same party?' More laughter, and I forced myself to smile.

Together we turned back round the corner onto 62nd and as we walked to the building's side entrance I tried to shake the feeling I had just been mugged, or that the encounter had, in some respect, been a variety of rapidly unfolding assault.

The doormen in Meredith's building all know me, so I nodded a greeting and went straight ahead to the elevators, waiting for one to arrive as I heard the young man saying he had come to see Peter, who was expecting him, though by this time I had concluded it was as likely as not that this was the case, however horrific it seemed, horrific because it appeared, already at that point, to be part of a plan, the young man's plan, to insinuate himself into my life. I did not hear his name, but the doorman phoned upstairs, evidently got the confirmation he needed, and the young man was soon standing next to me, just as the elevator doors opened.

'I guess it is the same party,' I frowned, turning over in my memory our conversation on Saturday afternoon, looking for any clues that would tell me more about him, or what his intentions might be. 'I'm the hostess's father. Jeremy O'Keefe.'

'I thought it was you. I was at the wedding. Peter and I were in grad school together. I'm Michael Ramsey.'

The name fit my impression of his likely background, an old New England family, perhaps, though it was increasingly difficult to tell, and the prestige associated with such lineages no longer has much currency in wider society. Yet Michael Ramsey carried himself with an air of privilege assumed rather than won that I found off-putting, although some of my initial wariness was an instinctive aversion to his tone in our two encounters and, on this second chance meeting, the sense of resentment I felt at his intrusion into what I had thought of as a family event. In fact I knew Peter and Meredith were expecting some fifty guests for the parade breakfast and many of these people would be professional acquaintances, while only twenty were staying for dinner itself, all of whom would be close friends, I supposed, or family. I tried to calm myself down before we arrived at my daughter's door, making certain I was in the lead, so that I would ring the doorbell and be first inside and Michael Ramsey, whoever he was, would know his place.

It was clear from the introductions that, though invited, Michael was not a part of my daughter's intimate circle of friends and over the course of that morning I got the idea that even Peter did not know him particularly well, that perhaps Mr. Ramsey was one of those graduate school hangers-on who tries to wheedle himself into the life of his friends because his own is so dull.

'Where did you find him?' I asked Meredith when I got her alone in a far corner of the living room.

'He and Peter were in some club together. They fell out of touch for a while and then he suddenly surfaced a few years ago. Peter says he's harmless. He seems nice, don't you think?'

'He seems like a prick.'

'Oh, Dad, don't be such a grump. Have a glass of champagne.' She motioned to a waiter who glided across the room with a tray full of glasses.

'I think Mr. Ramsey is following me.'

Meredith turned back to me, grimacing.

'He doesn't even know you. You've never met him before.'

'But we have met.'

Again, a grimace—of disbelief or, perhaps, more accurately, a look of panic and unbelief, of total incredulity, as though the words she was hearing made my daughter believe in my own non-existence, as if in revealing myself as a paranoiac (not without cause, but she did not know that at the time, or at least I still trust, I want to believe, that she was innocently unaware) I had negated the image of fatherhood, of the parent-being, in which she always placed her trust, however compromised that trust might have been or felt—we have never really discussed it—when I moved out of the family home and across an ocean.

She took a glass from the waiter and put it in my hand, then took one for herself. We clinked glasses and she turned her head to look out towards the park and the parade as if she wanted to blind herself to her own unbelief in me, or perhaps, as if in no longer believing in me as the man she thought she knew, she could not bear to look at me, or even in looking found that the man before her was suddenly so unlike the man she thought was her father that she could not resist looking away, averting her eyes to protect an interior vision of the person she thought she knew, of the man I had once been, when still young and occupying a territory of sanity so vast I could not even conceive of it having reachable limits.

I regretted what I had said because it was obvious how happy Meredith was in having this party, to be able to host a room full of well-dressed and beautiful rich people, access to whom her mother and I could never have provided. This is not to suggest that Meredith is a social climber, she is one of the most grounded people I know, and yet I know and appreciate that because of the nature of her profession, having access to the enormously wealthy means the potential for a degree of success that might otherwise prove elusive or even permanently unattainable. Peter paid for her gallery space and start-up costs, and Peter made the introductions to collectors, but it is Meredith's eye and taste and business acumen that will turn hers into a leading gallery, I have no doubt. Like the dinner on Saturday night, the Thanksgiving-morning party was as much about business as a private social life. It occurred to me, looking at my daughter trying to reassemble the joy of the occasion after my odd intervention, that there was only a thin and quite porous boundary between professional and private in her and Peter's world. They run their home as a site of commerce, as the staging ground for relationships and events that work on behalf of their professional pursuits. It was as alien a concept to me as if they did the opposite, keeping their home instead exclusively for themselves, allowing no one inside except other members of their respective families. Ordinary, mainstream sociability was always the order of my and Susan's home. This was true of the homes she and I each grew up in, different though they were. Friends were invited for dinners and brunches, family came on holidays, but business associates were always something of a rarity, perhaps because our fathers, while professionals, were not particularly far up any corporate ladder and neither man was a striver, both of them disinclined to work hard for advancement, believing it was enough to be solid and reliable, not to appear to their bosses or upper management as if they had ideas above their particular station, so when colleagues were invited, at least in my own childhood home, they were my father's equals, and the gatherings were ones of friendship rather than any calculated attempt to solidify a professional position.

'What do you mean you've met?' Meredith was drinking her champagne too quickly and I knew I risked spoiling the day if I shared any of the thoughts I was then imagining might be true about Mr. Ramsey. Instead I sipped my champagne and watched the young man lingering near the terrace, talking to no one, but appearing rapt by the pageantry passing below on the street, as if he were in a state of wonder, a child marveling at the world and the giant balloon creatures floating just beneath the window and bent more than double because of the winds that day, staring as if he had never seen anything like it even though every American alive in the last few decades, unless he or she has lived in isolation without access to the media, has grown accustomed to the surreal spectacle of inflated cartoon giants floating down Central Park West in celebration of the national holiday.

Living in Oxford all those years, I found Thanksgiving produced the most acute feelings of homesickness and nostalgic longing, made worse by the fact that on those fourth Thursdays every November I would usually spend the whole day teaching, and often at least one of my students was an American and the two of us would look at each other in recognition of our displacement and the fraught togetherness produced by the holiday that we were both missing—or if there were no other Americans about, some thoughtful British student would usually wish me a Happy Thanksgiving at the end of the tutorial and ask if I was going out for dinner. Sometimes, I devoted part of my lessons on that day to the origins of the holiday. Thanksgiving, first recorded in English in 1533, a quotation from Tyndale, I would read out from my *OED: thankes giuyng*, and then, two years later, in a translation of the Bible, *thankesgeuynge*. *The Book of Common Prayer*, 1552, and then Shakespeare used it, *Love's Labour's Lost*, 1598, before the Pilgrims had their own in 1621. Lincoln made it national. One or two of the Colleges, although not mine, made a point of catering to the homesick longings of its American members and would produce an ersatz version of a turkey dinner. I attended such meals on half a dozen occasions but always found that instead of assuaging my sense of homesickness they only made it more acute. Surrounded by so many British people (many of whom seemed to think the whole affair vaguely ridiculous, sneering at any tradition, holiday, or manner of speaking that had grown up on this continent), I would forswear going to such gatherings in the future and might decline similar invitations the following year, only to find the experience of being alone in England and passing the day with no acknowledgment of the holiday was even worse than an imperfect celebration. In a way, there could be nothing more typical of Thanksgiving than a day spent in disappointment, or in only partial merriment, a holiday in which someone among the group irritates the hell out of you with his offensive jokes or rude behavior, but whose company you are obliged to tolerate for the sake of wider peace, or because he is your sister's new boyfriend or your daughter's husband or, as in Oxford, your senior colleague who exercises a different kind of power over your life. It was, after all, a holiday made official in a time of civil war, an occasion that was, perhaps in its broadest philosophical impulse, about bringing together opposing sides in a domestic conflict and letting them cease their fire long enough to break bread and tear a dead bird limb from limb, a holiday tradition built on giving thanks for the success of the first settlers' attempts to colonize.

This was my first Thanksgiving back in America, and part of me would have preferred to be only with family, taking Meredith and Peter up to my mother's house, or even going to Peter's parents' place in East Hampton (like my mother they were expected later in the day), instead of feeling like a grouch and a paranoiac in a room full of people as interested in mingling with potential business contacts as in watching the parade outside and enjoying the champagne and cinnamon rolls that circulated as if there were a limitless supply of both. I did not want to live in a world of fanciful abundance, of abundance predicated on a belief that nothing should ever run out for as long as there was someone ripe with desire. My own parents, children of the Great Depression, grew up with a sense of scarcity that made them frugal and practical, sometimes so much so it drove me nuts, but they also savored what was good, and enjoyed the large and small treats of life with a pleasure that was genuine. Looking around Meredith and Peter's living room, there was without question a sense of pleasure, but of a kind born in the expectation of such luxuries always being available. And there was Michael Ramsey, helping himself to more food, more drink, chatting to Peter, laughing as if they were old, close friends, although most of these people were already in high-gear party mode and everyone they met was potentially an old friend, someone they would have known forever if only they had been given the chance, provided of course that the person was worth knowing, could offer something in exchange for the friendship.

I was on the verge of explaining to my daughter why I was feeling so paranoid when Susan arrived. Meredith stood to greet her mother and I could see in the slight tremble of my daughter's hand how she was nervous about her parents meeting again for the first time since the wedding, though our divorce has been largely amicable. At the

wedding itself we had become almost—I liked to think at the time—
quite warm with each other, as if my ex-wife and I were both imagining a more serious rapprochement might be possible, such that one
day we could even contemplate reuniting. I had to remind myself I
had come for Meredith more than anyone else, the world did not
revolve around me, and at twenty-five it can still feel as though you
are the center of the universe and every event and relationship in your
life is ultimately about *you*. Meredith wanted me there, I was certain,
to support her in the face of her mother, and so I attached myself to
my daughter in the partial belief that I was supporting her with my
presence, even as I knew, at a more distant remove, that I could not
quite bear to circulate on my own, to risk spending another moment
alone with the strange Mr. Ramsey. Then, by one of those flukes
of social gatherings, I found myself separated from Meredith and
standing next to Susan, who has hardly aged in the years since we last
lived together, looking to my eyes as though she might still be in her
early forties.

'Where's your wonderful mother, Jeremy?'

'They've sent a car to fetch her from Rhinebeck. She won't be here
until after noon.'

'What a shame. She'll miss the balloon animals.'

'You know my mother hates parades.'

'Still cultivating her misanthropy?'

'As attentively as her African violets.'

'She'd be much happier if she could just decide to like people.'

'She always liked you.'

'But I was such a bitch to her.'

'She thought that meant you respected her.'

'You know I've always been mean to people who scare the shit
out of me.'

As we smiled at each other I felt for a moment that the previous decade had never happened and when we left the party we would go home to the same apartment at the top of a converted brownstone on 75th Street and when I went to bed that night, overstuffed and satiated, I would be going to bed with Susan, and there would be nothing strange about this, no *resumption* of what once had been but a *continuation* of what had always been, as if my decade in Oxford were only some transient series of hallucinations, one vision piled on another, all unfolding over the course of a single New York night.

I knew, however, that Susan was content with her life and had no interest in returning to me. Paranoid I might have been, but delusional I was not. She was drinking a cup of coffee and I watched her lips curl in to take the hot liquid, careful not to drip, and a light smear of coppery lipstick adhered to the white china as though the cup were a soft and susceptible skin. Her gaze turned away from the room and we looked at each other as we had not really looked for more than fifteen years, since in the final months of our living together she averted her eyes whenever I stared too closely, as though she feared my scrutiny, or as if the experience of being observed by her husband caused pain instead of pleasure. Now, however, she smiled and warmed under my gaze and it was that response, her evident enjoyment of my company, that allowed my mind to wander off and imagine what it would be like to live with her once again, to make all our lives so much less complicated than they had become since my departure.

'Nice to have you back, Jeremy.'

'Do you really mean that?'

'Yes, it's good to have you here. I've missed you.' She punched my arm in the way she always had, with more force than she realized, and the slight pain of impact was as familiar and welcome as her ageless face. This, I thought, this is someone I can trust, no matter how much time passes, I will always be able to come back to her, even if we are no longer living together she will listen to my panics and hallucinations and paranoia and know exactly what to say to calm me because there were so many years spent together and so many hours learning the habits of the other person's mind that so little now needs to be said to find our way back into the territory we shared, and which—it seemed then, in our daughter's apartment—began to expand once again the parameters of my own sanity, to make that boundary recede into a remote and nearly unreachable distance, because Susan has always, since we first met as graduate students at Princeton, given the impression of being among the sanest people I know, despite her choosing to bring our marriage to an end, which felt at the time like an act of insanity, or at the very least a bout of passionate violence. I had believed up until the time when she began to avert her eyes every time I looked at her that we shared a perfect life, because there was so little hidden between us, or because I believed, wrongly as it turned out, that she knew everything of substance about me and that I knew everything of substance about her.

'Is there anyone now?' I asked.

'No, not now. Not since before the wedding. You know me.'

'Choosey.'

'*So* choosey.' She shook her head and looked down into the lipstick-rimmed china cup, swirled the dregs, and finished the coffee. 'And you? Found anyone?'

'Not now, not anymore.'

'But there was someone?'

'At Oxford. A few flings, and one that lasted longer. More serious.'

'But came to an end.'

'Yes, I think, although there may still be fallout, of a kind, I don't know. I'd rather not—'

'I'm sorry. That must have been—'

'It's not your fault. It wasn't anything.'

'That sounds like a lie.'

'Yes, it is. It was something. And I was foolish.'

'God, you sound so British now.'

'Don't say that. I haven't changed, not fundamentally.'

'Poor Jer.'

'Please, Susan, no pity.'

'What's wrong? You look—'

'I—' At that moment I was about to tell Susan what had happened in the previous few days, believing she might have some insight into the matter, or at least be able to share in my worry, but then I saw Michael Ramsey come across the room towards us and I felt as though I could say nothing for as long as we were that close to each other. He was wearing a white button-down shirt and black sweater so that from behind he might have been mistaken for a particularly hip class of priest. 'Do you know that man?' I whispered to Susan, nodding in Ramsey's direction, hoping she would offer some reassurance that he was a harmless asshole friend of Peter's, another trust-fund frat kid with too much time on his hands but nothing really out of the ordinary. Instead she shook her head and scowled as if the very look of Mr. Ramsey left a bad taste.

'I've never seen him, but the truth is I don't know anyone here except you and Peter and Meredith. I think I recognize a few people from the wedding, but no one was very interested in me then and I don't expect they'd be interested now.'

'So you don't know him?'

She shook her head. 'Who is he?'

'A friend of Peter's. I've encountered him twice in the last few days, on Saturday, down in the Village, and then coming here. I suppose running into him on the way here isn't really the same, but it seemed like a weird coincidence.'

'What, like he was following you?'

'Sound crazy?'

Susan shrugged. I wished she had not shrugged but had instead told me it was completely crazy to be so paranoid about the friend of our son-in-law, or had at least been more dismissive, less ambivalent, less willing to countenance the possible sanity of my paranoia. It is horrible to begin to imagine that what seems like paranoid delusion might be anything but, that suspecting you are being followed and monitored and manipulated is, in fact, the height of sanity, perhaps the very definition of sanity in today's world. What is crazy is to imagine we are living private lives, or that a private life is a possibility any longer, and this is not just true for those of us living out our sentence in the developed world, but anyone anywhere, except perhaps those hidden underground, for the satellites we have launched into space and the aircraft, manned and unmanned, patrolling the air above the earth, gaze down upon us, producing finely detailed images of all our lives, watching us, or perhaps you could say we are merely watching ourselves, or at least the governments we allow to remain in power are watching us on our own behalf, as well as the corporations who do so only for their own behalf, even as they insist on the public service they claim to provide, and which we use, often for free, spending nothing to look at satellite images of our neighbors' own backyards and roof terraces or street views of their front windows and doors, trading this free access to all knowledge of the world for the recording by such corporations of the habits of our activity and making ourselves susceptible not only to the collecting of this data and its potential monetization, that is to say its sale to other entities collecting their own kinds of data about us, but also to be bombarded with advertising that, however much we may struggle against it, inserts its messages deep into our thoughts, influencing us one way or another, even though I insist I am not receptive to advertisements for fast food establishments where I haven't set foot since I was in my teens but nonetheless, and despite the fact I no longer eat meat, I look at those burgers and *have* to struggle against the desire their images produce.

'I don't think much of anything sounds crazy these days,' Susan sighed, switching from coffee to champagne. 'But I don't see how one of Peter's friends would have any reason to follow you, unless he actually works for Peter, and Peter is checking up on you on Meredith's behalf, through this proxy, whoever he is, but that's kind of a fanciful explanation, don't you think?'

'Or the explanation of a fantasist.'

'You said it, sweetie, not me.' She patted my arm and gave me such a look of sympathy, a look the like of which I had not seen since our marriage began to unravel, that I felt my eyes water and throat harden. The relief of having such a rapport again, however little we said, allowed me to believe things really might not have changed, or the clock had been reversed and it was still fifteen years ago and we were only stumbling but could see how our relationship was going off the map and we had to correct our course and keep within the known limits, because the wilderness of any relationship is a place both of potential and profound existential risk. Leaving the charted territory between you can either lead to the kinds of adventures that will reinvigorate a dying relationship or, quite the opposite, take a thriving and more or less happy one and nudge it into a place of peril out of which it is impossible to escape, a slough of despond, a bog, a wasteland of quicksand and mire. I had no knowledge of the relationships Susan might have had since the end of our marriage, just as she had not been privy to the details of my affairs, such as they were, and because I had never confided much in Meredith, who at first was too young to be told about matters that would only upset her and later because I was waiting to see if the relationship took hold and was going to be permanent enough to publicize, to make a part of my daughter's own life, because she had never even known the names of the few women with whom I shared a bed in Oxford I was fairly certain Susan did not know either, possibly could not imagine that I am able to count those foreign relationships on two hands and still have fingers to spare.

The life I led in Oxford was, for most of my time there, an isolated one, a bachelor existence in a world surrounded by many other bachelors (of both sexes), though there were the occasional one-night stands, nothing that lasted longer than a few hours or days before it became clear to both parties that it was either deeply unwise because of professional complications (they were often colleagues, like Bethan) or because these women had husbands or partners or boyfriends or lovers. They each of them used different words to describe the men on whose territory I was trespassing, though they themselves would have recoiled at my description of the situation in these terms, not wanting to be regarded as the territory or possession of anyone other than their own selves, and while I respect such a position I understand too the attitude of the men whose women were cheating on them with me, men who would have believed they had a claim at least on the loyalty of those women if not on the women themselves, although the distinction is perhaps a rather Jesuitical one, the species of sophistry I learned to appreciate in what I began to think of as the Oxford intellect, the endlessly supple reasoning that could so often bend logic to self-interest or, scarcely more nobly, self-defense.

There were one or two occasions, perhaps more, when my entanglements with these otherwise committed women of Oxford became quite painful for me, for them, and for their husbands or partners. It's not that I was helpless in the face of my own desire, although one husband in particular felt compelled to intervene because his wife was threatening to leave him for me, despite having never asked me whether I was interested in a permanent relationship with her. The poor man turned up, hat in hand, quite troubled, at my doorstep on

Divinity Road, pleading with me to break things off after having failed to convince his wife to do so herself. I showed him into the house and we sat down in the dining room where I poured him a drink. Quite apart from being aggressive or defensive, this fellow, Bryan, a medievalist who chewed his fingernails, nearly wept, saying that his wife, Anne, one of my colleagues in History, was threatening to take the children and move in with me. I could not imagine anything worse than having to share my life with Bryan's children and wife and the messy complications of this arrangement, so promptly got on the phone and told Anne it had to end. She was so devastated that the Chair of the Faculty Board asked me to try to control myself in a way that suggested I had somehow been at fault, when in fact it was Anne who had made the first move, following a gaudy at her own College where I happened, by coincidence, to be the guest of another colleague. After dark on one of those extraordinary Oxford spring evenings when summer seems already to breathe its warm airs across the rivers and the overgrown grass of Christ Church Meadow, Anne and I were alone in the Fellows' Garden of that College, or at least felt ourselves alone in the dark, in a corner, talking about Foucault or having the kind of inanely philosophical conversation fueled by excellent wine and incomparable port and the romance of decay forestalled by money that surrounds and encourages such encounters, when she reached a hand across in the dark and rested it against my left breast, pressing to feel the beating heart beneath my clothes and skin and ribs. I thought for a moment that she had reached out for balance, for she seemed to be swaying, but then she leaned in, and, being taller than me and I suspect quite a bit stronger, pushed me against a sandstone wall and prized my mouth open with her lips and tongue. I could not have imagined that our hurried fling in that garden, or the subsequent fucks in her rooms in College, or the weekend she spent at my house when Bryan had taken the children to his parents in Stoney Middleton, would lead to her developing a fantasy of a new life with me.

Anne and Bryan—troublesome though they were, and a lesson in how never to get involved with colleagues—could not have been the reason anyone might wish to pay such close attention to my life, nor could the aborted affair with Bethan in my first year at Oxford, nor, I hoped, my entirely professional run-ins with students like Jayanti, who threatened suicide and caused trouble for no reason and who was, I now feel, never serious in her threats, was making her threats in fact to terrorize me. No, I was certain—I remain convinced even now, as I write these pages, directed to my heirs, perhaps, if you have occasion to read them, or perhaps brought forth one day in my defense in a court either open or clandestine—that none of those people was the reason for the intense scrutiny of my entirely innocent activities.

I know the reason, or at least I suspect, have a ghost of a suspicion, as fleeting as the face I continue to see in the assemblage of text on a page, between the dark veils of those last moments of unconsciousness before waking each morning. By that Thanksgiving morning, talking to Susan, observing Michael Ramsey, and thinking back on my Oxford years, I should have begun to realize that it was not just one thing I had done, no single activity or stray word, not only my departure from home to live in another country, not just my choice of friends and lovers, but the enfolding of all these elements to create a kind of destiny.

'AND THEN THEY TOOK me into this tiny room and I sat there for ages,' the man was saying. He was one of Peter's acquaintances, a South African lawyer from Johannesburg. 'With the Americans you know where you stand. After three minutes the woman at the American Embassy smiled at me and said, "okay, thanks, dearie, there you go," and I got my visa. The British make you wait and wonder. They ask you a million questions, as if they're trying to catch you out, and then at the end of the interview the snide little man said, "now look up at that camera in the corner of the room." This thing was minuscule, I hadn't even noticed it was there until he mentioned it. I looked at the camera and the man said, "now, please say in a nice clear voice, 'My name is Mark Wald.'" It was the first indication I'd had that my visa interview was being recorded, but I guess it shouldn't have surprised me. What I don't understand is why they would have me do that, the looking at the camera and saying my name.'

A man in an adjoining group, who'd had his back to Mr. Wald during the story, suddenly turned around. It was Michael Ramsey. 'Facial recognition,' he said.

'Sorry?' Mr. Wald said, looking displeased.

'They do it for facial recognition. Now you're on file. You could be walking down the street in central London and some technician or law enforcement officer will be sitting at a terminal and maybe they zoom in to get a closer look at you, and the computer can tell instantly that it's Mark Wald, he's on such and such a visa, he entered the country on such and such a date, he's the son of X and Y, he specializes in whatever it is you do, etc.'

'How do you know all that?'

'Conspiracy nut,' Ramsey said, smirking.

'Well it's fucking terrifying.' Mr. Wald accepted another glass of champagne. 'But that's not the end of it. So I'm on the plane to New York from Heathrow, after the meetings in London are finished. I'm in Business Class, and as we're boarding a man sits down next to me, around my age, balding, and I could tell even before he opened his mouth that he was American.'

A round of appreciative laughter rose as Mr. Wald continued.

'So we exchange courtesies as we're getting settled. Hello, good evening, etc. I take a glass of sparkling wine from the flight attendant, but my American friend is on orange juice. Okay, I think, he's a health freak. He's in great shape, very lean, like he's at the gym every day or running thirty miles a week. Not like me.' More laughter. 'The plane takes off, and as the meals are delivered, he starts making conversation, but from the beginning he addresses me by name, "Mr. Wald." I think, fine, he must have seen my ticket, or the tag on my case, or something, but then it becomes clear he knows who I am, what I do, where I live, who my wife is, how many kids I have, even who my parents are. This man is sitting next to me for a reason. It's all prearranged. He asks me about the state of things in South Africa, what I think of the government and the president, and I'm getting even more uncomfortable, although my answers are almost certainly the ones he wants to hear. I don't like this government, the president is corrupt, the country risks sliding towards chaos. By this point we've been talking for an hour or so. The meals have been cleared, he's let the conversation ebb a bit, and then they dim the cabin lights and people around us get lost in movies and the like, and when he's certain no one is listening, he leans close to me and says, not in so many words, that the US government would like me to spy on the South African government, "for the greater good," and it's my duty as a citizen of the free world to accept.'

The people listening looked surprised, some laughed, some nodded in ways that suggested they had new respect for this Mr. Wald or that what he had revealed confirmed their suspicions about the operations of the American government, while others fidgeted, began checking their phones, and slipped away, making excuses.

'So what did you say?' Michael Ramsey asked.

'I said I was flattered but no, that was something I could not do in good conscience while continuing to practice law.'

'Why not?'

'How could I possibly stand in front of the Constitutional Court and argue a case knowing I would also be informing on the people around me, on my fellow lawyers and the justices? That would be antithetical to my idea of democracy.'

'Democracy would crumble without spies. You should've said yes,' Michael Ramsey said, in a way that was far from friendly. At that moment Meredith pulled me away to speak with a friend's daughter who had applied for early admission to NYU. My Thanksgiving morning passed in that way, ducking in and out of random frag-ments of conversation, watching people come and go, and then, when I thought again to look for him, I discovered Michael Ramsey had already left. Good riddance, I thought, and thank goodness he won't be staying for dinner.

My mother arrived, and Peter's parents, various aunts and uncles and cousins on his side of the family. We ate in the middle of the afternoon, though we had never really stopped eating. There was great amusement at my not having a smartphone; even my mother has one now, a gift to herself. 'They're so intuitive,' she said, 'I do everything with it.'

I asked her whether she realized that everything she does on her phone is recorded somewhere, stored on a database, perhaps many different databases.

'Who cares? I'm an old woman, I have nothing to hide, I don't break any laws, I just talk to my friends and send emails and watch funny videos of animals. Why the hell would the CIA or the NSA or whoever it is give a damn about any of that?'

'The fact is, we can't possibly know what will pique their interest.'

'Don't be so paranoid, Jeremy! This is still a free country. We have due process and the Bill of Rights and the best democracy in the world. Why should a law-abiding citizen worry? Even if they're watching us, they're doing it for our protection. Frankly I'm all for it.'

I wanted to lean over and whisper in her ear, 'you have no idea what you're talking about, you cannot imagine how quickly you could be affected by, for instance, my own activities, how this new regime of data collection does not see innocence first but assumes guilt by algorithmic association. How much do you know about all the people you claim as your friends? What do you know of their connections? We have remade the social landscape without understanding the ramifications of this remodeling.'

But of course I said nothing, smiling with what an English friend in Oxford once called my 'shit-eating grin,' and accepted another helping of mashed potatoes.

Peter's parents were staying for the weekend so I agreed to take my mother back upstate on Friday morning, which meant she would be with me overnight, no great burden since we get along well despite her occasional obstreperousness, and in fact when I bought my house outside of Rhinebeck earlier this year I knew there would be a certain pleasure in locating myself close enough to my mother to be able to see her easily without ever having to stay under the same roof. Some parents and children adapt to their mutual adulthood and find ways of living together, or spending extended stretches of time in their respective homes, and this has as much to do with the children learning how not to act like children as the parents learning how not to treat their children like children in constant need of correction and advice, which is to say that both sides have to learn to respect each other and the fact of their mutual adulthood, at least until the parents, if this should chance to happen, begin that terrible descent into their second childhood, during which they may wish, quite sincerely, for their children to become parents to them, as payback for that earlier relationship of care and protection and nurture.

My mother and I have reached the stage where I can happily have her stay in my home for a few nights and stay in hers for a similar period, but more than that and we risk killing each other because my mother has never quite believed in my adulthood, and, although she was happy to accept a car service from her granddaughter for the trip to the city, is wildly independent at the age of eighty-three and so remarkably intact both physically and mentally that I have not yet been faced with the prospect of assuming a greater burden of care.

Now, I wonder, should that stage ever come, will I be at liberty to assume the responsibility, or will it fall to my daughter? More likely, I think, now more than ever, my fingers aching from the effort of this composition, moving the pen across each sheet of paper, Meredith will bear the burden for us all, her parents and grandmother, the choices we have each made throughout our lives, our chickens all coming home, at once, to roost.

'You're looking well, Jeremy,' my mother said after we had finished dinner and moved to various corners of the living room for coffee and *digestifs*. 'You look like you've lost weight.'

'My weight is not open for discussion.'

'It's a compliment!'

'It's a backhanded compliment, mother. It's a compliment that implies the person being complimented was once fat and has now improved himself.'

'Don't be so stuffy!'

'It's not polite to talk about people's weight.'

'But you've always struggled with your weight, Jeremy, so I thought I was giving you a compliment. You look slimmer.'

'I have not always struggled with my weight.'

'Well, you did yo-yo while you were in England. All that ale, I suppose, and the fish and chips.'

'I ate fish and chips once in a decade and probably drank one pint of beer a year, if that.'

'You don't have to be so defensive. Why are you so defensive with your own mother? Can't I talk about my son's health?'

It went like that, circling round the same misunderstanding, or shifting perception of the offensive thing my mother had said. This was usually the tenor of our conversations, for as she has grown older she has, like a child, lost her filter, says whatever she thinks regardless of the feelings of the people around her, and yet, also just like a child, is so quick to take offense if she herself is criticized that we can very quickly come to grief if we spend too much time alone. There was the strong possibility that one day soon she would say something offensive over the phone—for instance threatening the life of a politician in a completely unthinking way—or write something similar in an email, which would draw the attention of whoever might be listening and recording. Is it so fanciful? I no longer think so.

By that morning, having listened to Mr. Wald and Michael Ramsey's curious intervention in the conversation, I felt certain that my paranoia was not misplaced. Perhaps in not so short a time my mother and I will both be detained, required to prove our innocence or, worse, to reveal whatever we know—which, I am sure, is nothing. Would you—whoever you may be who eventually reads this, either friend or foe—force my mother to scribble away in a room her account of me, of what she knows of my recent life, even if it was clear she knew nothing? Or is clarity a quality in which people like you no longer believe? Do you require that the world is endlessly gray, every person potentially shading into the categories that merit your attention, all of us, every one, people of interest?

Thanksgiving was in fact quite a happy day, without any arguments or serious conflicts, the presence of Michael Ramsey that morning being the only wrinkle in an otherwise unremarkable gathering, and I had no doubt that I was the only one disturbed by him.

Before leaving Meredith and Peter's, my daughter drew me aside in the kitchen and asked what had happened during my appointment with the neurologist, Dr. Sebastian.

'There's nothing physically wrong with me. The scan—I mean I haven't had the results, but nothing is going to show up.'

'Oh good, what a relief. Did she have any thoughts about what might have happened? It still seems so strange.'

'She advised me to see a therapist or an analyst. It's not because I'm crazy, but she thought it was possible that something traumatic might have happened recently, or because of some past trauma—I don't know—my memory might have blocked out the exchange with my student on Saturday. The brain does funny things.'

Meredith scrunched her nose, almost as if she'd drunk too much and was struggling to focus, though I knew this was not the case. She was making faces because she was concerned and during such intense family gatherings her emotions tend to rise even more powerfully to the surface. I knew she preferred not to cry in front of other people, even her family, and it was this she was trying to forestall, as much for my sake as to protect her dignity, perhaps precisely because it happened so frequently in the past, crying was as much a part of her childhood and adolescence—though I remind myself how much of that latter period I missed—as was laughter or ordinary sulking, but in the years of her adulthood I had seen her cry two or three times at most, out of frustration and concern rather than sadness, and I did not want to force that response again, especially not on Thanksgiving of all days, when the kitchen crying-fest between parent and child is as well worn a cliché as the drunken relative who makes a scene before passing out in the guest bedroom.

Meredith made a look halfway between disgust and despair, as if she were considering the possibility that rather than being afflicted by a degenerative disease, her father might instead be crazy, and imagining all the implications of this alternative decline and diagnosis, the ways in which I might suddenly be inaccessible to her just when she thought I had returned as a full participant in her life. One wants to offer reassurance in the face of such paralyzing alarm and since I was certain there was nothing physically or psychologically wrong with me, and the confusion with Rachel was the result not of my own mind but of some incursion into my private messages, that the real issue was the fact of my being surveilled and followed and fucked with by persons and entities as yet unknown, I reached out to my daughter to give her the comfort and reassurance I thought she needed.

I hugged her and whispered into her hair, 'I promise I'm not crazy. I mean I'm all kinds of crazy in an ordinary way, but I am not *crazy*, or at least not any crazier than most people. Paranoid a little, yes, and perhaps I have a persecution complex, and sometimes I have difficulty with impulse control, but I'm not any crazier than most people who have spent the bulk of their lives in New York, or Oxford for that matter.' As I said it, I thought of the many crazy people I had known in Oxford, and in particular about the one person who, the more my thoughts returned to him, seemed potentially to be the cause of this sudden strange turbulence in my life.

'But you'll talk to someone? I mean, it couldn't hurt, could it?'

'Yes, sweetheart, I'll talk to someone, just to put our minds at ease.'

MY MOTHER AND I refused Meredith and Peter's offer to call a car service and took a taxi back down to the Village. During the ride my mother began to nod off, though it was only a little after seven in the evening, and she woke with a start when the cab stopped outside my building. The doorman on duty was not someone I recognized well enough to know his name. He was wearing no badge and seemed more interested in watching a video on his phone than on making sure we were supposed to be going upstairs unannounced. Since it was a holiday I decided not to make a fuss, although as we waited for the elevator I felt a rising urge to say something, which my mother said for me, speaking in a stage whisper the doorman could not help hearing, 'If it was *my* building I'd want the doorman to check who was coming and going. In this day and age you can't be too careful, but I guess he must be *obsessed* with football, or maybe he's watching *pornography*, you know that's what most of them do these days.'

The elevator doors opened and I stepped inside without looking back to see the face of the doorman, poor guy, poor chap I would have said only six months earlier, to have to be subjected to my mother's hit-and-run commentary is never pleasant. I put her to bed early with a glass of whisky, which can be relied upon to make her sleep through the night, although I myself was feeling wide awake once more, and thinking back on the people I had known in Oxford, the man and woman on whom my mind was actively avoiding settling throughout that day and the previous few days, knowing nonetheless they were undoubtedly at the root of what was happening—what is *now* happening as I write this account.

That is to say, I had begun to suspect that Stephen, who I have been trying to forget, and Fadia, whose face hardly ever leaves my consciousness no matter how much a part of my mind wishes to place her beyond memory, were somehow the cause of the persecutions I was suddenly facing. These are the people you care about, I think, and for no greater reason than because I knew them, allowed myself to become involved with them, to entangle my life with theirs.

IT WAS NOT until the start of my second year at Oxford that I met Stephen Jahn, his return to the College after a year's sabbatical transforming my own slightly haphazard social life. Our first meeting was at a High Table dinner when we were seated across from each other, an unusual night when there were only six or so Fellows dining on the dais at the far end of the eighteenth-century hall with the students in their gowns seated on benches at the great long tables. They would sometimes clamber over these to reach the benches nearest the wall, it being impossible, given the length of the tables, to move them such that enough room could be made for someone to take a place further down an otherwise full bench, and for some reason there was a perverse habit of leaving blank spaces and of those who did so refusing to make room, or even to file out and file back in so that the space could be filled without putting filthy shoes on the tables where one was about to eat. But this was Oxford, which delights in the precarious balance of decorum and iconoclasm.

Stephen was a short man, not unlike Bethan's father in that respect, and he was perhaps five years older than me, but totally bald, and I could see, despite his gray three-piece suit, carefully tailored or *bespoke* as the British say, that he was muscular to the point of looking almost like a bodybuilder but with none of the usual bulk. In other words, he was short and sinewy, so that, at the knocking of the grace, when he was standing up, he looked as slender as a sprinter. It was only seated, bringing his arms forward to eat, his spine always very erect, that I sensed how physically fit he was. He had a pug-like face, pugnacious, popping eyes, and wore narrow, Germanic-looking glasses that made him resemble a *kapo* or even a *capo*, a Neapolitan *consigliere*. At any rate, he had the face, body, and style of a fascist.

Our first meeting was one of those odd dances of half-deception and barely concealed interrogation. Initially I could tell nothing about his origins, although it began to be apparent that he was, like me, an American, but one whose displacement was longer standing than mine. His accent had drifted farther off course, or rather, like my own, it retained all the sounds of American speech but none of its rhythms and few of its idioms.

At first, I seemed to have been more opaque to him than he to me, although as time went on and we became friends after a fashion, I suspected that had only been a ruse, that in truth he knew a great deal about me before we had ever met.

'Oh, are you *also* American?' he purred, looking just to the side of me through his very thick lenses. This peculiar Oxford—or perhaps more generally British—affectation, to have a direct conversation with someone while refusing almost all eye contact, never failed to unnerve me. 'I thought for certain you must be German, although of course the kind of German who has spent most of his adult life in England.'

'But I don't have a German name.'

'Oh? I didn't catch your name.' We had all been introduced in the Senior Common Room before processing into the hall, gathering and robing ourselves in preparation for that parade past students who must, I always thought, have looked upon us with a sense of resentment, or a few perhaps with some desire to join us, to be one of those graduate students who occasionally earns the privilege of dining at High Table, the Junior Dean and such, who are often more interesting and stimulating company than the aging Senior Fellows.

I reminded Stephen of my name and told him my field and area of expertise, what I was working on at the time, my interest in film as well as in history. As I spoke he ate his fish, using his fork and knife in the European way: fork in the left hand, tines pointed down to spear the food, knife in the right to cut and trowel a mouthful's worth onto the back of the fork. When I had finished talking about my work, he put his utensils down on the plate, and before he had stopped chewing dabbed at the corners of his mouth with the large white napkin drawn from his lap.

'Jeremy O'Keefe. O'Keefe. No, no, no,' he shook his head. 'That doesn't fit, not really, you're not a Jeremy, or perhaps you are, though you seem more a Jeremiah to me, you have an Old Testament voice and look like the kind of man the Tetragrammaton might raise, but O'Keefe is completely, but *so* completely *wrong*,' and here he glared at me, made brief eye contact, studying my face so closely that his gaze registered almost as a tangible weight on my skin. 'There's nothing Irish about you, Dr. O'Keefe. Not even anything very *Celtic*. No, you have a quite Teutonic face and a number of New Canaan ancestors. That is my guess. Am I right? Have you done one of those DNA tests? Finding your roots? Who do you think you are? Are you half Berber?'

Despite myself I found Stephen's assessment flattering. That sharp-edged flattery, I later learned, was his most dangerous charm.

'Entirely wrong, as far as I know.'

'Saxon, then, a slew of Saxon ancestors way, way back, but your grandparents grew up in New England.'

'That's correct, but not New Canaan. Southern Vermont and Poughkeepsie.'

Stephen clapped his hands with pleasure.

'Poughkeepsie! How divine! You see! I knew it! I *knew it*! I *always* win at this game!'

'And you, Dr. Jahn? Where'd you grow up?'

'Please, we must now be Stephen and Jeremy to each other,' he whispered, leaning towards me across the table, 'for we are Americans, little though we sound it. No, my dear, I grew up on Long Island, Port Washington, or near there, though do not jump to false conclusions. My father and I are very much *nouveaux pauvres*. Thank you, Matthew,' he said to the College Butler, who always waited at High Table and was clearing away the main course dishes. 'Tell Chef the fish was perfection.'

'I will do, sir,' Matthew said, adding another plate to the bow of his left arm.

As soon as Matthew had left through the door to the kitchen Stephen leaned even farther across the table and whispered, 'They had to bail Matthew out of jail last week. Brawling. In a student pub. Luckily none of our members was involved. If they had been, he'd have got the sack for sure. Now, though, it's perfect. Even if he wanted to leave he couldn't. He'll be indebted to the College for the rest of his working life. You know what these English peasants are like. West Country farmers.'

Stephen could get away with saying such a thing that evening because there was, by chance, not a single British person at the table and the undergraduates were too far away and too engrossed in their own raucous conversations to overhear. On that first meeting, after the dessert, and then the second dessert in the Senior Common Room dining room, and the passing of the port round the table, always clockwise, and the increasingly befuddled and self-aggrandizing or self-recriminating or self-exculpatory conversation that threatened to compromise all assembled if anything was remembered the following morning, I thought of Stephen Jahn as merely one more colorful

barnacle on the boat of my Oxford life, which is to say I was amused
by him, by his pomposity and the ways in which he had embraced
a European life and lifestyle, how he had affected habits that most
Americans would find distasteful if not immoral, but believed that
our acquaintance would never become more intimate, since he was,
first of all, patently a homosexual and I had, at the time, no close
gay friends (in retrospect this now seems more like a failing on my
part, a failure of my own ostensibly liberal credentials, than anything
else), and secondly because it was apparent even on that first meeting
that although he might have been something like a Centrist Democrat
in America, in Britain he could only be a Conservative, and I had
forsworn friendship with Tories because too often I found that conversation quickly foundered on the rocks of my own sense of political
correctness (yes, I know, that absence of gay friends makes my own
position at the time slightly indefensible), so it seemed impossible to
be relaxed around men and women who were so dispiritingly inclined
to say offensive things about women (yes, even the women), people
of color, Africans, Asians, not to mention Southern Europeans ('the
Latin is racially distinct, you can tell by the way he treats his women,'
a Fellow in Anthropology once told me), homosexuals, transsexuals,
and, sometimes most of all, Americans. From the Tory perspective
Americans were gauche, ill bred, poorly educated, little better than
children, and yet useful geopolitical allies. From the perspective of
the hard-left ranks of Labour, Americans were racist hoodlum mili-
tarists seeking to take over the planet. There was, I once told Stephen
Jahn, nowhere for someone like me in British politics. I voted Labour
because I could not stomach the Tories but I did so holding my nose,
as the British like to say.

Some years later, however, Stephen suggested we 'and a couple
of other bachelor members of the SCR' keep watch on the High
Table reservation list and try to find a night when a small party of

sympathetic souls might dine alone. 'And then, after dinner, you must come back to my flat to try some very excellent single malts.'

I remember nothing of that dinner itself, nor of who else might have dined with us, though it was likely one of the Fellows in English and his boyfriend, and possibly the Fellow in German, but at the end of the dinner Stephen and I quickly departed, walking down Turl Street, across High Street, down Alfred to Blue Boar, along to St. Aldate's, all the way past Christ Church and Pembroke and the line of cutesy Alice in Wonderland-related shops, past the Music Faculty and the grungy police station, down to the unromantically modern brick structure of Folly Bridge Court, where Stephen owned an apartment that spanned the top floor, on one side overlooking the Thames and that island in the river clustered with a number of buildings, and on the other a Victorian school converted into flats.

Stephen's place was modern, with a plush off-white wool carpet (we both removed our shoes), a bathroom whose walls were lined in white subway tiles, a kitchen with a slate floor and shiny white cabinetry, two bedrooms into which I was not allowed to look, and then a large living and dining space, with views to the north and the south, furnished with a glass and steel dining table, steel chairs with black leather seats, an assortment of black leather couches and chairs, and the walls covered with metal bookshelves and packed with books as well as a large collection of DVDs, all in the same gray plastic covers, numbered rather than labeled with titles. The DVDs gave me a chill, for they suggested to me, in my naïveté, a collection of pornography, and Stephen Jahn seemed exactly the kind of man who might be in possession of such a comprehensive-looking assemblage of vice.

He directed me to the couch nearest the south-facing window, though it was impossible to see much without going right up to it since the apartment was effectively in the attic of the building and all the windows were angled into the slanted roofline.

'Let us begin with a young specimen, before we move on, in care-fully judged stages, leading up to our arrival at a place of greater maturity. We'll begin with a ten-year-old,' and with that he crouched down in his socks to remove several bottles with labels I did not recognize from a black-lacquered sideboard, along with two crystal glasses of a suitably modern turn. He poured us each a glass, removed his jacket so he was only in his white shirt sleeves, gray waistcoat, and gray trousers (black socks, of course, because the understatement seemed to suit him; he was not, like some assimilated migrants to Britain and many homegrown British men, given to wearing brightly colored or patterned socks with sober suits), and sat down on the couch opposite like a schoolboy, or perhaps like a maiden aunt enter-taining her first suitor in twenty years.

His jacket was draped over the back of a chair, though he had done this with considerable care, making sure to fold it along its central seam and laying out the sleeves so they would not be rumpled. I wondered, however, why he did not just take a moment to hang the jacket in his closet in one of the bedrooms. Perhaps because he did not want to leave me alone to snoop around his bookshelves, although I had little interest in Stephen Jahn's life or whatever secrets he might have held. In fact I felt distinctly as though our acquaintanceship had evolved in sudden spurts of parallel but unequal growth, so that by the time of my visit to his Folly Bridge flat I understood, perhaps only at the edges of consciousness, that I was much more interesting to my colleague than he was to me. Why this should be so I could not then imagine, and there was no element of false modesty in that feeling, for I was, apart from the fact of being an American abroad like him, and being employed by the University of Oxford and one of its constituent Colleges, also like him, no more remarkable than any other academic anywhere else in the world, and arguably less remarkable because I had, to my own discredit, failed to make tenure at Columbia University, where I would have remained in all happiness for the rest of my working life had I been allowed to do so. It was possible, I supposed then, that Stephen Jahn was attracted to failure, or to failure rehabilitated, which was how I then thought of myself: I had not made a total secret of my shipwrecked career in American academia and the ways in which this move to Oxford was in a very real sense an escape from a more robust and more discriminating system, to one that was more fluid, less secure, and far worse paid.

And yet he was not a man who asked direct questions, or did so only rarely, offering instead statements to which one was expected and on many occasions compelled to respond.

'Now, this one,' he said, swirling his glass, 'you probably won't have heard of. It's from the Isle of Mull's Tobermory distillery, called Ledaig, made with burning peat. Distinctive, I think you'll agree.' His eyes popped a little as he nodded, taking a sip. 'Saline, *gracefully* peaty, almost dainty, like a bright little dancer, almost a very fine sherry, walnuts and the scent of pine forests, charred at the edges and regrown. Call me perverse but when I sip this whisky I think of that young colleague of ours, Bethan. A fine young scholar, very bright, quite intelligent, a little burned at the edges. Attractive, I should suppose, to those attracted by such types.'

I wondered if he already knew of my brief relationship with Bethan or if he merely suspected, or was entirely innocent, although Stephen Jahn gave no impression of being innocent of anything, no matter how little known or unexpected. Worldliness was his abiding character. I knew his area of expertise was the Middle East, particularly Arab-Israeli history and relations, and he was, by reputation, fluent in Hebrew and Arabic as well as Persian, French, German, Yiddish, Turkish, and Kurdish, and claimed to be conversant in Italian and Spanish as well. Such people are less uncommon in Oxford than elsewhere, and no doubt he had groundings in Latin and Ancient Greek, perhaps also—one never knows where the limits of such a person's mastery may end—even more arcane languages like Balochi and Azerbaijani.

'Yes, she is attractive, in her way.' Though I was conscious of not wanting to be drawn into deriding her, my relationship with Bethan had been professional if chilly since I fled her family's home that New Year's morning a few years earlier. We had devised an elaborate dance that meant, in the intervening months, we managed never to sit next to each other at a College meal, and if one of us entered the Senior Common Room to find the other the only person there, we would both pretend as if no one at all had appeared or been present. In America this would have been extremely strange, but in Oxford, in Britain more generally, it is possible, even common, to 'blank' people one knows, either out of an avoidance which is predicated on a fiction of not having noticed the presence of the other person and is therefore regarded as being polite, or out of a studied and unveiled desire to let the other person know that she or he simply does not signify, is not worth noticing, must be reminded of her or his subordinate place. It was a custom to which I could never wholly adjust, even in moments of falling back on the behavior myself, but in Oxford I had to learn—at least in the realm of the College—to raise my eyes discreetly, and if it was Bethan or someone else I wished to avoid, lower them again into whatever book, newspaper, or journal I was taking a few moments to read in those semi-public spaces and wait until the person had departed.

Stephen continued to swirl his glass, inhaling and sipping. 'Leather and cigars,' he said, as if I had not spoken, and then, once he had swallowed, 'I left this open for a week after acquiring it. You would not imagine the difference it makes. I believe some women are like that, Bethan for instance. If allowed to breathe, in the right company, with the right degree of . . . openness . . . she too might become sublime.'

'I don't think I would put it like that, Stephen.'

'No? You're so politically correct, Jeremy. I can see how unwilling you are to talk about your women as if they're anything less than equals.' So he did know, I thought, he knew exactly what had happened between us, perhaps from Bethan herself. 'It's admirable but rather exhausting, don't you find? Not every person one has sex with need necessarily be one's equal. It is fine, I would suggest, to seduce one's social and intellectual inferiors, knowing the act of seduction and resulting congress gives them just as much pleasure as it gives you. Your very superiority is what makes you alluring.'

'That's an unpleasant way of seeing it. I don't remember ever going to bed with a woman I didn't regard as my equal or better.'

Stephen clicked his tongue. 'Politically correct *and* modest. We'll have to do something about that. I have a young Egyptian friend, Saif, you don't need to know his surname, who works for the government there, you don't need to know in what capacity, but he was assigned to me as a minder on a visit I made a couple of years ago and during the course of last year we spent a considerable amount of time together, though you understand that in such societies, and given my own position as well as Saif's, one has to be very careful.'

I was unsure whether Stephen meant for me to understand that Saif was a lover. It seemed somehow unlikely while also being the only possible conclusion I could reach.

'We've become very close friends. He's even taken me to meet his mother, French, a lovely woman, very elegant, an excellent family, quite wealthy, to whom I must have appeared something like a doting uncle. The father is impossible, but that is no surprise.'

I must have nodded, or perhaps just took another sip of the whisky, which despite Stephen's description and grandiloquent claims I found rather acrid, taste so often being subjective, and yet I forced myself to finish the glass he had poured and perhaps because of this I drank it too quickly and then tried to conceal the empty glass in my hand, thinking it was time to go home, back to Divinity Road and the house I had recently bought, which I was still in the process of redecorating and remodeling, turning the dingy old kitchen into a bright airy space with a dining room at the end and doors opening onto the long narrow garden.

'Of course, Saif works for the Egyptian government and while Egypt is a friend of the West there are, necessarily, some problems we would wish them to improve, in respect of democracy and human rights, although really these are quite minor concerns when measured against the value of a stable and cooperative Egypt, if you see. But of course you see. Anyway, how did I get on to Saif?' He paused, glanced up to the ceiling, and then fixed me with his odd little smile. 'I see your glass is empty. Let us move on to something rather more interesting. Poit Dhubh, from the Isle of Skye, twenty-one years old, and thus fully legal,' he smirked, taking a tall bottle with a black label from his sideboard and pouring a large measure into a new glass. 'Sweet and soft, only slightly peaty, I saw you grimace at the first one, peat is too strong for some less seasoned palates, I made a mistake with the Ledaig but this you will find sublime, and very drinkable. In fact it's a vatted malt, various ones mixed together. Aged in sherry casks, which helps neutralize some of the sharper peatiness. This is a little candy bar of a whisky you can chew and suck, nutty and fruity with a tender note of vanilla. Sixty pounds a bottle, so still very, very respectable. Inhale.'

I raised the new glass to my nose but by this time I was beginning to feel quite seriously drunk and impressionable so that the aromas wafting up to my brain suggested some strange combination of fruit and caramel and roasting nuts and wood fires in old houses with stone floors and vanilla puddings cooking in the tops of double boilers. I sipped and although it was not a true single malt Stephen was right, it was sublime and comforting and almost as substantial and pleasing as an entire meal, a whisky as if invented by Willy Wonka for connoisseurs with only enough for a single good bottle that might satisfy them for many a night without ever having to go in search of anything more refined.

'I *knew* it, I knew that would be the one, but don't worry, we won't stop there,' he laughed, pouring himself a glass of the same and doing a scurrying jig as he came back across the room, pausing for a moment to glance out the window overlooking the Thames. 'Oh, please, won't you excuse me,' he said, and abruptly left the room.

I took the opportunity to stand and examine his bookshelves. As I was doing so I happened to turn and also looked out the window, across the river, to the island and the tall yellow house upon it, where, on the middle floor, lights were on and the curtains open and a young man and a young woman were having sex on the floor, he on top of her, both of them athletic, almost certainly university students, undergraduates or graduates, perhaps postdoctoral Fellows, but it was clear that whatever their rank they felt no qualms about being watched, or perhaps were so lost in the moment of passion they had forgotten the curtains were open and the lights on and the hour was so late they might have imagined the rest of the city was asleep and assumed they were not being observed.

By instinct I turned away and tried once more to study the bookshelves, but found my head kept turning and the couple were still very much engaged every time I checked over my shoulder. Stephen remained absent, though I had no sense whether he was in one of the bedrooms or in the bathroom, on the side of the flat facing away from the river and the copulating young couple. Fifteen minutes passed, the couple finished, and I heard the flush of the toilet down the hall. Stephen returned, acting as if he had been absent only a moment. 'How is your drink?' he asked.

'I'm fine, thank you, Stephen. I should be heading home. Do you have the number of a taxi?'

'What's the rush, my dear? We still have to move on to the thirty-year-old, which, I assure you, is quite unmissable. And in the meantime I think you should have another drop of the Poit Dhubh.'

'I can't, really, I'll never get up in the morning if I do.'

'But tomorrow is a Saturday, so no need. It would be an insult to refuse what I so generously offer.'

'Just a drop, then.'

'A wee dram,' he smiled, speaking in a broad caricature of a Highland accent. His eyes disappeared into folds of lean skin as he smiled and I noticed he had rolled up his sleeves, exposing his fore-arms, which were hairless, muscular, and roped with thick blue veins, as if, in his absence from the living room, he had been doing vigorous pull-ups. 'Are you still having a relationship with Bethan?'

I choked. 'You're being very indiscreet, Stephen.'

'I shall take that as a *yes*.'

'No! It's none of your business, but no, I had a brief fling with her but it's over. Entirely finished.'

'And does that mean the two of you have a difficult working relationship?'

All of a sudden I could see Stephen Jahn was heading somewhere, with a specific destination in mind. What he wanted, though, I could never have predicted. Above all, you must understand that whatever has happened subsequently, I was, at least initially, Stephen Jahn's dupe. 'It's a cordial relationship, but we don't allow ourselves much opportunity to interact.'

'You avoid each other?'

'Not by any agreement. It just . . . ended up that way.'

'You were badly behaved?'

'Listen, Stephen, I like you and respect you as a colleague, but this is none of your business.'

'I ask as a friend.'

I was unsure whether Stephen Jahn was the kind of friend I wanted, but he smiled with such ingenuousness I found myself persuaded to speak, or perhaps it was merely the whisky. 'I didn't end it as elegantly as I should have.'

'You left her for someone else? You *dog*! I *knew* you were a dog!'

'No, it's not that. I just left. But I didn't say I was going. I was visiting her parents and left without telling anyone.'

Stephen clicked his tongue and wagged a finger at me, but beneath the disdain there was a smile that said he had found the information he wanted.

'I want you to do me a favor, Jeremy. Make it up with Bethan. Not romantically, don't worry, just professionally. Go and apologize. Women appreciate a sincere apology even if they do not, initially, seem to accept it. And tell her you know you were badly behaved but frankly since the two of you have to work together for as long as she's at the College, which will be until next summer, and undoubtedly she's the kind of young woman who will find a permanent place here in the Faculty and in one of the other Colleges, it only makes sense that you should have a cordial working relationship. Get on your knees if you must, but make her see the apology is sincere.'

I was baffled by this request, since it demanded a kind of self-abnegation out of keeping with my character. Also, I did not see how a few glasses of expensive whisky put me so deeply in Stephen's debt. 'Why should I?'

'Because, as I said, I need a favor.'

'To do with Bethan?'

'Bethan is merely a component force in the performance of the favor. You and she are interviewing candidates together in December.'

It was true, though I had allowed my mind to draw a veil over this small irritation in my academic life, for it meant a rather tedious two days spent interrogating bright and not so bright adolescents who wanted to study History in the College and by bad luck—or perhaps, I now think, by Stephen's design—I had been paired with Bethan for the interviews. In practical terms, it only made sense that I should try to patch things up with her in advance. I nodded and held out my glass, which was empty.

'Time for the thirty-year-old. This is a very special whisky. I'm not going to tell you where it comes from or what it is, because it wouldn't mean anything to you anyway, but I have never quite had its equal myself, and I pour you this drop,' he said, filling the bottom of yet another new glass, 'with liquid of great rarity and expense. It is, quite literally, worth its weight in gold.'

I took the glass and raised it to my nostrils and was instantly over-come with an almost hallucinogenic vision of a great library, such as Duke Humphrey's in the Old Bodleian, full of exquisite leather bindings, but a library that is also a gentlemen's club, with a whiff of fine cigars, excellent tobacco, and perhaps, wafting round the edges of the room, a sublime and subtle perfume, like those made by Santa Maria Novella in Florence, such as the scent of ambergris and pome-granate blossom, and then, as I tilted the edge of the glass between my lips, those scents merged together and were transformed into an astonishing and dizzying rhapsody of taste that coated my tongue and filled my mouth and floated again into my nostrils, going down my throat with an absolute smoothness and clarity unlike any alcohol I had tasted in the past.

'My friend in Egypt, Saif, he has a younger sister, whose name is Fadia. She will be coming to the College to interview for a place. Her marks are unspectacular, but she is bright. She will be impressive in interview but perhaps not as impressive as some and not quite as impressive as she ought to be to make up for the marks. Nonetheless, I want to be certain she does not leave this College without an assurance that she will be able to come here to study. You and I will head up the two interview teams and it is, therefore, as much in your hands as in my own that we end up with the proper result.'

I inhaled the aromas of that extraordinary whisky and let Stephen's request settle, though as I did so I was conscious that what he had just done was to give me a gift (fine drink) in expectation of me doing something to merit his generosity, and that this act of meritorious behavior prospectively rewarded would, quite likely, compromise my own position in the College and the Faculty if this Fadia proved to be embarrassingly ill-equipped to study at Oxford.

'You want me to rig it? I can't rig it.'

'You are senior to Bethan. She, perhaps, feels wounded by your behavior. You will be supportive of Fadia in ways Bethan will find persuasive. In any case, she might herself be on Fadia's side, but you understand that given Bethan's junior position in the College and the Faculty I cannot possibly approach her in the same way I trust I may confide in you.'

'And pressure me.'

'Pressure is too physical a word. We are not men of physics. I have been observing you and I know that we both understand how, from time to time, certain individuals need help. Fadia is one such person. She needs to come here, she needs to stay out of Egypt. I thought you, of all people, would understand. Mubarak's Egypt is, in many respects, not unlike East Germany. There are more than a million security staff members monitoring the citizens of Egypt, who number less than eighty million. Egypt under Mubarak is a police state, nothing less, and a very nice one for tourists, provided they don't find themselves on the sharp end of terror. And in some quite important ways Egyptian society is not as disunited as some police states, but it is, I would argue, a police state nonetheless—one in which life can soon become untenable for those holding the placard of democracy and freedom of speech, as young Fadia has rather rashly been doing every time she goes home on holiday. As I said, her mother is French, and the spirit of revolution is hereditary. Fadia needs the protection that life in Oxford can offer. She needs exile that does not look like exile to the authorities. She needs to be able to come and study and remain studying until such time as things change in Egypt or she can be persuaded to remain in Europe on a permanent basis. What I am asking you to do is to make allowances for a young woman of fierce intelligence who has lived a rather coddled existence, who has never been forced to work hard. Do you see?'

The finger's depth of brown liquid in the crystal glass sat heavy in my hand. I swirled it to release the aroma before holding it again to my nose and mouth. Stephen was, I could see, almost desperate for my help and had approached the problem in perhaps the only way a man like him knew how, by trying to leverage influence through the imposition of a forced sense of gratitude. It was as unseemly as it was pathetic.

'I ask you again. Why should I?'

Stephen's eyes popped and his mouth spluttered. He had not been expecting resistance. Perhaps in his world men like me do not defy whatever demands men like him make, and in thinking this I realized I had already been making assumptions about the kind of person he was, and I mean not just ordinary conclusions about character but a more profound level of supposition that Stephen Jahn was only notionally an academic and was, chiefly, something else altogether.

SITTING IN MY living room looking over Houston Street on Thanksgiving night, swirling a glass of much less interesting scotch than those Stephen once served me in that room overlooking the

Thames, listening to my mother's snores resonating from the guest room down the hall, snores of such depth and volume they made the floors vibrate, I understood that the real beginning of this story was not my departure from New York, not my arrival in Oxford, not my brief affair with Bethan, but allowing myself to be suckered into a compromising acquaintance with Stephen Jahn. He admitted that night to observing me. For how long? And why? Was he looking for a pawn? Now I begin to see how that moment, the night in his flat, and everything that has unfolded thereafter, all the ways in which Stephen and Fadia came to inhabit my Oxford life, has been haunting my return to New York.

'Why should I do what you're asking?' I said again to Stephen that evening in Folly Bridge Court. A moment earlier I had put down my glass on the side table and without speaking he reached across, lifted the glass, and slid a black leather coaster beneath it.

'Because I've asked you in the nicest possible way. I've demon-strated how you would be doing me a great favor. I've given you, I have to say, a substantial amount of very expensive whisky over the course of the evening. What else can I or should I do now but threaten you if you refuse to be reasonable about it? You want money? That would be unwise. Money can always, but always be traced. Help me in this way and I will make your life easier than you can possibly imagine. Give me time, and I'll even get you back to New York, which I know you miss more than you want to admit. I will look after your daughter and even your ex-wife in ways you would not think possible.'

'Is this about something more sordid than just helping out the sister of a friend of yours?'

Again he spluttered. 'This is about grace and doing the *right* thing in the *right* moment for someone who may be more important in the long run than we can now conceive.'

This was, I felt certain, about sex and nothing more: Stephen wanting to do a favor for a man with whom he was in love, or perhaps a man, this Saif character, who might himself have been threatening Stephen with exposure, or blackmail, or some darker vengeance.

I rose from my chair and began walking towards the door, hearing behind me the wheezing of a man unaccustomed to failure.

'Can I trust you?' he called out. 'Can I rely on you? Or do I have to take other measures?'

I turned around, half expecting to find him holding a gun, but there was nothing in his hand apart from the glass of whisky. 'No one has ever tried to intimidate me like this, not in my whole life.'

'That is not an answer, Jeremy.'

In his expression I saw a quality of ruthlessness that made me afraid not only for myself, but for Meredith and my mother, even for Susan, for everyone I loved and had ever loved. There was no question that this was a man capable of delivering on his threats.

'I promise to judge the candidate on her merits,' I said, and knew I would not.

Outside, on the Abingdon Road, it was frigid and I didn't find a cab until I had walked almost all the way back to Carfax and then, going home, drunk several times over but still trying to hold my mind together, I played back the conversation in my head, imagining other responses I might have given and ways I should have turned Stephen's demands to my advantage. I went to bed but did not sleep, aware of all the sounds around me, bumps coming from the adjoining house, cars in the street, the whisper of the ring road encircling Oxford and the drone of military aircraft overhead, planes on their way to and from Brize Norton.

Those memories returned to me in New York with clarity and the recollection of our conversation kept me awake as much as my mother's snores, rumbling across the parquet while I made my dark perambulation through the living room, fighting an insomnia that had come to stay over the course of recent days, as disobliging as an unwanted guest.

Out on Houston Street, in the lamplight, taxis braking and lurching, a man in black stood still, staring up at my window, and when I switched on the light, as if to acknowledge once more the fact of being watched, he turned around and ran.

THE DAY AFTER THANKSGIVING my mother was up before dawn cleaning my kitchen, although it was immaculate, and intermittently reading *The New York Times*, which she had gone out to buy, while listening to *Morning Edition* on National Public Radio. An Egyptian pro-democracy blogger had been arrested, while a court in Alexandria had sentenced to prison a group of women and girls who had protested, armed only with balloons, in support of the deposed Islamist president. It was not what I felt like hearing first thing in the morning. I did not want to be reminded that people I knew—had once known—might be affected by such distant events. From world news, NPR switched without pause to reports of the Black Friday shopping frenzy that burned across America.

'I *hate* all this consumerist craziness,' my mother said. 'People were lined up at Macy's overnight! They opened at 8pm on Thanksgiving! What is the world coming to? What are we doing to ourselves? *Everything* for the almighty dollar! Do you want some coffee? I just made a pot.'

'It's not even seven. Our train isn't until ten.'

'I needed to get organized!'

'There is nothing whatsoever to organize. I have organized everything already.'

I found myself watching my mother, anxious she might break a glass or complicate a process I felt I had perfected, for instance the making of coffee, and as I drank a cup of what she had made, I found it at once too weak and too acidic and then made a show of pouring out her pot and making a new one according to my own plan, and when she drank a cup of mine she grimaced, saying she preferred it her way.

'Yours is too strong. Too bitter.'

'If you don't like it, you don't have to drink it.'

'Don't be so goddamned huffy, Jeremy.'

I know that my time in Britain, my partial acculturation there, means that the emotional diffidence I internalized and accommodated to my own personality seems now, to my mother, like a form of rejection or a kind of filial abrasiveness, but there is little I can do to change it. Perhaps in time I will again be American in a way that I was once American, and yet I doubt such reversal is possible.

At eight-thirty we took a taxi to Penn Station, and throughout the ride my mother fidgeted, searching her purse.

'What did you forget?'

'Nothing, nothing.'

'Are you missing something?'

'No!' She coughed, and it was clear she was lying. Then she leaned over and said in a low voice, 'I just wish you would have let us leave half an hour earlier.'

'Mom, it's fine. We have plenty of time. If I were going alone I would've left half an hour later.'

As it was we had to wait in line for the better part of an hour, standing in the snake of people who know from habit which track the trains heading up the Hudson are likely to depart from, and though the station has changed somewhat over the years there was a great familiarity, even comfort, in standing once again in the same spot, checking over my shoulder at the Departures board and listening to the clacking changeover of times and destinations, the old-fashioned-sounding announcements of track numbers and stops along the various routes, and I noticed the way people bound for upstate New York, particularly those going north of Poughkeepsie, look more like Midwesterners than New Yorkers, so often unfashionably dressed as they are, or at least not dressed like people who live in the city, the businessmen in their poorly fitting khakis and navy blue blazers hiding ample waists, the frumpy government workers checking their smartphones and holding loud conversations, the older woman who arrives and asks if this is the train to Albany and then strikes up a conversation with my mother, assuring us she is not crazy but 'waiting on line in Penn Station makes me so nervous, you know what I mean?' and we all know that this old woman, who lives in Vermont and worries about terrorists without saying the word is voicing the fear so many of us have learned to contain in lives that demand travel, but this woman, this Vermonter who is expecting a niece to pick her up from the station in Rensselaer and drive her to Bennington where she and the niece both live, does not come to the city frequently, although she used to live here, was born and grew up in Brooklyn, spent all her professional life working in Manhattan, then retired to Vermont just after the attacks, deciding she did not want to spend the rest of her days worrying about being blown up when she was just minding her business, and the whole story spilled out as we stood there, 'on line' as New Yorkers say, the way she had come down simply to have Thanksgiving with her sister and brother-in-law, and that got my mother talking about Meredith and Peter, though she did so without giving their names or divulging where they live or what they do, since a great many people would recognize who they are or be interested in the glittering lives they lead and such knowledge could put them at risk because by revealing our proximity to Peter in particular we might be seen as useful targets for kidnapping or worse.

'This is my son, he's a professor at NYU,' my mother said, and I was forced to meet the woman from Vermont although she did not introduce herself and promised she would not sit next to us on the train, 'just in case you're afraid you can't get rid of me,' she laughed, and I was, somewhat to my shame, grateful to her for saying that as the track was announced and we waved our printed tickets to the Amtrak employee before descending the escalator and hurrying along the dark platform towards the middle of the train, where I helped my mother into one of the seats at the front of a row so she could stretch her legs, as was her preference, and look out the window onto the Hudson River while the train chugged in its occasionally unreliable way northward to the town where I have made my investment in long-term stability.

After leaving Penn Station, entering and exiting tunnels that took us in and out of darkness, offering glimpses of Riverside Park and then more distant views of the Palisades across the river, a man I thought I recognized from the back passed through our car. There was a familiar quality about him—a certain agitation in his walk—without my being certain that he was who I thought he might be, and for a moment, without this thought registering fully in my consciousness, I became convinced of the *possibility* that it was Michael Ramsey.

There are people who are not instantly recognizable once you have met them, so if you glimpse the person from behind, or see only a small part of his or her profile, their identity remains uncertain. I had only met Ramsey twice at that point, and on that day after Thanksgiving when much of America was hurtling towards shopping malls to buy quantities of unnecessary gifts and my mother and I were sitting in a train car, bad capitalists failing to participate fully in the life of our economy, it was conceivable to me, at some proximate remove from full consciousness, that Michael Ramsey was with us on that train.

Because my mother had been tired the previous night, and I was not in the best of moods that morning, I did not speak to her about the three boxes of material that seemed to betray the disturbingly close examination of my life, at least my life insofar as it is lived through the internet and over the phone, nor did I mention my encounters with Michael Ramsey, or the presence of that young man at Meredith and Peter's party, an appearance which had, in retrospect, ruined the holiday that means more to me than any other. All I wanted on that first Thanksgiving back in America was the comfort of sheltering with my family as autumn closes in, fog settling in the hollows of the Berkshires and Catskills and Adirondacks, those hunchbacked mountains of the northeast that, in October and November, seem more American to me than anywhere else. But there, in the season's final hours, my interloper had appeared, as if to send the message that I was no longer secure in the country of my birth, suggesting I was right to feel paranoid, because my period outside of America had left me vulnerable to questions about my loyalty and habits, even my patriotism, as though treason could be caught like a virus, acquired by removal from home, a disease transmitted by long-term exposure to the unfamiliar.

In the first year I was at Oxford, as America coiled for war, I found myself falling into arguments over email, insisting to friends back home that they did not understand the way the rest of the world saw our country, how we were squandering the sympathy and good-will of the international community, that my time in Oxford—then only a scant few months—had already 'radicalized me.' I used the phrase without knowing how 'radicalize' would become a keyword in the grammar of America's War on Terror, how the media and polit-icians would describe terror suspects as having been 'radicalized,' and as these thoughts came back to me on the train heading north along the Hudson, the trees around us having lost nearly all their leaves, ice forming in the shallows of the river's wide expanse, so unlike anything in Britain, I wondered whether, in the box of internet addresses sitting in my apartment, there was a link to the email in which I described myself, more than a decade earlier, as 'radicalized,' and whether that self-description was the first flag I might have raised, if that offhand remark alone stained me red and started the process of tracking all of my communications.

Was it possible, I wondered, feeling the rhythm of the train and looking at my mother reading her issue of *The New Yorker*, cackling at the cartoons, that Stephen Jahn was *sent* to find me in Oxford? I had assumed his presence in College pre-dated my arrival and that in my first year he had merely been absent, but I did not know this for certain, I never had a conversation about Stephen with any of the other Fellows. There was a sense in which he was never fully present in the life of the College, as though, if I had not known him and spoken to him and been befriended by him (however menacingly), his presence would not have been noticed by anyone else.

From the station in Rhinecliff my mother and I took a taxi to her house, where I had left my car the last time I was upstate, some weeks earlier, so she could use it if needed. In fact she now rarely drives, being close enough to the center of Rhinebeck that she can walk to see her friends or get groceries at the natural foods store she loves, only driving if she needs to see her doctor or one of her more distant acquaintances in Hyde Park, but I feel more secure knowing the car is not sitting in the garage of my empty house outside of town, down a quiet road and set back on the property, a tall hedge hiding the house itself, so it would be easy for a thief to get inside without being seen from the road and take whatever he found there. I had resolved that I was going to have an alarm system installed in the new year, and perhaps also a series of internal motion-activated surveillance cameras as Peter had recommended, which would allow me to

monitor the house from Manhattan and, he claimed, receive a noti-
fication if the cameras were triggered to record. 'They'll even email
you the video they've taken, so you can see if it's nothing at all, or if
there's an intruder walking through your living room.' It sounded like
science fiction, but Peter insisted the technology was cheap, although
there were some concerns about privacy, given that the email service
meant the video would be sent through a third party and there were
no guarantees, none that mattered at any rate, that 'some asswipe in
Bloomington isn't looking at a live feed of your living room whenever
he feels like it.'

My mother and I agreed to meet for lunch on Saturday. Though
my preference would have been for a weekend to myself with no
social commitments, my mother was still reveling in the novelty of
my return. On Sunday I would drop off my car in the late afternoon
and walk to the station, or if the weather turned out to be bad she
would drive me. That Friday, she showed me the changes she had
made since my last visit, although the house looked the same as it had
for years, in good order if more cluttered, filled with calendars and
greeting cards and tchotchkes given to her by friends and neighbors,
and while her style was not my own it was gratifying to know she
lived with a sense of community, people looking out for her, noticing
if she failed to bring in the mail or newspaper, if her lights were on
late at night or her curtains not open in the morning, stopping by to
ask if she needed anything from the store or offering to take her to
lunch. She lived within the eye of the town, at the center of its social
life, very near its geographic center, and in its constant vision. I could
return to Manhattan believing my mother would be fine because she
was not ignored or forgotten.

On the way to my house I stopped at the grocery store on Route
9 to get a few odds and ends so that, apart from seeing my mother
for lunch the next day, I could spend a stretch of hours reading and

perhaps also thinking about my recent past, about Stephen Jahn and Fadia and Saif and the way that trio of people had come to dominate my world.

THE HOUSE, OFF a long rural road north of town, sits on a plot of land surrounded by small farms. My closest neighbor is more than half a mile away and the road itself is little but a paved farm track, wide enough for one vehicle, so it often feels more remote and removed from the world than it is.

I unloaded the groceries into the mudroom and was relieved to find the house in good order. Watching the garage door go down and the gray afternoon light give way to the white glow of lamps, I felt calm again after the events of the week, and relieved to know I could retreat to this kind of space away from the city, from students and colleagues, even away from Meredith and Peter, for this felt like the locus of some future retirement, a sample of what my own old age would be like, though unlike my mother I could not imagine placing myself at the center of any community.

Whatever may happen in my own case, now more uncertain than ever, it has always seemed to me that elderly women are more likely to be looked after by friends and neighbors than elderly men, who are perhaps by nature more disposed to retreat into themselves, less adept at reaching out for support. Perhaps people assume men are better able to see to their needs, a symptom of an old sexism that does as little for us as it ultimately does for women, men being thought capable and thus ignorable and so declining more rapidly, women thought incapable and thus in need of a cossetting that assumes only one way of growing old correctly, although one might well think that women, in the end, get the better deal out of such assumptions. Or perhaps this is not true, perhaps people assume the opposite, that men cannot begin to know how to care for themselves domestically while women, as they age, are assumed to live lives focused around the domestic, ruling an arena over which they have long been masters (or mistresses), and therefore can be left to themselves. In truth, too many old women and men are forgotten and ignored and prejudices one way or another do much to hurt both. Perhaps a little watching in such cases is no bad thing.

For now I am happy to be alone and ignored, perhaps even forgotten, although I know Meredith does not forget me, and I am not elderly, only in my fifties, in perhaps the September of my life, or if we are to believe the predictions for our own longevity, even the early July. It is comforting to think I still might have half a life more to live, another five decades to set right what I sometimes got spectacularly wrong, in particular where it comes to my relationships with women, and not just Susan and Meredith, and to a lesser extent my mother, but with Fadia, about whom I feel a profound and troubling sense of failure, of having not only failed her but having actively done wrong, quite regardless of the complex circumstances. Even where matters were not straightforward I know it is possible I might have done better than I did.

There are times now—sitting in this apartment on Houston Street, unsure how long I may yet come and go with a sense of freedom—when I wonder if I have already slipped past the boundary of life, and if this current situation might be, for the historian, the academic, the pursuer of other people's stories in the archive of recent history, the only version of purgatory I could have earned, an accounting of my failures, recorded in anticipation of an audience about whose character, identity, composition and purpose I can but speculate: the authorities, my heirs, some future historians concerned with the ways this nation has contorted its gaze back on itself.

I SPENT THAT Friday afternoon, the last one in November, installed in my warm living room, gazing out at the lawn and the garden to which I did very little this year, promising myself that in April or May, when the ground has thawed, I will hire someone to make a garden requiring minimal maintenance and little watering, a garden that can be left to grow regardless of the seasons and immune to my oblivious eye, and between those spells of watching the garden disappear into shadow and my own reflection grow more distinct in the windows through which I was looking, turning on lights so I would not be in the dark, I read, flipping between my former colleague Timothy Garton Ash's memoir *The File* and Simon Menner's *Top Secret*, which chilled me with its polaroid images of the homes of people who had been subject to surveillance. At the end of Menner's book a series of photos shows the head of the Stasi's Phone Surveillance Unit in his gray suit going down on one knee, tapped on the shoulder with the blade of a sword, and bestowed with an ornamental pendant featuring a red telephone receiver. The honors of surveillance, the spy's secret accolade. Would my own watchers be so garlanded?

When I found myself dozing I turned on the television, trying to slip into one of those thoughtless moods when the mind can rest on lives and concerns other than one's own. I must not have found anything sufficiently distracting because my thoughts kept returning to the events of the week, trying to separate the fact of the surveillance to which I was subject (my God, someone is watching me at all times!) from the purpose (why would someone wish to track me so closely?) and the revelation itself (*who* would want to make me aware of this surveillance and *why* would they do so?).

I had almost accepted the fact of the surveillance, and had a sense, now, that whatever I did, wherever I went, if I did so in ways that could be tracked (facial recognition software, financial traces, even my MetroCard, not to mention my online and phone activities), then someone would be collecting the data even if they were not necessarily analyzing it to look for patterns of behavior or suggestions that I might, in some preposterous way, be regarded as a threat to national security. I picked up the handset of my landline and spoke to the dial tone, or anyone who might be listening, insisting to them as much as to myself, 'I have done nothing wrong, I am a blameless, guiltless person, a Professor of History at a reputable university in one of the world's great cities. Why should I be concerned about the government monitoring my habits and communications and financial transactions if I have nothing to hide? A student said to me not long ago that privacy is for criminals, that only a criminal would think to demand privacy of his or her communications. I am not a criminal and still I demand privacy. I demand the right to be left alone, to be forgotten, to be a nonentity.'

Of course I knew this had something to do with the people I had known in Oxford, and perhaps also with what I had read online or carelessly written in emails or said over the phone during the course of the last decade. Over the coming two days I would begin to see these reasons with growing clarity, as I see them now, or suspect I see them, regardless of the ongoing imponderability of all that has happened. But at the time, on the last Friday in November, it was beyond my powers of analysis or imagination to guess who would wish to make me conscious of the surveillance and why he or she would risk alerting me to such an intrusion.

My first thought was that it must be directly connected to someone who already knew me, such as Stephen Jahn, who knew how to access my records and wished to do me the favor of warning me that I could not be assured of my privacy, as if he understood my sense of vulnerability when it comes to these matters. No, that is not the most accurate way of putting it. Rather, as if he understood that I have a particular neurosis about privacy, and one that, in the best Freudian fashion, took root in my childhood, in relation to my father.

Is this, I wonder, the kind of trauma that Dr. Sebastian might have had in mind?

Though I loved him dearly, my father had an altogether different sense of privacy from my own, perhaps because he grew up poor on a farm, the middle child of seven siblings, so poor he shared a bed with his two older brothers and must have grown accustomed from a very early age to not having any true privacy. I, however, grew up with my own bed in my own room. Although not strictly my own, there was a family bathroom (one of four in the house), which I used by habit, where I bathed and showered, brushed my teeth morning and night, shat and pissed and, in my adolescence, masturbated. My father had enjoyed no such privacy as a child. His body was observed by his siblings, his pissing and shitting the business of the whole family as their pissing and shitting was his business, there being nothing but an outhouse for the first several years of his life, only later indoor plumbing arrived, and with it a competition for access that meant uninterrupted use of the facilities by one person was rare.

Because of this difference in our sense of what privacy meant, when I was a young child my father would come into the bathroom without knocking, even when the door was closed, even when I was on the toilet, and with no sense, initially, that this was strange or anything that should upset me until I began to lock the bathroom door whenever I went in. Oddly, rather than understanding what was going on, my wanting to shit and piss without worrying about whether the door would open during these most private activities, my father became irritated and demanded I not lock the door because there were, he insisted, 'no secrets in our house.' There followed a period of negotiation initiated by my mother and at last my father acquiesced and I was allowed to lock the bathroom door, satisfied that when I was at my most vulnerable no one was suddenly going to walk in and disturb me. There was, of course, a strong element of bodily shame at work. These intrusions coincided with my sense of not wanting my parents to see me naked, but while my mother seemed to understand this instinctively, for my father it remained almost incomprehensible. His own father and brothers had routinely seen him naked until, I suspect, quite late in his adolescence. The psychological consequence, for me, was longstanding, not to say permanent, so that whenever I use a public restroom I feel compelled to be sure the stall door will lock, or if it is a single unit that the door to the rest of the establishment locks securely. Similarly, visiting friends, I am often anxious about whether the bathroom door will lock, and when there has been no lock I have often gone to rather ridiculous lengths to make sure people know I am going to use the bathroom and if I find myself on the toilet in an unlocked bathroom and hear movement outside the door I will loudly cough or clear my throat so the person passing will have no doubt the room is occupied. A more well-adjusted man would simply not care, since what one man does in a bathroom is what any man or woman does, give or take small variations of habit and biology, but this neurosis about toileting privacy *is* ultimately about embarrassment and shame; while my father had no sense of bodily shame and no natural sense of privacy (at least in the domestic sphere) my mother was and remains a deeply private woman whose bare shoulders I do not think I saw until I was in my teens and the three of us took a vacation to Florida. Until that time I had never even glimpsed her in a swimming suit and was surprised, when the opportunity came, to see her shrink in on herself, pained by having to expose even modest amounts of skin.

Was it possible, I wondered, that the person who had tipped me off to the ways I was now being monitored had a sense of my neurosis in this matter? If that was the case, then he or she must have been someone who knew me well enough to have observed my behavior or to have been present when, for instance, I was lecturing on surveillance in East Germany, my field of expertise being, arguably, the most revealing thing about me. That someone should choose to focus his professional life on the history of surveillance in a particular country surely suggests he might be obsessed by ideas of surveillance and privacy to more than an ordinary degree. Of course, it struck me—later perhaps than it should—how anyone might take note of my neurosis about privacy simply by examining my scholarly record, accessible for anyone to see online at the department webpage, on any number of websites for conferences where I have spoken, in the catalogs of countless libraries where my books may be cross-referenced under various revealing subjects, not least among them being 'surveillance' of various forms and in several contexts, not limited of course to East Germany, which is to say I might be regarded not just as a surveillance neurotic but as one of the world's leading experts on surveillance, and yet this is, somehow, not a central part of my mental world. I do not walk around thinking of myself as a surveillance expert, but rather as a historian of twentieth-century Europe and to a certain lesser degree as a political theorist or even philosopher. I had to acknowledge, though, sitting in my living room outside of Rhinebeck on a cold November afternoon, which had fallen into an even colder evening, that if someone wanted to make a point about government surveillance then I was, in a sense, among the most useful people to contact or target or make an example of, depending on what the impetus might be.

With these thoughts spiraling round, I made dinner and poured myself a glass of wine. I had just sat down to eat and watch the news when I heard the sound of steps on my gravel driveway, a person walking towards the house at a fast and determined pace, followed by the sudden ringing of my doorbell. I put down my fork on the tray, placed the tray on the floor next to the couch where I had been sitting, and walked out of the living room to the front hall. In the foyer I pulled aside the curtain in the window next to the front door and looked out onto my porch where a young man stood fidgeting in the light. It was Michael Ramsey, as ever in black, his face thin and wind-chapped.

I opened the door but the screen door was still between us and although it was little more than flimsy aluminum and mesh I knew it was secured because I always leave it locked when I go away and I had not yet been through the front door since arriving. Ramsey pretended to look surprised but there is no such thing as coincidence three times in one week, particularly in New York, and I knew that, whatever he might say, he was at my house for a reason, just as he had been at Caffè Paradiso the previous Saturday and at Meredith and Peter's the day before.

Although not naturally inclined to rudeness, in fact my parents were so assiduous in their training I find it difficult to interact with anyone, even clerks or cashiers in stores, without saying 'Hi, how are you doing today?', faced with Mr. Ramsey for the third time in a week, and confronted by him there on the front steps of the place I had come to think of as my retreat from the world, I found my reserves of politeness suddenly emptied and in their place a bursting store of rudeness. 'What the hell do you want?'

'Hey, it's—hey, you're Meredith's dad. What's the likelihood?'

I did not answer except to raise my left eyebrow, which arches more dramatically than the right.

'I, uh, I'm staying in the house down the road.'

'Yes?'

'The power's out.'

'Is it?'

'I don't have a car, and when I saw lights through the trees I thought maybe, you know, you'd have some candles or a flashlight I could borrow. Even just a wind-up radio, you know?'

'No.'

'No you don't have any of those things or no I can't borrow them?'

'I don't have any of those things. And if I did have candles one cannot borrow candles since they are a species of thing consumed in their use, not that batteries in a radio or flashlight aren't as well, but it is, I would suggest, a different order of use. One may receive candles, like eggs or a cup of sugar, with the understanding that one will replace such things or else enter into a reciprocal agreement with the person who has provided them such that he may, when next finding himself without candles, eggs, sugar, or a pound of butter, come knocking on the other man's door and ask for one of these items in kind, as repayment.'

Ramsey looked nonplussed.

'So you don't have a spare flashlight? It's really dark over there. The trees, man, they're kind of creeping me out.'

'You walked here in the dark. I'm sure you'll be fine. You can catch up on your sleep.'

'Come on, Professor, you must have a spare flashlight. I just got here. I came up from the city because I wanted to get away for the weekend, you know, and my friends, they said I could stay at their place, but I don't know, maybe they forgot to pay the electricity bill or something. I get here and there's no power and no heat and it's really fucking cold tonight, and I've been looking around for hours trying to figure out what's wrong. They said the temperature was gonna be the same in Rhinebeck as the city, but shit, man, it's way colder when you get out of the city's microclimate. Have you noticed that? Manhattan's always warmer than surrounding areas, I guess that heat island effect or whatever they call it, the cars and the subways and all that glass and concrete and steel, it produces its own, like, ten-degree boost or something. You'd think the weather service would take account of that but I swear they don't, or their monitoring stations are, like, up at the tops of buildings and get way different readings. Shit it's cold out here. Could I come in and warm up before I head back?'

'It's only a ten-minute walk. You'll warm up on the way.'

'That's not very hospitable.'

'Maybe I'm not a very hospitable person.'

'Come on, I don't think that's true, you're just—I don't know—'

'I'm what? You have a theory about me? You don't even know me.'

'Maybe you're a little paranoid, Professor.'

'Maybe I am. Maybe you should go back to your friends' house.'

'Your neighbors.'

'Yeah, see, I don't know them. Haven't met them. I don't feel obliged to help one of their guests.'

'But I'm a friend of your daughter's.'

'I don't think so, Mr. Ramsey. I think you're Peter's friend and I don't think you're an especially close friend. I get the sense you're some distant hanger-on who turned up in their lives because you realized my daughter and son-in-law might be useful.'

'That's not very nice. Come on, man, can I just get warm for a few minutes? That house is fucking frigid, and if I can't figure out how to get the gas and electricity working I'm in for a cold night.'

'It's not too late to catch a train back to the city. Tell you what, I'll call you a cab.'

'I don't give up so easy, I'll rough it out if I have to—if I could just get warm.'

Even through the obstruction of the screen, it was obvious he was shaking, and perhaps he was a good actor or perhaps he was genuinely cold, but whatever the case something in me began to thaw against my own better instincts and I unlatched the screen door, standing aside as Michael Ramsey walked into my house. In retrospect it is possible I had figured it out already to some extent and wanted to see how things would unfold, hoping if nothing else that inviting him in might give me answers, or that he might reveal his role in the drama unfolding around me.

'Listen, thanks, man, I'm really grateful.' He shivered as I closed the front door, locking it from the inside so he could not leave without momentary obstruction, as if I wanted to make him think he was my hostage as well as my guest. 'My phone's out of juice and I wondered if I could use yours to call my friends and ask them what's up with the power? I don't even know if they're home but they said they were staying in the city tonight and they were going to come up tomorrow to join me, but, you know, I'd rather not spend the night in a cold house if I can avoid it? There must be some really simple explanation like a switch that just needs to be flipped, I don't know, circuit breakers or whatever, maybe there was a surge and things went down, but you didn't have any problems with your power when you arrived? Did you come up last night or this morning?'

'I came up today, this morning. Everything was fine. The house was warm, the lights worked, they still work, as you can see, so I don't think there's anything wrong with the power supply in the area. I don't think a transformer has blown. If there's a problem it's in your friends' house. What are their names, anyway?'

'Phil and Sara Applegate.'

It sounded improbable but I nodded.

'They bought the place a couple years ago and completely redid it. She goes in for primitive design, you know, so it's, like, I don't know, colonial, like walking into the eighteenth century or something, all really simple, but shit it's cold in there.'

'Maybe they don't have electricity. Maybe they only use oil lamps and candles and heat the house with a woodstove. There are people like that up here. You'd be surprised how many. They don't want to live on the grid. They dig a well, chop wood, lead a pastoral life. I think it would be exhausting myself.'

'Totally. Wow. Can you imagine? You'd be working all the time just to stay warm.'

'Simpler existence. Zen-like, or something.'

'You're a funny guy, Professor.'

'What did I say that's funny?'

'*Zen-like, or something* . . . beat, beat, beat. I like your comic timing. Very post-ironic. I never noticed that about you before. So, can I use your phone?'

'Why not?' I pointed with my forehead at the phone in the corner of the living room and Michael Ramsey loped across the floor, I could see he was in what seemed to be his trademark outfit, all blacks and grays, wools and cottons and leathers, as if he had internalized some outsider's sense of the limits of Manhattan chic, how a Midwesterner might imagine a New Yorker should dress, and then in an elegant movement he picked up the phone and dialed. He was skinny and elastic, and I thought again that he was too thin to be healthy, the body of a junkie or anorexic.

'I know their number by heart,' he said, turning to address me over his shoulder.

'Photographic memory?'

'Eidetic. Especially for numbers and addresses and shit. Hey, Sara, it's Michael . . .'

I listened or half listened as he recounted his discovery of my neighbors' cold and dark house and his inability to make the heating or lights work and then the revelation that he was phoning from my own house. It became evident within a few further sentences that Sara and Phil (I later confirmed those are, in fact, the names of my neighbors) had no idea why the power should be off and were hopeful that Michael would be willing to stick around on Saturday for someone to come have a look at things and perhaps they themselves would think twice about coming up for the weekend, which suggested that either the Applegates were assholes or they were not as friendly with Michael Ramsey as he wanted me to believe. (I still have not got to the bottom of that.) At last he hung up the phone and turned around to find me standing at the edge of the living room rug, my toes just touching the tassels, one of my hands resting on the back of a chair while the other searched the inside of my pants pocket for any indication of how I should handle the situation, but cloth offers no answers and a pocket is all too often merely a pocket.

'I guess I'm kind of screwed. Are you sure you don't have some candles or a flashlight? I'll bring them back tomorrow. Or, I mean, I could buy some more candles tomorrow to replace whatever you . . .'

If it was an act he was a convincing liar. He seemed almost bereft, stricken by the prospect of staying in a cold dark house, nearly as horrified as I might have been if faced with the prospect of having to use a toilet in the middle of Penn Station with strangers passing around me on all sides, bumping my bare bottom and shanks with their rolling suitcases and snickering as they watched me reach round to wipe myself.

'I'll see what I can find in the kitchen. I don't think I have candles but I may be able to spare a flashlight.'

'Thanks, anything would be great, you know, even a pen light or whatever.'

As I was about to leave the room I realized I did not want Michael Ramsey to remain alone and unobserved in my house, just as, I imagined, Stephen Jahn might have felt about me those many years ago in Oxford, when I visited his flat in Folly Bridge Court.

'Come with me. I'll make you a cup of tea if you like.'

'Oh no, that's okay. I'm fine, really, I don't want to put you to any trouble.'

'It's no trouble. Come on, I'll make a pot.'

I stood in the vestibule between the living room and the hall that led to the kitchen, making it clear from my stance that I was going nowhere without him. He shuffled across the rug, nearly tripping. I wanted to tell him to pick up his feet and be sharp about it but I just smiled, stepping aside so he could go first into the kitchen. As I did so I imagined pushing him down the stairs into the basement, which was just ahead, the door to that staircase open, the cellar dark, and if I pushed him down those stairs, as I suspected I would have little trouble doing given his slender frame, he would almost certainly die. I stuffed the thought away and followed him into the kitchen, where the lights were still on, leaving my dinner sitting on the tray in the living room, the television flickering in silence.

Michael stood in the middle of the kitchen floor taking in the stove and the open bottle of wine and the cupboards full of plates and cups and glasses, the drawer I had left open, heaving with a second-hand set of silver-plated cutlery bought at a tag sale in Hudson.

'Smells good, man, you cook this yourself?'

'Have you eaten?' I asked, all of a sudden feeling the power in pretending to be hospitable. Rudeness is limiting. Sometimes a false hospitality can be even more dangerous, as any reader of fairy tales must know. The stranger's house in the woods which is suddenly opened and well stocked, the well-laid table of the old woman who smiles and offers a chair at her hearth, the graybeard who pours you a glass of grog and tells his tale, these people all want your life, at the very least, if not your immortal soul, for they may be demons in disguise, Satan in the skin of a man, a hag in the wig of a crone.

'No, but really, that's nice of you—'

'I'm not necessarily offering.'

'Oh, sorry, I thought—'

'Just kidding. Have you eaten?'

'No, but like I said . . .'

'It's no problem. I have plenty. You have a house without heat or electricity. As you say, it's a cold night. You have no car. You know my daughter and son-in-law, therefore custom, as you have reminded me, says I should be hospitable.' I took a plate from the cupboard and dished up a mound of pasta and a helping of salad and a piece of garlic bread, then poured a glass of red wine and smiled at Mr. Ramsey in a way I hoped suggested I was not entirely happy to be doing this but accepted it was the only humane thing to do, or perhaps the most humane act I could have chosen to do short of inviting him to stay the night, which I had no intention of doing. I put the plate on a tray and handed it to him, taking the glass of wine and leading us back into the living room, where I resumed my place on the couch and motioned for him to sit in one of the hard-backed wooden chairs I had acquired at that same tag sale in Hudson where I bought my upstate cutlery from a couple of on-the-make young homosexuals trying to transform another corner of rural poverty into a land of antiques and artisanal cheeses.

'This looks great, thank you,' he said, and for the first time I thought I sensed he might be anxious or was suffering second thoughts about the wisdom of accepting my food and the risk of putting in his mouth what I had prepared, though he must have realized I had not been afforded any opportunity to poison what he was eating unless I had done so in advance. I took up my own plate, with my now cold portion of pasta, and put a forkful of penne with tomato sauce rich in eggplant and garlic into my mouth. After I had swallowed he also ate a forkful and took a sip of wine and nibbled at the garlic bread and all at once looked both exhausted and relieved. We went on eating in silence and as he ate Mr. Ramsey seemed to become ever thinner and younger, more childlike, vulnerable, so that, far from being in his early thirties, as I guessed was the case, he became in my

sight someone half that age, and though he knew my daughter and
son-in-law, and we had met twice before, I was struck by the strange-
ness of having this very immature-looking young visitor seated in my
living room eating my food, intruding on my privacy after having
noticed, through the half-mile of woodland between the house where
he was staying and my own property, the lights of my home at night.
It meant he had been looking for a solution, or perhaps there was no
solution needed, and he knew all along that I was coming here, and
then it occurred to me he might not even be staying with my neighbors but had arrived from town in a taxi, which could have dropped
him off half a mile away so that I would not have seen its lights, and
walked through the cold in the dark to arrive at my doorway with a
story of staying at my neighbors' house when in fact that might have
been as fabulous a concoction as if I were to tell him I had once gone
to bed with an Egyptian princess.

'Peter tells me you lived in England.'

'That's right. For more than a decade.'

'Why'd you come back?'

'My daughter's here. And NYU made me an offer I was in no
position to refuse.'

'More money?'

'Significantly more. And less work.'

'*Nice*,' he said, in that way of his generation, drawing out the
word, making it sound unpleasant or even immoral, a not entirely
justified victory or an advancement won by less than impartial favor,
as though both NYU and I had been compromised by the offer made
and the fact of my accepting it. 'But Oxford's a better school, right?'

'These things are hard to quantify. If better means older and more
selective then Oxford is better, certainly, but as I say, it is difficult to
judge abstractions of quality. You and Peter were both at Harvard,
weren't you?'

'Yeah, I had such a blast.'

'And before that?'

He hesitated for a moment. 'Um, Columbia,' he said, with a rising intonation.

'Also a great school.'

'No doubt, no doubt. I didn't have such a good time, though.'

'Sometimes we end up where we don't belong, and it can be difficult to extricate ourselves.'

'You speaking from experience?'

'Perhaps. Perhaps not.'

'Most Americans, you know, they say *maybe*. I think of *perhaps* as being very *British*.'

I smiled, watching him finish the last bites of the dinner I had prepared for myself, making enough to have leftovers for the following evening so I would not have to cook twice over the weekend, though it was just as likely that after having had lunch with my mother I would find reheated pasta too depressing to eat. I allowed myself to think Michael Ramsey was doing me a favor by consuming half the food I had prepared for myself, and yet watching him eat hungrily but carelessly, as if the operation were one of mechanics rather than desire, of the need simply for sustenance with no attention paid to flavor or taste, no savoring of the meal I had cooked, I began to resent not only his imposition but also my quixotic desire to be helpful to someone adrift in a cold upstate night, and my urge to make myself useful—even, strangely, to befriend this young man. He put down his fork on the tray and looked at me in a way that seemed to expect I should make the next move, and when I said nothing while continuing to stare, unsmiling and silent, he squirmed in his chair.

'I guess I should get going.'

'Before it gets too late.' Although it was still quite early I was anxious to be rid of him, so I stood and walked towards the door.

'You sure you don't have a flashlight?'

'I forgot. Let me go look in the kitchen.' I nearly left him alone in the living room when it occurred to me it would be unwise to assume I could trust him even for a moment. I stopped in the doorway and turned back around, looking down my nose at him from across the room. 'Why don't you help me?'

I waited once again as he walked ahead of me into the kitchen and stood in the middle of the floor. Trying to keep him always in sight, I went directly to the utility drawer with its assorted screwdrivers and spare nails and other bits of household detritus, and at the back, in a cavity that remains perpetually darkened by the over-hanging countertop and can only be accessed by tilting the drawer off its casters, I reached and searched around until I found not one but two different flashlights, both offering rather uncertain illumination, as though they would not last more than a few paces never mind half a mile back along the road or through the woods, and even if they did Ramsey would still be left alone in a darkened house, assuming his story was true. I searched for batteries in a cupboard but found none. There was an antique oil lamp upstairs in my bedroom, which I had filled in case of power outages, but I was not going to loan it to some stranger. Candles I did not possess, and so I shook my head and said I was sorry but he would have to make do with the flashlights and have an early night.

'Thanks, that's helpful, I'll bring them back tomorrow.'

'Only if you get the power back on.'

When I opened the front door and the cold blasted my face I felt a spasm of guilt. If Meredith turned up in a similar predicament at the home of, say, Michael Ramsey's father, if such a man exists, would I not wish for her to be treated with greater care than I was showing this young man?

'Let me give you a lift,' I offered. 'Maybe I can look at the fuse box.'

'No, no, no, I don't want to bother you any more than I have. I'll be okay for the night.'

'Why? Are you not really staying there?'

'I don't understand—'

'If you don't want me to come look I assume that means you're not actually staying at my neighbors' house and you just made up that story to get in the door, because I don't think you're considerate enough to care whether you bother me or put me to any additional trouble or not.'

Michael Ramsey smirked. 'I'm staying there, man. I've got the keys, see?' He pulled a ring from his pocket, but the keys could have belonged to any property.

'I'm curious to see if one of those opens my neighbors' front door.'

I took my coat from the peg in the foyer and told him to wait outside on the porch. Alone again in the house, I locked up and looked for my phone but could not find it so gave up and went out through the garage.

'What, no vintage Merc?' Ramsey asked as he opened the passenger door.

The road was empty and black, glinting with ice crystals, and the lights of the car picked out trunks of bare trees lining farmland on either side, so I knew as I drove that no one was observing our passage. I could, if I felt like it, drive Michael Ramsey off to a remote location and kill him, though I am not and could never be a killer, and yet, not for the first time, the thought of eliminating him floated round in my thoughts, bobbing like a red and white plastic fishing float that might get dunked under the calm surface if the bait at the sharp end felt a purposeful nibble. Nibble, Michael Ramsey, I thought to myself, nibble my bait and see what happens, see what I am capable of doing.

'What exactly do you want from me?' I asked.

Apart from the sound of the car and the wheels on the asphalt, the grinding of gravel thrown up by rubber and the crunch of a shallow ice puddle broken by the weight of the vehicle, there was total silence. I asked the question because I had convinced myself that Michael Ramsey's sudden and repeated appearance in my life over the course of the week could not be chance: he had come for a reason and it must be related to the three file boxes delivered to my apartment, related to that and to my time in Oxford. I was convinced this was the case without possessing any evidence apart from my own suspicions.

'I don't know what you mean, you offered to come take a look at the fuse box. If you don't want to then you can let me out here and I'll walk the rest of the way. I don't want anything from you. Jesus.'

In the darkened car I could not see his face clearly but he sounded panicked in a way he had not in any of our other conversations, either that night or Thanksgiving morning or on our first meeting the previous Saturday afternoon, and I thought perhaps there had simply been a series of coincidences that led to our meeting three times in a week, and Michael Ramsey had nothing to do with whatever else might be happening in my life, in other words the boxes of phone numbers and web addresses might have originated from someone else entirely, from someone connected to Stephen Jahn. I remembered again how Ramsey had described himself as a 'corporate shill.'

'What is it you do? What's your job?'

'Huh? I don't—'

'I'm interested in what you do for a living. You know what I do, but I have no idea what makes you get up in the morning. You're well dressed, you move in circles that include my daughter and son-in-law and those are, if you'll forgive me saying so, rather exclusive tiers of the social hierarchy. I'd like to know what you do.'

There was a pause, as if he was trying to think of an answer.

'I guess I'm, you know, kind of a librarian.'

'You don't look like any librarian I've ever met.'

'A corporate librarian. I work for a corporation. I'm in charge of the company archives and files, so you could say I'm an IT expert, but I think of myself as a librarian, or an archivist.'

'I would have thought all those systems were digitized by now.'

As we arrived at my neighbors' house I sensed Michael Ramsey shift in the passenger seat. For a moment we sat looking up at the black windows and I wondered if he was about to make some further and unpredictable move, if perhaps he really was not staying there and I was about to reach the end of my life.

'Mostly they are. You've got instant access to everything in the company archive, for everyone, you know, provided it's not restricted to upper management. All of it's encrypted behind a firewall. But things still go missing, and if we lose a file or a volume it means a lot more than if your college library misplaces a copy of *War and Peace*. Once the files are all digitized, they're easier to track. I can see which employee has accessed which files at what time, which pages they've looked at and for what duration of time. Imagine if you could do that with your students and keep track of who's been doing the reading, see how long they spent reading—I don't know, what do you work on?'

'Twentieth-century German history.'

'So imagine you assigned Anna Funder's *Stasiland*—' he said it so easily I thought he must have been looking at my syllabi, '—and it was a requirement for students to read it as an e-book and you had the technology in place to see not only *if* they had done the reading but how long each person had spent, whether they had marked up the text, what kinds of notes they had taken, whether—assuming a socially interactive reading experience for the class—they had bothered to look at the notes and comments of their fellow students and contributed to a conversation or debate about the reading before class.'

'You'd need an army of people tracking all those digital markers. Who could manage so much data?'

'It's simpler than you think.'

'Frankly, it gives me chills. Privacy is the last thing we have. Privacy with a book most of all. When I sit down and read a book I don't want anyone else knowing how long it's taken me to read a page, what I've written about it, whether I've skimmed a paragraph too quickly to recall its contents clearly. You're imagining a world where even thought is a matter of public record. It's grotesque.' Ramsey's lips popped with a burst of air, as if in surprise, or exasperation. 'What, you think I'm just a dusty old-fashioned professor, a leather-sniffing bibliophile who naïvely thinks privacy still exists?'

'It's endearing.'

'I wouldn't ever want to know all that information about my students. I'd rather trust them and be disappointed. I could never police them in that way. It's antithetical to a university environment to keep tabs like that. I want to believe in truth, Mr. Ramsey. That is, I want to believe my students will be motivated by faith in the value of truth, of being truthful, not only with me, but with themselves and with each other and with the whole world. That must sound ridiculously romantic to you.'

'Truth may be beautiful but it lacks the artistry of lies.'

He opened the car door and I followed him up my neighbors' driveway to their house and front porch, hanging back as if I expected him to turn on me with a gun, or knock me over the head, and I watched as he took the keys he had dangled before me in my own house, found one on the ring, fumbled with it, dropped it, reached down to the mat and picked it up again—had he made an exchange of some kind, I wondered?—slipped the key in the lock, turned it, and pushed the door open before swinging back round to smile at me, as if to say, 'you see, Professor, I really am staying here, despite your paranoia and suspicion, I have not told an artful lie,' although possession of a working key did not prove he was a guest of my neighbors, there being many ways to acquire a key, for he might have been a highly skilled burglar able to copy keys, or have convinced a local locksmith to let him in and produce a replacement, he was the kind of young man who could persuade an unsuspecting stranger of his right to access, insisting he was sure he had brought the keys with him from the city and perhaps even claiming the neighbors were his aunt and uncle or cousins and the local locksmith, perhaps not knowing my neighbors very well, would have looked at this young New Yorker and either believed him completely or, if he suspected some deception by Ramsey, would nonetheless have gone ahead with making the new key because he feared having to deal with a sophisticated Manhattanite in black who might make an unpleasant fuss and threaten to phone the cops if the locksmith did not do as he was asked. Nonetheless, Ramsey walked into the house, flicking on one of the dim flashlights I had given him. As I followed, I tried the first light switch I encountered, thinking it might all be a ruse, even down to the absence of power, but nothing happened, the rooms remained dark but for the faint beams we held in our hands. At the end of a hallway Ramsey paused.

'Where do you think the fuse box would be?'

'Either the kitchen or garage. Maybe the basement. The basement is more likely.'

'Let's check the kitchen and garage first,' he said, almost as though he feared what I might do to him in the dark of the basement. 'You don't have a light on your phone?'

'I left it back at my house. What about you?'

'It's out of charge, like I said.'

He led me into the kitchen, whose cupboards and surfaces were visible in the moonlight that came in through the window, or at least this is how I remember it, perhaps there was no moon that night but I recall being able to see enough between the dim beam of the flashlight and the glow from the windows to discern the kind of space I was in. A modest kitchen, not unlike my own, a place of wood and stone.

I aimed the flashlight round the room, squinting my eyes, though I've never understood why squinting should improve one's vision since it seems to reduce the optic field and the amount of light reaching the eye itself, and I began opening cupboards, looking for a recessed hatch, I had in mind one of two kinds of circuit boxes, either large and gray and plastic and relatively new, installed in the last twenty years, or an old one with a metal cover and heavy black switches as I remember from my childhood, but after five minutes of searching we both seemed to understand this was not the place.

'Maybe the garage.' Ramsey opened a door that led from the kitchen down a few steps. It was an ordinary garage as such spaces go, with a few garden tools, a riding lawnmower, and a dusty Volvo I assumed must belong to the neighbors. We swept the lights over the walls and searched the shelves and cupboards clustered near the kitchen door. Again, no sign of anything resembling a fuse box or circuit breaker and having realized this was the case it was almost as though, in silence, we acknowledged the necessity of putting aside whatever tension had marked our exchanges thus far and descending to the basement, though my own mind was working its way through various scenarios, thinking about how and whether I might over-power Michael Ramsey if he thought, alone with me in a dark cellar, he could knock me out or tie me up. I entertained any number of possible schemes, imagining this was an elaborate way to confine me or even do away with me, though I could think of no logical reason why this should necessarily be so, why Michael Ramsey might hold a grudge against me.

'Did we know each other before?'

'What? I—what do you mean?' He turned around just as he was climbing the stairs back into the kitchen and held the light such that it pointed towards my midsection. Light on the soft spot. See the target. I moved out of the beam. I could not see his face, but I sensed his surprise.

'Did we ever meet before we met on Saturday, in the café?'

'Why are you asking this now, Jeremy?' It was the first time I was conscious of him calling me by my first name and in his tone I heard a familiarity that unsettled me more than almost anything else that had happened since our meeting at Caffè Paradiso the previous Saturday afternoon. He said 'Jeremy' as if he had said it before, or as if he knew so much about my life, felt so intimately familiar with the details of my past, that to go on calling me Professor O'Keefe would have been an act of deception so great not even he, who so plainly regarded himself as an artist of fabrication, who saw lies as an art to be mastered, could possibly continue in that vein, or perhaps he felt some sympathy for me in my confusion and alarm.

'Answer the question.'

'I'll answer it by asking another. Why is it you fail to remember *me*? Are you sick, do you have early onset dementia or Alzheimer's, or are you oblivious? Are you just an asshole who doesn't pay any attention to the people who pass through your life?'

'I don't *know* you. You talk now as if I do. We might have met, one meets lots of people and it's possible to forget those meetings if they fail to make an impression, but I do not *know* you, Mr. Ramsey.'

'Let's look in the basement. My light is fading.'

He walked back up into the kitchen and though I was deeply unsettled by this exchange I followed him, feeling I could not abandon the conversation until he had made himself clear. His flashlight was flickering and I steered myself down the hallway to a door, watched Ramsey open it, then stepped along behind him as he descended to the basement. This was one of those fully finished cellars with carpeting and 1970s-era fake wood paneling, a utility room with the furnace and hot water heater, another room with the washer and dryer, a bathroom, a kind of craft counter, a shower, a dumpy midcentury sofa. We searched the area around the furnace and water heater and at last found, in the farthest corner of the basement, a gray plastic box mounted on the wall, and when I opened the door I could see in an instant that the main circuit breaker had been thrown. I pushed it back in the other direction, heard it click, and we listened as the furnace began to rumble. The water heater made a hissing, gurgling noise, and upstairs the refrigerator in the kitchen came on, but the rooms were still dark.

Ramsey turned and walked back to the door leading into the utility room, fumbled and flipped a switch at the wall. A single bulb lit up and I could see his face clearly for the first time since we had left my house, at most only half an hour earlier, and yet he seemed transformed into someone quite other than who he had been when he arrived on my doorstep that night.

A student, I thought, Michael Ramsey was one of my students at Columbia, just as Fadia was a student at Oxford. Is it so inconceivable that I would not have remembered him before that moment, or that even then, when he told me I had been his teacher, I could not pull a memory of his face from the back of my head, I had no memories of the previous meetings, I could not imagine him as he would have appeared in his early twenties, nor can I even summon the names of most of the students I taught at Columbia, it was now so long ago and I was a different person with a different brain, one already jostled with too many claims on its finite capacity to remember. Michael Ramsey was a stranger to me, who wished to present himself as a familiar, if not a friend, someone to whom my own life was connected, it would seem, by the chance of him enrolling in courses I once taught,

the subsequent chance of him belonging to the same organization—
whatever it might have been—as Peter when they were both graduate
students at Harvard and my daughter was an undergrad.

I thought then he might be some kind of stalker with a grievance,
a hacker who had monitored me after I had spoken too sharply to
him in class one day back at the dawn of the millennium.

LOOKING OUT ON the city as I scratch at these pages, another day
ending, lights warming up in the adjacent buildings and Houston
Street clogging with traffic, sidewalks fuller than at other times of
the day as students released from class hurry to assignations or the
banalities of part-time work, I know how profoundly wrong I was
about Michael Ramsey. That weekend in Rhinebeck I was thinking in
the mode of the campus melodrama, a middle-aged professor targeted
for vengeance by a student scorned. That, I now see, was the wrong
genre entirely.

What, though, is the right one? Even now I am not entirely certain.
Are the events that have reshaped my life, which feel increasingly
as though they are demolishing the border that once kept me from
wandering outside the territory of sanity, any less realistic in their way
than the vagaries of melodrama? Is the mode of paranoia (particularly, perhaps, paranoia confirmed by events or evidence as nothing
more fantastic than sensible caution duly justified?) any less a form
of social realism than some lyrical testament of love or friendship or
loss? My own story, I know, is not only about a state of paranoia at
last proved warranted. In the accordion-squeeze recollection of my
past, the distant events coming closer during the moments in which I
examine them only to recede as the expansive air of inattention pushes
them further away again, I sense that in the end the more universal
experiences of romance and separation may yet prove my innocence.

Fadia, of course, is the key.

WHEN SHE CAME TO interview at Oxford, Fadia was in her final year of high school or secondary school, in fact I should have no trouble remembering, it was a *lycée*, because she was at school in Paris and for some reason it had been decided that Oxford would be a better place for her than one of the French universities. Although she spoke with a distinctive French accent, her English was flawless, and she was, from first sight, one of the most striking young women I have ever met. She had thick dark hair worn long, sometimes up in a chignon, other times falling to her waist, held back with that implement that in England they call an 'Alice band' after the Tenniel illustration of Lewis Carroll's heroine, as if all girls who wear such bands are somehow participants in a vast apparatus of Alice-dom, as if even the men who dare to wear Alice bands—and there were quite a few in my early days in England, a footballer having made such gender transgressions possible—were themselves participating in the emulation of that precocious blonde child.

Fadia was tall and slender and gave the impression of being constructed of pure self-assurance, a confidence so bold it blinded her to her own failures and made her irritable with others whose qualities she regarded as shortcomings, even when she found them in figures of authority like teachers or, indeed, university professors interviewing her for a place in their College. If she believed she was right, I could see in that first meeting, it would take very inventive persuasion to make her see she might be wrong, and this fact was, without my realizing it at the time, one of the most attractive aspects of her character. She was not conventionally beautiful, either, for she had a prominent nose with a slight arch, rather closely set dark eyes, and while her height and slenderness suggested a contortionist more than a great beauty, she held herself as if she were nobility dressed in a pants suit, which, on a less confident girl, would have looked like a loan from a corporate mother's wardrobe. On Fadia it was as natural as her skin, fine and smooth with the red-gold sheen of amber.

In our first meeting at that admissions interview her insights were workmanlike and she was bullish rather than receptive. She seemed too confident, almost arrogant, to be a natural choice for a College like ours—I would have sent her off to St. Hilda's, or even Christ Church—and yet I remembered Stephen Jahn's request, and so asked encouraging questions that I hoped would lead Fadia towards answers which would make it easier for me to persuade Bethan we should give her the kind of score—we scored all the candidates and then compared notes with the other interviewing team at the end of two days—that would make her, if not one of the top candidates, someone solidly in the middle of the pack, about whom there could be no doubts. Perhaps it was the nature of that year's pool of applicants, a trick of dumb chance or mere coincidence, but without having to say anything to anyone, Fadia was offered an unconditional place, although Bethan thought her a potentially 'difficult' girl, while Stephen made a point of mentioning the wealth of the family and the prospect of a substantial donation to the College at some future date, the sort of donation that might, in fact, allow for another post in History or the provision of grants for female students from disadvantaged backgrounds. Even less flattering, there was an unspoken understanding that, from a public relations perspective, it would be no bad thing in the wake of the terrorist attacks in London over that summer for the College to demonstrate its commitment to educating Muslim students, as an indication of its longstanding investment in a liberal humanist tradition. At the time I thought no more about it. Fadia was one of a group of young people, no more than that, although I looked forward in a remote way to seeing how she evolved in the coming years, by which I mean my interest was pedagogical and observational rather than emotionally inflected.

Fadia arrived as one of the freshers in October the following year, but because of the way the undergraduate History degree is structured at Oxford and how the College organized its teaching, I had little to do with her until the year after that, by which time I had been promoted to a full professorship (although I had not been particularly confident about my application), and so returned to teaching with a renewed sense of purpose.

When I began seeing her in weekly tutorials, she reminded me, for the first time in what was then no more than our passing acquaintance, of an Egyptian boy I had known in my freshman year at Georgetown. Though I was not friends with him, we lived in the same dormitory and I often saw him at events since we were both in the School of Foreign Service, to which I had foolishly committed myself, thinking I might have a career in diplomacy or government. I have forgotten the boy's name, perhaps it was Amir, but I remember being astonished that an Egyptian could be blond, as he was, and unsettled in my own mind by the curiosity I felt about him. I think we never spoke, but on several occasions I found excuses to sit next to him in classes and lectures, or behind him on the bus that ran from Georgetown to Dupont Circle, and on one occasion, in the middle of a warm spring day, I remember sitting next to him in a lecture and being conscious of his odor, which was not unpleasant, but rather a mix of cologne and the smell of his body, an aroma unlike anything I had sensed in the past and yet there was something curiously familiar about it, almost familial. When Fadia began appearing in my tutorials, I caught that same scent, a note that was recognizable without my being able to place the association.

At first, Fadia was a serious if unexceptional student. Her work was skillful and her arguments efficient rather than sparked with genius in a student body that often produced undergraduates with genuine intellectual fire. In the summer before her final undergraduate year, something happened, as it often does to young women and men as they push themselves over that last cusp of youth and into adulthood. When she returned to College in October she had become another person, as if at last her body had grown into its features. The occasional arrogance had vanished and in its place was a more attractive self-assurance, as though over the space of a few months she had become the noblewoman she always seemed to know she was. Alongside this I also noticed the emergence of a furtiveness or anxiety I had not observed in the past. In tutorials she always sat in the same chair and would glance out the window every time there was a flutter of movement, even if it was nothing more than a pigeon. When I saw her around College or in the libraries, or simply on the streets of Oxford, coming in and out of clothing stores on Cornmarket or standing in line for a sandwich in the Covered Market, she was often looking over her shoulder, as though she feared someone might be following her. I began to suspect she had suffered a trauma over the holidays but did not feel we were close enough for me to ask what might have happened. On occasion she came unprepared to class and called in sick more than once, although on those very days of illness I sometimes saw her in town, looking fine. So while she became physically more impressive her academic standing slipped. And yet, because of my history with Jayanti, or perhaps because of some finer quality I sensed in Fadia, I did not chivvy her to work harder.

Then, one dark November afternoon, she stayed behind after a group class to ask if I would support her application to read for a two-year MPhil.

'I'm not convinced postgraduate studies are the right choice for you, Fadia. I don't want to be patronizing, but you don't seem like the graduate school type. It requires a huge amount of self-direction.'

'You don't understand, Professor. I *have* to do this.'

From her tone and the panicked expression on her face I understood there was more than learning at stake.

'Is this a way of staying?'

'I don't understand what you mean.'

'I imagined you might go into a job immediately after finishing.'

She looked shocked, as though a 'job' were so pedestrian a proposition as to be unthinkable.

'Is it so surprising I might be interested in the subject?'

'You've not demonstrated much in the way of enthusiasm. Your work is competent, but I confess I have never been astonished by it.'

'You're saying I'm a bad student?'

'Not at all. You've been a very good student up until the last few weeks, but you don't make yourself noticed.'

'Maybe I will make myself noticed from now on. Will you write me a reference?'

She reminded me what courses she had taken and explained that, in fact, her interests were in the area of my own research, Germany after the Second World War.

'Your work on the Stasi has been very illuminating for me,' she said, with an earnestness that kept it from sounding like empty flattery. 'It makes me think about Egypt differently.'

'That's nice of you to say.'

'But your book on East German cinema—that is what has inspired my own thinking. I have become fascinated by leftwing European terror movements. You know, Forças Populares, the Brigate Rosse, but especially Baader-Meinhof.' Though her tone remained serious, almost static, I liked to think I saw a spark of passion—perhaps no more than intellectual inspiration. 'I want to think about terror and media, or the relationship between the media and leftwing terror.'

'Quite a lot of work has already been done in that field.'

'But what do you think of Fassbinder's films? Have you seen *The Third Generation*? It's so absurd and yet there's something about the alienating quality of its form that speaks directly to the concerns of the Red Army Faction. What were they trying to do if not make West German consumer society see the artifice of its own construction, just as Fassbinder tries to make his viewers experience the artifice of the otherwise realist film they are viewing by terrorizing their ears through his use of that horrible non-diegetic soundtrack?'

'I haven't seen it in a long time, but yes, what you say sounds sensible. You don't have to settle on a topic right away, of course, there will be time for that, assuming you're accepted for the MPhil. Are you thinking of a doctorate?'

'If the Faculty will let me.'

'And this is really what you want?'

'You think because I'm a girl—'

'I don't think anything of the kind. But I hadn't realized you were so eager.'

'Does it surprise you so much? Did you think I was some lazy Muslim girl who was just going to marry a sheik and go live in a penthouse in Dubai?'

'I would never think that. But neither did I want to presume to know.'

'I'm an atheist, Professor O'Keefe. Culturally mixed up. Half-Muslim, half-Catholic.'

'I didn't imagine...' I said, and trailed off, feeling the precipitousness of the conversation we were having, the vertigo of knowing we had stopped talking about her studies or about history and had moved on to her life. I did not, as a rule, like to speak with students about their lives, not after the experience of Jayanti. It seemed too loaded with risk to know what they loved or believed, and perhaps as a result of this caution I failed in my pastoral duties, which are taken as seriously at Oxford as one's intellectual work.

To get Fadia out of my rooms that day I agreed to write the reference, knowing she would almost certainly be admitted to the MPhil program if she had my support. Despite the recent blip during that term, her results had been strong and she was likely to do well in her final exams, which turned out ultimately to be the case.

When she was awarded a first-class degree, she came to thank me for my support. It was one of those peerless long afternoons Oxford delivers each summer, lingering with a carelessness as intoxicating as the perfume of linden blossoms.

'I'm looking forward to the autumn,' Fadia said, handing me a heavy parcel wrapped in thick silver paper and tied with a blue ribbon.

'What's this? What have I won?'

'It's just a small token of thanks, for your help with the reference, and for your teaching.'

Gifts from students were sufficiently rare that I was quite overcome by the gesture and moved to an almost childish excitement. When the paper came away there was still a box, and then another box within, and only on removing the inner box from the outer could I see it was a bottle of that thirty-year-old whisky Stephen Jahn had served me some years earlier, a whisky that had made me swoon with its magnificence such that I agreed to do what he asked—namely, whatever I could to ensure Fadia was admitted to our College. As I pulled the bottle from its inner box and held the liquid up to let the summer light break through and illuminate the color, I knew there could be no question of coincidence. Stephen himself might have paid for it, or perhaps merely made the suggestion and Fadia followed through on it.

I wondered about the transgression of a young Muslim woman from a good family giving a non-practicing but nonetheless Christian man of a certain age—an American no less—a bottle of expensive alcohol as a gift. It seemed somehow doubly wrong, and yet the transgression made the gift all the greater, as if Fadia were saying to me, 'look what I am prepared to do to show you the extent of my gratitude. Imagine what my family would say if they saw me buying the bottle, or if they knew that, even worse than me drinking it myself, I was going to give it to you, my professor?' Although perhaps it would have been judged far worse if she had meant it for herself; I knew so little of Islam I could only begin to guess at the weight and scope of any particular taboo and, apart from the occasional sliver of information Stephen had let drop over the years about Fadia's brother, I knew nothing of the family, whether they were secular or devout, of ordinary or extraordinary wealth, if their money was earned or inherited, even what the parents did. I knew then that Saif had somehow been employed by Mubarak's government (although I remained unsure, at the time, in precisely what capacity) but Fadia's own politics were democratic, progressive—even, one might reasonably say, leftwing—and I knew that she was, by her own assertion, an atheist. Perhaps this was why she had been sent abroad in the first place, to protect her from the government in which her family was enmeshed, or perhaps to protect *them* from the embarrassment and risk of her political activity.

There was an evening that summer, just at the end of Trinity term, when Stephen Jahn and I again found ourselves alone after dinner in the Senior Common Room and he suggested returning to his flat.

I declined the invitation because I had an early meeting the next day and no great desire to be alone with him.

'Professor O'Keefe,' he muttered, 'so very busy now that you have a Chair. You see how you have been duly rewarded . . .'

'Duly rewarded? In what way do you mean?'

'Rewarded for doing your duty. Rewarded for doing what was asked of you.'

'I don't think I understand, Stephen.'

'You fulfilled what was required of you. You did it well. People are rewarded when they do what is asked.'

'Are you talking about Fadia?'

Stephen, in his incomparable way, spluttered, eyes popping, apoplexy overtaking his whole wiry bald person, as if he might transform, by sheer force of outrage, from gristle and bone to a column of fire.

'I am talking about doing one's duty, Jeremy, and nothing more. *Nothing more.*'

He blinked several times and then, rising a little unsteadily, as though he might lose his footing at any moment, bid me goodnight. Was it possible, I wondered, that because I had, in my quite passive way, helped Fadia get her place in College, Stephen had stage-managed or finessed my promotion? What more might be given in reward if I continued to look after this young woman? And why, if this proved the case, was she so important? Could it be nothing more than because she was the sister of Saif, the man I believed Stephen loved in his peculiar way, whether or not that love was reciprocated? I had no answers and still, thinking it over now, I cannot entirely puzzle my way through the possibilities.

IN THE BASEMENT of my neighbors' house north of Rhinebeck that cold Friday night the last weekend in November, Michael Ramsey

stared at me, and in his appearance of torment and disbelief I saw
the echo of expressions that had once exploded in Stephen's face, his
eyes growing larger and darker than they were, muscles between the
eyebrows knitting together and drawing down into a V, mouth blis-
tering as a wound.

'You were my student, once.'

'Yeah. You really don't remember?'

'No, only—yes. I can see your face now, in my memory I mean, as
a young man.' This was a lie, I could not, I had no way of imagining
how he might have looked more than a decade earlier.

'But other than that?'

'No, I'm afraid not. I'm sorry.'

I watched as he turned and disappeared back up the stairs. It
could not have been a case like Fadia. I have no interest in men, my
fascination with Amir—or whatever he was called—aside, and in that
instance it was interest in an otherness that felt inexplicably familiar.
Perhaps, though, it occurred to me standing there, Michael Ramsey,
like Stephen Jahn, *does* have such an interest, and perhaps, just
maybe, I was the object of his obsession, a father figure, a daddy to a
fatherless boy. Melodrama again, a campus intrigue, a gay romance.
I was thinking in the wrong genre.

In the kitchen we stood some feet apart, not quite staring at each
other.

'Thank you for your help, Jeremy.'

'I'm glad we found it. The house should heat up quite quickly.'
An apology seemed out of order, even excessive. For what did I have
to apologize? Why be sorry for the failure of one's memory? 'I should
be going, Michael. Have a good night. Perhaps I'll see you again, at
another of Peter and Meredith's parties.' I paused to let him speak but
he said nothing. 'I'm sorry I didn't remember you at first.'

Not wanting to wait for his response I showed myself out the front door. My car was already cold though the engine had not been off very long, so I sat in the driveway as the steering wheel lost its chill. Ramsey was moving around inside the house, his shadow crossing the windows as he pulled curtains closed one room after another. I watched, as if in watching his movements some gesture or tic might bring back memories of him, but nothing returned. He was like any other thin young man. I could read neither his sexuality, nor his politics. As for age, he would have been at least in his early thirties, if not older, unless he had been some kind of wunderkind, not impossible at Columbia but unlikely nevertheless. His face still had the youth of a man in his twenties, younger looking than Peter, who must be his near contemporary.

When I got home I pulled into the garage and stayed in the locked car until the door had closed, climbed out after a moment's hesitation and locked the garage door before entering the house, checking all the doors and even some of the window locks, as if someone might be moved to push a window open and crawl inside, padding damp footprints across my floors and carpets before hunkering down next to my bed. These are things I imagine without much effort, though I have never suffered a break-in, and neither has my mother or anyone in my extended family. We have been singularly untouched by crime, so much so that one might think we were overdue for an intimate encounter.

Before going upstairs I checked the front and back doors once more. I think now that I had not closed the curtains on the second floor, so before I turned on the lights I must have gone from room to room, pulling curtains shut and for a moment looking out on the surrounding farmland under the blue-white shimmer of moonlight. To the south, I could see the lights burning in my neighbors' house, where Michael Ramsey might have been watching television and drinking a beer, or perhaps doing something far less innocent. It was early, not even ten, and I felt a heaviness settle on my shoulders as I stood in the dark bedroom with my bare feet on the wooden floor, its smooth polish interrupted by a scattering of dust that created the impression of life, the world beyond human effort struggling to overtake us. Through the trees I could see the forward march of memory, an army worn down by long battle, forgotten by its generals, creeping forward to deliver their report.

IN ERNST BLOCH'S *The Spirit of Utopia*, written in the midst of the First World War, he suggested in a section entitled 'The Egyptian Volition to Become Like Stone' that in Ancient Egypt's 'spirit of stone'—that 'total dominance of inorganic nature over life'—'Man . . . sees his future, but sees himself dying,' and consequently 'a nameless fear of death dominates . . . every Egyptian face.' Although undoubtedly exoticist, and infected by the cultural assumptions of his own time, as any historian must be to a certain extent, Bloch's lines sang through my thoughts, rearranging themselves into new formulations as I came to know Fadia, until at last I could no longer see her without hearing his words. A consciousness of death's proximity had been carved into her face, or so I imagined, until there was, in the firmness and clarity of her features, the quality of stone.

Nothing happened between us when Fadia was an undergraduate. Nothing happened during her MPhil, and although I was conscious of her beauty—it was something one could not help noticing and on occasion I found myself distracted by her poise, by the fine strong arch of her nose and the dark hair she kept long, sometimes braided, often spilling loose around her, straight hair that seemed to resist all curl except around the face, where fine tendrils flexed themselves into spirals to frame her features and at times stray into the soft pucker of her barely open mouth—I can assert to myself and to anyone else who might ask, I had no intention of pursuing her. This has never been my style, unlike a great many male academics who find themselves single or simply away from their wives—or even their husbands nowadays—I was never inclined to seek affection from my students. Perhaps this comes from an old Puritan impulse or merely an aversion to mess and complication, but however much I might have noticed women in my classes over the years, and I can recall some great beauties, I never imagined trying to seduce any of them, except, perhaps, in the course of daydreaming, an exploration of erotic possibility unblemished by anything approaching concrete intention.

Then, one January, in the first year of her doctoral studies, Fadia's world came unstuck, by which I mean that the world of her parents and brother, who remained in Egypt, began to fracture and crumble. On what in Egypt was celebrated as 'Police Day', a holiday commemorating the sacrifice of police officers who resisted British occupation in 1952, the people rose up against the government, and even against the police themselves and the whole repressive apparatus of the Ministry of the Interior, which had placed political activists under surveillance, among many other breaches of civil liberties. By chance I happened to pass the College MCR one evening after a High Table dinner and noticed Fadia and a group of other graduate students gathered to watch rolling coverage and analysis of the unfolding events or crisis or revolution, as it became, although a revolution that seems in the end to have been forestalled by a coup d'état.

But that January evening, as I paused outside the MCR, I remember how Fadia looked up at me hovering in the doorway, her face lit by a strange radiance of hope intermingled with fear. She appeared to be torn moment to moment between poles of elation and concern, triumph and defeat, and from the little I then understood of her and her family, the division that I already assumed existed though I would later come to see how the fracturing was more complex than simply along the fault lines of age, I sensed she was happy for the overthrow of a regime she despised but also terrified about what this shift in her nation's history would mean for her parents, brother, and extended family. Perhaps she did not then know where Saif really stood. Perhaps Stephen Jahn did not know either. Perhaps Saif himself did not know, although I should say, I want to record it clearly here now, on this page, in this document, that I have never met or communicated with the man, or with any other member of Fadia's family. Of that charge I remain innocent.

Stephen was absent from College in those months, as he often was during crises in the Middle East, and I had begun to intuit that his role was only marginally collegiate or academic. I suspected he was entangled in a web of government and global intelligence, whether working for the CIA or MI6, although I could not then say and still do not have an answer. He acted like my idea of a spy and so I began to believe he must be one, clip-clopping down Turl Street in his three-piece gray suit and his matching homburg, little round spectacles perched on his nose, feet in brogues handmade by Duckers, so he looked as though he would have been more comfortable at the beginning of the twentieth century than in the second decade of the twenty-first, a spy in Vienna or Berlin in the 1920s or '30s rather than a spy of the present, and yet perhaps that was the greatest disguise of all, to make himself up as a walking antique who was, in fact, nothing of the sort. By that point I had been in Oxford for nearly a decade and had learned over the years that if I ever had computer problems, at home or in College, Stephen could be relied upon to sort them out faster than anyone else and with no expectation I should do anything in return except perhaps stand him a drink in the Senior Common Room. How early did I first seek his assistance? If only I could pinpoint that date and cross-reference it with the start date of the files delivered to me here in New York, I might begin to find an answer to the questions I seek.

By chance, I saw Fadia the following day in Brasenose Lane, as I was cycling into College from home. It was still dark enough in the mid-morning January gloom that I had turned on my bicycle light so the yellow beam cut through the fog and fell against the outline of her body. She was wearing a long black coat with a white scarf trailing in folds and swags across her shoulders and down her back. Despite the cold and a sky that threatened to open, we both stopped, shifting our weight on the slick cobblestones.

'Is everything okay with your family? I wanted to ask last night—'

She took a breath and blew it out in puffs of vapor. 'I wish I could be there. I feel I should get on a plane, but I can't. I mean I could, but my mother has forbidden me. Things are too uncertain for them. It's very complicated, Jeremy, as I'm sure you can imagine.'

Somehow, during the course of her MPhil, we had graduated from her calling me Professor O'Keefe to using my first name. This was not so uncommon, some Fellows are happy to have undergraduates address them by their first names from the start. I had never made a policy myself, simply allowing individual students to speak to me in whatever way seemed appropriate to them, provided it was respectful, though disrespect is still a reasonably rare occurrence in an Oxford College. She said my name with that distinct French inflection she had, making me sound more like a *Jérémie* than a Jeremy, allowing me to imagine myself as a man louche yet soigné. By subtle measures, Fadia was already transforming my sense of my own self. I now see this as one of the first steps on the path I was following towards a more conscious attraction.

'But are they safe? Your parents, I mean, and you have a brother?' I knew she had a brother. We play at ignorance to appear less knowing, to act as if we have not already spent hours looking at her profile on various social media platforms, all of them public, open for anyone to see. I knew what music she liked, what films and books (the works of Edwar al-Kharrat, Ahdaf Soueif, and Amina Zaydan, Hélène Cixous, Frantz Fanon, and Jacques Derrida, but also Hilbig and Calvino, Poniatowska and Lispector), her pet passions (animal rights, democracy, freedom of speech, the overthrow of censorship, the environment, the rights of women and children, the fight against female genital mutilation, not to mention Monty Python and Asterix and Tintin). I knew all these things and had them circling behind my eyes as I pretended not to be certain whether or not she had a brother.

All at once, in that alleyway between Lincoln and Exeter, Fadia seemed to struggle against tears. Her eyes reddened, but she maintained her composure. I might have touched her upper arm or shoulder, trying to reassure her, and I remember suggesting she come to my rooms for a cup of tea instead of carrying on to the Bodleian, as had been her intention, for she seemed in no state to sit in the low wooden chairs of the Upper Reading Room, and I had sufficiently acculturated myself that I was now reasonably persuaded a cup of tea and a biscuit were a balm for most ailments. So she accompanied me back to College, through the lodge, across the front quad and up the staircase to the Senior Common Room, where I made us tea and collected some biscuits before we went back down the stairs and across to the Chapel Quad, climbing another staircase to the rooms I now occupied, overlooking a square of lawn so trim and green, even in winter, it seemed an act of gardening alchemy or artifice, a performance of life rather than life itself.

I remember the gray floorboards creaking under our weight as we sat across from each other by the fireplace, which had never been lit during my time. She put the cup and saucer on the coffee table and unwrapped herself, dropping the black coat and long white scarf on an empty chair, swinging her loose hair round to the front of her body. I no longer recall what she was wearing under the coat, but

I imagine it was something like a creamy silk blouse and a black cashmere sweater and long tapered black wool trousers with black leather boots. As she progressed further into her graduate studies the glimmers of color I had seen in her wardrobe in earlier years began to disappear, giving way to a palette of grays, whites, ivories, and blacks, arranged in inventive permutations so that, in time, I would see her in a shirt or sweater I did not recognize even though it might have been part of her wardrobe for some months. She was nothing less than an agent of transformation, though in the beginning— that is the beginning of what became our stronger, more intimate attachment—I did not entirely appreciate how powerful this art could be.

The story of her family came out over that cup of tea on a dark January morning, how her father and uncle were high up in Egypt's Ministry of the Interior, how her brother had worked for the same division but had now aligned himself instead with the Muslim Brotherhood, while her mother, Jeanne-Alice, born and raised in France, was, like Fadia, in favor of secular democracy. At that particular moment, it seemed as though such a hope was not naïve. It was her father, Khalid, and her uncle, Samir, who were the locus of Fadia's concern. As close as they were to Mubarak, she worried about their safety.

'They are talking about leaving the country and coming to London, which they could do, but it does not look good. I know what my father and uncle have been doing. I know, of course I know, that this government has been all wrong for a very long time. Why do you think my mother sent me abroad for school and university? She saw I could not stomach what was happening and I was going to continue to be a problem, an even bigger problem if I stayed. And now, Saif, he is also a problem. I have terrible visions of my parents trying to flee and getting caught by an angry crowd, finding themselves suddenly face to face with people who hate my father, or what he stands for, and with total justice they hate him, though I do not believe he is a bad man, and I fear that seeing him try to flee they would stop him and kill my parents, both my mother and father, and I can imagine how easily I might be in one of those crowds, how I might get carried along by the turmoil. I know Saif is out there, protesting and camping and he like others might surge forward at the sight of men like my father fleeing with their wives and find the rage ungovernable such that he, my own brother, might be a bone in the hand that pulls the trigger that kills my mother or the wrist of the hand that makes the knot that lynches my father. This is what I see when I walk past the gates of Trinity in the morning, when I open a book of German history, when I try to sleep at night in my College room on Museum Road, and it is what I see when I turn on the news and watch my people and my country, this people and country that feel both closer and further away from me than ever before, because I know them and yet now I do not know them, I've spent so much time in France and Britain that I have become French and British. I have to remind myself that I *am* half-French, that I am as much European as Egyptian, and this division in myself, sometimes, Jeremy, it so overwhelms me that I want to go back to Egypt and forget the person I have become while living in Europe, to be Egyptian in an uncomplicated way and fight for the country that so many of us believe it could become. I look at you, and I don't know how you do it, how you have spent so many years away from your home. A decade away from your family! How can you stand it?'

'I get on a plane.'

'That's easy enough.'

'Except the money.'

'Of course, always that.' When she looked away I knew she had never been made to think about budgets.

'Have you spoken to your brother?'

'He doesn't answer when I try to phone. He doesn't reply to my emails or text messages. I don't know him anymore.'

I could not help wondering where Stephen Jahn might be in all this, what role he had assumed. His complexion was such that he could pass as Egyptian, though his features were Italianate and I thought I remembered there was an Armenian grandmother as well. Might he have been there, among the crowds of protestors, or moving like a ghost between the putatively democratic and the unapologetically despotic, reporting the identities of the demonstrators to those men still clinging to power? And what of Saif, the man I was sure Stephen loved, for the name had continued to blow into his conversation over the years, often late at night in the SCR, when only he and I and perhaps one or two sympathetic others remained, deep in our cups after a High Table dinner, and someone, as often as not myself, would venture to ask how Saif was doing and whether Stephen had seen him recently, and then Stephen would almost invariably nod his head and say, like the doting uncle he imagined himself to be, or the lover of a much younger mistress, 'he is doing very well indeed, thank you for asking, though I worry about him sometimes, there are people . . . who could make things impossible for him, so one must be very careful. Discretion.'

Still, such conversations gave almost nothing away. Stephen never said in so many words that Saif was his lover, and to assume this was the case would, I think now, be to fall into a certain kind of trap, perhaps a trap of Stephen's own design.

A week or so later Fadia reported that her parents had fled to London, and though her mother came up to Oxford for a day, Fadia did not go down to see them until the break between Hilary and Trinity terms. When she returned for her exams that last summer term of her MPhil she had lost whatever glimmer of innocence I might have detected in the past. I do not recall any conversations over the course of those months about the status or welfare of her parents, though I knew that other Egyptian officials who had fled the country were having their assets frozen by the British government; the policy seemed to be applied in a typically patchy and inconsistent way, as if some former despots were better friends than others. Stephen Jahn came and went and seemed, although it might have been my imagination, to avoid speaking with me. Whether he and Fadia saw each other—if indeed they ever saw each other—I could not say. Stephen's flat at Folly Bridge Court was in a part of the city I rarely had occasion to visit unless someone happened to propose meeting for a drink at the Head of the River pub or if I decided to go down to support the College at Eights Week when that stretch of the Thames known locally as the Isis is fat with lean young bodies pushing wood through water.

THE HISTORY FACULTY accepted Fadia's application to read for a doctorate with the understanding I would supervise her further research into the role of media and cinema in the formation and critique of leftwing European terrorism. British doctoral studies are significantly different from what happens here in America, where a committee of academics looks after a student's progress through the writing of his or her dissertation, and only then after two years of demanding coursework and oral examinations. In Britain, a doctoral student has only one or at most two supervisors for her thesis, and there is no coursework, only 'pure research.' In practice this means that, depending on the supervisor, things can either go very well or very badly—or, as in the vast majority of cases, the student muddles along in an unexceptionally adequate and thus eminently British way.

Over that summer, Fadia moved out of her rooms on Museum Road and into a College-owned house on Divinity Road, across the street from my own house. She had been assigned the bedroom on the top floor, its bay window facing the street and thus, also, my own master bedroom and living room, both of which were at the front of my semi-detached redbrick Victorian. Divinity Road is a street of multiple characters, and in our particular stretch—up the hill but still on the straightaway before it begins to curve round to meet the Warneford Hospital, originally the Oxford Lunatic Asylum on its foundation in 1826—it was so narrow it felt as though the people across the way were almost as proximate as those on either side.

At first I thought nothing of our being neighbors, supervisor and student, members of the same College, our lives drawing closer together as years passed, two lives intertwining as naturally as the tendrils of a climbing rose find their way through the bars of a trellis. One of my colleagues in Anthropology had let a room in his house to one of his doctoral students, though no one in College seemed to think this was a particularly good idea and I remember now that the student in question found the house so dark and cold and my colleague of so eccentric a disposition that she left well before the period they had agreed she would stay.

As autumn closed in and winter once again approached, fogs rolling in off the rivers and filling the streets of Oxford with a ghostly mist, I happened one night to wake with a start. I got out of bed, shuffled down the hall to the bathroom, and returned to the bedroom. I was about to get back into bed when I noticed a light from outside. Drawing my curtains aside, I looked out on the street awash in yellow lamplight and in the house opposite Fadia's blinds were open, her lights burning. She stood in the window, wrapped in a white robe, speaking into her phone. There was no mistaking that she was upset, her shoulders and arms moving with agitation, and after ending the call she sat down at her desk in the bay window and stared out at the night.

I stepped backwards into the deeper shadow of my room but her head lifted as if she had seen me standing there, or at least had been aware of my movement, of an observer shifting out of range of her observation. My heart lurched and I held my breath, perhaps even cursed myself, but did not immediately retreat to bed, instead standing in the dark and watching my student watching me. Her gaze soon turned away from me to follow a cyclist flying down the hill towards the Cowley Road. Then, with a movement that seemed too casual not to be considered, she closed her blinds and put out the light.

Doctoral supervision at Oxford being what it is—sometimes no more than one meeting each term—I did not have occasion to see Fadia alone until the following January. By that time, I confess, I had started making a habit of noticing when I went to bed whether her blinds were open or closed, when she was home, what she had been wearing that day, if she took a shower before bed or first thing in the morning, whether she went out every day to work in the library or chose to stay home and sit at her desk, when she had friends come to visit for tea or lunch or dinner parties with her other housemates, and if she went out with young men, or indeed with young women, for I did not presume to know the nature of her affections, or, to be blunt, her sexual self. In all those days of watching I never saw her alone with anyone, but always in a larger group.

Stephen Jahn returned to College around the same time, and I discovered that he had been in Egypt for almost the whole of the previous year, only coming back to Oxford for short periods since the beginning of the revolutions that had rippled across the Arab world. When I asked what he had been doing during his time away, he implied that it was official and highly classified government business.

'Which government?' I wondered aloud, sitting alone with him in the SCR late one February evening.

'Which do you think?'

'You're American, so I assume it must be ours, and at the same time I think it would be naïve of me to assume anything about you or your affiliations is straightforward. Do you work for ours?'

'Ours? My dear Jeremy, for gentlemen like us, such allegiances are pragmatic and fluid. You have taken dual citizenship just as I have taken dual citizenship. *Which* government I work for is a matter of context, moment, and intent.'

'And discretion.'

'Always,' he smiled, pouring me an indifferent whisky from the SCR drinks tray.

'How is Saif?'

There was a hesitation I had never observed before in Stephen, as though he was weighing how much he could tell me, or as if the question of Saif was the most serious question of all.

'I'm afraid I don't know. I can't see him anymore. Probably never again. He's no longer in Egypt. I believe he may be in Syria.' His mouth cracked into a marionette's smile before clapping shut. 'How is the sister?'

'She's making good progress. I'm happy with her work. I wouldn't have imagined when you told me five years ago—or six, whatever it was—to be sure she was admitted, that she would be as constant and consistent as she has turned out to be.'

Stephen blinked, his eyes dead.

'I don't know what you're talking about.'

I was so bewildered by his response that for a moment I did not know what to say. I looked hard at him, trying to see if he was joking, or playing a game of some sort, but he continued to stare in a way that offered nothing in reply.

'You told me one night, at your place, after getting me very drunk, that I had little choice but to see to it that Fadia was offered a place. You threatened me.'

Stephen sipped his drink and I understood, as moments turned into minutes, that he would admit nothing.

'You should be careful of her,' he said at last. 'It is not a family—'

And then he stopped himself, as if he had thought better of whatever he might have been intending to say.

'It's not a family that what?'

'Just don't,' he said, 'if you have any sense.'

'I'm sorry, Stephen, but I don't know what you mean.'

'One can see you find her attractive. I am telling you it would be foolish, not only because she is your student. There are other reasons to keep it professional. Think of this as the warning of a friend.'

Perhaps I shook my head or thanked him, or perhaps he merely stood and left the Senior Common Room and we said nothing more about it, or perhaps I left first, offended that Stephen should presume to offer advice about the intersection of my private and professional lives, and perhaps I left the College and walked down Turl Street to High Street and caught a taxi back to Divinity Road where I saw Fadia's bedroom light burning and because I had her number in my phone I sent her a text message asking if she was okay and if she might, for a change of pace, despite it being very late, care to come across the street for a nightcap. In any case, that was what I did, whether it was that night or another, in the spring of last year, and the drink we had in the dining room at the back of my house, looking out on the garden at night, was, without question, the beginning of the next phase.

LOOKING OUT THE window of my house in Rhinebeck, staring at the light of my neighbors' house where Michael Ramsey had come to spend the weekend, innocently or not, the lights suddenly went out and I was left standing alone in the dark, gazing out at the moonlight and starlight and the ambient light of the distant town filtering

through the trees. I felt, not for the first time in the last decade, a
sense of such wrenching loneliness that, under other circumstances,
I might once again have sent a message asking a relative stranger to
join me for a drink, except that Michael Ramsey was not Fadia. I was
not interested in becoming his friend, much less his lover. I wanted, if
anything, to open a greater distance between us, and yet I suspected
that, given a further hour alone with him, I might get answers to the
questions raised by the events of the previous week.

Standing there in the dark it occurred to me that I had not yet
found my misplaced phone, and out of a desire to sleep without
such a small detail niggling at my unconscious, I began searching
the house, turning on all the lights, groping through drawers and the
pockets of clothes, checking everywhere logical. There was no sign of
it and I turned at last to the kitchen, rummaging in cupboards and
pantry shelves, until there was nowhere left to look but the refrigerator, and there I found it, inside, sitting squarely on the top shelf, next
to the milk. I had no recollection of putting it there, and tried to think
whether it was possible I had given Michael Ramsey opportunity
sufficient to hide it in this way. I knew I had turned my back on him
at least once, possibly twice. I was moved to phone him, then realized
I did not have his number, but as I touched the central navigation
button at the top of the phone's keypad, the screen came back to life,
and there, in a message composition field, were two words, written, I
was certain, by Ramsey himself. My hands were shaking as I set the
phone down on the kitchen table. The screen went dark and then I
touched the navigation button to light it up again. The two words,
black on a white field, were written, if such a quality is possible for
text of this kind, with what looked like insouciance, or perhaps it
was instead a kind of rushed telegraphy, no time to write more than
he had, because I had been about to turn around from whatever I
was doing when he snatched my phone away. I could imagine how

the scenario must have unfolded behind my back, Ramsey hurriedly thumbing letters into the device.

I looked at the screen again.

'Phones listen,' it said.

THERE WAS NO SNOW the following morning, but the trees were coated in ice and frost had formed on the windows, refracting the light. Michael Ramsey would be stirring himself while I was sipping my coffee and thinking how, even though the temperature had never been so low during all my years in Oxford, I had been colder there than anywhere else, shivering in those drafty houses with single-pane glass in the windows and inadequate insulation, standing on a train platform at Oxford or Didcot, even in London's great Victorian stations, like St. Pancras and Paddington, open to the elements at one end; though it would make sense to raise a wall of glass to protect the waiting areas, no such thought seems ever to have occurred to anyone, even today when the winters in Britain are becoming more and more unpredictable, icy wind punching off the North Atlantic, in some years dumping snow and crippling a country that still imagines itself temperate. Such discomforts alone were enough to make me think of returning to America, to a house like the one I have bought in Rhinebeck.

That cold November morning just weeks ago I was content, in other words, to be back in New York in my insulated home with its double-glazed windows and forced-air heating flowing through the vents. I have been planning to install a solar array, following the example of neighbors in the area, and to invest in various other technologies that would make the house not only warmer but more efficient and sustainable. Now those plans seem, at the very least, uncertain. How long will my house be my own? In the absence of answers, I can but hope that whatever may happen, however com-promised my liberty, I will not be stripped of my property.

During the years in Oxford, even when I owned my house on Divinity Road, even after, halfway through my time there, I had acquired dual citizenship, I felt a near constant sense of insecurity, a premonition of the ground beneath me suddenly giving way or of finding myself, however innocently, on the wrong end of a system of laws that seemed designed to catch one out in wholly unpredictable ways. Sometimes I imagined my life past retirement in a community where I had friends but no one sufficiently close that I would feel I might phone him or her in the middle of the night if I needed rescue. When I returned to Britain after being away for any period, I often said to myself, 'I could disappear tomorrow and no one would really care.' I felt unanchored, drifting and ignored, or at least uncared for by the people around me. There seemed little neighborliness in Britain, at least not of a kind I could recognize, not in cities like Oxford or London. It may be different in Scotland and the north of England, but in Oxford people keep to themselves, and my sense of social isolation was compounded by feeling that the longer I spent there the more powerfully I missed Meredith, the more I wanted to be back in the ambit of my mother's life and the lives of my extended family, the aunts and uncles who were in their eighties and nineties, the cousins I had not seen for more than a decade.

Whenever I looked online at the photographs of friends gathered for family reunions or making cross-country road trips from Kansas to California to visit siblings or grandparents, I felt such an acute sense of dislocation that the desire to leave the life I had built in Britain grew so intense I no longer felt invested in it, I no longer cared whether I did all that was expected of me, I wanted only to write books that would get me noticed by American universities, to publish in the right kinds of scholarly journals, to give the sorts of plenary lectures and conference papers that would make the senior members of leading History departments in the US turn to each other when they thought of who they might wish to add to their ranks and say, without having to pause more than a few seconds, 'what about Jeremy O'Keefe?', and another of their colleagues would say, 'wasn't he at Columbia?' and 'didn't he fail to get tenure?' and 'yes, but he got very lucky, he's worked hard, he put things back together at Oxford and whatever happened at Columbia is old news, just look at his publications, a list of books and articles the length of my arm, and his monograph on the private lives of informants was pathbreaking in its archival scope and intellectual cogency.'

Self-regarding, certainly, but that was the tenor of my thinking as I sat in my Victorian semi-detached house on nights of bone-numbing damp when the temperature dipped to just below freezing, gazing out my bedroom window, sometimes lying in bed with the curtains open wide enough that I could see into Fadia's window, the lights of her room burning late, blinds open as she worked at her desk, often curled up in the drapery of that great white robe, and this all after that night when I first invited her over for a drink. It must have been February or March last year, the calculus of time is not insignificant in this case, but my calendar and diary reveal nothing specific. For a historian, I find the dates of my own life always blur and fragment the harder I work to pin them down. Perhaps it was then, perhaps later. What matters is that I reached out, she responded, and our course was set.

She came to the door some fifteen minutes after I sent the message, giving me just enough time to change out of my pajamas and back into jeans, a shirt and sweater, put on a spritz of cologne and deodorant, pass a comb through my hair, and when I opened the door she was standing there in one of her black coats with no scarf, neck exposed, eyes slightly red round the lids, as if she had been crying some hours before, or perhaps was just tired and cold, and in her hands she held a box of chocolates, the kind of fine Parisian confection that might have been a gift from her parents (who by that point, she had told me, were established in Mayfair, in a house as tall and narrow as an obelisk, just around the corner from the Saudi Embassy), or perhaps something she herself kept in stock for sudden invitations necessitating a gift for the host. It was a perfectly square white box containing sixteen chocolates decorated with such precision they achieved the quality of art. I was expecting no gift and the appearance of the box, the finish of its paper on my fingertips, changed my understanding of what was happening. I felt, truly, as though I was the one being wooed.

'Chocolate at night,' she coughed, 'I suppose it's not so good for one, but perhaps it's also what the hour demands.'

I draped her coat on a hook and led her down the dogleg hall, imagining as she walked behind me what she must be thinking, that her supervisor was trying to seduce her, that he was lonely, desperate, desiring, or that he was concerned for her wellbeing. Perhaps, supposing she knew little of American habits, she might have dismissed the hour as some odd cultural affectation, a New Yorker's refusal to believe any city ever slept, and yet those chocolates told me that whatever I was feeling, she also felt an attraction of some kind, although in retrospect I can see how she might have brought chocolates simply to be polite, because I was her professor, her supervisor and mentor, in a sense also her patron, and if invited by such a man to his house at night, what could a young woman like her do but accept? Did I give her the choice to say no? Did she even think it possible? Such questions now haunt me, although what happened between us was not, I am certain, a matter of coercion.

The lights were on in the galley kitchen and beyond, in the large addition I'd had built not long after buying the house, a room that doubled as a dining space and library. As she moved to take a seat at the table I pulled the curtains closed, though someone would have had to climb over the garden wall to see us.

'Why don't you sit there?' I pointed to a couch on the other side of the room. 'What would you like? I still have that single malt you gave me.' I knew by then that Fadia was sufficiently westernized to drink alcohol, as seemed to be the case with most of the young Muslim women I had encountered during my years in Britain, many of them having been educated at British boarding schools, with parents who split their lives between London and the Middle East. Although she had declared herself an atheist I had the sense that culturally she remained Muslim to a degree. I knew, too, that other Muslim students and colleagues I encountered often took what I thought of as a Roman Catholic approach to their faith, picking and choosing the ways they might adhere to the rules of Islam; some even ate pork, I had seen it at College dinners, and very few wore headscarves or veils—at least not at my College, though the numbers of women in Oxford, and particularly in Cowley, where I lived, who were completely covered seemed only to grow year to year, while the men with their beards and traditional clothes congregated in crowds that increased by an even larger factor. I would be lying if I said I had been wholly comfortable among them and yet I wanted, always, to try to keep an open mind. A taxi driver, taking me home from the station after I had returned from London one day when a number of men in Birmingham were arrested on terror-related charges, cursed throughout the journey, 'I been fucking living here forty fucking years and I never seen fucking anything like this fucking nonsense. Always this fucking minority fucking up everything for the rest of us. This is fucking nothing to do with us, you understand, Professor? All this fucking terrorism nothing fucking *at all* to do with *us*! All I want to do is go home, I so fucking tired, have a quiet drink,' the man had laughed, 'so my wife and children don't see. I'm a *bad* Muslim!'

'Whisky, no, it'll keep me awake,' Fadia nibbled her lip in a way that made me feel guilty. There was something nervous, even childish about the gesture, and I asked myself what it really was I thought I might be doing. Was I thinking of trying to seduce my student, or was I offering no more than innocent late-night hospitality, if that is not a contradiction in terms, hospitality of the kind I would extend to my daughter if I happened to see her passing my apartment late one night, alone and looking miserable as Fadia had so often appeared when I caught sight of her through my bedroom curtains. 'Do you have any wine?'

'Red or white?'

'With chocolate, I think it should be red, don't you?'

'Banyuls? Or would you prefer port?'

'Banyuls would be lovely.'

I poured, we clinked our glasses, and I took a chair next to the couch where Fadia was sitting. I am certain she was wearing some variation of her usual monochromatic uniform, gray wool slacks and a white sweater, mohair, with a cowl neck, and a glimpse of a delicate silver necklace against her skin. I opened the box of chocolates and offered her one. Some part of me believed a woman as slender as Fadia would decline a chocolate, but she took one without hesitation, her long index finger and thumb closing around its contours.

'My mother would like this,' she said, taking a sip and smiling. Not a smile of invitation, I thought, but one of gentle exhaustion and pleasure in good things.

'Your parents are well? They like London?'

'They seem fine, as much as they can be. I hate London myself. My father's assets were frozen, but not my mother's, I don't quite understand why, and they are living in a house owned by my mother's parents, so things are all right for now, although in fact my mother doesn't have that much money. Economies have been made, though they still live like rich people. They both feel they've come down in the world. On the one hand I pity them but I also find the complaining insupportable.'

'Do you see them much?'

She shook her head, swallowed, and ran the fingers of her left hand through her hair, sweeping its length behind her ears in a way that struck me, for the first time, as unconsciously flirtatious. It was a gesture I did not remember seeing her make in the past.

'It's strange of course to live with the knowledge that one's father has probably done terrible things, torturing people, making them disappear, but has done them so—I don't know—so *cagily*—is that right?' I nodded. '—So cagily that I suspect he may never be called to account, and also there's no extradition treaty between Britain and Egypt, so he's safe here, and I wonder whether that was the reason they wanted me to end up here in the long run, instead of France, as if they had foreseen what has happened and feared that families might also be implicated. I don't know. It's a strange thing to consider. I can't really look at my father anymore, not, you know, direct eye contact, because every time I do I imagine what he might have done. It would be better almost to know exactly what he did than to live with such uncertainty about him, but somehow I can't bring myself to ask, and if I did, I don't really believe he would tell me the truth. I didn't even understand what he was, not properly, until I moved to Paris for school. And then it was my grandmother—I lived with my grandparents in their apartment, on rue Visconti—she helped me gradually to comprehend. Nothing was said directly, but there would be these articles left lying around about human rights abuses in Egypt, and then friends from school said things that made it clear. I was so naïve. Before I moved to Paris I thought everyone had servants in tuxedoes. I thought everyone had a driver and a police escort. I thought all little girls went on shopping trips to London and New York and Paris. Or at least, I thought this and yet I didn't think it. I knew that the servants and the drivers, the people living in the poor neighborhoods I passed in the car as a child, were not living as I did, and yet I never thought about poverty, not in any considered way. I couldn't even see it properly until I moved to Paris and began a life less chaperoned than what I had known in Cairo. And then, after I began to understand the nature of my family's life, I found it difficult to be alone with my father, even to let him touch me. I have grown to hate the smell of him.'

'And your mother? Can you speak with her?'

'They have separate bedrooms, which is new, and I believe she will leave him if she can be sure of her security. I don't just mean financial. I think she worries about what he might do if she left, or what his former colleagues might be persuaded to do. I don't know whether this is paranoia or not. What do you think?'

'Truthfully, Fadia, I have no idea. I'm not the person to ask. Where would she go?'

'I think she will try to return to France, perhaps to live with my aunt or my grandparents. I love her so much but now that she is here she is always coming up to Oxford to take me to lunch. I've eaten everything on the menu at Gee's and I just want to tell her to leave me alone so I can get on with my work but she is almost beside herself with panic, this weird anxiety that I totally understand given the circumstances but which I don't know how to manage or help her overcome. How can you conquer anxiety like that, when your life is upset so quickly and people you love just disappear, or you disappear from them? Because of what we believe, my brother will no longer speak to us, and that is because of what he himself believes. *Je crois que la foi elle-même est une sorte de terreur. Vous comprenez?*'

'Just about. You've heard from your brother?'

At this she made a face, a reflex grimace of disgust and suspicion. 'Did Stephen tell you to ask me?'

'No, of course not.'

'I know you know, Jeremy, it's okay. Stephen has been badgering me for weeks, as if I would know anything. I keep telling him I don't.' She sipped her wine and reached for another chocolate. 'The heart does strange things to the head, and Stephen has a very strange heart.'

'Then you're still not in touch with Saif?'

She shook her head. 'Why do you care?'

'Curiosity. Concern. He's your brother. Don't you worry about him even if you disagree?'

'You understand, we were never close. He's fifteen years older. It was like I got all my mother's genes, or at least her sensibility, and he got my father's. He was, you know, to all intents and purposes, a member of the security police, so as soon as I understood what *this* meant, which was also pretty late in my life, only after I left for Paris, we did not get on. And now, having turned his back on all that, he's found religion and in a way I find that more terrifying. I haven't heard from him for a year almost. He just, I don't know, he vanished. I bet Stephen's spoken to him more recently than I have. Maybe he's in Syria. That's what Stephen thinks. My parents haven't heard from him either, and I know they would tell me, or at least my mother, she's terrible at secrets. My father would too, I think, since he feels betrayed by Saif. It would be a kind of victory if he had confirmation . . .'

She trailed off as though unsure which outcome might be the worse betrayal. I cannot remember now whether it occurred to me in that moment that Saif could have been a terrorist, a member of one organization or sub-group or another that kept springing up and coalescing, subdividing and reproducing, an organization that went by so many names, *ad-Dawlah al-Islamayah* or *Da'esh* or any number of others. I suspect my mind shuffled Saif into a mental file of men who were anti-government freedom fighters and thus thought no more about it. In my naïveté, I remember thinking we should do something to arm the Syrian resistance. How foolish that now seems. How *real* has become my *politik*. Stay in bed with the dictator you know rather than give succor to groups so unpredictable, so little understood, groups which may just as easily turn back to attack the hand that first fed them.

Whatever my thinking at the time, I poured my student another glass of fortified wine, a smaller one this time, since she raised her hand to stop me, and we each took another chocolate. Neither of us was drunk, at least I know I could not have been, except perhaps drunk on need and loneliness and the chill of a dark night in the early English spring, and I assumed that a little dessert wine would not make Fadia drunk either, Fadia whom I had seen cavorting with fellow students such that I believed she knew how to handle her drink and did it well. Half-French, I reminded myself, an adolescence in Paris, intellectual relatives, the grandfather was a prominent critic, the grandmother an economist, Fadia would have been allowed wine at dinner, champagne on special occasions, I was sure she knew how to remain in control.

'Why did you invite me over, Jeremy?'

'I wanted to know how you were. We haven't seen much of each other, and I saw that your light was on. Isn't a supervisor supposed to provide hospitality to his advisees?'

'Not at midnight usually, at least not when it's just the two of them, and the supervisor is a man and the student a woman.'

'Are you calling me inappropriate?'

'No, no, I am calling you nothing. I am merely observing that this is an exceptional situation and I would like to know your intentions.'

'To be hospitable. To pass the hours. I can't help noticing how much time you spend alone in your room, however often your mother might take you to lunch. You seem to be working hard. Sometimes it's not a bad thing to relax and leave the desk. *Mens sana* and all that.'

'I relax. I swim at the university pool four times a week. An hour each time.'

'Then I guess you have no need of my hospitality. You're free to go. You should not feel obliged.'

She put down her glass on the side table between the couch and my chair. 'Don't be English like that. You're not English and English manners don't suit you. I prefer the direct American you are in your other affairs. I prefer the professor who tells me when the work is bad and who praises me when it is good, not like these English people who hum and haw and expect you should read between the lines and know that when they say something isn't *quite right* they mean it's fucking terrible and when they say you've done *quite well* they mean you're exceptionally brilliant. I find it grotesque and dishonest, all this indirectness and euphemism. It makes life unhappy.'

Whatever was said next I no longer remember. I have a distinct memory, though, of standing up and lingering at the step leading into the kitchen. Perhaps I gave Fadia a meaningful look, but however it happened she followed me back along the dogleg hall and upstairs to the master bedroom at the front of the house, where the curtains were still open just wide enough that we could both look over to the windows of her own darkened bedroom.

'Do you watch me every night?'

'Not every. Many. Did you know before now?'

'I wasn't sure. I thought I might have been imagining it.'

Over the next hour my mind submerged itself in the beauty of what was happening, sinking happily in the shallows at the same time I was conscious of the more terrible depths close to hand: terror at what I had allowed myself to become, this predator of younger women, of someone who was in my power, whose life I could make difficult if I chose, though I could not imagine doing anything so cruel, and then, as we lay next to each other in the dark, I was conscious of her eyes on my body, the force of her gaze on my skin, and I thought of Ham and Noah, and that first sin of voyeurism, the way I had opened my body, my person, made myself vulnerable, like Noah lying *uncovered within his tent*, how I had allowed her to penetrate me nearly as profoundly as I had penetrated her, that in seeing me like this, looking upon my nakedness, she had entered me just as I had entered her. I reached across to take her hand and hold it.

'Is this the beginning of something?' I asked.

'Shared hospitality, you called it. Does it have to be more?'

We slept beside each other but she left before dawn, slipping out as the milkman came whirring up the street in his electric cart. Alone in bed I inhaled her scent on the sheets, and the face of that blond Egyptian boy at Georgetown came back to me: same smell, same unfamiliar familiarity. I am living in a novel, I thought, watching as Fadia appeared in her window across the street and quickly closed the blinds against me. In my case, however, the campus melodrama leads to something else, to a different genre of complication.

Over the course of the next few weeks we met every night or two, always at my house. There was no expectation on my part that sex would necessarily follow the drink and conversation we shared, and on each subsequent meeting I waited for Fadia to signal if she wished for something more, allowing her to lead us back down the hall and up the stairs. Once or twice we left it at a drink and nothing more.

'I feel I should clarify,' I said at one point, perhaps a week after the first meeting, 'that whatever it is we are doing, this shared hospitality, it will in no way impinge on our work together.'

'You mean that if I say to you I want to stop this, you won't suddenly make my life difficult, Jeremy.'

'Precisely. I want you to feel in control.'

'But I am in control.' I can see her, as I write this now, sitting up a little straighter on the couch and finishing a glass of wine. 'As a test, I'll say goodnight to you and leave you wondering if there will even be a next time.'

'Is that a test for me, or for you?'

'For us both.'

After more than a dozen such meetings, in the course of which I began to imagine continuing in this way until we felt ourselves able to go public, perhaps even until I asked her—or she asked me—to formalize our relationship, whatever the consequences for either of us, Fadia abruptly stopped responding to my messages. One day communication, a bantering exchange of plans, and then, without warning, silence from her end, the blinds in her room always closed, although I could tell when the lights were on, was able to watch her shadow passing, and observed her coming and going from the house in the mornings and evenings, feeling all the while I could not in good conscience—not if I were to mitigate my breach in decorum and ethics and policy (God knows I must have broken countless University and College and Faculty statutes by sleeping with a student)—ask her to explain herself, demand to know why I was suddenly being locked out, why she would no longer acknowledge me. Look at me, I wanted to say, look at me and tell me what I have done wrong.

A month passed in which Fadia maintained her silence and I my watchfulness, waiting for a shift, just as sudden as the first, to bring me back into favor. I did not want to become the obsessive professor knocking on the young student's door or hectoring her with emails and text messages, trailing her to the library or, indeed, the university pool, though I found myself one day thinking of buying a new swimming suit until I realized the destination of the route along which my mind was leading me. Professionally there was no reason for us to meet until later in the spring and I was confident we had parted such that when we did meet again there would be no awkwardness, however odd in retrospect those nights together began to seem, the invitations extended, each evening's seated dance of seductive hospitality, the frank business of retiring to a bed.

And although I had invited her over in the first place, and was the first to lead us up the stairs, the passing weeks without message or phone call began to make me feel, perversely, as if she was the one who had been using me. This was not so much unpleasant as surprising, for I had never felt it before with any other woman, certainly not with Susan, who seemed to suffer the mechanics of sex with patience and goodwill rather than enjoying the act, and while this was a small factor in our gradual growing apart it was not the force driving the ruptures which had opened between us over the course of many years. Or, I wonder now, was I misreading the situation with Fadia entirely? Was her aloofness an indication that what we were doing was not, in fact, something she desired?

During that month of silence I became more assiduous about dressing and undressing with the curtains closed, hiding my nakedness from Fadia in her room across the street as much as from the rest of the world. Oxford is a small enough city that anyone might be passing—students or colleagues, other employees of my College or the university.

One evening in April last year, although it could already have been May, Fadia sent me a text message asking if she could come over, and surprised as I was by the communication I immediately wrote back and said yes, of course, she was very welcome, I had no other plans, would she like dinner? No, she had a dinner engagement already, but might she drop by later, for a drink? Of course, I replied, that would be lovely. And yet the vulnerability of my assertion, or the way in which asserting the loveliness of seeing a student I had slept with not so long ago created a sense of vulnerability in my own psyche, of opening myself to the feminine, unsettled the ground beneath me once again, so that I had, as seemed to happen more often the longer I remained in Britain, the sensation of standing on two opposing plates, one moving east, the other west, my balance becoming ever more precarious the longer I tried to remain established on both.

NOW, OF COURSE, I understand why she went silent, and I was beginning to think of Fadia's sudden return to my life after that absence of four weeks as I looked out on the frost-covered trees in the land between my house and my neighbors, in the clear morning light of the last Saturday in November a few weeks ago, heat chucking through the vents and warming my feet on the linoleum floor of my kitchen, knowing I would have to take my mother to lunch at the Beekman Arms. This was exactly why I had wanted to come home to America, to enjoy these casual weekends in the midst of family, to be able to dart from my daughter's to my mother's, to see my ex-wife on a whim as if I thought for a moment she might find it in her power to take me back after my years of geographic and romantic straying. I imagined how much ground would need to be covered, the confessions I would have to make, revelations of my intimacy with Bethan and Fadia, the flings with half a dozen other women, and I had come through it all without disease (which I had feared more, for some reason, than I ever did in America), although not without complications of perhaps greater order than the species of infection that might be trusted to respond to antibiotics.

From the moment my mother got in the car I knew something was wrong. She fidgeted with her purse and confessed she had forgotten to make a reservation. We would instead be going to the Italian restaurant at the Culinary Institute of America, which was half an hour's drive away and not what I felt like.

'Is everything okay?' I asked, hearing my own impatience as she continued to scramble in her purse.

'Mmhm, yes, yes, yes.'

'Did you lose something?'

'No, I'm just organizing,' she sang, in that tone I had come to associate with an array of artificially bright moods that could crash into darkness without warning.

'It's distracting, Mom.'

She huffed and closed her purse. We drove in silence, or rather I drove and neither of us said anything more until we arrived at the CIA campus. At the restaurant she complained that our table in the window, with its views of the grounds, was far too cold, there was a draft. The whole place was done up in an ersatz Tuscan style that made me queasy. My mother ordered the eggplant parmigiana to start, while I chose the octopus salad and we both decided on the fish of the day with pistachio couscous (not very authentic, I thought, but I kept that to myself). As we waited for the first course my mother looked around in her distracted way.

'Tell me something. How's that class you're teaching? The film one.'

'What do you want me to tell you?'

'I don't know. You're so secretive, Jeremy. You never tell me anything. Tell me about the students.'

'It attracts a mixed group. Conspiracy theorists and philosophers and nursery anarchists with barbed-wire tattoos, and then a few serious-minded cinema philosophy boys who want to talk endlessly about Deleuze and movement-image and I know nothing about any of that really. I'm more interested in the films as documents of particular social moods.'

'I don't understand what any of that means.'

'Of course you do.'

'But you talk so *fast*, I wish you'd explain it better. I don't know how your students follow any of it.'

'I'll explain it another time.'

'You always say that.'

'Is there something wrong?'

'It's nothing. You'll just get upset.'

'Upset about what?'

'What I'm about to say.'

I had a premonition that whatever she was going to reveal had something to do with the events of the previous week, of that Saturday a week earlier when I sat in a café on MacDougal Street waiting for a student who never appeared because I had, or had not—someone else perhaps had—sent her an email rescheduling the meeting. Whatever my mother was about to say had to do with the boxes delivered to my apartment. It had to do with Fadia and her brother Saif and Stephen Jahn, and ultimately, I felt certain, in a single cold blast of panic, it had to do with Michael Ramsey.

'I got a phone call.'

'From whom?'

'He didn't say.'

'But it was a man?'

'It certainly sounded like a man. Most of the time I know if it's a man or a woman, Jeremy, however demented you think I am. I haven't lost my marbles so as I can't tell a man's voice from a woman's.'

'Don't talk so loud.'

'Nobody can hear!'

'Just tell me what he said.'

'He said I should know that you were not a good person, that you were a very bad man—' here she began to get choked up, '—that you had done *terrible* things, that you were anti-American, that you were a friend of the enemy, that you believed in terrorism and had financed jihadis, that you were working against the interests of this country, all kinds of things, I mean, really awful, it was so upsetting, and then he said—I don't even know how to put it—he said you had been intimate with a young Muslim woman at Oxford who was linked to extremist organizations. I know none of this can possibly be true, but I didn't know what to say, and I started shouting at the man on the phone telling him he was lying and then he said if I wanted to open myself to a life of terror then that was my choice, but he advised I never see or speak to you again, and I hung up the phone. It was *awful*,' she said, and by that point a mess of tears had misted across her cheeks. 'It's not true, is it?'

As she spoke I felt my skin go clammy, my stomach lurch, my legs rush with a feeling of vertigo. In falling, I thought, my exposure would be complete. Exposure as what? As a man who cannot control his desires? As a man who has accidentally allied himself with terror? As a man on the wrong side of history? As a man less than the man he—I—wish to be. My face was betraying me: my mother's expression registered what she saw before her, my shame and culpability, my panic, a sense of terror opening before me.

'It's not true,' she said again, as if trying to convince us both.

'Of course not. Probably just a disgruntled student. There's absolutely no truth to it. Zero.' The words came easily but I struggled to master my tone. 'Did he say anything else?'

'I told you, I hung up the phone. I didn't want to hear any more.'

'But before that, he didn't say anything besides what you've just told me?'

She shook her head. 'Not that I can think. Did you know a young Muslim woman at Oxford? I thought I remembered you had an Egyptian doctoral student, didn't you mention her? Fawzia?'

'Fadia.'

'That's right. I thought you'd spoken about her. But she was just your *student*, and I know you would never do anything with a *student*, would you, Jeremy?'

'Of course not, no, I'd never cross that line.'

I tried to remember whether I had always been able to lie to my mother so easily, words and whole fictions tripping off my tongue, but I could not recall any great lie I had ever told her, no series of moments in my childhood when I tried to get away with vandalism or played hooky, no faking of illness, no holding thermometers against light bulbs or heating pads or under hot water, that was simply not the kind of boy I was, perhaps because my parents were themselves inflexible with the truth, I had never seen them tell white lies to anyone, and their truthfulness had often come at great social and professional cost, alienating friends by declining a dinner invitation at the last minute because one or other of them no longer felt like going, or my father phoning in to work every few months to explain he would not be coming in that day because he was tired of his life's routine and needed a break and the two weeks of vacation he was allowed each year were simply not enough to see him through the other fifty weeks.

The only time I remember telling my mother a significant lie was when Susan asked me to leave. Out of some misplaced sense of loyalty to my wife, I told my mother that I was the one who needed a change, I was the one in crisis, I had elected to leave the family home, to turn my back on wife and daughter, though in time I admitted to my mother this was not the case, and in retrospect I can see how the original lie had less to do with wanting to protect Susan, and more with wanting to protect myself from the shame of admitting I had been judged an inadequate husband who was asked to leave.

'What did he sound like, this caller? What age?'

'I don't know. Fifties?'

'American?'

'I couldn't say. No, not American. Or a very old-fashioned kind of American. You know, like a movie star from the '40s. Cary Grant.'

'Cary Grant wasn't American.'

'Wasn't he?'

'British. Deracinated.'

'Then I suppose this man sounded like Cary Grant. Do you know anyone like that?'

'Not that I can think . . .' Of course I did know someone whose voice fit that description, despite my never thinking of it in those terms. 'A colleague with a grudge. Or someone whose book I gave a bad review.'

'It was so specific.'

'I'm sure it's nothing.'

While I lived in Britain, I did not learn to lie, but I learned to tell my family—my mother, my daughter, even my ex-wife—much less about my life, delimiting whole regions of relation and acquaintance as top-secret zones. It surprised me that my mother remembered Fadia, for I felt I would have kept her off the map, just as I had kept Bethan and every other woman secret despite my mother's occasional questions about my love life over the years, soft-pedal queries about whether there was 'anyone special' or if I had been 'seeing anyone' or if I imagined I might 'settle down.' And with impatience I would tell her I had no plans in either direction and however removed I might be from my former life in America, I had certainly 'settled down,' I was as settled as it is possible to be, with a house in my name and money in multiple banks and the security of a permanent job. 'How should that be any less settled than if I woke up next to the same woman every morning for the rest of my—or her—life?' And then my mother would huff and promise not to ask such prying questions and she might keep that promise for six months or until whatever part of her mind became concerned about my wellbeing caused her to ask once again, in a tone that made the question irritatingly pregnant with expectation, whether she might ever hope to have another daughter-in-law.

We passed the rest of the meal in relative silence, poking at our food, before fighting over the bill and then browsing through the CIA gift shop, where my mother bought a flowery French tablecloth she almost certainly did not need. On the way home she stared out the window, preoccupied in a way that made me suspect she had not believed my denial. Although it was possible Michael Ramsey had phoned her, perhaps disguising his voice, there was little doubt in my mind that Stephen Jahn was responsible.

'I'll see you next weekend.'

'Yes,' she paused, 'I'll have to check my calendar. I might have a lunch.'

'Both days? What about dinner?'

'Do we have to decide now?'

'No, we can speak during the week. What do you have planned?'

'Pilates on Tuesday and Spanish on Wednesday, and I want to start thinking about Christmas. Do you have any ideas for Meredith and Peter?'

'Give them books. Or a tin of your gingerbread men. That would mean more than anything.'

'Isn't it strange how fast everything changes? One year I was worrying about Meredith and all of a sudden I guess she must be worrying about us.'

'Honestly, Mom, there's nothing to worry about.'

'No? Well, I'm glad to hear it,' she said, and kissed me goodbye.

As I drove away from my mother's house I rehearsed the accusations her anonymous caller had made against me, and while they were crass and predictable, and almost entirely wide of the mark, they were so unsettling—not to say offensive to my own political and ideological sympathies—that I heard them like a litany, but a litany only in the later sense of the word, which overturns and subverts the original, not a prayer of supplication but an enumeration of curses, droning a raga in my head, and always in the voice of my mother, though I tried to shift the register, to hear the accusations in the tone of Stephen Jahn, as if that change of timbre might defuse all the false assertions, or the curse of a man were somehow less powerful, less killing, than that of a woman.

I am no lover of terrorism, although in high school I had a brief romantic flirtation with the *idea* of the IRA and Irish independence, attending Celtic music festivals upstate where representatives of various fraternal Irish organizations would display bumper stickers and paraphernalia with slogans like 'Our Day Will Come' and 'England Get Out of Ireland.' I admit to buying those very bumper stickers and slapping one on the back of my car, although I never had so much as a honk of acknowledgment. Later, when I moved to Britain, it occurred to me how my purchase of such stickers might be construed as supporting a terrorist organization. This came home to me even more acutely when someone like Bethan's father all but proclaimed his hatred of the Irish, or when, in Oxford, I began to notice how my name sometimes elicited hostile responses from clerks in shops and banks, people who would be perfectly friendly until they saw my last name, and then it was as if, at the sign of a name beginning with O', a curtain fell and whatever association or memory the individual might have held—perhaps, as with Bethan's father, of a loved one killed or injured, or perhaps of his or her own intimate brush with IRA terrorism—made them see anyone with an Irish name as a potential enemy, or at least as an unwelcome reminder of past suffering.

A LITTLE OVER A year and a half ago I was sitting once more with Fadia in my dining room at the back of the house. The daffodils were finished, the tulips in bloom, the ornamental cherry trees clotted with heavy pink blossom, but all that color faded to a dim impression of charred pastels in the dark.

It would be romantic to say I noticed she looked different, but in fact I suspected nothing at that point and noticed no change in her appearance. She was as lovely as she always seemed, though in retrospect I might be moved to say she had even more life about her, or that her face glowed with anticipation, but I don't think this was the case, because if anything she was preoccupied, in a state of agitation and in need of reassurance.

'Can I offer you something to drink?'

'Peppermint tea?'

'Nothing harder?'

'No, Jeremy. Just the tea.'

'How's the work? Have you looked into visiting the Fassbinder Archive?'

'I've been rather busy so, no, I haven't been able to think about the Fassbinder Archive or anything else for that matter. Not yet. Maybe this summer. Berlin is best in summer, when one can swim.'

'As long as you get there sometime this year you'll be fine. Honey?'

'No, just as it comes.'

We sat as we had on all our previous meetings in my house, I in the chair, Fadia on the couch, though she had kicked off her shoes and curled her feet under her. I sensed this was to be a different kind of evening but did not, at that moment, have any notion what was coming. We sipped our tea in silence and it felt like an hour passed, though it can only have been a few minutes at most. I think I said nothing, waiting for her to take the lead. It does not flatter me, but I admit to wondering whether we might again retire to my bedroom, although I also feared she was going to rebuke me for some failing, or thought perhaps she had come to clarify the nature of our relationship.

'I have something to tell you, Jeremy.'

'You don't sound very happy about it.'

'I don't exactly know *what* I feel . . . *Je ne sais plus. Je suis confuse.*'

Perhaps, I thought, she wanted me to meet her parents.

'Has someone said something?' I asked, fearing a friend of hers or colleague of mine might have suggested they knew about our liaison.

'Of course not. But—I don't want you to argue when you hear what I have to say.'

'I can't imagine wanting to argue with you.'

'I don't want you to convince me it's anything other than what I know it to be.'

'You're being so mysterious.'

'No, I just want to lay the groundwork. You're not to argue or ask questions that throw doubt on what I tell you.'

'I accept that.'

As she took another sip of tea I noticed her lips against the rim of the white mug and thought, not for the first time, what it might be like to enmesh myself in her life, to meet her parents, who were not much older than me, eventually to meet her brother, unless he was, in fact, the fundamentalist Fadia feared he might be, in which case . . .

in which case I knew not what. I contemplated what it would mean to my own life, to my career, my livelihood, and the life of my mother and daughter and even my ex-wife, if I came to be known as the professor who had married a student who happened to be the sister of a terrorist and the daughter of a despot's crony. What would it mean to divorce myself from the life I had known, even the strange life I had adopted in Oxford, and to marry into a life of utter foreignness, and one divided on itself? It would mean, I thought, being stopped at borders, finding that trips by plane suddenly acquired new complexities, perhaps even being placed under forms of surveillance both visible and invisible by the security services of any number of governments, not just British and American, but also Egyptian and Israeli. I sensed Fadia looking away, as if she could not quite bear to maintain eye contact with me. Who knew what else loving her might mean? I knew nothing of her culture or country, almost nothing about her life up to the point she had become my student, and still I knew scarcely more than that which concerned her academic progress and daily habits, when she rose and slept, that she went to the pool on Iffley Road, how she always dressed as a woman of maturity and style.

I cannot say whether this, now, this situation in which I find myself, writing these pages, is the stage preparatory to a more serious set of consequences for the way my life has been drawn into the lives of Fadia's family. Do I force myself to write this account because I slept with a woman innocent in her own right but implicated by relation and association? I do not have an answer. I write and write, and, I have no doubt, someone at some point will read these pages, reach a judgment, and perhaps, if they find against me, seek to impose some form of punishment—against my person if I am still alive, against my legacy if I am dead. I have come now to expect, in the course of the last week—is it only a week? have I written so much in a matter of days? how much in fact have I written? I count the pages, my handwriting is large, there are three hundred sheets at least but I cannot guess how many words—that I await a consequence which may never come, that I may go on writing this account of my innocence and see it sit unread until such time as I place myself more unambiguously on the wrong side of the law, or until someone, perhaps Stephen Jahn, informs on me in such a way that the authorities have no choice but to take action. Stephen has all the qualities of an informer. I know the type. Are the doormen to be trusted? The woman who comes to clean my apartment? My daughter, my son-in-law, my ex-wife and mother? Is it possible that any one among them is an informer?

Despite that initial formulation of my misgivings, as I sat there in my Oxford home with Fadia, I also felt a kindling of *will*, a new desire to accept the opening, the further step of establishment, which I had convinced myself Fadia was about to offer.

'I missed my period,' she said in an unemotional way. 'I bought a test kit, one of those horrible plastic things, and then I went to a doctor at a clinic in Reading. I couldn't go to the College doctor, and I didn't want to risk a clinic in Oxford or London in case someone saw me. The doctor in Reading confirmed it. It's still early, but there's no doubt. Do you understand?'

The sudden fillip of joy I felt in my chest seemed out of synch with her tone. There was no smile on her face, no great happiness. What had happened was a complication in her plans, I understood that much, and one requiring more than the usual care to negotiate. I wanted to handle it correctly, to make right what I had made wrong in the first place. We had used protection, but these things happen. Meredith, in fact, had been conceived under similar circumstances. I understood that Fadia did not want me to question her assumption of my paternity. She was not, I believed, the kind of woman who had many partners. Certainly I had seen no evidence of other romantic entanglements.

'So what does this mean? I don't want to presume a greater role than you'd like me to take.'

'I wanted to ask what you think. That's why I'm here. If it were straightforward in my own mind, one way or another, then, forgive me, I might have chosen not to involve you, depending on the decision of course.'

'Is it rude of me to ask if you want to keep it?'

'Yes, I suppose it is rude in a way, but I appreciate the frankness. The answer is that I don't know. I haven't decided. I wasn't planning on having a child now, but I do want children, it's just that I imagined having children with a husband and being a few years older, maybe even a decade older, after I'd had time to establish my career and do a little more living.'

'We could get married.'

She smiled, indulging me for a moment. 'The fact is, as much as I like you, Jeremy, and as much as I find you attractive, and I don't regret what happened between us, I can't imagine being married to you. I hope that doesn't offend you too much.'

Of course I was disappointed, but I tried not to show it. 'The age difference, for one, and I suppose—I mean, we come from very different places. The cultural gulf . . .'

'Yes, those things would be difficult. My father, and my brother, if he ever comes back into my life, it would be impossible for them to understand, even though my father has always been quite secular. When I was little it felt like he was spending more time drinking and playing squash at the Gezira Club than he did at work. He is very liberal in many ways, I mean in the way he lives his life, not in what he believes, and on this point he would not be understanding, I feel certain. Even my mother would be difficult.'

'And the other alternative?'

'I don't have an objection to abortion in principle. I have my mother's rational pragmatism in that way. But I'm not sure it's what I want, if it's the decision I would necessarily take, and yet I would never consider giving up the child for adoption, so either I have the abortion or I accept that I will have a child, and that means having a child with you, in some way, however that might work.'

'I can't make the decision for you.'

'I appreciate your saying that. I mean, I appreciate you respecting my right to make the decision. But it would be helpful to know what you would be prepared to do, in either case.'

'I will support you, whatever you decide.'

'What does that mean exactly? Emotionally?' She paused, wrinkling the bridge of her nose, her eyes disappearing for a moment behind a veil of dark hair. 'Financial? Or would you be prepared to be a father? To be present in the life of our child?'

'Whatever you decide, I will be there, if you want me to be there, or I will disappear, if that is what you prefer. If you choose to have an abortion, I will pay for it. If you decide to keep the child, I will support you as well, and take whatever role in his or her life you wish me to take. I am not a bad person; at least I don't want to be a bad person. Perhaps it was a mistake, but I want to do whatever I can to make it right, or to do what is right, what is best, from your perspective.'

'Do you have your own perspective? Do you want a child with me, even if we have separate lives?'

It was not a question I had expected. After Meredith's birth Susan and I had made a conscious decision not to have more children, in the belief that it was the ethical thing to do, not to contribute to the overpopulation of the planet but also to think sensibly about our means as two academics living in New York. Circumstances had changed, for I suddenly found myself, later in life, with significant financial security, and no worries about Meredith's own situation. In other words,

I could afford to support a child. What would it mean, though, if it were a child with whom I might only ever enjoy a tenuous connection, a boy or girl living perhaps in Egypt, or France, or even in Oxford, such that I might see him or her every week (I had not, at that point, been approached by NYU, so had no thought of returning to New York any time soon)?

'I have a child, of course, a daughter around your age. She got married last year, younger than I would have expected. I know what that sounds like.' How easily I said it then. I wonder if I would find it so easy now.

'As you say, these things happen.'

'So I've had the experience of fatherhood. It's not a need I feel in the way a younger man might, but that's not to say I would do anything other than welcome a second fatherhood, even a distant one, if that's what you wanted.'

'The idea of a child appeals to you?'

'Yes,' I said, without hesitation, and my own certainty surprised me. 'Have you thought how it might work, if you keep it?'

'I don't know that it *can* work, this is the problem. If I keep the child I will have to find a way of explaining to my parents. My father will want to know who the father is. He might even want to . . . I don't know . . . To me I don't think of him as a violent man, but suddenly I have visions of telling him and then watching as he grows enraged and flies from the house, driving to Oxford, breaking down your door, and strangling you in your bed, or stalking you to the ends of the earth, making life hell for your family in America, and I believe he might be capable of doing this. I have seen these scenarios in my head over the last few days. So I don't know how I would handle this. Perhaps I could lie and say it was a fellow student, or that I was drunk and had gone to bed with someone and didn't remember who it was. But I think, for now, it would be impossible to tell them it was you.

Even if he didn't want to kill you, my father remains well connected, especially with people in America.'

'But would I have a role in the child's life?'

'Yes, I would want that. I don't know how or when. I haven't decided. I need some time to think about all the ramifications, but it is useful to know where you stand. I appreciate that.'

'Are you sorry this has happened?'

'Sorry? I don't know. I think I need to be alone for a while longer. But thank you, Jeremy.' She stood and handed me her empty mug.

'Should I wait to hear from you?'

'Yes, that would be best, for now.'

'If you need . . . What I mean is, if it requires taking time out from your work, all of that can be arranged.'

'Yes, I know. Don't be so English.'

'I will do everything I can to make this right, whatever you choose. If you have the baby you can take a break. If you don't have it you can also take a break. If you need money, there is money.'

She turned and glared at me for an instant. 'I wish you would just say what *you* want, without any equivocation.'

I did not have to think. 'Keep it. Keep the child. That's what I want. We'll find a way.'

She looked at once surprised and furious but almost reflexively leaned over to kiss me on the cheek, twice, just next to my lips, either side of the mouth, and then she turned and was off through the kitchen and halfway down the hall. By the time I reached the front door she was on the sidewalk and raised a hand in farewell as I called out goodnight.

Alone in my Oxford house I felt a surge of warmth as I imagined the child she might have, though I held myself back from thinking of it as *my* child, since I had no faith at that moment whether, despite my role in its creation, she would ultimately want me involved, or would even allow me to have contact such that I might think of myself as a parent. Alongside this feeling there was a sense of isolation, of being unable to tell anyone what I had just learned, not only because I wanted to protect Fadia, whatever her decision, but also to protect myself. I feared the scandal that might result if the College or university discovered I had impregnated one of my students; it would make my position at Oxford untenable if it became public, and might even end my career anywhere, worse than any failure to get tenure would ever do. I imagined seeing out the rest of my working life in some backwater state university or community college, perhaps even fleeing to one of the remote Anglophone corners of the world and teaching History in a small Asian university or African technikon where no one would possibly know what I had done. Britain has a great tradition of sending its scandals away, once to the empire or the colonies, and even still one hears stories of the failed son of a good family packing off to Kenya or South Africa or Australia to try to make a life for himself where his diminished state will cause no embarrassment to the family remaining in Britain. There is no real American equivalent, perhaps because Americans are in a way more forgiving of failure and the country is so large that the idea of holing up in a remote western outpost always floats along as a possibility in the mind of a man who fears he may not have strength sufficient to live out the life his parents and community have imagined for him; it remains possible to lose oneself in North America in a way it has not been possible in Britain for many centuries.

Such trajectories played about in my head while I stood, feeling a little breathless, in the hallway of my house on Divinity Road, contemplating the prospect of again becoming a father. How, I wondered, would my daughter react? Or my mother, for that matter, suddenly presented with a new grandchild, a baby to fuss over and adore when she no longer had any reason to expect the appearance of one? I tried to calm myself, to assume nothing, but the feeling of warmth spreading through my limbs was born as much from the anticipation of loving a new daughter or son, as it was a feeling of expectation in the creation of something good, a new life unmarked by acts or deeds.

DRIVING AWAY FROM my mother's house I turned on the heat, stretched out my hands to feel the hot air blowing against my fingers, and steered north towards my own house, which was now not only house but home, although I had not entirely assimilated it into my revised and endlessly revisable sense of my place in the world. This small upstate town, this wooded acreage, this solid if modest building were the places I thought I would spend the rest of my life, attended by my daughter or the people she paid to support me when I could no longer look after myself. That was what I imagined, naïvely thinking that I had left the complications of Oxford behind me, or that they would somehow be amenable to forgetting because of the kind of arm's-length management I established earlier this year to look after them. Now, of course, I know that not to be the case.

It was a short drive, hardly long enough to consider what I was doing, or I might have thought better of it and simply gone to my own house rather than pulling into that driveway half a mile south and stopping the car outside my neighbors', sitting in the subsiding warmth of the vehicle and feeling, with some surprise, the quickness of the heat loss, as my fingers started to smart with the cold air that crept through the vents. The temperature was too low to sit there for long and I knew Michael Ramsey must have been watching. Before I could ring the bell he had opened the door and was standing there, smirking. 'I thought you'd be back.'

'Can I come in? It's frigid.'

'Are you armed?'

'Of course I'm not armed. What a stupid thing to ask.'

'Just wanted to find out if I'm putting myself in danger by letting you in.' I could not tell whether he was joking.

'I thought perhaps I was the one who should be afraid.'

His smirk disappeared. 'You could call the cops.'

'I left my phone at home.'

With that he stepped aside, allowing me to enter the house I had first explored in such unusual circumstances the night before, bopping around in the dark in what might, I thought in retrospect, have been little more than a ruse to gauge the limits of my fear.

My neighbors' taste for primitive American furniture was so obsessive that all the furnishings and art were from that period, arranged in a tightly curated palette of colors and forms. The couch where I sat was firm and uncomfortable, meant for a body shorter and leaner than mine.

'You said last night you were my student. When exactly did I teach you, Mr. Ramsey?'

'My junior and senior years.'

'You were in more than one of my seminars?'

'Yeah, like three.' He sounded shocked by my failure to remember him, and objectively, it was true, I had quite clear memories of several students who had taken more than one of my classes, at least I could see their faces even if I could no longer remember their names, though I think this is less a failure of memory than a natural process by which a teacher, confronted with dozens of names and faces every year—sometimes different groups from semester to semester—might remember the students for a necessary period of contact with each other, but at some point not long after the student has moved off to the next phase in his or her life, the teacher's mind must begin to purge the files, to manage the data of memory such that room is made to remember other, more important information in the space taken up by people with whom one has no permanent relationship, or people with whom that brief moment of relation was not significant enough to create lasting memories.

'Forgive me, I've tried to remember you, but I can't.'

'I was such a good student, too,' he said, grimacing, and the way he said it made me think for the first time that I might not be dealing with a man in his right mind.

'Are you being facetious?'

'No, I was really good. Solid A, every course, all four years. Summa Cum Laude.'

'You have to understand I've had lots of students over the years.'

'Not like me.' A smirk twitched back onto his lips.

'You were a troublemaker?'

'Let's not talk about me.'

'Why? I find it interesting. I'd like to know more about you, Michael. Can I call you Michael?'

'Call me whatever you like, Jeremy.'

'You said you were a librarian, I think.'

'Something like that. Corporate archivist would be a better description.'

'And you majored in History at Columbia?'

'With a minor in German Literature and Cultural History.'

'And your master's degree, when you met Peter?'

'International Relations.'

'And yet you're an archivist. No degree in library or information science or anything like that?'

'Maybe I trained on the job. Or I did a diploma or a certificate, an online course in that other stuff.'

'Can you tell me why we've been meeting?'

He smiled. 'Chance.'

'Is that possible?'

'These things happen in New York.'

'So, according to you, we spent a number of hours together in a Columbia seminar room more than a decade ago, over the course of several semesters.'

'Three semesters in total. *And* you were the advisor for my senior thesis.'

I tried not to let this shock me, and it still seemed possible he was making up all of it, just to unsettle me or to see what the effect might be. The question in my mind was this: if Michael Ramsey was behind the three boxes of internet and telephone records that were sent to my apartment, and if he was somehow stalking me, then what was the point? Was he trying to demonstrate his power to hurt me, because of some old grievance, or was he trying, in a more complicated way, to help me, to warn me that I was in the crosshairs of a much larger entity? Michael, I considered, might be more ally than adversary. Or was it possible for someone like him to have warring intentions, to want to help at the same moment that he might have wanted revenge, to show his hand at the same time that he remained concealed, perhaps not even present? And then there was the possibility, the very real possibility, that Michael Ramsey had nothing to do with any of it, that his appearance in my life over the course of the week was indeed pure chance, and someone else altogether—a someone who could only be Stephen Jahn—was trying both to threaten and discredit me.

'Did you phone my mother?'

'I don't know what you're talking about.'

'You deny phoning my mother?'

'Yes, I deny it.' He said it without hesitation. 'What reason would I have for calling your mother? Anyway, I wouldn't begin to know how to find her.'

'I think that's a lie.'

'An understatement maybe. Sure, I could find out who she is and where she lives, unless she's in witness protection, and even then there are ways of locating such people. But no, I mean, in an ordinary sense, I don't have a clue where your mother is, what her name is, whether she's divorced or married or widowed, owns a house, has an unlisted phone number or Swiss bank account. Zip, nada. I don't know anything about her, Jeremy.'

'Why are we meeting?'

'You tell me. You came to the door.'

'Why are you staying in this house?'

'I told you, it belongs to my friends, the Applegates. They were supposed to come up here this weekend. We were going to do upstate things!' He punched the air with his fist in a mock-heroic gesture that seemed to signal a change in register as well, or perhaps this is only a failure of my memory. 'I don't have any family nearby, man. Friends are my family. It was just supposed to be a chill weekend, not a frigid one. Anyway, at least the heat's working now. Thanks for your help last night. I'm sorry if I freaked you out.'

'Did I do something to you? I mean, did I do something when you were my student, to make you angry?'

'I'm not angry with you, Jeremy.'

'I thought . . .'

'Dude, no, you were a good professor. I was a smartass and you had patience, I mean, you'd tell me to shut up sometimes, not in so many words, and you kind of flaked when I needed references—'

'Sorry about that.'

'It's okay, it's not, I mean, it didn't stop me from getting where I wanted to be, I still got into Harvard, and that's all I really cared about, you know, going to the Kennedy School and whatnot, it was my dream, and you helped me get there even though you didn't write a reference and I had to scramble at the last minute and shit, but yeah, it's okay, we're cool. I don't hold a grudge or anything. Did you think I was stalking you?'.

'Such a string of coincidences . . . it's enough to make a person suspicious.'

'Or paranoid.'

'So you're not following me?'

'Of course not.'

'And you never stood outside my building this week, at night, looking up at my window?'

'Why would I do that?'

'I'm asking *you*, Michael.'

'No, shit, the answer is no. We ran into each other a week ago in that café, then we ran into each other going to Peter and Meredith's party, and then I happened to ring your doorbell last night.'

'You have to admit it looks like a pattern, one might see it as a kind of gradual approach.'

'If I wanted to stalk you—and I don't—I'd be much more subtle about it. You wouldn't even know I was stalking you until it was too late. And what would be the point, anyway? I don't bear you any ill will. You were a decent professor and our lives have happened, by *chance*, to intersect again. I had no idea that you were Meredith's father. I don't really know her. Chance, see. It's like on these social networks—'

'I don't use them much,' I said, although this was a lie.

'Well, if you did, you'd see, it gets really creepy, the way chance plays a part in our lives, or maybe it isn't chance, but not a week goes by that I don't discover two of my friends, from completely separate parts of my life, people that I never would have put together in a million years, they know each other independently of me. For instance, my freshman roommate at Columbia, nice guy, works for the State Department, I discover that he knows a filmmaker I dated

during a year I spent in Berlin, or I find out that my cousin, who I
don't really know that well, we didn't get along as kids and—that's
another story—anyway, this cousin lives in LA and I find out she's
now best friends with the wife of one of my colleagues. It's chance,
it's random, or if it's not chance, then we're all unconsciously moving
in the networks we've somehow designed, or that we don't even know
we're designing every time we decide to be friends with someone or
take a particular job or go to bed with a new partner or get back in
touch with a friend we haven't seen in ten or fifteen years, or, and this
is even creepier, we're being moved around on the chessboard of the
world, we don't really have free will, we're just players in someone
else's simulation, and the rules and teams and relations, the *real* relations between us are invisible to us, or they have been until now, until
we can begin to see precisely what our own network looks like, and
if we were to map it, if someone chose to map all the networks of
relation between us, it would be possible to begin to redraw real maps
and real borders. And *then*—no, stay with me, I know it all sounds
a little crazy—there are all those people out there, a whole long list
of them, people with whom I have like ten, twenty, sometimes even
more friends in common and yet I've never met the person; I know
who he or she is but we've never been introduced, never written to
each other or spoken to each other or had our lives intersect long
enough to make that connection despite the mass of connections
that *should* be drawing us together, and maybe one day *will* draw us
together. You and I, I'm guessing we're *supposed* to know each other,
whether it's chance telling us this is the case, or maybe some crazy
genetic history—maybe we're actually related, they say you share a
huge number of genes with your closest friends even when you don't
think you're related, and you can smell, actually smell, people who
are even quite distantly related to you—or else something, someone,
some entity, call it the universe or God or the players controlling

the simulation we might want to suspect is our collective life on this earth, is moving us towards each other to see what happens. Now we can't be certain, neither you nor I, that we're necessarily on the same side of whatever game is being played, assuming there are even sides and it's not just a free-for-all clusterfuck. Every o and 1 for itself. Bing bing bing bing bing!'

At the end of his little speech he was almost breathless, sitting on the edge of his chair and leaning forward, palms pressed together and fingers pointed in my direction, like a Jesuit trying to convert the benighted.

'That's all very interesting. Thought-provoking theories, I don't know what to call them. I guess we have nothing else to say to each other for now. Maybe we'll meet again.'

'I think we can both fucking count on it, Jeremy.'

Walking to the door I paused and turned, and was surprised to find him so close to me, standing right there as if he'd been creeping up behind me on tiptoe.

'So you didn't phone my mother?'

'Shit, Jeremy, I swear to you, I didn't.'

I wanted to ask him if he had sent those three boxes to my apartment but some pestering little voice made me pause. I believed he had not phoned my mother, or if he had it was some other part of him that had done so, because the man in front of me in that moment seemed, strange as it felt, entirely benign towards me, he seemed to wish me no ill will and I considered it was perhaps nothing more than chance that had brought us together, and whatever was happening with the boxes of records and with the manipulation of my appointment with Rachel a week earlier, he did not wish to hurt me, if he was even responsible for those things. Fadia's family, however, was another matter. The phone call to my mother might have been made by some friend of Fadia's father or by one of her own friends in Oxford—

even, I considered once more, by Stephen Jahn, trying to smear my name now that I was safely away from the city where Fadia and our child, my son, remained.

IT WAS ALMOST DARK by the time I got back to my house. In the past I would have closed the garage door only after getting out of the car, but for the second time in as many days I waited until the door had rolled shut before unlocking the car, and then made a point, again, of locking the garage door, double-checking all the locks in the house, and closing the curtains, wondering as I did so whether drones or satellites might be zooming in with their long lenses to catch a glimpse of the habits of my completely ordinary life. Again I wondered what I had ever done to attract the attention of whoever might choose to monitor my activity, and rehearsed my crimes, such as they might be perceived by people hostile to me:

A. I had moved abroad in a time of national crisis, within days of the attacks on New York and Washington; a patriot would have changed his plans and remained to look after his wife, however estranged, and his young daughter; if I was not a traitor I was, at the very least, a selfish man;

B. During my years in Oxford I had become friends with a man who was almost certainly a spy; I assumed he was on our side, whatever and whoever *our* side might be (American, chiefly, but also, subsequently, British, for I am, according to the law, loyal to both countries, having sworn an oath to the Monarch

and all the heirs to the throne, though in fact I crossed my
fingers in my pocket at the time);

C. In the second half of my period in Britain I taught and subsequently had a dozen or more assignations with an Egyptian
student whose brother is now by all accounts involved in
a terrorist organization trying to establish a new caliphate;
her father, moreover, was until recently wanted for crimes
committed during the twenty years leading up to Egypt's forestalled revolution;

D. The fling with this sister of a terrorist and daughter of a
despot's henchman has resulted in a child who, far from being
aborted before the statutory period in which terminations
might be performed under British law had passed, was carried
to full term, arrived seven days after he was due, and named
Selim.

Was that ethical charge sheet enough, I wondered, to imperil
my privacy, even perhaps my liberty? As far as I could see, I had
committed no crime, unless giving money to Fadia could itself be
construed as a criminal act. Laws change so rapidly it is difficult to
know when the ordinary business of one's life, the way one governs
one's affairs in a fashion that has long been legal and seems innocent
enough, might be proscribed overnight by the whim of a few hundred
men and women in a stuffy room. Ignorance of the law is no defense,
and yet it seems, so often, that the lawmakers themselves have only
a partial understanding of the statutes they pass. Is the *sister* of a
terrorist now as good, or bad, under the laws of Britain and America,
as being a terrorist herself? Have I jeopardized my liberty by doing
nothing more than seeking lawfully to support my son?

Last night, in the hours between finishing one page of this text
and beginning another, I fell in and out of sleep, splayed across the
daybed here in my home office, nothing but white walls and the Neo

Rauch I bought years ago hanging above my desk, and dreamt I was in a similarly sparse white room, sitting alone, with a stainless steel toilet and sink in one corner, a window too high in the wall for me to see out of it, a door with a slot through which I pushed the papers I wrote, through which was pushed back more blank paper and pens when my writing grew faint, a slot through which I received my three daily meals and a ration of water. In the dream I could hear no one else, and knew nothing of where I was. Once every two days in the course of the dream, where the passage of time was uncannily easy to judge, a voice instructed me to sit on the floor and rest my head against the slot in the door. Hands then reached through, passing a hood over my head before the voice instructed me to stand with my hands on the back of my neck. When I had done so the door would open, someone grip my arms and twist them round to handcuff me behind my back. The man, I assumed it was a man, led me down a hall where the handcuffs and hood were removed and I was left alone in a shower room, given ten minutes to wash before the man returned and instructed me to stand, back to the shower room door, hands on my neck as the hood was lowered once more, and my wrists were cuffed. The dream seemed to last for weeks, perhaps even months, and every two days I was allowed to bathe, but was otherwise left alone to write my account, the account I am writing now, in a more realistic way, at this very moment. When you read these pages, whoever you are, will you pity me? Or will you wait for a confession I cannot provide? To confess my participation in crimes about which I have no knowledge would itself be an even greater crime according to the edicts of my own philosophy, which, for me, stands in the place of that religion I have eschewed, finding, like Fadia, that faith itself is the greatest form of terror.

That last Saturday night in November, sitting in my house outside Rhinebeck, having just spoken with Michael Ramsey, having eaten lunch with my mother and being told of the harassing phone call she received, I made myself a drink, thinking of my son, Selim, who is now almost a year old. I raised a glass to his health, toasted the secret I was keeping from the rest of my family, one I had even begun keeping from myself, burying all thought of the boy as deeply as I could because Fadia had made it clear that, for the foreseeable future, she did not want me involved, although she made promises about trips to New York, and I continue to live in a state of suspended hope that some other future might in fact come to pass, and we could perhaps find a way to establish ourselves as an unconventional American family, a very New York-style family, one that would not be out of place in Manhattan or Brooklyn, that might in time come to feel at home in Rhinebeck, although the more I have allowed myself to imagine these future lives and the more weeks and months pass in which I hear nothing from Fadia and my phone calls and emails go unanswered, I realize how I am nursing a wound I have little hope of healing. She is unlikely to come around, and I know, I made the bargain, that we would do this on her terms. In a sense, she saved me from professional oblivion, from the technikon in Limpopo or the university in Chhattisgarh or indeed from the likes of Staten Island Community College, places that have little use for a man whose entire career has been built around an obsessive examination of one country's past.

Fadia told her parents an invented story of a party and getting drunk and not being able to remember who the father was, and in so doing she saved me embarrassment and much more besides, taking all the shame upon herself, nobly enacting the part of single mother with a baby boy and no father. At least this is what I understand, what little she has told me. I am under no illusions: I know the shame was great, perhaps so profound that she has risked the love of her family, although she insists they have stood by her, inasmuch as they can given their own reduced circumstances, her father's accounts remaining frozen, her mother's resources dwindling. When I asked her how her father had responded to the news of her pregnancy, I remember she said, 'He was furious, as you might have expected. He threatened to have me followed, he said we should get DNA tests to track down the father, but I knew, in the end, he would do nothing like that. My behavior was a defeat for him more than anything, and I realized, in the few days of ranting that followed the news, just how toothless he has become. My mother is the one with all the power now.' And then, not long after the birth of our child, Fadia told me of her father's near total transformation. 'Selim of course is *his son*, *his boy*, he sees his own features in Selim's face, as if he himself were the father, as if Selim were born of father alone, and no mother. It makes me furious.'

In exchange for Fadia's deception I vowed to support her with a monthly payment transferred automatically from my British bank account into her own. There—I suspect, I feel with increasing certainty—is the reason I am being monitored: money to a woman whose brother is a terrorist, whose father was on the side of a regime now out of favor with America, this is enough to make the intelligence services in London and Washington and Tel Aviv sit up and analyze your affairs with the probing long lenses of their remote gaze, to rifle your virtual drawers with their digital fingers, every trace a sequence of binary code. I should not have been so naïve as to think a standing order to Fadia could remain a matter between the two of us.

I have kept my bank account in Oxford open for the sake of convenience and with half a thought that I might one day need to return there if America sinks itself and Britain, by some miracle, remains afloat. I left enough money to cover the monthly payments to Fadia for the next several years, and planned that when it was exhausted I would simply transfer more, or, greatest and most deeply hidden hope, imagined she might at some stage agree to move to America and be my wife. Such a dream suggests I love Fadia well enough to imagine spending the rest of my life with her. It did not seem so preposterous then, and as I watched her grow over the summer and autumn of last year, her body blossoming and expanding in ways that surprised and mesmerized me (Susan's pregnancy with Meredith had been one of illness and discomfort by comparison), it was possible to think we might become a couple of the kind who would joke about the difference in our ages: as I grew older, I might turn a blind eye to Fadia's dalliances, allowing that she would want a younger man to satisfy her sexual needs, whereas I would be faithful to the last, never looking at another woman but basking in the gratitude that must warm a man when a woman of greater beauty and intelligence condescends to love and accept him on whatever terms suit her, and that this love—or fond tolerance, call it what you will—would create a child who might see between his parents the crackle of energy that produced him and know it to be the essence of his own being as much as it would always remain mysterious. How could this man and this woman have come together to make *me*?, he must think, as we all wonder to some degree about our parents. How could these two people who perhaps he would love in differing degrees, find infuriating, exasperating, even repellent, have seen something in each other that fired the spark required to produce his own life?

My conversation with Michael Ramsey left me with a sense of relief compromised by the conviction that if he was not tormenting me then someone else was. I knew I had not lost my mind, and I know it now, with near total certainty. The boxes that came to my apartment were not imagined, their contents no hallucination. I know I did not forget the correspondence with Rachel: that was undoubtedly the intrusion and creation, the malign meddling, of someone else. I knew my mother was not lying to me about the phone call, and I believed

Michael when he said he was not the one who had placed it. Michael Ramsey might, as he insisted, have nothing to do with any of what was happening, or, and this possibility intrigued me more, he was trying to help me in the only way he could manage.

THE NEXT MORNING I called a cab to take me to Rhinecliff. After punching in the first few digits of the number on my landline, I suddenly got a dial tone, as if I were phoning from within some larger network and could not get an outside line. I tried several times with the same result, four numbers in and the dial tone would return. I hung up and tried my cellphone, and although I was able to dial the complete number, the phone rang and was answered, but when I spoke I heard only my own voice in reply.

'Hello?' I said.

'Hello?' I said back to myself from the other end.

'Is anyone there?' I said.

'Is anyone there?' said my recorded voice.

I ended the call, tried again, and the same thing happened.

'Hello?'

'Hello?'

'Can I get a cab as soon as possible?'

'Can I get a cab as soon as possible?'

Again I hung up, dialed a different company, got an answer and a voice other than my own, a woman who said a taxi would be on its way in fifteen minutes. On the drive to the station I phoned my mother and made some excuse about needing to be back in the city early to see an old friend, or some other easy deception, I no longer remember the lie, except that my mother's voice was clipped, as if she had other matters on her mind, or could no longer speak to me without thinking of the anonymous caller and the accusations he had made.

As I waited for the train inside Rhinecliff Station, an early twentieth-century brick pavilion with elegant slatted benches, a waiting room with a high ceiling, warm and dry and so unlike any British station I ever visited, something Stephen Jahn once said came back to me. It must have been the last conversation he and I had, perhaps in January this year, not long after Fadia had given birth. Stephen and I were in the SCR one day after lunch, and once everyone else had left the room he shifted towards me, stepping over the carpet as though he was half-drunk or had difficulty seeing, his body moving so ponderously I wondered if he was about to collapse, but then he sat down across from me, gazed up through his little round glasses, and nodded his head. I had not confided in anyone about Fadia's pregnancy, during the course of which I had seen her regularly, but always in College, or in the company of other doctoral students and colleagues if she came to my house. No one knew, as far as I was aware, that I now had a son, and as a consequence the elation I felt was tempered by a sense of isolation from the rest of the world.

'I should give you a cigar,' Stephen whispered. 'Or perhaps you're the one who should be giving out cigars.'

'I don't think I understand.'

'Yes you do, but that's all right.'

'Honestly, Stephen, I don't have any idea what you mean,' I said, though of course I did.

Stephen's eyes goggled and shut. When he opened them again there was a hard little light burning just off center in both pupils. I knew it was nothing more than the sun refracted through his glasses, but it made me think of a jinni. A puff of air popped from his lips. Three wishes, I thought, what would my three wishes be? Return me to New York, assemble my family into a new constellation, and then disappear forever from my life, Stephen Jahn. He muttered something to himself that I could not hear and then spoke in a low voice bleached of affect.

'In the next few days I predict you will receive an email inviting you to apply for a position at an American university. Perhaps more than one. I advise you to make applications. I further predict you will be offered a position, again, possibly more than one, and when you are you would be wise to accept whichever offer you prefer, and give your notice here, to the College and Faculty. It will be straight-forward enough to arrange your affairs in Oxford. This is a seller's market, and the house is in excellent decorative condition, as these British realtors like to say. I suspect you'll achieve over the asking price, and you'd be a fool not to accept such an offer, although I see now that you are a greater fool than I first imagined. Never mind. When all that is completed, you will move back to America, as you have long wished. Do you understand?'

'What game is this, Stephen?'

He brushed the wrinkles from his gray wool trousers and pursed his lips.

'It is not a game, Jeremy. Don't be so bumbling. I have made it quite clear—'

And there he broke off because another Fellow suddenly appeared, nodded at us, poured herself a coffee, and left.

'I have made it clear, time and again, that it all matters,' Stephen continued. 'This is not a question of jest. I don't understand how a historian like you could be so blind to the workings of contem-porary history. *This* is history, Jeremy. You have involved yourself in a narrative that is already in progress, and which threatens to sweep us all to one side. What do you know of the girl? What do you know of her parents or her brother? Have you bothered to discover anything about them beyond what she has told you? Have you sought independent verification of anything she has said? She talks fondly of the *shabab* as if it were just a group of youthful revolutionaries seeking democracy but how can you be certain she does not mean something else as well, like *Al-Shabaab*, which is another thing entirely?'

Perhaps I sat with my mouth open, a little stupefied, but looking back on that exchange I think I said nothing in response. What could I have said? Do you, my readers, whoever you may be, not see how naïve I was? I could not conceive of doing what he asked, and so I stood, turned my back on that little man, and left the room.

A few days later, the email came from the chair of NYU's Department of History asking me to apply for a professorship. There were other invitations as well, at least half a dozen, universities up and down the eastern seaboard. It was the first time such a thing had happened. I sent CVs and letters and a list of references. I had interviews, three campus visits in the spring, and in the end it was NYU that made the best offer. I gave Oxford my notice, sold my house to a woman who offered just more than what I was asking, and returned to America, knowing that, in some real sense, I was doing exactly what Stephen Jahn had insisted I do. Except I was not, not entirely, for I set up the monthly bank transfer, and I kept the lines of communication open with Fadia, and I was intent, then and now and forever in the future, to know and support my son. Does that make me a traitor?

Over the course of the months leading up to my departure, I saw Fadia and Selim several times, always in my College rooms, where it would not seem odd for a student to be showing off a new baby to her supervisor. We had polite sessions in which I was allowed to hold and play with my son, although I felt always the necessity of locking down my emotions, fearing that Fadia might be alarmed by any outward expression of the significant joy I felt. Alone I cried, overwhelmed with happiness, trying to believe it was no different than the jubilation I had felt at Meredith's birth, but if I am honest with myself, and with my children (if you, Meredith and Selim, ever chance to read this), then I have to admit feelings of another valence altogether, perhaps because my son was the product of a relationship that was in so many ways forbidden. Gender alone was not a factor. I did not spend all the years of Meredith's life up to this point longing for a son. But the circumstances of Selim's arrival meant that there was in each of my interactions with him a charge of excitement I had not felt in the same way at any other point in my life.

Each time I watched Fadia gather Selim up in her arms and put him in his pram and then walk round the quad and disappear once more through the main gates of the College, I felt certain there would be no next time, that at any moment she might disappear without explanation or forwarding address. I made a point of not hectoring her, always waiting for her to contact me by email or text message to arrange our next meeting until the final one before my departure, which I took the risk of requesting, inviting them over to my house one evening in late July this year, the day before the movers came to pack. Selim was by then seven months old and although not yet crawling he was turning over and alert, and, I liked to think, happy to see me. As we sat in the garden I held him in my lap and he dozed, sucking the tip of my index finger.

'He's growing fast.'

'His parents are tall. And his grandparents. At least mine are. Yours must be, too,' Fadia said, though I realized we had never shown off photos of our parents or other family members to each other. I had looked up photographs of her mother and father on the web but they had not seemed particularly tall to me. Saif I had not risked searching for, afraid, even then, that entering his name into a search engine might raise a red flag to whatever powers of monitoring might be at work.

'Reasonably tall. Both under six feet. I don't know where I got my height.'

'Better diet.'

We had made a custom of this kind of small talk, but I knew there was too much politeness about it. It was not the conversation of people who had slept together more than once, and who were now living with and loving the unexpected result.

'I leave at the end of the week.'

'I remember.'

'So this is goodbye for now.'

'Indeed,' she said.

'Can I hope to think you might come to visit New York?'

'He doesn't have a passport yet.'

'That's easily sorted.'

'Don't pressure me, Jeremy.'

'I didn't mean to, honestly.'

'No, I understand. You want to see him again. I want that for him, too.'

They stayed another quarter-hour and then she said it was time to go, he needed a nap, and she hoped to do some work. It was the last time I saw them. All my subsequent messages, my emails and text messages, my phone calls, even the physical letters I have sent through the mail, have gone unanswered, unacknowledged. I assume she and he, my ex-student and son, are still in Oxford, although I know it is possible they may have moved on, to London or Paris, or, though the prospect terrifies me, to Cairo. Each month the money slips from my British account into hers. It goes and it goes, and I hope in a way that perhaps makes me worse than a fool, that it goes to support my son, and that wherever he is, Selim is growing up with the knowledge of me as his father.

All this unfolded in my mind on the train back to the city from

Rhinebeck, only weeks ago, the tails of my coat spread behind me like wings, the Catskills receding as I was propelled backwards towards the city and my own uncertain future, moving away from the past I have been contemplating, staring at the frozen waters and the storm blowing down from Canada, gaping at the wreckage of my life that remains heaped before me.

ALTHOUGH IT WAS a Sunday and her gallery was closed, I knew there was a chance Meredith would be there, working, as she often was. When I arrived I could see her standing inside before a large canvas composed of millions of small dots depicting a street scene in what could have been New York, although it was impossible to tell for certain, an image like a pixelated shot taken by a CCTV camera aimed down from a lamppost to record half a dozen women and two men walking in either direction, one woman with a phone pressed to her ear and oblivious of the man whose hand was reaching into the bag slung across her back. I missed the opening of the exhibition in October and knew nothing about the artist, a French painter called Guillaume Pari, whose name was painted in three-foot-tall gray letters across one of the gallery's white walls.

As my daughter let me in, kissing me on both cheeks, she turned back to the painting, the surface of which looked machine-made, each dot of acrylic paint raised and beveled along its perfectly square edges.

'I can't stop staring at it. I really had no reason to be here today but I wanted to come look at the paintings by myself, without any members of the public or collectors or, you know, my employees. I wanted to be alone with the work.'

'I can leave if this is a bad time.'

'No, Dad, that's not what I meant. You're not other people. What do you think of the paintings?'

'Very precise. Not like the work of a human hand.'

'It's done with a CNC machine. Pari takes images from CCTV cameras and manipulates them on his computer, degrades them, and turns them into these impressionistic visions of the *now*, like Pissarro or Seurat. We forget the Impressionists were painting contemporary life, no more classical or biblical scenes, and that in itself was revolutionary, their drive to make the ordinary into art, to demonstrate what painting can do that photography can't, although we might argue about that, I guess maybe that's what Pari is doing, demonstrating how the degraded photograph is effectively no different from what can be achieved in paint, or that painting is itself a kind of mechanical process whose effects are ultimately no different from photography. When you take a picture with your phone or your tablet and then use a program to alter it and it comes out looking pretty convincingly like a painting made with a brush, it's hard to be categorical about what is and isn't art. Anyway, when Pari has finished manipulating the images, the computer spits out the commands to the machine, which makes the painting.'

'Is it art if the artist isn't the one controlling the paint?'

'But he is controlling it. It's his design, his program, just a machine doing the actual application of the medium. I don't know that it's any different in the end, only a matter of degree. I think they're beautiful, and creepy, however they're done.'

'How does he find the images?'

'They're licensed from all these different law enforcement agencies. At least that's what his gallerist in Paris tells me. I've never met Guillaume in person, and I kind of suspect he doesn't actually exist. There are *no* photographs of him anywhere. No one I've talked to has ever met him, not even Marie-Edith, she's the French gallerist. The paintings are delivered by a van to her gallery in Paris but the driver picks them up from some warehouse in the countryside and Marie-Edith says she even tried to track down the owner of the warehouse but could only find a holding company, and then another holding company, and then a shell corporation, like a Chinese box or something—and get this, the warehouse is on a street in the middle of nowhere and there's no CCTV watching it. Whoever Guillaume Pari is, he's found a way of making himself invisible. He might not even be called Guillaume Pari. He could be some other person, not even an artist, or it could be a collective of artists or activists. It's kind of wonderful, all the uncertainties, the invisibility of the artist who makes work entirely about visibility. I wrote an essay along those lines in the catalog. Did I give you a copy?'

'I haven't had a chance to read it. I will today, this evening, when I get home. Are we completely alone here?'

'Why, are you going to kill me?' she laughed. It seemed an odd joke.

'I just wondered if you had time for a coffee.'

She led me through the three white rooms of the gallery, which opened off each other in the converted Chelsea warehouse located within spitting distance of the Hudson, and at the back, through a white sculpted door that is itself a work of art, a piece by Castellani probably worth more than what Meredith pays her assistant each year, we came to the offices and the kitchen where she pressed a button that ground beans and made the coffee, drizzling into two stainless steel cups.

Her office always reminds me of an artist's sunny Parisian atelier, the roof half given over to windows. We sat in the sunken lounge area under the window with the early winter sky above us. It was a room in view of the satellites, the NSA and others able to look down on me having a chat with my daughter in her place of work. I knew this was not fanciful. A friend from Georgetown who until recently worked in the White House told me a few years ago about how they had been testing new satellite technology in the West Wing and called up a live image of another staffer's children playing in their backyard. Recently my mother showed me on her tablet a map of Rhinebeck in three dimensions, so detailed it gave me a sense of her house and her neighbors and my own property in a way that seemed astonishingly intrusive. How long, I wonder, before each of us can call up live images of the streets where we, our families, our friends and ex-lovers and enemies all live? We are all being watched, all the time, whether we want to believe it or not.

'How was Rhinebeck? Is Grandma doing okay? She seemed distracted on Thursday.'

'You know large groups are difficult because she can't hear well enough to follow the conversation, but she's in good health.' I paused, glancing up at the sky as a helicopter passed overhead, and the sudden arc of a gull rose from the direction of the river, bird looping machine. 'In fact I'm here for selfish reasons. I came to talk about myself.'

'You're being very cagey.'

'Don't worry, I'm not sick or dying. I didn't lose my job. All things considered, everything is fine. I shouldn't be in this panic and I probably shouldn't be as anxious as I feel. Look at my hands, I haven't been like this since I submitted my doctoral dissertation.'

'Are you having money problems? You know we can fix that.'

'It's nothing like that, but thank you, darling. I want you to understand that what I'm about to tell you does not change the fact that I love you more than anything or anyone. I am so proud of all you've accomplished. And you're still so young! You don't even know how amazing you are to me. I was a hopelessly lost graduate student at your age and you have a career and a life and everything organized in ways that make my head spin.'

'You're flattering me, Dad.'

'Stop being so modest. And stop interrupting. I have to say this before I think better of telling you.' She looked at me then, her brows crinkling into a brief flicker of displeasure so that I could imagine, for the first time, what it might be like to see Meredith truly angry with me, or disappointed, and it was a horrible thought that only worsened my anxiety, tugging a bout of nausea from my gut, as though after years of being a teacher I found myself again in the position of the student, the child being governed and chastised by an adult who has promised to fix whatever is wrong, provided I am suitably penitent. 'When I was in Oxford I had a student, she's a little older than you, but not much. She and I became close, I taught her for several years, and by chance she lived in an apartment across the street from my house, so we saw each other outside of the usual College contexts, tutorials and lectures and meals, all that kind of thing. This isn't so unusual in a place like Oxford. It could happen in any college town.' I was short of breath and paused to inhale deeply a few times, conscious that Meredith's look of displeasure had settled and deepened. 'One night I asked her over for a drink. I guess you can imagine what happened, but one thing led to another.'

Meredith sat up straighter in her chair, raising her hands. 'Please, Dad, why are you telling me this? I don't—I really don't want to hear this.'

What must it feel like, I wondered, to hear that your father has embraced someone your own age just as easily, just as thoughtlessly, as he abandoned you in the first place? Why, I suddenly thought, would Meredith possibly want to meet Fadia and Selim? What right did I have to expect such magnanimity from my daughter, from whom I have already taken so much?

'Believe me, darling, if I didn't have to tell you, I wouldn't.'

'So you slept with your student. I can't—'

'She was my doctoral student at that stage, but yes, I slept with her. It happened several times, over the course of a few weeks, and then I didn't hear from her for a while—'

'Wait, *what*? I don't understand, if she's living across the street—Was it consensual?'

'Of course it was consensual. How can you ask me that? In many ways she took the lead.'

'It just seems strange that you would sleep with your student and then not speak to her, like she was avoiding you, or you were avoiding her.'

'It didn't seem strange at the time. She's very independent.'

'Oh, Dad, for fuck's sake! Did you call her?'

'Please don't shout, Meredith, this is hard for me. I didn't want to appear aggressive. I was trying to do the right thing. I was trying to think about what *she* would want. And eventually I did hear from her, maybe a month after the period when we were seeing each other.'

'Fucking hell. Can I guess what happens next? I can't actually believe this . . .'

'I'm trying to do this as well as I can.'

Meredith raised her hands again. I didn't know whether to read it as a gesture of capitulation or dismissal.

'She came over to tell me she was pregnant and there was no chance of anyone else being the father. It could only be me.'

'And you just believed her? Jesus, Dad, that's the oldest fucking trick in the book.'

'If you knew her, you'd understand. She isn't given to telling lies. I'd go so far as to say she lives according to the most fervent belief in truth, and in fact what happened between us has forced *her* into a compromising position. She has lied to protect me. I know how distasteful that sounds. In any case, she and I discussed the various options available and I promised to support her regardless of her decision, accepting it was ultimately a choice only she could make. After several weeks of deliberation, and further discussions about the way we might proceed, she decided to keep the child.'

Meredith's mouth knitted into a firm tight line. Her eyes had grown large. She raised a finger to the corner of one eye.

'She gave birth not quite a year ago. I saw my son, your half-brother, a number of times before I moved back. He looks exactly like me as a baby. Since our last meeting, back in July, she has stopped replying to my messages, although I have every reason to believe Fadia is still in Oxford.'

'Fadia? What kind of name is that? Are they Arabs?'

'Meredith, please. They're Egyptians, Franco-Egyptian. Fadia's mother is French, and the boy is, of course, an even greater mix, half of what I am.'

Meredith stood and walked up to her desk on its raised platform, opened a drawer, took out a bottle of scotch, found a glass, poured herself a large measure, and drank it in one. I could see her chest rising and falling as she tried to calm herself, a vein pulsing in her neck, her hands now flat on the desk.

'I wish that was the end of it, but it isn't.'

And then I told her about the deliveries I'd had over the course of the previous week and the other strange occurrences, the multiple meetings with Michael Ramsey, the phone call my mother received, and my bewilderment at why anyone should wish to track me so closely and then tip me off to the fact that I was being watched in this way. 'I can only think it's because of the money I send Fadia, because her brother used to work for the Egyptian government, and then after the revolution he became a member of the Muslim Brotherhood, and then he simply disappeared. The last time Fadia and I spoke about it she thought he was fighting in Syria, and all I can guess is that someone in some intelligence service has noticed the money going from my account into Fadia's and perhaps, for all I know, she's been giving money to Saif, that's her brother, or, I don't know, maybe she doesn't have to give him anything for it still to look suspicious, me giving money to the sister of a man who might well be regarded as a terrorist. I guess I'm asking for your advice. What do you think?'

'You're giving her money?' Meredith moved behind her desk and wrinkled her nose.

'It seemed like the right thing to do. She did not ask for the money but I volunteered, and by law I am obliged, although it is not an obligation I would try to avoid in any case.'

'Have you spoken to a lawyer?'

'I haven't done anything illegal.'

'You need a lawyer. I'd say you could use one of ours but I don't think that's a good idea. Peter wouldn't . . . I'll ask Barry to make a referral. You need to sit down with someone tomorrow, before this goes any further.'

As she poured herself another drink, I noticed her hand shaking. She was trying to control herself, but was angrier than I had ever seen her. What I had done with Fadia was despicable, I knew that, or understood how it could appear so to my daughter, although I felt what Fadia and I had done was the product of loneliness and attraction, certainly of mutual respect, and the consequences were what made it so complicated, placing us in positions that were now threatening to derail my life. I also knew that no matter how Meredith might try to prevent herself from getting involved, she would almost certainly want to see her half-brother, refusing a future in which Fadia and Selim carried on with their lives outside of her influence. They would be drawn into the fold, incorporated, made to sever all ties with their own family for the sake of ours. At least, that was my hope, that an American sphere of influence might replace an Egyptian one.

'So you don't think I'm paranoid? You don't think I'm making it up?'

'If someone is sending you evidence that you're being watched, then no, I don't think you're paranoid.'

'But I'm no one.'

'We're all *no one* until we do something to turn ourselves into *someone* and you, Dad, have made choices that do just that. These days it takes so little effort to put yourself on the wrong side of the law. In the past it must have been way more difficult to do something really seriously bad, but now you can blink and end up in jail.'

'Maybe not. Handing a letter to someone for whom it wasn't intended. Gossiping. Mentioning to an informant, whether you knew it or not, that your neighbor was seen speaking to someone already suspected of wrongdoing. I don't think it's so different. It's always been easy to drop oneself down a black hole. The only difference is the degree and speed of response by the authorities, whether you are coerced, arrested, executed. Michael Ramsey—'

'I don't think Ramsey has anything to do with it, Dad. He's the dullest person Peter knows.' She paused, staring at me with that awful look of disappointment. 'You understand that Peter has to know what's going on. He and I are both implicated by association with you.'

'You make it sound like you're the children of a terrorist.'

'You can't joke about these things. This is the reality of our world, and you stepped across the line, whether you meant to or not.'

I wanted to shout at my daughter, who had never made me angry in her life. What could I do? What could I have done? I had no choice but to give Fadia money. It was the only moral, ethical move I could have made, and yet in giving her money I was also, potentially, breaking the law, whether implicitly or explicitly, depending on what she herself was doing with the money, depending on whether or not she had renewed ties with Saif, depending on whether she was now, by some terrible act of chance or a delusion of conscience, giving aid to her brother the terrorist. I should not have gone to bed with her in the first place, not only because she was my student, but because of what I knew of her family. I could not govern my desire. Surely that is my worst failing?

When she began to show, there were whisperings in College and the History Faculty, though I never heard an accusation leveled against me by my colleagues, except of course by Stephen Jahn, who by then was again spending greater stretches of time away from Oxford on government business. I often watched the news expecting to see his face, either as a talking-head Middle East expert, or lost in a crowd in Egypt or Syria, standing alongside whatever person or entity America and Britain had elected for the moment to support. If colleagues other than Stephen knew or suspected that I was responsible for Fadia's pregnancy I never heard such rumors.

It was arranged for a colleague of mine to take over the supervision of Fadia's thesis after I announced my return to New York earlier this year. At our final meeting in my garden on Divinity Road this past July, Fadia asked me to wait for her to be in touch, not to phone or email or write until then, but as soon as she left my house I knew I could not possibly honor her request. It pained me too much to hand my boy back to his mother without knowing whether I would see him before he was old enough to make his own decisions. I felt compelled to write and phone as a way of demonstrating that my door would always be open to her, and to him. As months pass and my messages continue to be ignored, I fear there is little hope of ever seeing either of them again.

ONCE MORE, LAST NIGHT, I dreamt of the white room, a place that seems half-modeled on my home office, half on the black sites of secret detention which must exist in America—perhaps in smaller numbers—just as they do abroad. In this iteration of the dream I am hooded and handcuffed before being led down the hall, suspecting a shower awaits me as it has on previous occasions. Instead I become aware of arriving at a larger space, an echoing room with a high ceiling and distant walls. My hood is lifted, exposing my ears, nostrils and mouth, but the rough material is then cinched across the bridge of my nose to prevent me from seeing anything more substantial than pinpoints of light through the crosshatch of fabric. I hear rustlings of paper, metal chairs being pulled across a linoleum floor—two chairs, I think, and three sets of feet: two people seated, the third the one who led me here, who has lifted my hood, who stands behind me, his hands on my shoulders, radiating a warmth that, for a moment, fills me with a strange goodwill towards the man. I recognize his scent from other dreams, know that he is the one who habitually takes me to the showers, whose grip is firm but never cruel, who watches as I bathe, never saying a word.

Without waiting for a sign from my jailers, I speak.

'If detention is what this is, it fails to meet my expectations. I am almost disappointed. Can you not do worse? Make me suffer bodily, give me a pain I can feel on the skin, tug at my fingernails, force death in my eye instead of this isolating torment. It's like being made to sit alone after class, wondering when the teacher will ever return.'

'We could do those things you suggest,' a woman says. 'Is that what you deserve, Jeremy?' When she says my name, I know the woman speaking is Fadia. I squint into the pinpricks of light and her face comes into focus. 'We could continue to treat you as a misbehaving child, or we could make it much worse. *Notre régime pédagogique est assez doux.* We want only that you should reflect on what you have done.'

The man behind me, the guard with warm hands, leans over and whispers in my ear. 'This is already more serious than a school detention,' he says, squeezing my right shoulder.

'That never happened to Jeremy,' Fadia says, as if she has heard the guard's whispers. 'He was a good boy. Never naughty.'

'That's right,' I say, 'not a single detention in all my years of education. Does my daughter know about my detention? Does she do nothing to fight for my liberty? What can you tell me?'

'Your daughter knows,' a man says. 'She learned her lessons, unlike you. Her mother brought her up well.'

'I had a hand in that, too.'

'Indeed?' the man laughs, and as he does I recognize it is Stephen Jahn. 'She can do nothing to liberate you. We have been watching for too long.'

'I never thought—'

'We should all assume someone *may* be watching, Jeremy, even though we cannot know for certain if or when they are definitely watching. We have made the world a virtual panopticon.'

'So freedom is illusion,' I said, working an equation in my head, a formula that, in the dream, burned neon through the burlap hood covering my eyes: *Detention < Suspension < Expulsion.* It was the ladder of punishment, above which remains only *Execution*, if we the criminals or suspected criminals are unlucky enough to find ourselves in a state with capital punishment, or a state without due process that does simply as it wishes, behind closed doors, regardless of what its laws may say. Substitute *Disposal* for *Expulsion* and the matter is soon handled, no need for a higher category.

I woke with the equation on my tongue, clear enough that I could use it as a key to the remainder of the dream, to the formulations my unconscious assembled into a dialogue. I lay in bed looking out at the white sky, the reflections on adjacent buildings, the painted advertisement across the street. Though not in a state of detention, I am at least in a state of suspension: suspension of belief in the possibility of liberty. In other words, I believe that one day soon, perhaps today or tomorrow or the next, I may no longer walk free in the world, left with nothing but the memory of an illusory freedom once enjoyed with too little appreciation for its rarity.

There is a kind of similarity between the detention I may face, in some cool white room, and the after-hours detention a misbehaving student suffers in school halls. In both cases they are attempts to coerce the detainee back into good behavior. Some petty disobedience is punished by an extra hour in confinement under the eye of the teacher, a first step on the path to suspension, always an odd punishment, a penalty that must seem like a gift to some children, being able to stay home for days or weeks, and ultimately, if such corrections fail, expulsion, the permanent exclusion from school, which must result in assignment to a different or special school. I was never close enough to anyone expelled from school to know where he or she might have ended up. Such people disappeared and in the cruel way of the young I made myself forget them. (How quickly might those I love manage to forget me?) School breaks us in with its threats of existential violence and removal from the herd, preparing us for the more profound violence of adulthood, the long stretch of life when only a verifiable claim of insanity might spare us punishment for slips of behavior that fall afoul of the laws we have ourselves allowed to be written to control and organize our lives. I once made myself a student of Althusser, finding in the latter's formulation of Ideological State Apparatuses—schools and churches and the like—a picture of my own childhood, my experience of social indoctrination and control. Go to school and learn the lessons of society and law. Go to church for the added moral edification, inculcation of the Ten Commandments, the lessons of the Gospels, all of it preparation for submitting oneself to the Repressive State Apparatuses of the police, the courts, the military, surely also the intelligence services.

If I am detained, will there be a trial? Will I stand before judge and jury, listening as the case is argued for and against my liberty? Perhaps such trials no longer allow for the attendance of a defendant, due process judged unduly lenient. The prison sentence that might follow a less formal detention would be not unlike a suspension from school, although the metaphor begins to crack because prison removes one *from* home (home as the ostensibly free world outside its walls) rather than from the institution, the school, the body public, in the expectation that one's parents would confine one *at* home. (Would I want, now, to be confined by my mother, the parent assuming the duties of the state, *in loco imperium*?)

Pushed far enough, I can imagine a scenario in which, prison itself failing to correct my behavior, the country of my birth might try to expel me, sending me back to Britain, or even—unendurable though I would find it—to the state, which is to say the realm, the territory, the geographic kingdom of terror, land of the new caliph, whoever he may be, who decapitates his enemies as warning and sport. Then, I can imagine, my American family would think itself free to eliminate me with a specially targeted drone attack, a two-foot-long individualized missile painted with my face, steered by a boy suffering from remote PTSD in a control center somewhere deep in the wastes of Nevada.

No one in my family has ever been arrested. No one I know has ever been to prison. A citation for speeding is the worst infraction I know at close hand. No one I know has even been interrogated by the police, all of us, family and friends, the whole rippling circle, so boring and law-abiding. Crime has touched the life of my family and friends only in the form of minor victimhood: my mother's last car sideswiped, an uncle once mugged in Central Park, a friend—the Swiss postdoctoral Fellow whose rooms were across the landing from mine that first year at Oxford—had his bank accounts emptied by Nigerian identity thieves. I imagine that if I am detained, either in America or Britain, there will be abuse, torture, some kind of physical coercion such as one imagines has been inflicted on other detainees in the first years of our new millennium, this age when humanity begins once again to dehumanize itself in the same moment that it struggles to assume total control over the planet. The historical mind thinks not only in details but also in ages, epochs, the macro as well as the micro. The Anthropocene. We are imagining ourselves into dystopia, sleepwalking into fantastic nightmares made real.

So far I have had it easy. Threat is brutal to the mind but not the body. Physical pain I fear more than mental. I can imagine how the hood so routinely placed over my head in these recurring dreams might one day be cinched tight round my neck and water poured over the cloth so that I would experience the horror of drowning on dry land only to have the sentence revoked at the last moment, mortality teased again, another reprieve, the torture of death approaching and retreating, *fort, da* . . . And perhaps they would go too far, death arriving by accident so that I fall into her arms blind and suffocating, wet cotton sucked deep into my mouth and nostrils as we rush, Death and the Dying, along the black fringed tunnel, away from the light, into the light.

Isolation itself might be construed as torture. Am I, like Louis Pierre Althusser, no longer of sound mind? (Does my knowledge of him make me suspect? Is the Gallic too foreign?) Could I, like Althusser, strangle someone I love to the point of death? Should I also be given shock therapy? Perhaps it would have been better if I had remained at Oxford (where once every century men chase a wooden duck round a quadrangle), living in College, restricting my life within the walls of academia where eccentricities are tolerated, even valorized, just as Althusser lived out his life between the *École Normale Supérieure* and mental hospitals. Unlike Althusser, I am no *éminence grise*, no great mind revered by his nation. If I killed my ex-wife or my son-in-law there would be no excusing my crime, no one to argue my value to society as counterbalance to the horror of my acts. I am no one, a dabbler in history and philosophy, a dilettante, a movie buff who pretends to cinematic philosophy, a failed lover, a father of children who do not and may never know each other, a divorced man, a predatory teacher, an ogre who sees a desirable woman and cannot stop himself, who has no apparatus for self-control, who needs Althusser's Repressive State Apparatuses to keep him in check, to prevent him from turning himself, however unwittingly, into a traitor not just to the state but to every individual around him.

I TICK OFF the days on a laminated paper calendar, but the ink smears against the glossy surface and I begin to wonder how many days have passed since Thanksgiving weekend, if my shaking hands have smudged the marks or if someone else, perhaps the woman who cleans my apartment, might be working for those who watch me so closely. Some evenings I think I hear voices coming from upstairs or downstairs or out in the hallway, but whenever I stop to listen or open the door there is no one, and I fear these whispering men and women may only be in my head.

Is it possible that even my family, those people I remember as my daughter and mother, my ex-wife, the student who was my three-week lover, the boy I call my son whose face I see as a memory of my own face photographed in infancy, are all just figments, from Latin, *fingere*, to feign, to fashion (in other words to make *or* to falsify), all of them inventions that are also fictions, a catalog of frauds. Figment is a word Shakespeare never used; search the corpus. But not Hobbes, he understood its force, compare his theory of personation: 'An Idol, or meer Figment of the brain, may be Personated,' which is to say, *represented*, or acted, even performed, 'as were the Gods of the Heathen; which by such Officers as the State appointed, were Personated, and held Possessions, and other Goods, and Rights, which men from time to time dedicated, and consecrated unto them. But Idols cannot be Authors: for an Idol is nothing.'

What if, my dear Jeremy—myself, me speaking now to my loony-tune reflected mind, for who knows if anyone else will read these words—my family and my past are mere Hobbesian idols, figments of my brain, that I have been personating to myself? What if the hand of the artist has taken faces of passing acquaintance, manipulated them, and allowed the machine of my thoughts to turn them into a slideshow of false memory? What if I have been in a cool white room all my adult life, ever since leaving high school or college, confined for observation, medication, electroconvulsive therapy, and found still to be so dangerous to himself and others that he must be kept in isolation in a padded cell, handcuffed, blindfolded, allowed only to shower alone, never even seeing the faces of the men and women who jail him, that is me, the first sign of madness the dissociation from self, I no longer know, cannot say with certainty, the pen, in any case, has run low on ink and the machined metal nib scratches, slicing through the flimsy gray page, made not from cotton but wood pulp, reams of the stuff, susceptible to quick decay, so that the text itself might soon disappear, disintegrating long before I have finished this testament.

I REMEMBER SPENDING THE rest of that Sunday, the first of December, with Meredith and Peter in their apartment, and then, because they insisted on including her, with Susan as well. Though she was only a twenty-minute walk away, Peter sent a car to fetch her, wanting her there quickly, as if I were a bomb and my ex-wife the only person with the knowledge to defuse me.

The four of us sat in my daughter's living room overlooking Central Park and I was forced to explain, several times, the nature of my failure and indiscretion, submitting myself to their interrogation.

'Have you slept with other students?' Susan asked, her face as apoplectic as Stephen Jahn's once was, goggling eyes and crimson cheeks, Judy for a Punch. But could I kill her? No, not possibly.

'Please, Mom, that's not what's important,' Meredith sighed.

'I think Jeremy should tell us whether this is habitual behavior or if it was just a one-time fuck up.'

'It has never happened before and will never happen again.'

'Damn right it won't. They'll put you in prison,' Susan hissed.

'I did nothing illegal.'

'I'm not sure that's strictly true,' Peter interrupted. 'If you've been giving money to support a terrorist organization, even indirectly, I think that *might be* illegal.'

'But Fadia is not a terrorist organization. She's not a terrorist.

She's estranged from her brother, and we don't even know for certain that Saif—'

'Jesus, will you listen to these names?' Susan muttered.

'Mom! Enough.'

'Nonetheless, you don't really know, do you, Jeremy?' Peter continued. 'Did you ever see a bank statement for Fadia's account? Did you ever confirm it was her account alone? Do you know for certain there isn't a co-signer? Are you sure her dad or brother isn't on that account? How do you know it isn't in fact the *brother's* account and this Fadia is just a co-signer? What if she's nothing more than a front for terrorist fundraising? You could be just one of dozens, scores of men similarly duped.'

I hesitated. They were reasonable if unpleasant questions. I had never checked any of those details. 'I trusted her. I was in the hospital room at the birth of my son. I felt—I was in love with her. You trust the people you love, don't you?'

'What a moron, Jeremy. You can't trust people like that!'

'Honestly, Mom, you're not helping.'

Susan snorted. 'I'm glad to see nothing's changed. All the old loyalties . . .'

For a moment no one said anything and then Peter and Susan continued haranguing me in a tag-team relay that suggested a kind of understanding between them I had not expected.

'I think you're lucky—we're all lucky—that you haven't been arrested already,' Peter said at last, as if that was the final and most important point. Through my behavior I had risked not only my own reputation and liberty, but the reputation and liberty of my entire family, even perhaps my friends and colleagues.

'Peter, honey, that's not fair. What Dad did was foolish, but I don't think we need to go farther than that. He's apologized.'

'There's the legal issue.'

'We can take care of that,' Meredith said. 'I'm sure we can take care of that. We're not the kind of people who have problems like this.' I was grateful for my daughter's words but also aware of the desperation in her voice.

Although they tried to convince me to stay overnight I finally insisted at eight o'clock that I wanted to go home and we would continue discussing the matter on Monday, since Peter had been unable to reach Barry and did not want to speak to any of his other lawyers about such a sensitive issue.

He took me by the arm as I was standing to go, his hands squeezing through the cloth of my coat. 'I want you to see a psychiatrist. If there's something wrong, we need to get you medicated or treated or whatever it takes.'

'Electroconvulsive therapy?'

'They say it's not such a bad thing.'

'Who says, Peter?'

'Dad, please,' Meredith interrupted, and led me to the door.

'I was stupid.'

'Yes, you were. But we'll find a way to fix it.'

'I thought no one would ever know about it. I kept it a secret because that's what Fadia wanted.'

'That's enough for now. You've told me all I need to hear.'

'I'm not crazy. Do *you* think I'm crazy?'

'I think you're stressed, and anxious.' She paused, trying, I thought, not to look away from me. 'Maybe you'd benefit from some medication.'

'Hollywood Housewife regime. You want to turn me into a pill popper? I've only had antibiotics half a dozen times in my life. Nothing harder. I only smoked pot once!'

'Go in with an open mind.'

'Do you think I should take a leave of absence from work?'

'No, that wouldn't be wise. Don't do anything to make it look as though you think you're guilty of something. Carry on as usual. Go to class, finish out the semester, and hopefully, by then, we'll know how to proceed.'

They had called me a car service and as I traveled down to the Village, shock absorbers taking the jolt of manhole covers and potholes, brakes silent in a way that suggested whatever livery company operated the vehicle understood its customers expected the illusion of traveling in a bubble of comparative silence approximating the security of their well-protected homes, I thought of Fadia and Selim going about their lives in Oxford, the two of them sleeping in a flat almost certainly paid for with the money that slipped each month from my account to hers, childcare paid for with that same money so she could continue her doctoral studies under the supervision of my former colleague, a humorless woman raised in the western half of divided Berlin who was undoubtedly giving Fadia better guidance than I could as she continued to plumb the philosophical and historical ramifications of the media's construction and treatment of left-wing terror in Europe during the twentieth century's long Cold War.

Meredith and Peter and Susan were the first people I had told about Fadia and Selim, and while I understood their shock and anger at my deception, at what might reasonably be regarded as the failure of my own moral compass, no one among them had given any indication they were going to reject me. No one had said they never wanted to see my son or his mother. Everyone, even Susan, seemed to believe the onus was on me to take such actions as might prove necessary to right whatever had gone wrong. Action of some kind must be taken to clarify my situation with the authorities. This I remain willing to do. If you require further evidence, you only need ask. I will do all that you demand.

WHEN I ARRIVED BACK at my building the doorman Ernesto was again behind the front desk, back from whatever short holiday he'd had with his sister in Queens.

'Professor! You got another delivery. Looks like the same kind of thing. With the last one, you know, you didn't have any problems?'

'Nothing I couldn't handle. Did you remember—I asked if you could take a picture of the delivery person?'

Ernesto nodded, sliding the index finger of his left hand back and forth across the surface of his phone. He held up the device for me to see the image. 'That's your guy. Not a nice dude.' The man was in profile and while it might have been Michael Ramsey, I could not be completely certain.

'Did he say anything?'

'Nope. Some of these delivery guys are like that, but you know this time I was looking at him and I realized this dude is no bike messenger. Gear's all wrong, the clothes *and* the shoes. This guy's, you know, at least not like a regular messenger. I thought maybe a student intern or something, but he looks too old for that.' He paused a moment. 'You recognize him?'

'I think we've met before. Where's the new package?'

He pointed across the lobby to the floor near the mailboxes, where a box like the others, perhaps a little larger, sat alongside a plastic Christmas tree that had grown up during my absence over the weekend. This fourth box was heavier than the first three, and I carried it into the elevator with a tug of dread that seemed to pull my feet down through the floor and dangle me over the bottom of the shaft.

As soon as I was inside my apartment, without opening the box, I went to check my voicemail, but there were no messages. Perhaps whoever was making trouble for me with my mother was not given to leaving messages, or was nothing more than a troublemaker, someone in Oxford, a new boyfriend of Fadia's, even her brother, perhaps her father—more likely, as I thought earlier, Stephen Jahn himself. My number in New York is unlisted while my mother has always kept hers in the phonebook, concerned that old friends be able to reach her if their memories should fail them. At some point in the past I must have told Stephen that my mother lives in Rhinebeck, might even have mentioned her name.

Though the new box glowered at me from the front hall, I tried to ignore it, fixing a sandwich and opening a bottle of wine, but as I ate in front of the television and struggled to put the box from my mind I kept catching glimpses of its reflection whenever the screen went black until finally I put my food and drink aside, took a knife from the kitchen, and sliced open the flaps of the box.

Inside was not a stack of papers, as in the first three cases, but a second box, which contained a series of file dividers. I reached into the first section and pulled out a bundle of photographs. It took me a while to pick myself out of the crowds, but it soon became apparent that I was looking at a photographic record of my movements in Oxford and London in the months after Fadia first came to interview at my College. How young I looked! How naïve and full-faced and healthy! Only occasionally did I appear preoccupied or thoughtful, almost never scowling, and as I examined this record of my life from nearly a decade earlier, I felt something approaching gratitude for that reminder of the man I once was.

I dropped the photos back into their section and made my way through the subsequent divisions, each one bringing me closer to the present. There were photos of me on the street, sometimes in my car (the car I had sold before leaving Oxford, a car I only ever used to go to the grocery store or escape alone on drives into the Cotswolds), my face seemingly captured by a CCTV camera. There were photos from my travels, from trips home to New York, from research and conference visits to cities in Europe and North America. There was nothing, at first, that one would call incriminating or embarrassing, except perhaps the state of my hair or my weight or my occasional bad dress sense. There were no photographs of me picking my nose or scratching my crotch or digging in my ear. For the most part, I looked like an ordinary man of my age, if not always as suave or sophisticated as I liked to imagine I was. My jaw began to grow slack as the years passed, as if I was holding my teeth apart with my lips closed, my jowls became jowlier, the wisdom peaks in my hairline ate deeper into the scalp, my weight fluctuated, I could recognize the periods during summers when I was exercising and turned lean, and the winter months when, overindulging in High Table hospitality, I pillowed to fat.

There were pictures of Meredith as well, of the two of us together in Oxford and New York, images of my mother, of various colleagues, a photograph of me and Bethan taken long after our brief liaison, then pictures of me in the company of the few other women who made up the short inventory of my intimates during those years in exile. And of course, as I came quickly and anxiously to expect, the deeper I delved into the file, there were pictures of Fadia and me together, although these were always discreet, there was no indication we were anything other than student and teacher speaking briefly on

Turl Street for instance, or pausing in the Old Schools Quad of the Bodleian Library or meeting for a coffee in the café on the second floor of Blackwell's Bookshop on Broad Street. I congratulated myself on the public restraint I had shown. No sign of a hand straying to touch her hair, no fingers clasping, no kiss on the cheek. Nonetheless, there was a record of our acquaintance, and this visual record sent me back to the files of phone numbers and internet addresses and I knew from a quick glance that all our communications must necessarily be present there as well. And then I realized that somebody somewhere—Michael Ramsey, surely—must be using facial recognition software to search through an existing archive of images, just to demonstrate to me that I had long been observed and my movements recorded, as if, from the moment of first meeting Fadia that day she came to interview at College, I had placed myself on the radar of whatever entities are entrusted to watch over our security, and for no better reason than because of her relation to three men—her father, her uncle, her brother—who were at the time figures in Mubarak's government.

What else might yet come? Would I wake on Monday or later that week to find a box outside my door, kindly brought up from the lobby by Ernesto or one of the other doormen, and inside discover a complete record of all my electronic financial transactions over the past decade, a body of evidence that would suggest, if nothing else, a life lived abroad and, more recently, sympathy for this woman who was my student and is now the mother of my son?

I returned to the box, for I had not yet exhausted its contents, and in the final compartment found pictures from this past year, dating from just after Selim's birth. A sob tore out of my throat as I gazed at them, pictures of my son in his stroller pushed along the uneven Oxford streets, carried in his mother's arms, meeting with his maternal grandmother in the Grand Café on High Street, being displayed to cooing friends at a picnic under a beech tree in the University Parks, a beautiful child, a boy who looked without question like his father and mother drawn together and distilled into a new and vital image. It was terrible to look upon and I spread all the photos of mother and child out on my long dining room table, arranged so I could see how my boy had been growing in my absence these last few months, he was healthy and happy and no doubt meeting all the milestones as he should, and Fadia, whose face provoked more tenderness in me than I might have expected, appeared happy but also heavy with preoccupation or concern, I didn't know quite what to call it, a look of thoughtfulness and worry, perhaps only because she was finishing her thesis, or so I suspected, perhaps because of the disappearance of her brother, perhaps because all was not well with her father, perhaps because she knew that one day I would return, refusing to allow my son to carry on living independently of me. And then, near the end of the files, was a single photo showing Fadia on St. Giles, just outside the Taylorian, speaking with Stephen Jahn, and Selim in a pram between them. There was something in Fadia's and Stephen's postures that chilled me, as if the inclining of her head in his direction suggested an alliance and the glint in his eye a plot or a purpose. I looked at the photo again, knowing I could not reliably read the situation on the basis of a single image. They might have met by accident, and what appears to be alliance in one moment might in the next, the many unrecorded moments that followed, look like coercion or rejection.

As I was studying these images, feeling the tormenting pleasure at seeing evidence of the ongoing life of my child, and confusion about how Fadia and Stephen might still be in touch with each other, I was conscious of the weight of a gaze upon me, of someone looking, a still point in a field of movement, and when I glanced up and out of my window onto the dark glossy stretch of Houston Street, I saw Michael Ramsey, undisguised, staring up at me, a finger pointing at his chest, his head nodding as he watched me looking at him, as my gaze met his and together, in that shared moment of recognition, I knew that whatever else might be happening, whatever the strange complications my own actions had created in my life and might go on proliferating, Michael Ramsey was somehow trying to help me.

AND YET, HE TURNED away, and as he did I began to doubt it had actually been him. I watched as the man who might have been Michael spun on his heel and walked west along Houston towards MacDougal, perhaps to the café where we had met a week earlier. Thinking I would phone him, I searched the white pages online, but there were a hundred Michael Ramseys in New York alone. Calling each of them, and on a Sunday evening moreover, seemed preposterous. Then it occurred to me that I could simply ask Peter how to contact Michael, and yet, I knew that even if I reached him he would deny everything over the phone because if he was—or is still—working for the NSA or some other intelligence-gathering body, he would know his own line was being monitored (that must, I imagine, be one of the requirements for such a job, the relinquishing of one's own privacy for the sake of our national security).

Whatever he was doing, trying to help me or warn me, he had done so in a way, I was certain, that would not be discovered, or could never be traced back to him, or only with considerable effort. It was as though he wanted me to make myself into a victim who was willing to come forward, revealing how I was being watched by my own government for activities that were not, in point of fact, illegal. (Perhaps, I think in this moment, that is precisely what I am doing here, in these pages, revealing my own victimhood.) Michael Ramsey would not help me without first proving to himself that I had broken no laws, which meant that my payments to Fadia must be going to her alone, and that such payments could only, by the most doctrinaire mind, be thought to break any of the laws of America or Britain.

Given the conversations with Meredith and Peter and Susan, I had been considering stopping the payments, though I feared if I did so it would look as though I believed something was amiss in the first place. More importantly, I was afraid that suspending the transfers would jeopardize any relationship I might yet have with my son. It remains my legal responsibility to support my child. To follow one law is to break another. Catch-22. But I have, I remain confident, broken no laws. I do not think I am a fool. Desire undid me, yes, to that I make a full confession, but in trying to correct my failings I have done only what I believed to be legal, to pay for the support of the mother of my child, to pay for the support of my child as his mother has asked me to do. If the account into which I have been sending money to Fadia is in fact not her account but one belonging to her brother, a terrorist, or an account to which he has access, am I nothing more sinister than a dupe?

That Monday morning I tried to phone Fadia on the last number I had for her, but when the call connected a singsong British accent told me it was no longer in service. I sent her an email, and then another, as I had in the past, but she did not reply. Later that morning a messenger delivered a parcel, but this time it was nothing more menacing than a new phone, a gift from Meredith, 'To help us keep in touch,' her note said. I turned the thing on, following the directions to set it up, and dialed her number.

'I received your little gift,' I said into the phone. 'I'm calling you from it.'

'I know, Dad, your new number is already in my contacts. Do you like it?'

'It's a phone, darling, what's to like?'

'They're objects of desire.'

'Perhaps your desire, but not mine.' There was a pause on the line. I was disappointing Meredith, who only wanted to help, just as she did when she upgraded my airline tickets or arranged car services to fetch and deliver me, acts designed to insulate me from the realities and messiness of life. 'Sorry, I don't mean to sound ungrateful. It's a fine-looking thing. Very sleek. And I suppose it'll allow me to do all kinds of things I couldn't do before, like finding a decent restaurant in Midtown.'

Meredith laughed although she did not sound amused. It was not a laugh I recognized.

'Darling?'

I could hear her breathing, a quick exhalation, almost as if she were smoking a cigarette.

'It's—I just thought it would help us stay in touch.'

Once a landline was enough, and I wonder if, in the past, we didn't trust each other more, knowing there would be stretches of every day when we would not be able to contact our spouses or children or parents, trusting they were simply getting on with their lives and being faithful to us and whatever they later reported having done was true, or at least plausible. For each of us, the freedom of not being reached, of wandering untracked through the city, browsing in bookstores and libraries, living life in a way that the mind did not feel hunted or followed or simply distracted by the silliness of unwanted messages and the ability to check stock prices every thirty seconds or receive alerts of breaking news, must have meant that as recently as a decade ago we were thinking more and reacting less. Is it any wonder we have entered a more reactionary age? Our technology is teaching us to react rather than reflect, so that even the leftwing movements of the present seem no longer to be based in ideas as much as in the constantly shifting desire to respond to offense or inequality or injustice, and yet the discourse surrounding whatever the movement or outrage du jour might be seems too often founded on a wafer of historical and ideological ignorance. These were the kinds of thoughts I was once able to share with Susan—in fact such conversations were the foundation of our relationship when we were in our twenties, married overnight, with a daughter nine months later, and no knowledge of each other except the quality of our respective minds. How I missed the possibility of such talk, and in the spirit of spontaneity and the desire to see, perhaps one last time, whether there might still be the possibility of a more serious rapprochement, I got in a cab and went uptown.

When I spoke into the intercom Susan said nothing, but the door buzzed and I pushed my way back into that familiar old entrance, the tile floor a little grubby, the lobby sharp with the scent of aluminum mailboxes. Susan's dog, yapping from behind the door at the top of the building, reminded me of the dog we once owned together, that Westie we had named Lotte Lenya because she looked like the actress, dour face, mouth that was all teeth, a dog who dragged her heels every time we tried to bring her home from Riverside Park.

Seeing Susan's face again, and the little dark eyes of that very white dog looking up at me, I felt such a strong sense of hominess that I embraced my ex-wife without thinking and began to cry in her arms. Despite her anger the day before, she was, apart from our daughter, the only person I felt I could trust, since my mother is no longer as accessible as she was in the past. How comforting it would be to return to the life we once shared, to live again in this apartment, to make Riverside Park and this stretch of Broadway my territory again, after my years of exile. But then, as I stepped into my old apartment, moving down the hall to the living room, I was shocked to find Peter sitting on the couch. Seeing him there, so comfortable and sleek, I thought, 'this is like a Jew walking into a place of supposed safety only to find a member of the Gestapo lying in wait, welcomed by the hosts.'

Peter smiled, the same smile I had seen on his parents and one that, on occasion in the months since my return from Oxford, I had seen on Meredith as well. It was a smile with no heat.

'I've spoken with my lawyers, Jeremy. They've made a referral, and the other firm, you know, they can do it all at our place, this evening or tomorrow, although I think the sooner the better, don't you?'

'Do what exactly?'

'Go over the facts of the case as you've laid them out, look at the evidence, the files you've received and all your bank records if you have them. Maybe you could print them out and bring them, and then we can start to think about how to deal with the authorities, if that becomes necessary, I mean, if the lawyers think there's anything that has to be addressed. Can I ask, has anyone else seen the files you've received?'

'The doormen at my building.'

'You showed the doormen your files?'

'They saw the boxes I received. Which contained the files.'

'But not the files themselves?'

'No, not the files per se.'

'So you're the only person who has actually looked at the files, the papers I mean, with the words and numbers printed on them.'

'Yes, that's correct. They're, you know, they're very private.'

I thought he was concerned that other people might have discovered what was happening, but then, looking just off to one side, he asked, 'And you're certain the files are not, just maybe, something you sent yourself?'

'Why would I do such a thing?'

'I don't know, and forgive me if this seems rude, but are you certain these files don't contain, I don't know, scrap paper, or even blank pages?'

'Absolutely certain. And the record of phone calls made and received is not something I could have produced myself.'

'You could have noted down every time you made a call, who you were calling, the duration, the times. You could be one of those people who never deletes his browsing history and then printed it all out.'

'But I didn't. I wouldn't. I'm not obsessive compulsive, Peter, if that's what you're suggesting. Susan can attest to that.'

'It's true. Jeremy's too chaotic to be OC,' Susan laughed, though there was no delight in it. 'But he was always a very good liar. Why do you think he had to leave Columbia? Flexibility with the truth. Hazardous for a historian.'

'Enough, Susan. I'm not making this up and I resent the suggestion that I might be.'

'Why do you think you feel so defensive about this, Jeremy?' Peter asked.

'Listen, I could get in a taxi right now, go home, get the boxes, and bring them back, if that will convince you.'

'Is it important to you that we be convinced of your sanity?'

'Yes, of course it is. What kind of idiot are you?'

Peter paused. 'There's no need to be insulting. We're just trying to help you.'

'I'm not being insulting. I'm frustrated. You're frustrating me because you're casting doubt on what I'm saying. Why are you even here, Peter?'

'I was in the neighborhood and stopped by to see how Susan is doing. She was upset after your visit yesterday.'

Susan shuffled across the living room and stared out the window.

I found myself no longer able to read the language of her movements as I once could, the way a certain posture might convey assent, or a tilt of the head backwards and to the left would betray disapproval. 'We were all upset, Peter. Not just me.'

As always in that apartment I was conscious of the sound of traffic from the Henry Hudson Parkway and the click of the radiators that were so impossible to control that on some frigid winter days we'd have to open the windows just to regulate the temperature, and the dog, this new dog who was so like Lotte she could have been a clone, had given up on the three humans and stretched out her front legs, resting her white chin on them as those dark eyes, twitching beneath her brows, glanced from Susan to Peter as if she knew one or the other of them would eventually take her out for a walk. Why Peter? I wondered, why should the dog look at Peter with such familiarity?

'I know who's doing it.'

'Who's doing what?'

'The person sending the files. It's your friend, Michael Ramsey.'

Peter snorted. 'If you think that then you really must be crazy, Jeremy. Michael is a paper-pusher. He's like the most boring IT nerd.'

'You don't know where he works.'

'He works for a bank. I can't remember off the top of my head.'

'He works for the NSA.'

'You know this for a fact?'

'It's the only logical explanation. He's been standing outside my building on Houston watching me at night. Yesterday he sent me a box of photographs, images of me in Oxford and London and New York, pictures of Fadia and my son, and the doorman took a picture of Ramsey *delivering* the box. So I know for a fact it's him who's doing it. And if he's not doing it, then he's the messenger for someone else, but I don't think that's likely. Last night he stood out on Houston *waiting* for me to see him. He wants me to know but he's also being careful, because the NSA, or whoever it is, they're watching too. He can't email me. He sure as hell can't phone me. But he can stand out on the street and send me printouts of files and let me know what's happening. He knows there's no reason I should be watched in this way. He *knows* and he's trying to help me, Peter.'

Perhaps Peter shook his head, but he gave me the kind of look I associate with the condescendingly sane person who sees madness everywhere while remaining convinced they themselves must always remain of sound mind.

'And you're certain the photographs you received yesterday aren't simply your own collection of photographs from the past decade? Maybe something you shipped separately, from Britain.'

'The box wasn't shipped, Peter! Like the others it was delivered by *hand*, no postage. In any case, I don't own a camera. I haven't owned a camera since Susan and I split. She was always the photographer.'

'It's true,' she said. 'Jeremy had a terrible eye.'

'Besides which I'm *in* the pictures I received, and when I'm not, they've been taken in places where I have not been present on the dates they were taken. Don't you see? Why are you both staring at me like that?'

'We just think maybe you need help, Jeremy,' Susan said, her voice strained like it used to be when I could tell she was out of patience with the world. 'You don't look well. Your skin is gray. Your eyes—I haven't seen you look this way before.'

So I was wrong, Susan was against me as well, and it was then that I began to wonder whether she and Peter were colluding, and if, perchance, *Peter* might somehow be behind everything that has been happening. Perhaps he wants me out of the way. Perhaps I am too great an embarrassment for him and his family. Perhaps he has known about Fadia for some time, perhaps Stephen Jahn has not only been phoning my mother, but has been poisoning everyone against me, or perhaps Michael Ramsey is merely one of Peter's many employees. Whatever the case, I knew it was pointless talking to either of them, so I excused myself and said I'd be in touch if there were any further developments.

As I walked back up to West End Avenue I noticed the light in Dr. Sebastian's office was on, and nearly stopped to see if she had a moment to speak, but then thought better of it. I was not in the correct frame of mind, but I wanted to see her again, or felt, for a moment that flitted in and out of my passing thoughts, that seeing her might dismiss whatever remaining doubts I was having about my sanity, and it's true, I know this, that the questions Peter asked me were infuriating because they did make me wonder if I might be going mad. I took the subway home, and sitting in that rattling metal car I saw how easily I might become one of the city's legions of unhinged, a man muttering and unkempt, scribbling proof of his own life on scraps of paper, covering every surface of notebook upon notebook, ever convinced of his sanity.

But then, I came out of the subway at West 4th Street, and who was propped against the newsstand reading a magazine but Michael Ramsey. He was in his dark pea coat, with the collar turned up and a knitted black cap, looking like a Danish sailor. As soon as I was next to him Ramsey looked right up at me, as if he knew in advance the exact moment—down to the millisecond—of my arrival, as if he was tracking me on his phone, watching my progress through the city, a pulsing blue dot on the map. He smiled, and it was the smile that disarmed me. There was nothing smirking or menacing about it, nothing practiced, as in the smiles of Peter, or, it occurred to me, Stephen Jahn. Instead I read pity and concern, but also a kind of desperation from Michael that I should understand what he was trying to do.

I slowed down as I passed, waiting for him to speak.

'We have to stop meeting this way,' he said, and turned down into the subway.

ON TUESDAY I had to teach. My students were already half checked-out for the Christmas vacation but I tried nonetheless to draw them together, despite the blank stares and the expressions of fatigue, the excuses when it emerged that more than half the class had failed to watch Mohammad Rasoulof's *Manuscripts Don't Burn*. One girl who was sipping a bottle of soda and eating a bag of chips complained she had been sick, too sick to watch anything but reality TV.

'Lay off the soda and chips,' I shouted. 'Fruit and vegetables! Protein! Your body's sick because you're putting nothing but crap into it. You eat crap, you turn into crap, your mind becomes crap! You eat like that, of course you're sick. I don't want to hear any more excuses. You don't do the work you better be on your deathbed.'

The whole class flinched. A boy in the back of the room whimpered. I'd never said anything like that to any group of students in all my years of teaching. On the contrary, I have always tried to be the easygoing and sympathetic professor who students love. That day, however, I could no longer find the other, kinder Jeremy. He had retreated behind some anterior curtain, or perhaps I had at last allowed myself to step over that boundary in my mind, to run free in the great, perforated state that had long been encroaching on the enclave of my rational self. I struggled through the rest of the hour, teaching only to the brightest among my students, showing clips of the moments when the writers in the film are confronted with their tormentors, when one writer in particular speaks into a dead phone line knowing that someone is listening, that everything he says and does is being monitored.

On leaving the building I was unsurprised to see Michael Ramsey standing across the street, but as I walked towards him, he turned the corner and disappeared into a crowd of students. Was it actually him? Did he expect me to follow? Was he suggesting that here, on campus, we might find a place to meet that would be private enough to speak freely?

That evening a car collected me and my four boxes and drove me uptown where I spent several hours in Meredith and Peter's apartment with a team of lawyers, men and women, thirties to fifties, white and black and Asian, who grilled me and took away the files for forensic examination. I was told to wait. They would contact me in due course. For now, they suggested I should carry on as if nothing were amiss, although it might be wise, they cautioned, to delay any international travel. Borders can be tricky places. Leaving might not be a problem, but arriving elsewhere, or returning home, could prove difficult.

DAYS PASS. I READ and teach and wait. I take the elevator to the lobby, I speak with Ernesto and the other doormen, Rafa and Manu and Ignacio. I walk to the grocery store around the corner where I pay more than a dollar for an organic apple, sometimes I go in the middle of the night to buy cereal or cheese because the novelty of a truly twenty-four-hour business is still fresh, and walking those aisles at two in the morning, speaking with clerks who would rather be anywhere else, I notice the enclosed seating area where people can consume a quick meal, a collection of plastic chairs and fiberglass tables that is closed overnight lest the homeless or the destitute try to seek refuge.

I ATTEND A guest lecture in the English Department by a young Pakistani-American professor at Princeton who speaks about Jafar Panahi's films *Closed Curtain* and *This Is Not a Film*, both of which I teach in my Cinema of Surveillance course. There are only ten people in the room, no worse than you might find at a research seminar in Oxford, but not what I would have hoped for in a city like this. I go to dinner afterward with the host from the English Department—an Englishman around my own age who lives just downstairs from me in the Silver Towers—and the young professor from Princeton. We eat at a Malaysian restaurant and the next day I end up with food poisoning, which keeps me circling my apartment, orbiting bed and toilet and kitchen sink, and in so pacing my small quarters, I think how quickly I might accommodate myself to confinement.

EVERY DAY, EITHER in the morning or evening, sometimes at lunch, I encounter Michael Ramsey. Occasionally we greet each other, but often he pretends not to see me and simply walks away once I begin approaching him and then I ask myself if it is really Michael I am seeing, or if my brain is playing tricks. Sometimes I call after him, shouting his name, but he never turns around.

THE LAWYERS PETER engaged on my behalf have not returned the files, and so I remain in a state of uncertainty. How much could a group of New York lawyers determine about Saif's associations? Such matters would seem to be beyond their investigatory powers, but perhaps I am naïve about what is now possible. All I can hope is that Fadia's account, the account into which my money dribbles on the first of each month, ends up being in her name alone, and that the only serious issue is one of relation: Fadia's relation to Saif, and my relation to Fadia.

ALTHOUGH THE EXAM PERIOD finished on December 19th, I have decided to stay in the city for the holidays, hunkering in my warm apartment as the Polar Vortex again swings into force. One morning, a few days before Christmas, after a sober night indoors watching movies and eating takeout Vietnamese, Ernesto buzzes from downstairs to say that someone has dropped off a package for me, and so, on that frigid day, I open yet another box and find inside a shiny black plastic block, the size of a hardback edition of *War and Peace* or *The Collected Earlier Poems* of William Carlos Williams or *Crime and Punishment*, although in fact what it reminds me of more than any book is the humming monolith in Stanley Kubrick's *2001*. I notice the cables and understand this is some kind of external drive, and although I worry for a moment that connecting it to my computer may mean opening myself to a virus or some heretofore unimagined level of surveillance, I decide nothing could be worse than what I am already experiencing.

When I connect the drive and open the icon on the desktop, I am, at first, confused. There must be a glitch, because the window that opens presents an exact copy of the files and folders on my computer's own desktop. Only a few more clicks and I understand that the drive contains not only a complete copy of my computer's contents, but one which is current to this very day, the last changes being recorded at 7:52 this morning.

Assuming this is still the work of Michael Ramsey it is clear to me there is now only one possible meaning: a warning that everything I do, write, read, view online, even what I do *offline*, is accessible. When I am connected to the internet, whoever they are can read everything I have written, even the documents I regard as profoundly private: the diary I keep in a word-processing file document, drafts of occasional poems, pieces of correspondence that, in my old-fashioned way, I sometimes print, sign, and send off in envelopes to their recipients. There is no longer any such thing as privacy, unless one writes letters and diaries and poems longhand, as I write this document now, and even so, our government has long made a habit of scanning the exterior of all mail. It would be clear to the watchers to whom I am writing and from whom I am receiving mail even if they cannot necessarily discern the contents of the letters themselves. The phone Meredith gave me, this, too, has turned me into a trackable subject, someone whose location can be so precisely pinpointed that Michael Ramsey may now find me throughout the day, any given day, any-where I go. The phone, I understand, is why he has been showing up all over the city, not a bad penny but a red flag, mobile and rippling, trying to catch my attention. And then, I think of the message he left on my old phone, stashed in my refrigerator, on that strange evening a few weeks ago, a message that was also a warning: 'Phones listen.'

Even when turned off? Do phones listen even when they appear to be powerless?

I realize now that in writing this, in naming Mr. Ramsey, I may be putting him in some kind of danger of reprisal by whoever employs him. Although I did not think about the implications of revealing his identity at the start of this testament, how many days or weeks ago I began writing it, this was not my intention. I mean him no harm. No harm should come to him.

AFTER THE ARRIVAL OF the box this morning, I phoned Dr. Sebastian and asked if she could still make time to see me before the holidays.

'Come now, if you can,' she said. 'I'm going away tomorrow.'

As I walked from the station on Broadway to her office on West End Avenue, I stopped to pick up a token of the season, a basket of pears and nuts, almost as if I were a suitor.

'My patients do not usually bring gifts,' she said, leading me into the consulting room, which I remembered as more austere than it is. The white walls I had stored in my memory are instead dove gray, the wooden floors covered in Chobi rugs, the furniture a mix of nineteenth-century antiques and midcentury Danish chairs. African masks decorate one of the walls. I remembered none of it from my first visit.

'I wanted to make up for the short notice, and the time of year.'

'I am secular, Jeremy, but thank you nonetheless.' She put the basket to one side and rather than sitting behind her desk as she had on our first meeting, took a seat next to me in one of the two chairs intended for patients. 'So the scans look good. No anomalies. But perhaps, if there are still questions, you should see someone else. I would be happy to make a referral.'

'To a psychiatrist?'

'Or a psychotherapist. Or both.'

Friends suggested I go into therapy when my marriage to Susan broke down, but I concluded I was better off running and reading to deal with the depression. I stopped running at some point between deciding to leave Oxford and reestablishing myself in New York, and reading on its own is no longer enough to deal with the anxiety. Reading, in fact, produces its own forms of anxiety. Worries and pre-occupations suggested by some other person's prose start flurrying into my brain, preventing me from sleeping through the night. I realized I had been sleepless off and on for weeks, medicating myself with scotch and Miles Davis and midnight screenings of old Coppola and Alan J. Pakula and Sydney Pollack flicks from my childhood, telling myself that *The Conversation* or *Klute* or *Three Days of the Condor* were really research, preparation for the class I was teaching on the Cinema of Surveillance, and trying to convince myself that no one had thought adequately about the formal techniques used in the films, techniques that might be seen as outgrowths of a changing cultural landscape in the 1970s, the decade in which film, video, and audio surveillance were becoming commonplace, form and content united, a consequence of historical forces, as much about advancements in technology as the entrenchment and expansion of the military industrial complex and its imbrication with the intelligence community. This was what I did to help myself sleep. This is why, I am beginning to think, I remain unable to sleep. My mind will not stop churning.

'I'm not interested in talk therapy. I don't think there are any traumas that might explain what's been happening. I'm fairly certain I'm not delusional or suffering from blackouts. I'm anxious and a little depressed, but probably not significantly more so than most people who find themselves whiplashed by cultural dislocation. No worse, in fact, than most New Yorkers.'

'We could always try an anti-depressant, or even a mild anti-anxiety drug. Some people need it, others find they do not. People of high intelligence, like you, Jeremy—'

'For the sake of argument,' I said, interrupting her, 'if the problem *were* in my brain, what might it be?'

Dr. Sebastian raised her chin, holding my gaze as she moved her head, and at the same time her hands reached across to her desk for the ledger in which she had taken notes on our previous meeting. She glanced down, opened to the relevant page, and looked up again.

'It was just an apparent memory lapse, correct?'

'That was the first issue. Since then I've been receiving boxes of very intimate files. It has been suggested to me by some members of my family that I might have sent myself the files, to shore up my belief in what they judge to be a paranoid delusion.'

'You have no memory of sending yourself the files?'

'None whatsoever. Not even the faintest glimmer of a memory. Every box that arrives is a surprise, and a horror.'

'And so, you want to know if you could be doing this, sending yourself these files, and yet have no memory of it each time?'

'Essentially, yes. We're not talking about a single event, but a series of events, a suite of behaviors, if you like, about which I have no memory.'

'If that were the case, and I want to underscore my skepticism, then we might be looking at some kind of dissociative disorder, although I would certainly then suggest you see a psychiatrist as well. There are really no childhood traumas? Military service?'

'Nothing I would call traumatic. Mild, boring, a completely dull childhood in the suburbs. No broken bones, two loving parents who were married until my father died and never did so much as spank me. An adult life lived in libraries and classrooms and academic offices. Although I suppose that can be traumatic in its own way.'

Dr. Sebastian looked down at the ledger, as if it might contain an answer. 'Let me ask you some questions.'

'Shoot.'

'Shoot?'

'Go ahead.'

'Right. Do you ever find yourself driving in your car or riding on the subway and then realizing you have no recollection of the beginning of the trip?'

'No, nothing like that.'

'When you're talking to someone, do you ever have the sense, all of a sudden, that you have not heard what the other person is saying?'

'I suppose so, on occasion. Not very often. I try to be a good listener. Susan, my ex-wife, she used to complain that my mind would wander whenever she started speaking, that I would just grunt my approval without listening attentively, but no, for the most part, I am present when someone is talking to me.'

'Have you ever looked up and wondered how it is that you are where you are?'

'In an existential sense, or a physical one?'

Dr. Sebastian smiled. 'Physical.'

'No, nothing like that.'

She asked me whether I ever found myself in clothes with no recollection of getting dressed in them. No, never. Discovering objects in my belongings that I did not recognize as my own? No, not that I can remember. I know the contents of my life, my possessions and losses.

'Has anyone ever approached you, insisting they have met you before, or know you well, and you have no memory of this person?'

A cold sharp pain throbbed in my chest. 'Yes, that did happen recently. Thanksgiving weekend. I met a young man—I've been meeting him regularly, all over the city, even outside of the city—who insists he was my student, but I have no recollection of having taught him, or even of having met him, and yet we seemed to know each other—according to him—for a considerable length of time, at least two years, more than a decade ago.'

Dr. Sebastian scribbled in her ledger. 'Is this young man the only such person?'

'As far as I can remember.'

Question followed question, and in most cases the condition she described did not fit my own experiences, or my sense of those experiences, and yet enough of the questions did fit that I began to feel a swelling anxiety that manifested itself as shortness of breath. I described to her exactly what had happened with the boxes, how their content seemed to include material I could not objectively have produced myself, and how the files were now undergoing forensic examination by lawyers and private investigators.

'Let me ask you,' I said, after she had finished, 'if the authorities came to ask what you had gleaned from this single conversation, what would you say?'

'I might be required to divulge what I know, or what I have concluded about you on the basis of our consultation, particularly if I feel that you might be a danger to others.'

'In other words, you might tell the authorities I was crazy.'

Dr. Sebastian grimaced. '*If* that was my conclusion, and if I was required by a court to give evidence, then yes. And if it was a federal case, you should know that there is no doctor–patient privilege.' She paused, narrowing her eyes and inclining her head. 'Have you committed a crime, Jeremy?'

'That is the question. Whether I might have committed a crime, or whether I'm crazy, or both, I suppose. Every morning I get out of bed and try to go about my day, I cannot shake the feeling that I might be crazy. *Am* I crazy?'

'Let us rather not use that word. What I can say is this: your brain scan is normal, although that does not necessarily give us a complete picture. In some ways the technology is still rudimentary, and just because the brain looks normal does not mean that other psychological factors cannot be at work. On the basis of the questions I have asked and the answers you have given, it is possible that you have some kind of Unspecified Dissociative Disorder. *But*, and this is a very important qualification, the fact of the boxes, and the way you keep meeting this young man, the sorts of coincidence that do not seem like coincidence at all, as well as your demeanor, the way I observe you behaving, your general appearance, all that leads me to believe you are very intelligent and also very sane, as much as any intelligent person can remain sane in a world largely governed and determined by far less intelligent minds.'

'So what does this mean?'

'It means, I think, that you should trust in what you believe is happening around you.'

'But what if I don't know what's happening?'

'Then you have to find an answer.'

FLIPPING BACK THROUGH THESE pages, I find myself searching for a succession of clues that might lead to a place of certainty, rather than to further branching questions. The files and photographs I turned over to the lawyers still have not been returned. I understand the investigations are incomplete, but without those records I cannot help doubting all that I think may have happened. Only the monolithic hard drive remains, locked in my desk drawer, and who is to say I did not buy it myself and engage the backup system on my computer to create a perfect archive? Who is to say I might not have sent it out by messenger, and arranged for its immediate return precisely in order to buttress a delusion? Can the conscious mind partition what it knows, keeping one part in the dark as another part works frantically behind the curtain, turning gears and knobs, pressing buttons, amplifying and distorting the voice to deceive both its other self and those that encounter the physical person? Fireworks and smoke machines to distract the terrified, among whom might be included one's own true self. On the basis of Dr. Sebastian's questions, I find myself continuing to contemplate this as a possibility.

Each day, I see Michael Ramsey somewhere in the city. I follow, and the next moment, just as I'm about to catch up with him, I find he disappears. I stand at my bedroom window and look out on Houston Street, waiting for him to appear. An advertisement painted on a building, with images of palm trees and white beaches, instructs me: 'Find Your Beach.' Perhaps I need a holiday.

There is news of terrorists in Syria crucifying a girl who was the victim of rape. There is other news of terrorists in Iraq throwing half a dozen homosexual men off a building. I know this is not the first time such things have happened, and I cannot help wondering if Saif might be among those who conclude they have the right to pass judgment on the fate of strangers. Are such acts ultimately so different from the execution of inmates in American prisons, or the rape and murder of a teenage girl in Iraq by an American soldier? Surely that is part of the point these terrorists, in their evil, are trying to make.

A few days later, *The Journal of Modern History* asks me to review a new study about a group of leading British historians who were placed under surveillance by MI5 in the decades after the end of the Second World War, a decision made largely because those men were Communists or thought to be Communists or had simply traveled to Russia at some point in their lives. How like those men I might be, although I am no terrorist, and I have never even been to the Middle East, never traveled to Egypt, not even transited through the airport at Dubai on the way back and forth to one unremarkable destination or another. But perhaps logic does not rule the judgment of men in hidden rooms or standing on the tops of buildings, readying themselves to detain one man or push another to his death.

A NEW BOX arrives, this one, identical to the first three, contains all my bank records and IRS returns, beginning from the year in which I first met Fadia. This is not in my mind, surely, and yet, how easy it would be for me to order back statements, to pull up copies of my returns, to make the theater of my brain suspend its disbelief in the film projected on its internal screen, in the fiction—is it fiction?—that the projectionist has chosen from the reels at his disposal. Fiction or documentary? Campus melodrama or spy thriller? In what genre am I trapped?

I appear to be free for now, however imperfectly, and I give thanks for that at least, although I sometimes wake in the night shouting, asking to be released. Perhaps all I need is to see open country and an expanse of sky. I have not returned to Rhinebeck since Thanksgiving weekend and cannot recall when I last spoke to my mother. From the past two days there are dozens of missed calls from Meredith on my phone. I log into my computer, I read Meredith's plaintive emails but find no energy to reply. I look in my sent mail and discover messages that I myself appear to have written—not unlike the messages I supposedly wrote to my student Rachel—but once more I have no memory of writing them. There is an invitation from Meredith to join her and Peter for a Christmas Eve party at their apartment. My mother will be there, staying for several days, Peter's parents as well. I should feel free to come early on the day. I think of going upstate instead, absenting myself, but the desperation in Meredith's tone tells me I should simply accept, which I do. She replies in seconds, offering to send a car. No, on Christmas Eve it makes more sense to take the subway, traffic will be impossible. She replies again, offering that I could come early in the day and stay over, but no, I thank her, I would rather sleep in my own bed.

The night before Christmas Eve I spend alone, eating Vietnamese takeout and watching *Blade Runner*, the director's authoritative final cut, which seems to make Deckard more unambiguously android than the other versions I have seen over the years. Once, almost twenty-five years ago, when I was still a graduate student, I flew into Los Angeles one night for a conference. As we penetrated the clouds a landscape of orange lights, glowing through the darkness and smog, came into view, so much like the one Ridley Scott conjured that I imagined for an instant we had flown into the future. Can I see my own place in the system? Can I, unlike Deckard, know what I am beneath the conscious fiction I present to others as well as myself? Will the true instinct seek to express itself if placed under threat? What is it that I think I might be? An android, no, certainly not, but what is Deckard if not (or not only) an android? A revolutionary, an insurgent, a sleeper agent. Perhaps in walking blindfolded through this country of my birth, this motherland I love, the home I want more than anything to find homely, *heimlich*, the zone of my greatest familiarity, I will eventually begin to see with other eyes.

THE CAWING OF CROWS in wet winter air was England for me, and that crying through bare limbs over lawns which remain green beneath an occasional frost, moss growing dense on all that is still, never failed to hollow me out, leaving a husk of melancholy. In Oxford I avoided going out after dark. I feared the damp streets in greasy orange lamplight and the unpredictability of English men, the surges of violence that seemed to come from nowhere. For wearing a tuxedo, a colleague claimed he was attacked one night after a High Table dinner at Lincoln College, beaten on Ship Street in the center of town as bystanders observed, egging on his assailants, who had no interest in his money or possessions. It was all about class. That is a country in need of revolution, or perhaps every country now is, throwing over the old, the ossified, all the systems we use to destroy ourselves and our world. Burn it all to the ground, only save the art and the archives, the libraries, the knowledge of our past, and then build something better.

For a moment I allow myself to relax to the bleat of taxi horns. I exhale. I feel the warmth and dryness of the sheets when I wake on Christmas Eve day. I touch walls that have never been damp.

After so long with no word, I open my email and see a name that makes my heart flip. I click, hold my breath, and scan down the screen before returning to the top to read once more, slowly:

Dear Jeremy,

Forgive me for contacting you like this and please, accept my apology for not replying sooner. I read the emails and messages when you sent them but in your absence I did not know at first what to say, and still I do not entirely know how to think about what has happened between us, or what you did to me, and yes, I do think of it in that way, that you did this to me. Although I was a willing party, the balance of power, I think, means consent could not have been freely given, not absolutely, if you see?

I am making good progress on my DPhil. My parents are well, and my father talks of returning to Cairo, if a deal can be struck with those who are now in power.

I am writing because I think you should see your son, who has a few words, and sometime soon is certain to ask questions about his father. Whether next year or the year after, the day will come, and when he does ask I do not want to tell him that I have lost touch with you. If we came to New York, would you see us? Would we even, perhaps, be able to stay with you (most of my father's accounts are still frozen, and the money you give me, for which I am grateful, would not stretch to this kind of travel)?

I need to make clear that I do not envision the recommencement of some kind of relationship between you and me, or at least only insofar as we *are* related, as the parents of Selim, but I also do not want to stand in the way of you having a relationship with our son. It seems unfair to both of you—to him especially—if I were to prevent that.

Please will you tell me what you think, and how it might work? I would like to come for New Year, if that is not too presumptuous. There are other issues to discuss, potentially, which would be better done in person, things to do with the longer term, and what I see as the necessity of Selim's protection, and his multiple nationalities. I hope that is something we might sort out in America. Do you understand what I mean? I hope so.

Yours ever,
Fadia

I write back immediately, knowing as I do so that Fadia's message has been read, and whatever I type, perhaps even in the moment I type it, will be collected, reviewed, and judged.

Dear Fadia,

Please, do come, as soon as you can. I have transferred additional monies into your account to pay for the flights and whatever else you may need. Say if you need more. Come for as long as you wish. You may stay here, on your terms. There are two unused rooms, a guest bathroom, and you would be free to come and go as you wish. I understand all that you imply, at least I think I do, and I can only say, for now, that I apologize for what I did and yet, if there is a hope of knowing my son, I cannot feel regret about what happened, except for the way it has affected you. It is my hope that my daughter will want to meet you and Selim, and my mother as well. If you give me your new number I will phone you.

With all good wishes and sincerity,
Jeremy

As I click SEND it occurs to me that in inviting Fadia and Selim here, I may unwittingly be putting them in as much peril as I believe myself to be in, that all three of us might disappear if suddenly collected together again in one place, on American soil. Who is to say they will even be allowed entry? Nonetheless, with a selfishness I recognize as habitual, I am consumed by joy. All the way to Columbus Circle my heart is humming, a song in my mouth as I walk up Broadway in the winter twilight and then pause as I did on Thanksgiving morning to see what is playing at the Lincoln Plaza Cinemas. There is the face of that government whistle-blower, eyes downcast, advertising a documentary about his revelations, and while I stand looking at the green-hued poster I hear a voice behind me.

'Excuse me, could I borrow your phone?' says a man, and before I turn, I know it will be Michael Ramsey.

I pat my pockets and realize I have left the new phone at home. 'No such luck.'

'Smart man,' he says, and nods at the movie poster. 'We could see it together, ditch the party.'

'A chance to talk?'

'Something like that.'

'You going to tell me what's going on?'

He arches an eyebrow but says nothing, and then, as we walk to the Century Building, he draws closer to me. 'There are some people in this world who just gather information. They don't deal in consequences. But let's imagine that one of the information gatherers—let's call him the archivist—noticed a name he recognized in the course of his work, say it's the name of one of the archivist's former teachers, maybe someone who taught him in high school or college, and in seeing the teacher's name, memories of the man begin to return and the archivist becomes interested, he wants to know why his old teacher's name is being flagged, and so he starts looking more closely at the activity he can see.'

We arrive at the side door, announce ourselves, enter the elevator and ascend alone. 'The more the archivist looks at what his teacher has been doing, the way he's been living his life, and remember he can see just about everything, from spending patterns to travel to the kind of things his teacher has been buying with a credit or debit card, the more the archivist becomes convinced there is no real reason to be watching the teacher, but he knows, he can see, how other people might disagree and perhaps he even knows, this archivist, that other people, people who push the buttons that make the archivist do what he does every day, are in the process of disagreeing, very actively disagreeing, that the people around and above him are getting ready to act, assembling a case, drawing conclusions on the basis of associ-ation and little else. You understand what I'm saying?'

'And if the teacher became aware of what might be happening, and, say, consulted lawyers, and the lawyers did not seem to think there was any great need for concern?'

'Maybe the teacher has the wrong lawyers,' he says, looking ahead at the elevator doors, his mouth scarcely moving.

'So what should the teacher do in such a situation?'

'Let's say, for the sake of argument—' he pushes the button for the top floor of the building, '—that the teacher has a family connec-tion to one of the most powerful media figures in the country. Perhaps it's a relative by marriage, a brother-in-law or son-in-law. And that relative could be persuaded to run a story, put the teacher on the cover, exposing all his warts for the world to see, turning over all the evidence that might be in his possession for the public themselves to peruse. When the public looks at this teacher, they'll see a mirror of their own lives. The teacher is ordinary. Sure, maybe he lived outside the country for a period of time, and that puts him in a minority, but otherwise he is a completely ordinary American whose life is no longer private.'

'It sounds too simple.' We arrive at the highest floor, the doors open, and we stand for a moment looking out at the empty hallway before Michael presses the button to take us down to Meredith and Peter's floor.

'Simple is elegant. Simple is effective. To do it properly, you understand, the teacher would have to let strangers read absolutely *everything* that might have been revealed to him, no matter how embarrassing, and even then some: turn over every document in his possession, all of his papers, files, notes, publications, everything he has ever written, every photograph. He knows he's done nothing illegal and obliterating his own privacy is a way to prove this to the authorities, but also to make a point to the whole country.'

'It could make the teacher's life impossible. He might be asked to resign his position.'

'He has wealthy relatives. Money is no concern. He will be taken care of no matter what happens. How many people are in such a position? How many Americans can risk sacrificing their career and their privacy to make a point that people like the archivist believe has to be made but are too afraid, too precarious, to make themselves? The archivist is just a drone inside the system. It's one thing for a guy like him to tell people what's happening. It would be easy to call him a traitor and dismiss every allegation he makes.'

'And then put him in prison.'

'Exactly. Or force him into exile. But have a man like the *teacher* come forward, and it begins to look much more personal, more preposterous, but also more horrifying. People could relate to it, and in coming forward the teacher would also be protecting himself.'

'And if the teacher could not bring himself to do this?'

'The alternative is a country that looks nothing like the country we imagine we live in. A country without privacy is a country without freedom. The archivist does not want to live in that country. And if the teacher doesn't go public he makes himself disposable. Easily discredited, easily disappeared.'

'They wouldn't do that to American citizens.'

'Don't be naïve.'

The elevator opens and we turn, walking together down the hall to my daughter's door. Meredith appears before we can knock, standing in the threshold smiling.

Everything I do is predictable. I can go nowhere and do nothing without being followed—or worse, anticipated.

MY MOTHER IS already there and before I can say anything further to Mr. Ramsey, she draws me aside.

'Meredith's friends are only interested in one another. They never ask me any questions about myself. It's impossible to have a really meaningful conversation with them. All they want to talk about is business and I just find that all so empty and *pointless*. No one wants to talk about art or music or books, none of them care about anything unless they can buy it and watch it increase in value and then be able to sell it again. I sometimes wonder how you could have let Meredith marry into such a group of people.'

'She married Peter, not the people around him.'

'It's the same thing. Can't you see that? It's the same goddamn thing, Jeremy.'

'Have you had any more phone calls?'

'I get phone calls every day. Dozens of them. I'm on that Do Not Call list and they still call me. I had a woman saying she was from some computer company and there was a problem with my security and if I didn't give her access to my desktop—some kind of remote control thing—then I'd be opening myself up to being hacked, and I said I'm not doing anything over the phone, and she said, well then prepare to be hacked and hung up. I was so upset!'

'You shouldn't believe anyone who calls anymore. But remember you had a call over Thanksgiving weekend from someone who was slandering me.'

'Oh . . . *him*. Yeah, he still calls. He never stopped. He always says more or less the same thing, but I think he's a nut. Is he some student you failed?'

'Are you sure it's always the same person?'

'Oh yes. Fruity accent, neither British nor American, and I know him the moment he calls because there's always this slight clicking delay before he starts talking. I tell him to stop calling but he just keeps going on and on and I tell him Jeremy's nothing like what you say he is, and anyway if you've got a child with some Egyptian that's your business.'

'So Meredith told you.'

'Of course she told me. Why didn't you tell me the truth when I asked?'

'Shame, I guess.'

'But that's just stupid. Am I ever going to meet the kid? I feel a pain about it.'

'Soon. He and his mother are planning a trip to New York.'

My mother's eyes grow red. 'That makes me so happy,' she whispers.

'I can't make any promises.'

'What does *that* mean?'

'I can't promise she'll be willing to meet you.'

'She doesn't have a choice about it. I want to see my grandson.'

THE REST OF the day unfolds with such predictability that it is not in any meaningful way different from Thanksgiving's gathering, although I recognize how, taken together, the two holiday parties mark a departure from my old life or lives, the years in Oxford being accountable as a life unto their own. This now feels like a distinct new stage, one that continues to evolve in unpredictable ways.

As I read the most recent issue of Peter's magazine I contemplate outing myself to the nation, even the world, waking up one morning to find my face on the cover. My mother and ex-wife and daughter and son-in-law and my son-in-law's parents circle one another, falling off into clusters of conversation. How would they be affected? Would all our lives become impossible?

From time to time Meredith disappears to check on the kitchen and returns to the living room looking so singularly unflustered that I wonder how Susan and I could ever claim responsibility for the person she has become. Her self-assurance is a quality she found on her own; we never modeled anything of the kind. How, in the face of such calm, can I possibly present what Ramsey has outlined? In revealing myself, making public all the minutiae of the last decade or more of my life (and I cannot be certain Ramsey does not have further reserves of secrets to reveal), I would also be revealing aspects of the lives of my family and friends and colleagues, and those who would potentially suffer most from the exposure are Meredith, my mother, and, of course, Fadia and Selim. Is it worth the loss not just of my own privacy (however illusory it may prove), but also of my family's, merely to demonstrate to the world the extent and perniciousness of what our government is doing, or, more selfishly, to protect my own liberty? In the end, can I be certain beyond doubt that I have never done anything wrong? Am I whiter than white? Have I never strayed across the border of legality? Surely there is no one, anywhere, who is faultless.

Michael Ramsey leaves before I can speak to him again and I cannot help wondering where he will be on Christmas Day, whether he has a family in the city who cook for him or if he has returned to his office and is finding his nourishment by continuing to poke around in my life, or perhaps there is a girlfriend or boyfriend who will slave to make a turkey with all its accompaniments, or perhaps he is alone, in an apartment in Hoboken, eating Chinese takeout. No, I correct myself, I am certain he does not live in New Jersey. However he may have started in life, he is now a Manhattanite, one who can move with all the swiftness of mercury, element rather than god, the metal that measures temperature and just as easily poisons the well, making its victims crazy, emotionally labile, irritable, perhaps even paranoid. Has my own personal mercury made me mad as a hatter? And perhaps he is also my Mercury, my god of communication and messages, of trickery and thievery, perhaps even my conductor beyond this realm, to paradise or the underworld or whatever darkness awaits. If I were to believe in a god, I would have to choose Mercury, no other.

But must one do what a god commands?

ALTHOUGH I OFFERED to send a car to meet them at JFK, Fadia declined, saying they would get a taxi, there was no telling how long the passport queue or baggage claim might take and she did not want me paying exorbitant waiting fees. I expected them late this afternoon, and as the hours passed my anxiety grew, the shortness of breath, the cold stab near my heart. I tried the cell number she had given me but there was no answer. I texted and emailed, received no reply, and then, at nearly ten this evening, as the city was already churning with its celebratory New Year's mood, Ernesto rang the intercom to say they were downstairs.

For a week I have been imagining a new life with Fadia and Selim, envisioning the two of them established permanently in my apartment and half believing that the more clearly I see it the more likely it may become true. This is, I know, a particularly desperate variety of magical thinking. At first I picture us doing as Fadia suggested in her email, with no recommencement of our intimacy, but the longer she stays here I feel certain—I wish beyond logic or respect for whatever her own wishes might be—that she will look at me with greater affection, perhaps even love, and by such slow measures we will slip into being the family I confess to wanting since the moment she told me she was pregnant. So joined together in this way, as husband, wife, and child, all of the other issues, the problem of my uncertainty in the face of American law, must surely evaporate, for it would become clear to the authorities that Fadia poses no risk to anyone. Tracking her as I have been tracked, the intelligence agencies would see in her face and behavior that being related to Saif cannot possibly suggest anything about her own beliefs or loyalties.

As I stepped from the elevator I was aware of my own heartbeat, a vein pulsing in my foot, my hands gone cold. Fadia looked as she always has, a swirl of black coat, ivory scarf pulled up to cover her head, and there in her arms was our son, asleep, swaddled in white.

'Your country, Jeremy,' she sighed, rolling her eyes with a look of fatigue and exasperation. Without asking, she handed me Selim, who did not stir as she shifted him into my arms. He was plump without being fat, a healthy baby, his straight hair blond and yet dark at the roots, and on him I smelled that scent I had caught decades ago, during a warm spring day in Washington, DC, the aroma of an otherness that was at once strange and familiar, emanating from the boy who is now a man my age, a boy who, in my colander memory, might or might not have been called Amir, an Egyptian I assume later returned to his country, a boy from a good family like Fadia herself, a boy destined for public life as she herself might have been had she stayed. Who will Selim grow up to be? How, I thought in that moment, catching his scent, will I ever manage to let go of him? I will not do it willingly. I watched as Fadia managed the stroller and her suitcase, so practiced in her movements that I wondered if there had been other trips, to Paris or Cairo or who knew where else, trips that might have made the Department of Homeland Security look at her passport and wonder. What passports do they use? Egyptian? French? I still know nothing of such basic practicalities about her life.

'My phone doesn't seem to be working. Otherwise I would have called. I was interrogated for three hours at JFK. They took us into a little white room with no windows, and asked hundreds of questions, about my father and brother, about my uncle, what I was studying in Oxford, why I was coming here, how long I would be staying. At one point I didn't think they were going to let me into the country, or, worse, I imagined we were going to disappear, or that Selim might be taken. For a moment I even considered you might have tipped off the authorities in advance, just to take him from me.'

'I would never do that.' But how simple a solution it would have been, I thought, to sacrifice Fadia for the sake of Selim.

'No, I know that. I was exhausted and frightened. I told them I was coming to see you, that you were Selim's father, but we weren't married. I think they thought I was trying to stay here, and I said no, I showed the letter from College to prove I'm a full-time student, which seemed to satisfy them on that point at least. And a French passport is not without value, I guess. I demanded they let me phone the embassy and when they hesitated I started to panic and told them everything I know about Saif, which isn't so much, although apparently he is on a list, maybe several different lists. I gathered this from the questions they were asking. So I decided total honesty would be more prudent than any hint of deception or resistance.'

'I'm sorry it happened.'

'Why? It isn't your fault.'

'That doesn't stop me being sorry.'

She yawned and in the light of the elevator I saw how much the last six months have marked her. It was not just the flight, not even the work of motherhood, but perhaps the worry about how life is going to evolve in the coming years. There is a new quality carved into her face. The stone I once admired has become softer, more plastic, and the consciousness of death's proximity, which in the past I thought I saw in her expression, has been textured by a more nuanced aware-ness of the precariousness of life, the life she and I produced, the life she must protect. Or so I imagined. At the door I handed Selim back to his mother, and as he left my arms I found my heart was everywhere, torn and scattered between them.

'I bought a crib and put it in your room, although if you'd rather have separate rooms it's easily managed. I want you to be comfortable.'

'The same room is fine. He sleeps well. I won't be disturbed.'

I asked if she wanted something to eat, but no, she had eaten on the plane, she wasn't hungry, just a shower, she said, arranging our son on the mattress and already, swiftly, unpacking their things into the closet and chest of drawers. 'Pick him up if he cries.'

Not presuming to touch her or do anything that might make her feel ill at ease, I nodded, moving aside to let her pass. Tomorrow I should at least offer to put them in a hotel. 'No!' I imagine her saying. 'We want to be with you!'

As the water ran in the bathroom, I watched my boy's chest rise and fall, his nostrils distend, contract, the eyelids flutter, a sigh push itself out of his mouth. How like me as a baby he looks, the same blond straight hair. Only the dark roots are different, and the subtle olive complexion. Will my son be an American? Is that a choice his mother would allow him to make? Or will he always be foreign in the country of his father?

Now I sit here, fireworks exploding all over the city, as my son and his mother sleep down the hall, the fulfillment of my most profound desire since leaving Oxford, and the source of a pain I did not anticipate, the gnawing of an even greater desire: never again to be parted from either of them.

WHEN I WAKE ON the first day of a new year, the morning of my son's first birthday, Fadia is moving about in the kitchen, taking care to be quiet, opening cabinets, searching for something she cannot find, and then, in the distance, I hear the sharp cry of my son, the first time I have heard his voice since July, drawing me from bed and into the kitchen. Fadia sees me and smiles an apology, but this, I know, is what it means to live with a baby.

'Shall I go?' I offer.

'No, it's fine. I'm sorry I woke you. I was looking for the coffee.'

'In the freezer.'

'You shouldn't freeze coffee. It ruins the flavor.'

'Does it? I didn't know. I won't from now on.'

Fadia leaves the room as I make the coffee. A few minutes later she returns with Selim, who is awake and smiling.

'He needed a change.' Our son looks at me for an instant and then buries his head in Fadia's hair. 'Don't be shy,' she coos. 'Who's that? Remember? Is that papa? Can you say papa? He already says mama but I think he's confused. I usually speak to him in French.'

I reach out to touch Selim's hand but he pulls it away, tightening his fingers into a loose fist. If someone is watching us now, how banal they must think us, making coffee, changing diapers, getting to know each other once more. Surely the banality of our lives puts us above suspicion, or is banality no protection against algorithms and keyword searches and guilt by association?

We sit in the dining area, overlooking the street, which is still dark, not yet dawn.

'What would you like to do for his birthday?'

'It's so cold we could just stay here. Order in food. I don't like him being out in this weather for too long, and I have no urgent desire to see New York. I know it well enough already. All those childhood shopping trips. My parents used to own an apartment in the East 60s.'

'You don't like it?'

'No, I do, but you understand, everything shifts,' she says, adjusting her grip on Selim so she can sip her coffee more easily. She puts him down on the carpet and we watch as he crawls towards a collection of soft toys I bought in anticipation of his visit. 'That was thoughtful of you.'

'Making up for the last six months. He's not walking yet?'

'Pulling himself up. It won't be long. I'll need to get some things at the shops for him today.'

We linger over such nothings, watching our son until he needs to be fed, and then Fadia sweeps him up in her arms, raises her loose shirt, and supports his head. Let us be like this always, I think, so relaxed and at ease with one another, content and quiet in a life that might not be private but which proceeds as if it were, perhaps doing nothing to accommodate ourselves to the end of privacy except to live more ethically, to admit our faults, to assume transparency, but also to demand it of others, to insist on the right to know as much about the watchers as they about us.

'Do you ever see Stephen?' I ask, still not having told Fadia about the boxes, about Michael Ramsey, about the photographs of her life over the past months. I suppose it is a test, to find out if she will admit to the meeting I saw depicted in the photograph.

'I ran into him recently on the street. I don't like the man, but I greeted him, because it seemed impolite not to do so—it was ages since I had seen him—and he nearly exploded there on St. Giles, as if he could not believe I was speaking to him. I did not really understand why, unless it is because of Saif or my father and uncle, but it was like he did not even want to be seen speaking to me in public, and as if he thought I should know better than to approach him.'

So that is that, I think, there is no collusion between them, no alliance, nothing suggested by the single image of Fadia inclining her head towards him on the street outside the Taylorian.

'But then,' she continues, adjusting the angle of Selim's body in her arms, 'he starts phoning me. He never says his name, but his voice, you know, it is unmistakable. He says terrible things about me, I cannot bring myself to repeat them, and about my brother, and also about you. He was phoning every day, and the line was always clicking and full of static, as if he was using an internet connection or as though the line was being monitored, that is what I imagined. And then he started talking about Selim, saying that one day when I didn't expect it, I would suddenly find Selim gone. I would turn my back and he would disappear and I would never see him again. I could not tell if it was an empty threat, or if I should take it seriously.'

'Is that why you finally replied to my messages?'

'Maybe. I was frightened. I guess I could have gone to the police, but I never feel safe around them, at least the white ones. They see a woman who looks a little Middle Eastern and that is enough to change the whole equation. Even if I was the one being victimized I suspect they would find a way to turn it around on me, and then I might be interrogated, and social workers would get involved, and before I know it Selim really would be gone. Forgive me if it looks like I was running to you for help.'

The sun breaks against the building across the street. Our cups are empty and I refill them from the carafe, deciding now is the time to tell her about the boxes and Michael Ramsey, the phone calls my mother has been receiving from a man who must be Stephen Jahn, the way I have been moved to doubt my own sanity, on occasion to suspect a conspiracy involving my son-in-law, perhaps even my daughter and ex-wife, although now I no longer think that is likely, I believe whoever may be watching me has nothing to do with my family.

'Can I see the boxes?' she asks.

'I gave them to the lawyers. They haven't returned them.'

'And this Michael Ramsey? You can contact him?'

'My son-in-law would know how to reach him, but I hesitate to ask Peter. I don't entirely trust him. And obviously the phones and email aren't secure.'

'A sign in the window?'

'It sounds like a spy movie.'

'When did you last see him?'

'I think I see him on the street every day, but when I try to approach him, he disappears, or I doubt that it's actually him. For more than a month now I've hardly felt sane.'

'But the last time you spoke with this Mr. Ramsey, he said you should go public?'

'Yes, in a roundabout way, he suggested running an article in Peter's magazine, assuming Peter could be convinced to do it, or perhaps the publication of this,' I say, showing her this very stack of pages, where I write these words, watching my own life, reviewing my own recent history, just as others do. 'I only wish I could say with certainty who is responsible for watching me. I believe it is the government, but I have no proof. In the end I have no proof of anything, except the files, and those are no longer in my possession.'

Selim is on the carpet again, crawling around and entertaining himself with the toys, so innocent, so unaware of the complexities of his parents' lives. As I look at him, I vow to myself to be present in a way I was not for my daughter.

'Does it really matter who is doing it?' Fadia finally asks. 'There are some people who live their entire lives in the eye of a camera, broadcasting themselves for strangers to watch. You could do that, you know, install cameras in the apartment, present yourself for the whole world, to demonstrate how ordinary you are, how unsuspicious your life is, how you have nothing to do with whatever it is the government—or Stephen Jahn, or MI5, MI6, the NSA, the CIA, Mossad—think you might be doing. Show them your life, our lives together if you like, to prove the point that there is nothing here to see: just a man and a woman who have a child together, who happen, by no fault of their own, to have a connection to a man who would want nothing to do with them, who would look at the relationship you and I have and condemn us. I have little doubt Saif would do just that, or, like Stephen, threaten to take Selim away, to put me to death for the choices I made, to kill you for what you did with me, or *to* me, however we want to think of it. Why should we be judged for who Saif has become? I think you must go public, one way or the other. And we can do it together. I will stand beside you,' she says, her eyes fixed on me with a look of hope, or the intermingling of hope and purpose, and in the spell of her gaze I feel the determination to take what little power we have been granted by Michael Ramsey, if indeed he is the one responsible for all that has transpired, and turn that power back on the powerful.

This text may acquire a life beyond any I would have imagined, not a text solely for my children or my legal defense, but for anyone to read, at any time, on any platform, wherever they may be, whoever they are, if only to prove my ordinariness, my inconsequence, the way I am ultimately like anyone else, like you, coming to the end of this page.

'Are you willing?' Fadia says.

'Yes,' I say, lifting Selim up from the carpet and kissing his brow, 'yes.'

Acknowledgments

Noah Arlow, Kate Ballard, Rita Barnard, Glenn Breuer, Charles Buchan, Megan Carey, Sarah Chalfant, Zahid R. Chaudhary, Justin Cornish, Nadia Davids, Karen Duffy, Tim Duggan, Gail L. Flanery, James A. Flanery, Thomas Gebremedhin, Lucy Valerie Graham, Neville Hoad, Chris Holmes, Michael Holtmann, Suvir Kaul, Thomas Knollys, Ania Loomba, Peter McCullough, Beatrice Monti della Corte von Rezzori, Neel Mukherjee, Rebecca Nagel, Roger Palmer, Angela Rae, James Roxburgh, Adrianne Rubin-Arlow, Paul Saint-Amour, Deborah Seddon, Tamsin Shelton, Margaret Stead, Eddie van der Vlies, Nan van der Vlies, Undine S. Weber, Zoë Wicomb, Will Wolfslau, Andrew Wylie, Robert J.C. Young, Alba Ziegler-Bailey, and everyone at Atlantic Books, Crown, and The Wylie Agency.

Special thanks, as ever, to Andrew van der Vlies.

PATRICK FLANERY was raised in Omaha, Nebraska. He studied Film at New York University's Tisch School of the Arts and earned a PhD in Twentieth-century English Literature at the University of Oxford. He contributes articles to a number of academic journals and has written for *Slightly Foxed*, the *Daily Telegraph* and the *Times Literary Supplement*. He has published two novels to critical acclaim; *Absolution* in 2012 and *Fallen Land* in 2013. He lives in London.